THE
CORRONHELD
PASSING

The
Corronheld
Passing

K.E. Macleod

SgianDubh

SEATTLE

Book design by Alex MacLeod

Cover design and illustrations by Liza Modern Art Media

PUBLISHED BY SGIAN DUBH

Seattle, Washington

Printed in the United States of America

First Printing 2016

ISBN 978-1-945827-00-6

Library of Congress Control Number: 2016912391

www.kemacleod.com

PROLOGUE

...an ending begins it...

LONG PAST DAY she entreated, while he paced and it grew ever darker outside and in. The more words she expended, the fewer he returned until there was only silence and the terrible heaviness of irreversible enmity.

She knew she was right. He did not care.

He said, "I will hear no more, cousin. If you cannot see the power of it, then it were best you leave—and that quickly."

She said nothing then, but retreated to her sleeping quarters to consider what must be done. In the hour of false dawn, having decided her course, she returned, alone and in secret, to the workroom.

He was already there.

He said, "You have convinced me. I now see this differently. We will spell together, as you wish, to destroy the portal. Though," and he hesitated in the way of one who is reluctant, "to close it we must be at the portal."

His mid-moon change of heart troubled her; but to believe was what she desired, so believe she did. And moved next to him as he stood in front of the large, rectangular looking-bronze that had showed them places and times not their own.

"Then let us pronounce the spell and gain the door," she said in spite of the warnings that spoke of themselves in waves of fear. She raised her eyes to the burnished surface, holding her head high as if determination were a defense.

He bowed his head and said, "As you wish."

Together they began the spell done so many times before; together in words, together in motions that sharpened their focus, together in the path to the portal that opened to the otherwheres and otherwhens. Together. Until he struck at her. Until he added and changed, twisted and warped the spell, pushing her magicked personhood into the void.

Terrified, she grappled with him in the dim silence of the nothingplain. She summoned up visions of her beloved husband and children, the world she knew as home. These were allies to her heart and strength in her battle. But her past unwillingness to acknowledge the wickedness he had embraced gave him the advantage. Like a flood upon fire, death blew out the flame of her life and what spirit remained hung like smoke in the realm of the portal. All she had been drifted in the in-between, biding time, seeking a last chance to change what might be.

Into the void that remained where she had been, a creature was pulled through. A woman. More alien seeming because she was so little different. Screaming in rage. Clawing the air with foul, frenzied word-weapons even as he enveloped her with his reality and brought her out into his time/place.

Once back, and when he had spelled the stranger into momentary submission, he surveyed the workroom, took his bearings.

He had brought an alien through. She awaited his use.

Shattered by the force of the battle, the shards and ruins of the looking-bronze littered the workroom. It would never function again, even if he managed to find another blood relation to augment his magic.

And his cousin was dead, her soul lost in the portal's nothingness, her body pierced by unmerciful remnants of burnished metal, motionless upon spreading crimson.

He closed his eyes, tasting, savoring the smile that rose to his lips.

Chapter One:
CATHRYN

THE MORNING OF vacation day three began with luxurious stretching under the covers. Not exactly cat-like, but, as the old saying went, close enough for government work. Since Cathryn wasn't compelled to crawl out from under the comforter, she did.

Hopping on a cold floor. Putting a match…a couple…well, several…to the fire she'd laid last night. And presto, little crackles. A bit too much smoke, but success nonetheless. Now to get the heart started.

Though the cabin she was renting might, by a generous person, be raised to the category of rustic, it still came equipped with electricity and, thus, a pot to heat water. Grind the beans (she'd brought them with) in the grinder (also brought with) and add hot water in the French press. Oh, yes. While it steeped, she dressed in the layers of wool and fleece required for the cold, wet winter outside. Donned cashmere socks—pricey, but her vices were few and mostly cheap—and laced on decent boots.

Ding. The little steeping timer chimed. Perfect. She poured the brew into a china mug (also brought along, because coffee tasted better in china) and sat down in the comfy chair before the fire. Cup in one hand, a pumpkin scone in the other. No need to brace for the snarl that was a Seattle commute. No standing with glazed eyes in front of the closet trying to figure out what to wear, her choices restricted to clothes that were appropriate (how she disliked that word) when you worked for a bunch of insurance actuaries. Good lord, ten days away from the math nerds. She, herself, was a nerd; so that wasn't it. No, it was the math. Not a one of them a word person, which was why she was hired. The lone English Lit major. Writing annual reports, brochures, marketing materials that tried to explain the convoluted, esoteric stuff actuaries did for people-types.

She took another sip of coffee, ruefully concluding that two days of vacation was not enough to quit thinking about work. Yet. But day three of vacation was going to be absolutely and non-urgently lovely. She'd gone to the ranger station at Lake Quinault and equipped herself with trail maps and guides to the Olympic Peninsula. Having poured over them last night, she was convinced there was nothing this part of the Pacific Northwest offered that she was going to miss.

Fully caffeine loaded, she opened the cabin door to check on the weather. Fog. Drizzle. Gray. Cold. Just the right conditions for a walk in the rainforest. Even if it was cold, the fog would brush against her cheek like cool silk. She liked how the rain, caught in the highest branches of the huge cedars, slipped down to tap on the ferns of the deep forest floor.

An odd noise caught her attention. It got a bit louder. A rasping, soughing noise, as if a monster were exhaling. There.

Two yellow eyes the size of platters gleamed, getting larger and larger…

…until the feral eyes resolved themselves into the headlights of a battered pickup that lurched to a stop directly in front of the porch. The door of the rust-colored truck screeched open and a stocky man in a tattered orange mackintosh stepped out. He walked to the back of the pickup, lowered the tailgate with a thump, grabbed an armload of firewood and started toward the porch.

She worked up a no-problems-here-thanks smile to cover the ridiculous turn her imagination had taken when confronted by headlights in the mist. More firewood was now hers. If only her pulse would simmer back down.

Mackintosh man dumped the wood on the porch. "There you go. Probably get cold tonight. Need more wood, just leave a note on the caretaker's door." With a shrug, he turned back to his truck.

"Thanks," she called after the retreating orange slicker. The man just grunted. Clearly, he had found his true calling in the hospitality industry.

When the pickup had ground its gears several times and slowly bumped down the road and out of sight, she went back into the cabin for the last few preparations. Throwing on a rain jacket, she grabbed an apple, a small bag of trail mix and a bottle of water, settling them into one pocket or another. Remembering her father's lengthy and logical instructions for safe hiking when alone, she wrote a note indicating the trail she was taking and the time she expected to be back. She left it on top of the pile of books she'd picked out for vacation: a Teddy Roosevelt biography, a medical thriller, her battered copy of the complete works of Shakespeare and a paperback that fell somewhere in the disputed territory between science fiction and fantasy.

One last pat of her pants pocket to be sure she had the cabin key and a just-in-case book of matches and she was ready. On impulse, she unfastened her watch and left it behind. Not needed. Tell time by days, not minutes, when on vacation, right?

Outside, the fog was thinning even as she began her tramp toward the small wooden sign pointing to the trailhead. According to the map, this trail was just over 3 miles long and would be fairly level most of the way. Just about right for 39 year old office-toned muscles and desk-creaky knees.

In a matter of moments, the rainforest, the calm and temperate rainforest, began to surround her in earnest. Towering over her were cedars born before Lincoln, giants whose roots were embraced by fertile soil and whose highest branches indulged in the winter's rains. Beneath the lofty roof, the children of the stately trees stretched for sunlight, rooted in the heartwood of long dead ancestors. In the air there was a rich smell which could only be described as damp and green. And on the ground, in profusion, were ferns, stumps, rivulets of the water chuckling by on a journey from glacier to ocean, mushrooms in colors from blue-white to burnt orange and a carpeting of branches, twigs, needles, leaves and more. The debris of death, tamped down by time, to serve life.

The farther along the trail she went, the more the knots inside her began to undo themselves. A living system this huge, this old, put all else in perspective. Here, she was but one of many parts in an immense whole, each part intimately interrelated, each destined to be part of something much larger.

Rocks falling, boulders crashing one against the other. Loud. Noise that did not belong here. She stopped in the middle of the trail to listen. It was coming from behind her and to one side. Her first impulse was to move away from what might be danger. But neither the trail nor the terrain around it were steep enough for a rock slide, so she listened hard to get a direction.

Then there came a strangled cry, a person calling for help—a cry battered to silence in a clash of rock. Someone was hurt.

With no more hesitation, she headed off the trail toward the sound. Over moss-slick, downed cedars, through mist thickened ferns, half running, half falling, fearing what she might find.

The fog split open so suddenly, that she nearly fell over the eruption of rocks. Slabs the size of cement blocks, so jumbled they looked as if they had boiled up out of the dirt. A movement. There. A hand stretching upward from between the rocks. Trapped.

She grabbed the topmost chunk and heaved it from the pile. The heft of it made her grunt with effort. But she reached for the next one. And the next. Putting her back and surges of adrenaline into it, uncovering more of the arm, then shoulder.

An explosion of light so bright that it burned out her vision and paralyzed her where she stood. Nothing in front of her hands but cold stone. Nothing in front of her eyes but whiteness. Or was that…? Somehow, though she could see nothing else, she saw the hand, and then the arm that anchored it and beyond that a body appearing in her mind's eye. A woman. With arresting eyes washed in regret. Head haloed by an oval of bronze. Reaching for her through the stone-blindness, finding her hand, pulling her into the formless void. Whispering, "You must help them. I am sorry. It is all I can do."

Cathryn felt herself being pulled into—through—the stones. Struggling to break free. Melting into the rock in an arc of pain. The presence of others. A letting go. Agony…

✳

In bed. Sort of waking up, but eyes refusing to open. Something had happened.

Cabin. Coffee. That much was comfortable to consider. After that, it was dicey. There had been a brightness—brightness that hurt. Then coppery light that was different. An apology and a plea.

She shifted uneasily. Fiery lances of pain stabbed here and there all over her body. With the pain, the memory became so vivid that she was almost there again. Rocks. Buried but not dead. Panic. Arms trapped. Chest crushed under a slab too heavy for lungs to move. Air. God. Air. Help me.

"You are safe. Don't be afraid."

A cool, damp cloth was stroked across her forehead with a gentle touch. There was the slightest smell of mint. The voice was unfamiliar, but sounded concerned. Perhaps it would not hurt to risk a glance at the owner of such a voice.

It was an open face she saw, though a frown of concern had furrowed its way on to the young woman's brow. Nothing too scary about any of that. She ventured a longer look at her surroundings.

She was in a room lit by sun streaming through a large, curtained window. The sheets, buttery colored in the ambient light, felt and smelled like line-dried linen. Near the bed, a small wooden table sturdily held a tumbler and a pottery pitcher whose dripping sides promised cool water. Next to the pitcher stood a plain, deep-green vase with white flowers of a type she did not recognize.

To one side sat the girl. No, the person on the edge of the bent-branch chair was not a girl any longer. There was the head-high posture of the newly independent about her, created by equal parts of defiance, pride, anticipation and apprehension.

"How do you feel?"

She tried moving to a more comfortable position but once again it hurt and she winced.

"Battered." The expression of her pain reverberated on the young woman's face. The frown grew deeper.

"The healer says no bones are broken. If you could manage to drink this…" Laying down the damp towel, the young woman picked up a small cloth pouch and emptied what looked like tea leaves into the water tumbler. "…it will help the pain."

Good lord. Healer, not doctor. Herbs, not prescriptions. Had she been saved by some kind of off-the-grid sect? Bits and pieces of the rescue began to throw themselves at her awareness: Shouted commands she understood uttered in odd rhythms, snatches of discussions peppered with unfamiliar phrases, unsurprising faces and bodies.

The hands that had pulled her out from under the rocks were strong, competent and each had the requisite five digits with opposable thumbs. But the cadences and postures felt off in a way not yet definable.

The young woman was watching her—no, waiting. Waiting for her to drink whatever had been put into the water. That wasn't going to happen.

The girl frowned. "You should drink the potion. It will ease your pain."

The particular phrasing touched off another wave of uncertainties. Cathryn felt an urgent need for more information and time to process the questions that were bombarding her. She searched for a way to distract attention from the offered 'potion' when the door to the room opened.

Dark hair, sprinkled with gray, seemed to indicate at least an approach to middle age. And he was, in build and height, medium. But there the mediumness stopped. Hard to look average while wearing a garnet-colored cape. Cape? Really? She could not see his eyes yet because he turned first to the girl who, when she saw him, jumped to her feet.

"Father."

He moved across the room in a stride and, with fingers plain and careful, touched his daughter's cheek.

"I came myself as soon as I heard. I needed to see you well with my own eyes."

A tear ran down the face he touched.

"I am so sorry…" Even from Cathryn's vantage point, the guilt was plain to see. What had this young woman done?

"We will talk later. Our duty now is before us." The rebuke in his voice was mild enough and yet she could not imagine anyone disappointing him and not feeling terrible.

The visage of the parent was put away and, with a purposefulness that seemed integral to him, the man came, instead, to stand at the foot of the bed.

He scanned her face. His scrutiny was quick and intense, as if he searched for answers even she did not know she had. But his eyes looked shuttered from within and offered nothing in return.

For a long, uncertain minute no one moved. Then he did. His left hand touched his right shoulder as he made a courtly bow, purple leather cords at his wrist swinging slightly with the movement.

"You are safely in a House of Care, lady. The healer tells us you are not damaged in any serious way but need only to rest." This was a voice that would carry to the back row if necessary, though right now it was modulated to a personal level. "If there is any favor we might offer as you mend, you only need ask."

"Things seem fuzzy to me. I barely remember being brought out from under the rocks. I don't know…could you tell me where I am?"

"You are at the rock quarry half a day distant from Forché Keep." He frowned. "Perhaps you are more familiar with our neighbor provinces, Quarel and Kilder? Linton?"

A knot formed between her shoulder blades.

"I'm afraid I don't recognize any of those names. Could you just estimate how far we are from Quinault?"

Nothing.

"I'm pretty sure they have a hospital or emergency clinic there. It feels like maybe a rib is broken. So, if we could…"

His frown deepened and whatever was hidden behind his eyes retreated even further.

She felt an upsurge of fear. Where in all hell was she, and who were these two? Maybe one of those renaissance-fair-re-en-actment-whatever groups. That could explain this. The idea al-most made her let loose a panicky chuckle. Rescued by a bunch of urban nerds playing at being medieval. Perfect. Just need to get them to break character, because this ongoing charade was getting creepy and she was pretty sure she needed real medical attention.

He must have seen her anxiety, for the man threw her a rope by changing the subject.

"Forgive me, lady, we have not given you our names. This is my daughter, Lucette. I am Benedic, Duke of the House Forché. This country is called Corronheld, presently under the stew-ardship of King Reyfen. I have the honor of addressing…?"

"Cathryn Porter. Originally from…" This was horrible. What was she saying? "I mean I live in…" The words trailed away. She looked down at her hands. She compulsively twisted the ring on her hand. To keep still, she clenched her fists shut. Hard. The carved letters on the ring's surface pressed into her fingers.

"I mean, I have no idea how I came here. I don't even know

where 'here' is." She drew a breath and plunged on. "So, if you would please drop the act and tell me how I got here, how you found me. That would be the best favor you could do."

"Lady, how you came here we do not altogether comprehend, nor why. I will tell you all we know as plainly as I can. Lucette is a member of the Maker Guild, Rock Circle." He motioned toward the young woman who raised her arm to show the green and gray bands at her wrist.

"Something went wrong with one of the quarry crews she was assisting and three of the workers were trapped under rocks that fell by accident. Because my daughter's magic is strong, she easily lifted the rocks so two could be brought out. But in her desire to save the third," his eyes flickered before he went on, "she called on a type of magic forbidden to any outside the Esoteric Guild—she tried to reshape place. There was a great concussion of light. When the rescuers could see again, they found you. As you were injured, they brought you here."

All the world seemed to pause and hang motionless. For the space of three heartbeats, nothing moved. Then she closed her eyes, took in a deep breath and raggedly let it out. When she opened her eyes and looked up again, she had somehow summoned up enough grit to at least appear calm.

"I'm not so sure I should have opened my eyes this morning." She attempted a small, self-deprecating laugh. These people were deep, way deep into their delusion. The sunny room suddenly felt more like a prison.

Lucette took her hand. There were tears in her eyes once again.

"I am so sorry. The fault is mine alone. Our country has little commerce with the rest of the world, but I will make it my first and only task to find your homeland and see you safely there again. Whatever I can do, I will do. I swear it."

The young woman looked so miserable and contrite that Cathryn, even in her own state of distress, was moved.

"You were just trying to save your friend. And once I was here, you saved my life. Your voice directing the rescue was one of the sweetest sounds I have ever heard, believe me."

She could see Benedic's expression soften as he watched the effect her words had on his guilt-ridden daughter. She tried to say something else reassuring.

"Anyway, just because I don't know the local names doesn't mean we can't ask around and find out where I need to go. Everybody says the earth is getting smaller every day."

Her effort at pleasantries seemed to help Lucette, though at the end she looked a bit puzzled. But before the words had died in the air, something slammed shut behind the man's eyes.

The duke turned toward his daughter.

"Will you leave us a while, Lucette? I will come out to you again before I depart." Though his manner was courtesy itself, Lucette didn't waste a moment with her exit, His voice, though. It made her back teeth vibrate. What the hell? And when he turned back again, his eyes looked into darkness.

"You are hurt and you are alone. I would not be cruel, lady, but I must require an oath from you." Somewhere under the darkness, a fire built. "We do not call our world 'Earth'. There is only one place I know whose peoples named it for the dirt under their feet. Is that what you call your world? Earth?"

"Yes, but…"

"I learned of that place from another; yet, from the little I know, I hate it."

She tried to keep her voice level and low. "That sounds a bit extreme, don't you think?"

"Does it? Think of your world. Remember it all and then tell me, if you can, that you would wish it upon us."

"I don't know you. I don't know your world. I don't even know if I am in another…"

He refused to allow her the comfort of denial. "Your heart has already told you this is not home."

There it was. She was in a place she did not know and should not be. The conclusion hit her like a blow and took her breath away. But the stranger would not relent.

"Furthermore, because you are in a place where neither Earth nor an Earther should ever be, I must demand you keep the knowledge of the existence and nature your world to yourself. If you keep your oath, I swear I will turn every corner, every page, to find a way back home for you. And find it soon."

Giving an oath? Seriously? She tried to stall for time. Anything to keep that buzzing in her head from making her even crazier.

"You want me to keep secrets for you? But even if I agree to try, people may just come right out and ask where I come from. What do I tell them?"

His eyes narrowed in thought. "Tell them you are a nomad. Our stories say roamers do not name their encampments or claim allegiance to any country."

Rising anger announced itself to her by bringing heat to her cheeks. What a self-righteous, cape-wearing bastard.

"Let me get this straight; you figure that someone from this earth you know so very much about wouldn't hesitate to lie. Is that right?"

Duke Benedic shifted uneasily. "I only meant that, for what little time you must be here, it would be better for you and for us if the damage done by my daughter's rashness in the quarry were kept quiet."

He waited for her response. A thousand questions and a thousand more anxieties argued in her head. Too many to handle. She needed to know more, find out more. Escape and an MD were her priorities. Play along to get along. Keeping quiet to buy time was something she knew how to do very well. At least her knowledge of office politics might come in handy, damn it.

"All right. I guess I can do that. It is probably best that way."

Benedic kept his gaze on her a long moment more, then gave a very small nod and started toward the door.

"The healer says you may be moved tomorrow. Allow me to extend the hospitality of our home to you. I will send transport. Until then, we will let you rest." And just like that, the door closed behind the intense Duke of Forché.

The word 'earth' had changed him from reserved to hostile. But she was trapped, dependent on this stranger and those who served him for her immediate survival and any likelihood of getting back home.

Too much. She felt dizzy. Could concepts kill? Another world that wasn't Earth. And did he say magic? Total crap. Delusional. And, therefore, quite possibly very dangerous.

Lucette entered again, more cheerful, ready to talk.

"Father says you may come home with us tomorrow. You'll like it there, really. We have a beautiful garden, Cathryn, a perfect place to recover. I helped with the rockeries myself. And when you feel up to walking, we—"

"Lucette?" The interruption was a relief. "I hope you understand, but this is…I mean…thank you, but if I could just be alone…"

"I am sorry. Of course, I understand. If you need anything, just call out. There will be someone standing outside the door at all times."

"Thank you." Oh, a guard. Even better. "I'll just rest, you know."

Perhaps it was Lucette's last look at her, a compassionate look, that tipped the balance. Perhaps it was just that a person can hold only so much strain. Whatever the reason, as soon as the girl shut the door behind her, restraint broke. Though her mother had lectured often on the evils of 'colorful language', one benefit of extensive reading in all sorts of genres was the accumulation of gratifyingly crude swear words. She put every one of them to use, some more than once. Then she put her mind to work. It was her way.

From nearby Forché Keep, messengers left in haste in the dark.

It is so often true that, just after a difficult time, the world puts on an aspect of beauty. So it was on this morning. Over the quarry poured sunlight, clouds pearled through the bluest of skies. The verge between the surrounding forest and the outcropping of rocks fluttered with the songs and flights of giddy birds. Even the solemn trees, huge sentinels as wide as houses and tall as hills, seemed to look down with favor.

All of this Cathryn watched and noted from the window of the room. She'd washed her face, twice, just to get rid of the guck that had gummed up her eyes during the night. Must be hay fever. Not tear leftovers. Couldn't be, because she didn't cry anymore.

It had taken much wincing to discover the bathroom arrangements. Not too hard to guess that they were behind the door at the back of the bedroom; but the odd configuration of pipes and rope pulls required a mental—and actually some physical—agility she was hard pressed to accomplish before coffee.

Nonetheless, she emerged from the washroom scrubbed,

relieved, and wearing clean clothes that had been left for her; a long shirt with a billion buttons, loose pants and her own boots. An outfit similar to the one Lucette had been wearing yesterday. Clutching the bundle that held the remains of her other clothes, the few tangible remnants of home, she stood watching a world she had been told she did not know come to life before her eyes. It looked mostly familiar.

The transportation Duke Benedic had promised arrived as she watched. Two horses pulled a coach under the direction of a woman with a weathered and competent appearance. Almost immediately, Lucette knocked and entered.

"If you are ready, our carrier is come. Will you away?"

"I'm coming." She hesitated before stepping out into even more unknowns. Still, her character spoke quietly in her ear, telling her what it always told her: there is no way to go but forward.

Outside, the driver was already climbing back up in her seat. Lucette was saying good-bye to the healer, who was delivering small packets of herbs and a barrage of instructions.

"The blue packet for headaches, the green for aches and fever."

"I will remember," the girl insisted. "Our thanks to you again. Always you tend with a good touch." She bowed respectfully.

Cathryn was caught by the sense of ritual and the oddness of language. How very damn coincidental, convenient even, that she and they spoke the same language. Sort of. The rhythm of words and flow of gestures seemed stylized, restrained. It made her own speech and customs seem crude and raw. And it made her feel inadequate in thanking the healer.

"Thank you. Very much." It was all she could think to say.

But the healer smiled and told her he would be by the Keep now and again to check on her progress.

Clearly determined to make the journey a comfortable one, Lucette took her by the arm and helped her into the coach, fussed with several pillows, raised the cloth covering on the window to let in the sun.

"The trip is not very long. We'll be there by midday. See, already we enter the forest." The young woman pointed to the huge, wide-girthed trees that, once out of the quarry's open space, surrounded them. A deep, rich, loamy smell gentled in through the window.

"What kind of trees are they?" There was a comfort in small talk. And getting information.

"These are the redbark trees. Only Forché province has them. I think they are the most beautiful trees in the whole world. When the sun catches them just so, the bark glows with the color of wine."

"We have trees back home that look a lot like this. I love them, too. We call the place they grow a rainforest."

"Rainforest. What a lovely name." Lucette brushed an errant strand of hair behind her ear. The movement made the leather strips on her wrist catch Cathryn's eye.

"I'm unfamiliar with these bracelet things, but they mean something. At least I think that's what your father said."

"Yes. We call them bands and the colors tell what kind of work we do. The band nearest the palm is the guild band. Mine is green for the Maker Guild. We work with the basic elements gifted to the world—soil, rock and water. The guild is divided into three circles, one for each element. The second band shows the circle, in my case gray for rock, the builders. Water Circle sustains growing things and masters fishing. Soil Circle sees to farming and those things made from soil. Pottery, bricks, those sorts of things.

"Red firstbands belong to the Begotten Guild. It works with growing things, begotten not made. Plant Circle helps the farmers and tends the forests. Retha, the carrier taking us home, belongs to Animal Circle. Soul-bearer Circle tends to people. Our healer is one of them.

"Black first bands are Esoteric Guild. They work with what we cannot see, but feel: Fire Circle for heat, cold and weather. Spirit Circle for counselors and artisans. The Unseen Circle," here she frowned as she evidently remembered her recent and unfortunate lapse into unseen magic, "deals with place and time.

"And of course, the onebands of the Servant Guild are purple. That is the only guild not divided into circles."

"What do they do?"

"They serve others. It is the noblest calling and the most difficult. Those who tend children, innkeepers, teachers, order-keepers and rulers all belong. It is my father's guild."

Now that was interesting. Part of Cathryn wanted to consider what that perception of service meant, but part of her wanted to ask another question—one that had been tugging at her insistently.

"Your father said something about magic…"

"Yes, he said my rock magic is strong, and that is true. But I think it's only strong because I enjoy it so much." Lucette smiled to herself.

"No…I mean, some of you have, can do, magic? Spells and things like that?"

It was the girl's turn to look surprised. "Yes. Of course. It does vary from person to person. Most only have enough ability to do simple things—sometimes only enough that it seems more like an affinity than a talent. Others, who have it strongly, must study hard for a long time to learn to use it well." She stopped in perplexity. "Are you saying you don't have magic where you come from?" She made it sound as if Cathryn didn't have air to breathe.

"No, we don't. We have heard of it and there are a lot of people who want to have it. And there are some people who pretend to have it. But, no."

"Then how do you make things, or build?" The young woman seemed genuinely distressed.

"Well, we just learn how to do our work, and we make tools to help."

"And what about counselors and leaders? How can they work without the connection to others that magic affords?"

"We just do without. We rely on ourselves, alone."

"Your people must be courageous. To make buildings without binding spells, to lead without knowing the heart of the people led, to cut trees not knowing which are ready to lie down. Working in darkness must be fearful, and yet you say you do. Your people must be very brave, indeed."

"Brave? Well, that's one way of looking at it." Cathryn sat back against the cushions.

At this, the girl was quiet. The two of them watched the deepness of the redbark stands pass by. In spite of the beauty outside the window, every mile traveled took her closer to an ugly truth: Nowhere in the state of Washington, or any place she knew, was there this expanse of…of otherness. That knowledge, being too alien to contemplate and still stay sane, would have to be tamped down, buried, walled away. It couldn't distract her from the more pressing needs: To stay alive, to learn what she needed to get back home.

By midday Lucette was pointing out the stony hill crowned

by Forché Keep. The towering redbarks ended, in unison, at the base of a steep hill. The paving stones of the road continued ahead, a winding gray ribbon that curved around and up. Beside the ascending road were sturdy houses, also of stone but in many shades—some rose, some blue, some with deep green flecks throughout. Warm wine-colored shingles topped the roofs. And above it all, the Keep. It was not so very massive, yet it was unmistakably dominant. In the light of that day, it looked a radiant gold, as if it took the sun's own color. To one side of the entryway arch, like an honor guard, grew the largest redbark tree Cathryn had seen yet, so tall it stretched past the Keep's highest part.

Through the archway went the coach, and into the immense courtyard where, it appeared, a public market was in full stride. Set around the walls were wagons and carts with bright awnings stretching from their high, wooden sides. Under the canopies were the makings of trade: foodstuffs, clothing, cooking pots, books, shoes, chairs and stools, seeds, flowers.

Did it seem too quaint to be real? Yes. Well, no. It was hard to quibble with the wealth of details that made this feel a true place and less like what critics of the fantasy genre called 'sanitized medieval.' She decided that it would be more enjoyable to believe she was hallucinating. Too much reading and then a blow to the head. Then all she had to do was just wake up.

Even with all the bustle, the driver had little problem threading through to the huge wooden doors of the Keep itself, doors which were wide open and admitted all sorts of people who seemed to have business inside. Still painfully stiff from her bruises, she had to be helped down from the coach. As she and Lucette reached the first stair, a man stepped forward and made a deep bow of welcome.

"Welcome home, lady. We are so glad to see you safely back."

"Well met, Arilon." With one hand Lucette pressed his arm in a gesture of greeting, with the other she motioned to Cathryn. "This is our guest, Cathryn of House Porter." She looked flustered. "Have I said it aright? 'Porter' is how you say your house name?"

"Well, you pronounced it right, yes. This 'house' thing, though…"

"Good. This is Arilon, our castellan. He makes everything run as smoothly as water over rocks—and we thank him daily for it."

"You are too generous." Tall Arilon swept his long arm toward the interior. "Will you come inside?"

He wound his way past clusters of people moving about on various errands. Several rooms they passed held groups of children. A long hallway was lined with tables of charts and drawings being consulted by groups of men and women. In another room, there was clearly a mediation of some sort happening as there could be heard earnest debates by two parties set on either side of a patient-looking person in a dark purple robe.

Arilon led them up a stairway and then past a large library where a dozen people studied, surrounded by piles of books. That looked interesting, possibly due some further investigation. On and past they walked, and up another stairway. By now, they must be nearing the top and back of the Keep. The higher and farther back they went, the fewer people there were, until they stopped before a plain, wide door. The castellan opened it and stepped aside to let them enter.

A vaulted ceiling stretched high above them, and along one side of the large room, facing the light-shafted forest beyond, were tall windows spaced and held by delicate columns of rose- and blue-blushed stone. The sight quite took her breath away. Lucette, too, though she must have seen it a thousand times, stood still in regard.

"It is beautiful. I never tire of it. It amazes me anew each time I come home. And reminds me."

"Reminds you?"

"The ducal house," Arilon's words had the cadence of ceremony, "was made to remind those who live in it who they serve and why. The greater part of the house is given to public service—teaching, the doing of justice, study. These windows keep before the Duke's eye the province he serves and the living things in it, the burden and the blessing of his duty."

She moved toward the windows, fascinated by the blue-green river far below and the forest that swept beyond. The windows met the floor and when she stood next to the glass the view was so precipitous that, suddenly, she felt dizzy and reached out to steady herself. Arilon was beside her instantly and, in a motion of support, took her arm. But when he touched her, a sharp stab of pain shot up her arm—a pain so piercing that she gasped and jerked away.

"What's the matter?" Lucette ran over and caught her by the shoulders. "You are feeling your injuries. The fault is mine, talking all this while. Come, let me take you to your room. Arilon, please send up hot water for the healer's herbs."

"Immediately, lady." He did not, however, move to leave, but paused to put something back in a pocket. Lucette, who had turned toward a hallway in the far wall, could not have seen him do so. But, with a sidelong glance, Cathryn did. And she saw him eye her with an odd, indefinable look. Then the glance was gone and so, in an instant, was Arilon.

Screaming for air. Run…run…it's getting closer. Red air—blood red. Can't run fast enough. NO! It's closer. RUN. Trees in the dark clawing face, tripping frantic feet. Run. Faster. Help

me. There! A road—someone's there…with a car! Lights on—get there. Run. Woman with the car door open—get inside. Close the door—hurry, please, drive away, please hurry, its coming. MOVE! The woman in the driver's seat turns. Can see her face. Opens her mouth. No…No…NO! Blood pouring out, drowning…

"NO!" Cathryn yelled the word, waking herself to a pounding heart and the giddy terror of the nightmare. Fear shivered her. She clutched the blanket tighter, rocking…rocking, talking to herself.

"Clonk on the head. Nothing more. I'm okay." But reality was hard to hold in the dark, in a place she didn't know.

Sleep wasn't going to be possible for the rest of the night, that was certain. It might bring back the nightmare, bring back the disturbing face of the woman in the car. She felt along the top of the table next to the bed until she touched the object she was seeking. Remembering the instructions Lucette had given her, she stroked the base of the light in an upward motion. Each touch made the column of milky glass glow brighter. When the room was lit well enough, she got out of bed and pulled a long robe over the nightgown they had found for her.

Though the gown was a simple long-sleeved affair, the robe was made of yards and yards of what felt like cashmere. It was very soft and supple but, perhaps because this huge tower of rock was cold at night, it was so voluminous it felt as though she was wearing a blanket. Or two. Managing this much material was much harder than throwing on the oversized T-shirts and fuzzy socks she usually wore. But there was no alternative, so she awkwardly gathered up folds of material and managed to swirl it all through the doorway and into the hall.

Quietly, hoping to wake no one with her restlessness, she made her way down the main hall to the room with the huge windows. It wasn't hard to find.

Across the shadowed room, the shy lights of the night sky

drew her. A plump, peachglow moon balanced just over the feathery fringe of trees. Thrown all over the rest of the darkness were so many stars that she was reminded of summer camping trips to Montana when forever-large, starry nights leaped through the clearest of air. But these stars clustered themselves in constellations she had never seen, patterns that twisted themselves in her eyes. The combination of the remembrance of home and the unavoidably alien in the same sky tasted bittersweet.

She shivered. A mammoth fireplace took up most of one wall and a fire still lingered in it. She moved toward the warmth. A large, deep chair was near the hearth, angled toward the view out of the windows. Had she been back at the cabin, she'd probably be doing this very thing—wrapped up all comfy near a fire. At least this fireplace looked as if it was regularly cleaned.

She tucked up her feet, wrapped the folds of the robe up around her and tried to think of a way through her situation. But a cozy chair in a dimly lit room doesn't lend itself to sharp thinking. She didn't realize she'd been dozing until voices brought her up from sleep.

"...sleeping. Wait here, I'll wake him." The voice sounded like Arilon's.

Footsteps sounded, headed toward the hallway. Still drowsy, she drifted off again for several moments. But once more, conversation roused her.

"...so late, but the guildmaster felt it was of such consequence, it could not wait." She'd had never heard this raspy male voice before.

"A message doubly sealed shows the concern of the sender." That was the duke speaking. There were two small, snapping sounds and the rustle of paper. Then a silence. Feeling awkward about remaining unnoticed in the depths of the fireside chair, Cathryn decided she'd better announce her presence and had just concluded that a discreet cough was called for, when the duke spoke again.

"D'Clan's concerns are ours as well, but I would not send her elsewhere until the king decides our course. Tell Guildmaster D'Clan we respect her fears for us, but the woman will stay here until the king commands otherwise."

"My lord, Guildmaster D'Clan is so strongly concerned she sent us with a carriage to bring the woman with us this very night. Surely the Guildmaster's request is most prudent. It cannot do harm to take her to the guildhouse, and it could very well prevent disaster. We are prepared to leave immediately upon your consent."

Now she was wide awake. The duke and this unknown person were discussing her. No longer ready to reveal herself, she sat still, hardly breathing, trying to catch every nuance of every word.

"Your preparations have been swift. The messages I sent were to the king only, as is right. I wonder your guildhouse heard of this matter so quickly."

"I am only a senior apprentice in the Unseen Circle, my lord, but even I felt the disturbance in the void this incident caused. The very weave of our world twisted and tore with its violence. It is no wonder that word went out to every Esoteric Guild initiate seeking information regarding the nature and result of such a thing. Our information brought us to Forché; our concern brought us here quickly."

"Understandable. Yet, it is curious. There are presently no blackbands at the quarry or at Forché Keep. Our own D'Parl has been these last two months in Linton Province heat-warding for Duchess T'Meara. I wonder which Esoteric sent you word from here?" The duke sounded truly curious, yet under the curiosity there was a hint of something sharper.

"I only bring the Guildmaster's request. I bring what I am told."

A veteran of too many corporate meetings, Cathryn recognized a non-answer when she heard one.

"Then bring to Guildmaster D'Clan my greetings and thanks for her concern. Tell her that I value her advice and will take even stronger precautions, but that I await the king's reply. Arilon will provide a place for you to rest before you begin your return journey."

There was a pause, as if the messenger had more to say. But the duke's last words were so clearly a dismissal, the moment passed. When the door shut behind Arilon and the envoy, Benedic stood for a long time. Then he moved toward the fireplace. Painfully aware she had not revealed her presence, she tried to shrink back into the shadowy depths of the chair. On came the duke until he stood facing the fire, warming his hands. She tried not to even breathe.

"I'm warned you may be considerably dangerous." Slowly, deliberately, Benedic turned toward her. The darkness of the night and the backlight of the fire hid his face. "Are you a danger?"

"You knew I was here and yet you let me stay hidden to hear the message. That doesn't sound like you think I am a danger."

He remained motionless and silent for a long time. Each moment made her feel more and more deeply her isolation, vulnerability and, above all, her dependence on the goodwill of strangers.

He turned back to the fire and then spoke. "Above this mantel hangs a sword. How it came to be, no history can tell. But it did come to the first ruler of Forché Province and has been handed down to each succeeding duke and duchess since. The first duchess wore it to secure an infant province's new peace. The seventh duke went to war with it. The twentieth duke took it to the Queen he served and swore an oath of service that took him to Chymion Province where, at the Queen's command, he used the sword to slay another. Playing a vain, self-indulgent game of state, the Queen forgot her own oath of service, caring nothing for those that suffered under her treachery. When the twentieth duke realized his Queen's wickedness and his own part in it, he fixed the sword in the crack of a stone and threw his own life upon it."

He turned and looked up. There, on the wall, in a sheath of plain leather, hung the weapon. Even in the dimness of the room, the hilt caught the light and gleamed. "Tell me, do you think this sword dangerous?"

In the flickering light, the man and the weapon waited for an answer. No coward's way out, she thought. Only forward. She stood up from the chair and moved to face her questioner. Heaven only knew what would come of it, but with a Lit major and philosophy minor she could certainly frame an answer.

"We have that debate on earth, as well. Some say the sword is not a danger, only the person who wields it is. Others say that argument doesn't go far enough. The sword itself is a danger, they argue; its edges are sharp and may cut even an innocent person who touches it.

"You ask if I am dangerous. As a weapon? Or as a wielder? My answer to either one is that I may well be. But that is definitely not my intention. I mean no harm to you, your family or your land. I'm not a weapon, not yours or anyone else's. I'll take any oath you want. But, here's a thought—if you're afraid, why don't you use some of that purple-banded-magic-stuff and compel me? You do that with your own children, don't you? Even I can feel it when you put the have-to on them. Epic parenting, there."

Benedic yanked the sword from the wall and drew it. Dropping the empty sheath, he grabbed her hand and pulled it toward the blade. She forced herself not to waver, to keep her eyes on his. The edges of her vision saw only darkness and flames, but she heard him take a steadying breath and took that as a very small, good sign. When he spoke, it was with a measure of calm.

"Quarel Province," he said, "has a sword called Vengeance. The King's sword is called Justice. The name of the sword of Forché is carved on the blade. Swear by it, if you would swear." And he brought her hand closer, so close that her fingers felt the carved letters, so close that she could feel, as well as see, the name emblazoned on the flat of the blade in lettering so familiar it made her stomach lurch. Truth.

When she took in a breath to speak, she practically hissed. "Be careful what you ask and how you ask it. Truth may be a weapon in Forché, but it doesn't belong to you alone. Take your hand off mine—take it off. Now."

She could feel him struggle with himself. She could feel the moment of his decision as his fingers loosened their grip.

"Now, look at the ring I'm wearing. Look at it!"

Almost against his will, his eyes dropped to the silver ring she wore, had worn for years. And there, carved into the band, was one word—the same single word carved in smaller but identical script to that on the sword.

"How did you come by this?"

"Why? Do you think it's a trick, that I somehow found out about this sword story of yours and found a ring to match it? Look under the ring at my finger. See the groove it's made? Look at that pale skin underneath it. That skin hasn't seen sun for years.

"Listen, I don't know how I came here. I don't know who did it and I don't know why. I don't know why my ring and this sword have the same word in the same letters. But I can tell you I have worn this ring for more than 20 years. I've worn it because it means that much to me. So, go ahead, suspect me if you have to, but all I want to do is find out how I got here and—and if I can get home." The last word hit like a fist.

Abruptly, he stooped to pick up the discarded sheath, replaced the sword in it and put it back up on the wall. For a long moment he stood before her, searching her face. Then, wearily, he turned away toward the long windows and looked down at the land for which he was responsible.

"The new day is not far away. Some nights I think I can almost feel the world turn over in its sleep. Some nights it seems good to me, a tender turning. Other nights the turning feels more like a snake bending black water over its back. I live at the top of this house, but always, always, I know they are there. All those who live and move in Forché."

He reached out a hand, touched the glass. "I will not have one of them come to harm because of me, because of what I do—or fail to do." The hand became a fist, pressed against the cold pane. "Nothing that might threaten them can be allowed, and yet..." The duke turned from the window, gathering his robe about him against the chill. "And yet, simply because you are here, you have become part of Forché as well. I would not condemn any person without evidence. To do right by those I serve is my duty—my life—and even fear of the unknown will not keep me from it. Tomorrow we will, both of us, take up the quest for answers."

"Thank you...my lord...your grace." The honorifics sounded so awkward on her tongue that she smiled in spite of herself. A small bit of the stiffness left her shoulders. "I'm sorry, I mean no disrespect. It's just that we don't use titles like yours. Really awkward here."

"No apology is necessary. Our people set great store by courtesy. The order we keep is built on a framework of ceremony. It is a comfort to us because we have lived with it all our lives. But you have not, so if it is more to your ease, my given name is Benedic. I would be Benedic to you." For the first time, she saw a slight smile grace his face. It changed the moment completely.

"I would like that. You know, Lucette introduced me as Cathryn of the House Porter. But I have no 'house.' Those are my first and last names." She felt as if she were beginning to babble. The strain of fighting for her safety and the late hour had begun to tell.

"But you must be tired. Tomorrow will bring us much to do." Smoothly, courteously, Benedic offered her his arm. The gesture was so natural for him that taking his arm seemed only appropriate. Down the hallway they walked together until they reached the door to her room.

"Rest well, Cathryn Porter." He swept a small bow. "Until tomorrow."

"Good night. Benedic." His name, when said, had the taste of a strange spice.

Coming up from a deep, dreamless sleep. Drowsy in a warm morning bed. Where? Oh.

Something hurt.

She curled up on her side, sliding her arm under her head. Pain. Now fully awake, she sat up, pulling up the sleeve of the nightgown. From wrist to shoulder, all along her right arm, was a long, sharp-edged bruise. She touched it, and flinched. It felt kind of hard underneath the skin. She was glad to be left-handed because the right arm looked like it would be out of commission for a while.

With difficulty, she performed the routines of morning. Dressing was especially painful. Eventually, though, she emerged from her room and almost ran into Lucette.

"I'm so glad you're up. Come on—my brother's home. He got back last night. You must meet him." Lucette was a most enthusiastic morning host, herding Cathryn down the hall and out onto a balcony where a breakfast table was set out in the fresh daylight. A young man stood near the table, waiting for them, his aurora of dark hair marking him as his father's son, his energy a signal of youth.

"This is my brother, Corry. Corry, this is our guest, Cathryn."

"Your servant." The young man caught up her hand and executed an extravagant bow and kiss maneuver. His sister fairly snorted.

"Ignore him altogether—he's a scoundrel who knows no shame at all. I cannot believe he's my brother."

"Scoundrel?! I'm wounded, devastated, ruined. That my own sister should so malign me comes near to breaking my heart—" Corry snatched up a small loaf of bread and broke off a chunk "—like this."

"Poor boy, so sad," mocked Lucette. In retaliation, the boy lobbed the bread bit at his sister, who dodged it, caught it and threw it back at him. In a flash he darted behind Cathryn, using her as a shield.

"Sister, dear, you mustn't throw breakfast at our company. Terribly bad manners. Must apologize for her." He stayed close to her back. "What would father say, Loos?"

"I would say the birds that feast on these crumbs may be the only ones to profit from your homecoming." Benedic had come up behind the group while the baked-goods throwing was going on.

"Lucette started it."

The duke firmly drew his son toward the table. "Please attempt to be civilized for one meal at least." Safely protected from his sister's vengeance, Corry threw his arms around his father, who unbent from his reserve to warmly hug him in return.

"I am glad to see you home again, but when the two of you are together you do wreak havoc on decorum." The duke smiled at both his children. "Let's not torture our guest with any more food flinging this morning. Shall we eat?"

When the passing and serving had settled down a bit, the duke explained that his son had, until now, been studying music at the Esoteric Guildhouse.

"What he has not told us is why he is returned home."

"Why for the company of my loving sister, of course." Corry pasted a sickly sweet smile on his face.

"Corry." The duke was intent on getting the true story. The boy would not be able to laugh away that regard. Cathryn knew she was watching long habits of family relations. It actually made her feel better.

"The truth is, father, I'm as surprised to be home as you are to have me here. One day all was as usual, classes and studies and practices; the next day the entire guildhouse was bestirred. From the Student House, we could see more blackbands than we even knew existed. Three days we watched the comings and goings in and out of the Guildmaster's, and then our teachers announced a 20-day holiday. With no reason given. Never in memory has such a thing been done. Not, mind you, we students argued overly much. I, myself, was the first one packed and—" he helped himself to what looked to be a bunch of grapes though they were an unlikely bright orange color, "—here I am."

"How many days since the guild first was disturbed, son?"

"Oh, well…a three day's ride to reach here…three days before…six days in all, father."

"Lady," Benedic turned to her, "we have already learned a very important thing. Remember the messenger told us that those in the Unseen Circle felt time and place tearing?" She nodded, uncertain where this was leading. "He also said the guild sent messages to its initiates seeking information about the event. But they could not have done so. Three days it is from the guildhouse to here for the message, three days back with the reply and three days for the envoy to come to us—they did not have nine days."

Lucette sat upright. "That means Unseens knew about this from the beginning. There is no other way to explain it. They had their initiates already looking for the event—" here she looked over at Cathryn "—before I…"

"It means more than that, daughter. The tearing of time and place was so great that only the most powerful of the Unseen Circle could possibly magick it. Though you were under the strongest of emotions, the esoteric talent inherited from your mother is not that powerful in you."

"Then…it was not my fault, think you?" The duke's daughter tentatively reached for hope.

"You may have altered the result, my heart, but I never believed it was of your doing. Your brother's news gives us proof."

"Pardon me?" Corry wiped the last traces of breakfast from his lips. "I have no idea what you two are talking about. What tearing of time and place? Loos? Father?"

Father and daughter hesitated, looking over at Cathryn. She sensed their reticence to tell the whole story directly, Lucette from a sense of guilt and Benedic from his own private aversion. So she did the one thing she thought might put them more at ease—she told the story herself.

"If you like, I can tell it—or at least part of it—since it does touch on my stay here."

Corry looked even more confused, but politely adopted a listening posture. His sister appeared relieved. But Benedic sat silent and still, his eyes hooded.

"Six days ago, at the rock quarry, there was an accident. Three people became trapped and your sister was part of the rescue effort. Two of the workers were retrieved safely using rock magic." She looked to Lucette, who indicated with a nod that she had got the story right so far. "The third was more deeply buried. In trying to get him out, she drew on," she frowned a bit trying to get the wording right, "Unseen Circle magic. A talent she inherited from her mother, I think I heard. Time and space were already being ripped open by someone else and, when Lucette added her effort, the result was a person brought to here from another…place. Maybe even another time."

She sat back, relieved she had constructed the tale while still leaving her promise to Benedic unbroken. Clearly, he knew much more than he was telling and she would need his goodwill to get home.

"No! How can this be?" Corry was open-mouthed. "I've teased you too much and this is a joke you're playing on me. Isn't it?"

"Of all the people here, I am the one who believes the story the most." Cathryn watched the duke's face from corner of her eye. "I am the stranger from another place. What I cannot understand is who would want to do something like this? And why?"

"Think about it, Corry," Lucette urged. "What else but something this overwhelming would close your guildhouse?"

Corry and his sister were an affectionate pair of siblings, but it was to his father that Corry looked for a definitive word.

"Our guest has the right of it, son. And a careful hearing and seeing she's made to tell it so fully."

"Then, how wonderful. Tell me everything about your country, what it is and does and how they dress and speak and…"

"Enough." Benedic rose abruptly. "You intrude on the lady with your impertinent prying. We need, instead, to discover the who and why of this." He began to pace the balcony, a frown on his face and a certain coiled intelligence in his eyes.

Corry looked as if he could hardly believe his father's reprimand. The whole breakfast had taken a swift and awkward turn. Cathryn felt badly for the boy. He looked to be about 14 or 15, not an ideal age for what must seem like unprovoked anger from his father. She tried to turn the conversation to safer channels.

"Well, perhaps others will know more than we do. You mentioned that your wife has strong Esoteric magic. Could we start by asking her about this?"

Benedic stopped his pacing, his back to the three of them. She knew immediately that, somehow, she had just made matters worse. A lot worse.

Lucette jumped up with a hurried excuse about getting Corry a home-from-school haircut and in the space of a few seconds they both were gone.

After a long and tense silence, the duke finally turned around.

"My wife died some years ago."

Cathryn shivered.

"By your leave, lady. I must serve at a trial. I will send Arilon to you. Please let him know if there is anything you require. When the matters of this morning are concluded, I will return and we will again pursue the answers we both need." He turned his back to her once again and walked away.

She watched him leave, trailing unasked questions, unheard answers.

The sun had softened the morning's edges. Small yellow and rust colored birds chittered in and out of the balcony balustrades, gossiping over Corry's crumbs. It was tempting to just sit, forgetting everything and everyone else. The very rhythm of life in this place was different; more stately, a sedate pace, a greener melody with touches of foreign harmonies. A soft, pungent undercurrent to the breeze promised a warm afternoon. It would be so easy to stay here and avoid the difficulties that were stacking up. At least for a little while.

But she roused herself. There were things to do, pieces of the puzzle to find and fit. Time to get up and get going. She pushed herself up from the chair with both hands, and then cried out. At the small pressure of pushing upward, her right arm felt as if it had caught fire. She grabbed the tunic cuff and pulled it up. There, tracing up her arm, was a hard ridge that curled and twisted from wrist to shoulder. She touched it and was punished with another jolt of pain. But in that brief touch she could tell that the ridge was caused by something pushing up from underneath the skin.

Now she felt the onrush of real panic. Knocking over her chair in her haste, she fled inside for help, running through the corridor of the duke's living quarters, calling out for Lucette. For anyone. Something was squirming under her skin. Faster she ran, through the huge entry room and out through the doorway toward the public rooms—so afraid that she was breathless—had to force air into her lungs for a shout. A shout that never came. For as she turned a corner, hands grabbed, a black bag was jammed over her head. It smelled of something foul, something…

Chapter Two:
BENEDIC

LIES FLOATED THROUGH the sun-warmed air of the hearing room like a fetid odor. It offended his senses and his sensibilities. His anger, now roused, turned the intention of determining justice on its side. It became the need to see justice delivered. The bailiff rapped her staff of order sharply on the floor three times. "Rise to meet justice Tyg, forester of Forché, the accused. Rise to hear justice Kester of Chymion, accuser. Rise to deliver justice Benedic of Forché, duke by right, judge by law."

Carefully, deliberately, the duke raised himself from the chair in which he had heard this case. Carefully, deliberately, he raised his head, raised eyes of ice to pronounce the forester's fate.

"I have listened well," his words fell like heavy stones. "I have heard how you did conspire to demand, from one Kester of Chymion, fraudulent tolls; how you did obstruct free passage along the public roads of Forché and abused the oathbond of the forester to practice extortion. I have listened well. Now listen you, with most careful hearing, for justice will stand. And listen you who hold your oaths lightly, who stand in places of power with dark purposes, for justice will stand.

"Present here is a man who would turn honesty inside out, twist privilege to the purpose of greed and sell that brightest of birthrights—his own and Forché's honor. I would not live next to one who has broken faith with all neighbors and kin, and I do hereby command he be taken to the border and be given over to officers of Chymion Province, there to serve that ducal house in menial labor for seven years. We will not welcome you back when your years are served. You are, from this day, a stranger to us."

The onlookers who had come, curious about this inter-duchy matter, were completely silent. Then a small rustling brushed through the crowd. The bailiff and a sentry were walking over to where the accuser stood. The duke, too, turned to the plaintiff. The eyes that had so doomed Tyg warmed not at all as they bore down on Kester. "And I have heard your story, Kester of Chymion; how you did travel from the farthest fields of Chymion with seeds to trade in our home. I listened and heard something underneath your words that set my teeth on edge. So I sent a sentry to your wagon. He searched it well— and brought me this." He reached out and the sentry stepped forward to place a small bag in the duke's hand. When he saw it, Kester turned sickly pale.

"You look unwell, neighbor trader. Tell us your sickness."

The low voice got louder. "Tell us why you look so pale."

Louder. "Tell us."

Once the accuser, now accused, Kester flung himself on his knees. "I do admit my guilt, my lord, and plead for mercy. I beg you be merciful."

"The sons and daughters, mothers and fathers, young ones

and elders of Forché offer the same mercy you would have given them. I do command that you be taken to a house of healers and that, under their watchful eyes, the anagar seeds in this bag be given to you, four at a time, each and every night until the bag is empty. Two seeds, sold cheaply, trick the mind into baseless, silly dreams. The body craves more as more are eaten. Three seeds, sold more dearly, bring wild dreams. Four seeds, which you would have sold for gold to the ignorant, bring gibbering nightmares that beat, slobbering at the doors of sanity. Your twisted heart that first decided to seduce the people of Forché into this living death will look into itself, in the dark, alone, time after time after time. And when the seeds are gone and your body craves what it can no longer have, then pray the Creator have mercy on your soul—for we have given you all the mercy we have."

The bailiff once again rapped the staff of order on the floor. "Thus is justice delivered this day. Take heed of it, all of you."

Almost before the last words were uttered, Benedic turned and strode out of the courtroom. The case had so disturbed him that it took persistent effort on Arilon's part to get his attention. Matching his pace, Arilon walked beside the duke.

"Please, you must see this messenger at once. He will see no other and he comes from the King."

"At last. Where is this herald?"

"He awaits you in your quarters, my lord."

The day had started off well enough. Corry had arrived and any time both of his children were home brought him special joy. But Corry's homecoming had also been the trigger for the unpleasantness at breakfast. Then the court case. He never enjoyed dispensing judgments and this time he hated what had to be done. But he could not shirk his duty. And now the king's messenger. He feared the message because he feared the subject of it. He felt he knew too much and too little. But his loyalty was to the king and he would hear and obey.

With Arilon at his heels, the duke entered his quarters and found the courier in the long receiving room.

"Greetings from His Majesty, King Reyfen, first of servants to Benedic, Duke of House Forché." The herald made a deep bow. "I bring word from the King to you...alone." He looked at Arilon.

From years of counting on Arilon's cooperation, he expected his castellan to leave immediately. Instead, to the surprise of both the duke and the herald, Arilon simply stood, unmoving.

"Thank you, Arilon. You may withdraw."

Still, there was a pause between the expectation and the movement. Finally, however, the door closed behind the castellan. The herald and Benedic stood alone in the sunlight pouring in through the high windows.

In the expectant quiet, in whispered words both familiar and disturbing, the herald began the remembering spell. Weaving words and focus together, he pronounced the spell upon himself. He would remember the words he had been given to say for the space it took to say them. Before the spell, and without the presence of the intended recipient as a trigger, he could recall nothing of the message. And afterward he would remember nothing. But for the moment, words brought directly from the king fell from him and were caught in the duke's attention.

"Here are the words of our King to Benedic, Duke of Forché. First, greetings to our friend and our regard. Being charged with this matter must be truly difficult. Sure we thank you. We agree that the woman should be kept from general contact. Knowledge of her world, as you know too well, is dangerous in and of itself. She must not be allowed to tell too much. Yet, to deal too strongly or too privately with her might keep her from doing that which must be done. I therefore conclude that, though our court is watched closely, it is only here we can control her usefulness and secure her safety. Bring her to us in all haste. We rely on you alone, remembering your good service and suffering on our behalf in past days."

With a sigh that sounded almost sad, the herald finished. When his eyes again were clearly in the present time and place, he added words he had been told to speak openly.

"My lord, I will await your preparations. For I am told we are to return to court together."

"I thank you for the pains you took to deliver this message. Arilon will make a place for you to stay the night. We will leave in the morning, with a third traveler in our party."

"Thank you, my lord."

As if he had been just outside the door, Arilon entered hard on the herald's heels.

"The herald says there will be three leaving for CorronKeep tomorrow morning. I will make all preparations for travel, my lord, if you could just tell me who will be going and…"

The duke found himself staring at his castellan. It was as though the man were singing off-key. Something was not right. Was he sick? Afraid? If so, of what? And why? In all the years he and his family had known and relied on Arilon, there had never even been a question like this raised before. Dreading that he must do it and what he might find, Benedic began his spell. As Arilon finished his sentence, he finished the spell. And caught his breath at what it discovered. Guilt. The man was feeling guilty. Why?

"Yes, thank you, Arilon. There will be three of us: the herald, myself and our guest, Cathryn of Porter."

There it was again. The mention of Cathryn's name intensified the guilty feeling.

"I…she….I have looked for the lady everywhere. And I

cannot find her. Or find where she has gone. No one has seen anything, or so they say. I blame myself, my lord."

So that was it. Arilon felt responsible for losing track of the guest. The duke put reassurance into his voice. "It is not your fault the lady walks about. There is no blame."

"Thank you, my lord. I'll search again, though I do not think she will be found. Thank you." Arilon almost ran from the room.

Tired. Too many spells, too much that was distressing. And now the woman missing. Though he had been calm with Arilon, he was profoundly uneasy within himself. He walked over to the wall of windows, close and then closer to one of the long panes still bathed in shadow. His head aching, he leaned his forehead against the smooth coolness for relief. And in the coolness and the quiet, he remembered.

Remembered: Laughing with D'Shaar. Winter and throwing snow. Red, chapped cheeks and kisses by the fire. Married to his truest friend, deepest companion, the most agile intelligence and kindest spirit he had known. Wife D'Shaar, Esoteric Guild—Unseen Circle. Studying time and place with D'Brin, her cousin. Two of the finest minds possessed of the most potent magic trying to discover the undiscovered, uncover the hidden. Always in his books, D'Brin seldom came back to Forché's light and joy. D'Shaar, though also a scholar, could happily pull herself back to him. First husband, then children were the anchors that kept her close to the harbor of family. Days of good work for mind and hand, nights of sweet contentment and the signal flares of passion. Hair the brown of redbarks, eyes a dark, deep-sea green. Ten years gone and still the ache could sink through his bones.

Remembered: The day she returned from D'Brin's distant and isolated compound to tell him about other worlds. The two of them had stumbled on a way to see into places that seemed like cousins to this world. Only quick glances were possible in the bronze mirror that showed the faces of alien peoples and times. Some of the world cousins were benign or empty. Some were malignant and menacing. D'Brin was ecstatic. But D'Shaar had felt the cold breath of fear.

One world in particular chilled her, seeped its dreadful horrors into her nightmares. This world put people in ovens, heaped bodies in shallow ditches, turned neglect into a hideous weapon for the murder of the youngest. This world also held words of grace, art of great design and passion, buildings that thrust into the sky with cornices and conditions of amazement, and acts of that resilient and unnerving kindness which spoke of the divine. In that time and place, people swarmed over their world like frenzied insects. There was something at once energetic and decayed, cunning and blind, intelligent and yet extravagantly unbalanced about them. This world, this cousin, held D'Brin's attention in the same way a dying beetle torn apart by birds could hold him. The balance of fascination and loathing was precarious.

So D'Shaar came home to her harbor and, in the safety of their bed, poured out her fears to him. Where would this knowledge lead? What would happen to Forché and Corronheld when the skills of the killers were learned? Even a brief glance was as addicting as anagar seeds, for this cousin-world was both admirable and terrible.

The next day D'Shaar went back to reason with D'Brin, to beg him to stop this research before the unthinkable happened. A fortnight went by. Stars and sun swam the daily sea in disregard. Fifteen nights later, she came home. In a coffin. The sight of the wagon and the long, stark wooden box it carried seared itself into his brain. And broke his heart.

D'Shaar had reasoned with D'Brin for days. When she felt no agreement in the wind, she took matters into her own hands.

It was the spell she wove to break the bronze looking-eye that killed her. So said D'Brin when he brought the box. And then he left. Left in his wake a husband unanchored, children adrift. He felt, in the endless days that followed, as if he stood on the surface of the world—as if it were dragging his empty shell slowly around and around, day after day. It was a very long time before he came up through the fog of grief to question the words D'Brin had left behind. Eventually, he went to his pledged sovereign and unburdened himself of his questions and the very few answers he had. So the King became aware of other places, other times, alien ways.

But the questions came too late. D'Brin had disappeared, and with him went the chance to learn what really happened. Rumors surfaced now and again of D'Brin's whereabouts, but nothing was confirmed. And in all this time, no hint of that renegade magic. Until now. Now another world—that world— had ripped into his home again.

At least this time he knew how to start. It seemed likely that Cathryn might have gone back to the quarry, perhaps thinking it might hold the exit from this world, as it had been the site of her entrance. Though he chastised himself for the perverse enjoyment the decision gave him, he concluded that a cold night by a very long road might better shape the lady's future reception of his needful constraints.

So, first he would take to bed. In the morning, the herald would return to CorronKeep, alone, with explanations for King Reyfen. Forché Keep would be cared for by Lucette and Corry and Arilon. And he would take on the cloak of the traveler and begin his search.

His mind made up, he turned his back on the windows that now showed a darkening, lowering sky.

❋

If the sun were going to warm away the cold, it would have done so by now. Having left in the earliest and grayest of dawnlight, he had already ridden for hours. Mists smeared and insinuated themselves under his traveler's cloak, beneath overhanging leaves, around the wide expanses of redbark trunks and under the drooping arms of ferns.

He had bid his children farewell late last night, telling them almost nothing. They had fretted, prodding him with questions. All he could tell them, he said, was that Cathryn was gone and he, alone, would find her. The tending of the province he left, for the while, in their hands. If, somehow, the stranger returned to the Keep, they were to hold her there—for her own safety, he said—and send word to the King. It was all he could tell them and it was not nearly enough.

While the dark was still cold and insistent, he had risen and had taken on the look that, in his younger days, had earned him the title of 'the gray duke' from those who knew him. Made from the fine, gray wool of Chymion province sheep, his traveling clothes were all of a color, varying only in shades: blue-gray pants tucked in charcoal leather riding boots, soft gray tunic closed with silver-worked clasps, and over all the long, hooded cloak.

It had been years since he had dressed so. Years since he had taken to the roads, singular and unrecognized. Even though the task which took him outward was worrisome, the prospect of moving through his land unburdened by the press of daily duties tasted delicious to him in that just-awakening, wan morning.

But then, just as he might have left with the taste of freedom on his tongue, he had reluctantly made one more addition to his travel attire. From the wall above the guttering fire he had taken Forché's blade and, with a hesitant hand, bound it to his belt.

Even now, after hours of becoming accustomed again to long riding, the sword made itself felt, an uncomfortable presence that slapped quietly with every step. His horse seemed to feel the awkwardness, too, shying more often at imagined road-threats. Or was there something else causing horse and rider both to flinch?

Impulse took the duke off the road at a spot where no branches or bracken would be broken to point out his path to a clever eye. As quickly and quietly as he could, he dismounted, led his horse far into the forest deeps and tied it within reach of easy grazing. "A little quiet is what I require, Kell." He spoke to his mount in a low and soothing tone. "Be a horse and eat, but no noise. And then I'll come back for you with an apple if you warrant it." Kell, being only and still a horse, shook his head and set to eating.

Benedic backtracked until he found a depression hidden by a lushness of branches and moss. Gathering his cloak around him and pulling the hood farther over his head, he settled in to wait. Fog brushed him all over with dew until, like the forest things around him, he was blended by the dampness into the mists. Waited. Waited.

There. Coming. Too quietly. With a haste born of instinct and preservation, he wound a spell around himself. Servant's magic could be used to make the server virtually unnoticed. Being unnoticed seemed urgently desirable right now. Done. And none too soon. Two riders in black, on dappled mounts. How could they be so quiet? As they passed, he saw the horses' feet had been bound and muffled in rags. His quick eyes ran over the riders as well. Black hoods. And there. One of them switched a rein suddenly so his wrist was revealed for a flash of a moment; one black band, one gray. With that sight came a whiff of magic, laced with a bitter tang of need and something less healthy. These two were from Spirit Circle. They clearly belonged to that particular Esoteric specialty—the hunting and taking of persons. Nothing could be seen under the hoods, but the feeling came strongly that these hidden eyes and ears were sharply, wickedly, relentlessly searching.

In the space of a breath, they were gone; though the search they made was precise, the riders were swift. He sat in the hidden place longer, to be careful and to think. No Takers had been seen in Corronheld for almost two decades. Forbidden now by law, they had been disbanded. Were they searching for him or for the missing Cathryn? Had they been hired by the Unseens to find her, or had she gone with Unseens and then sent these two to keep him from finding her?

No answers waited along the roadside. It was time to move. Drops showered off branches and leaves as he uncoiled from the shadows and set out to reclaim Kell. The horse was there waiting patiently and, for a welcome change, quietly. That not only warranted the apple, but also a sincere, though brief, bit of brushing down with a handful of leaves.

"I hope you enjoyed that, my friend, because the way we must go now will soon put it all to ruin." He mounted and reined Kell in a new direction. The road wasn't safe anymore and his destination was new. If Takers were involved, then he knew he couldn't handle this alone. Expert help was what he needed—and right away. Three hours of hard, cross-forest travel brought him to a new road that headed more north than west.

By midday, he came upon the compound. It was a source of some satisfaction that he remembered his soldiering lessons so well that the gate sentry was surprised to see him ride into view. He caught the sentry's quick glance upward to the hilltop above. Some outguard would get stable duty for a month, if he didn't miss his guess.

"Your name and business here?" What she had neglected

in vigilance, the sentry tried to make up for in bristling officiousness.

"My name is T'Grayn, messenger from Linton Stand to see Training Masters Kern and Bayly." He swung off his horse and leaned toward the fuming sentry. "And if you run fetch them quickly, I may not tell them what an unexpected guest I was."

After a bit of sputtering, good sense kicked in and she took to her heels. In a matter of moments, the gate opened. Once inside the high stone walls, his horse was taken from him and he was led to a central building. His guide, a young man of few words and large arms, pointed to a door. Benedic smiled to himself and entered. While his eyes adjusted to the sudden dark of the room, he stayed close by the door and kept silent.

"Well, messenger, what brings you to us?" A man's voice, deep and grainy, came from the duke's left.

"Speak, for we are eager to hear your news." The woman's voice, strong and controlled, came from his right.

"I came to tell you that these darkened room games won't work with me, cousin." Straight ahead of him a light flashed on, showing the pair of training masters behind it. "Although I must admit, you are getting better at putting your voices where you aren't."

"Benedic! Cousin! Well met." The woman reached him first and nearly dented his ribs with her embrace. That was followed by an equally crushing one from the man.

"Well met, indeed." Benedic disentangled himself as best he could from his very, very healthy hosts. "Do you two do anything less than full bore? Let me see you, Bayly. You look as intimidating as ever, cousin. Though I think your husband is dwindling to a nubbin, don't you?"

Kern, who wasn't anything closely resembling a nubbin, laughed and pounded the duke's defenseless back.

"Your cousin keeps me fit, old man." Kern's voice seemed to rattle the windows. "No student can best her on the training course, and no one would dare to best her at home." While leering sincerely, Kern casually flicked a leg out in what should have been a bone-cracking kick. His wife dodged it neatly, though, and returned with a slug to his arm that made Benedic wince to even look at it.

"Enough, my love. We have company and he hasn't even told us why he entered here using the name of an old Linton border scout. Fetch us something hot to drink, Kern, while my cousin tells us what game *he* is playing."

Bayly settled the duke into the guest chair, the only chair in the room with a cushion. He knew it from his younger days—days of training for his three years of service in the militia. Back then, his cousin and Kern weren't married yet, but soldiers in training just like himself. They saw the inside of this building often enough, though, when all three were called before the Training Master for a nearly endless series of reprimands. Never any serious issues—even then they were careful. But there had been the matter of the birthday surprise for the fencing master in which cold porridge and high-topped boots figured prominently. Or the time the three of them snuck into the strategy teacher's classroom, removed all the desks and chairs and reassembled the classroom—in perfect detail—outside in the center courtyard. That no one had seen or heard them do it was a matter of legend by now.

Now his cousin was married to his best friend, a pair of masters both sandy-colored from head to toe: sandy hair and weathered brown faces, dun colored leather jerkins, pants and boots.

"I would play no games with you two for fear of losing my head." The duke watched while Kern poured kaffe into three mugs and brought them to the table. He watched Bayly as she watched Kern settle near her; the look that passed between them tore all the wind from his words. It sometimes happened like this; another's happiness in a mate would hit him like a blow. He ducked his head over the steaming kaffe.

"It must be serious then, cousin, for I can see you are shaken."

Benedic blessed Bayly's assumption. "Serious, yes, and of such a nature that I cannot tell all of it. This matter may be but a rift in a guild or it may reach to the crown. I know so little now and yet what I do know has, I believe, set Takers upon my trail." His frustration getting the better of him, he left the chair to pace.

"I regret coming here with so little to say and so much to ask. We have had no secrets in the past…and what I have come to ask will put you both in the way of a danger deeper than any we have known. I do not understand, myself, what is safe or true to tell you and yet I am asking…"

Kern laid his big, callused hand on the duke's arm. "Enough. We are engaged. That you have asked is all we need, or else what was our past about?"

Bayly added her hand to Kern's. Their solid, indestructible affection left him speechless. He could not ask them to face this danger with him, and yet he could not face it without them.

Bayly stood up and headed for the front door. Kern rose and headed for the back room, talking over his shoulder as he went.

"She will arrange for the masters and teachers to stand watch tonight. Our next in command is an able teacher—we won't be missed unduly. Just tell me if we'll meet the mountains on this trip; Bayly won't go near snow unless we take her fur hood."

The muffled sounds of packing drifted out from the back for a while. Then Kern reappeared with a blanket.

"I'll take first watch, Bayly will take second. We'll leave at last light and travel by night until well away. Get some sleep while you can." Kern pulled a chair around to face the door and window, wrapped up in the blanket and settled down to watch.

Benedic amazed himself by obediently going to the bed in the back room and actually resting. Only here could he feel so safe; safe enough that, within minutes, he was so hard asleep he never heard Bayly come back and finish packing.

The final glimmers of daylight lingered on the mounded hills. In the valleys, night already circled before it settled. Within the compound, interior lights began to ignite. Inside the central offices, Bayly took down a map. It was time to lay plans.

Benedic scanned the map as he spoke. "I've turned this over and over in my mind. Each time the same conclusion forces itself on me: The one we need to find first must be D'Brin. The stranger was brought by Esoteric magic from—" he stopped himself from even hinting Cathryn came from another world "—another country unknown to us. No one knows more of Unseen magic than D'Brin.

"The likeliest place to begin the search," he traced across the chart from the south to the west, "is somewhere in the foothills north of the Sentinel Mountains. I am informed that, when word goes out of interest to him, within a day's time he can be to the Esoteric guildhall or to CorronKeep. That must put him within this circle."

"Going directly by main road from Forché to the foothills is not wise." Bayly rubbed her jaw in concentration. Strategy and information gathering had always been her strongest skills.

"Scouring those foothills for a small enclave could be the work of a lifetime. Perhaps we would gain time by spending a bit of time." Her finger traced a cross-country route to the capitol, CorronKeep.

"If the wizard is truly a day away from the court city, then someone there has information we can use. We can't ask in the highest places if you want to keep your journey a secret, cousin. So I think it's time for a little tavern diving."

Bayly looked positively delighted at the prospect of mixing with tavern-goers. Since the three of them drank nothing stronger than kaffe, it couldn't be the wine that pleased her. The two men knew from long experience that it was the chance to listen to rumors, eavesdrop on foolish babblers, pry answers from stingy informers that made her eyes light up.

Kern, however, despised gossip. To him, those who played at rumormongering and court intrigues were, as he once elegantly put it, "nothing but a pack of dogs sniffing each other's hind parts." His preference was looking, not listening. No one matched Kern's ability to follow and observe unseen, to find a trail and keep it, to watch and understand the movements of others. With Kern and Bayly along, he knew he had the best eyes and ears he could ever hope to find in bodies trained in the soldier's arts.

"The daylight is gone. Let us be gone as well." Kern folded the map, tucked it away and slung his pack over a reassuringly broad shoulder.

"Shall we away, cousin?" Bayly spared not a single glance for the room and things they were leaving behind. Her whole demeanor said that, with Kern and Benedic beside her, all that was important was present.

Under cover of darkness, and with the stealthy cooperation of senior masters, the three left the compound on foot through a hidden gate. By plan, Benedic again cast a spell on himself so that, if there were Takers nearby, they would only sense two unimportant travelers. If the Takers actually saw them, then the spell wouldn't help. So Kern scouted ahead and watched and examined and prayed his skills would discover any threat before it came too close.

To Benedic, the enforced silence was loud with sound. Every tree frog, every cricket, each hoot of a nightlooker filled the dark with noise and the possibility of danger. Shadows tried to take on forms. Branches grabbed for faces and cloaks. Roots snaked up through dirt to ankle-bite. Night traveling was heart-thudding tedium.

Finally, when the first hint of pale cream rose to the lowest star, Kern called a halt. He had found a hollow that would both hide and shelter them for a while and they settled in to rest.

It was midday before Bayly roused them to start up again. When they emerged from the hollow, the sunlight shone on a field of flames. There, belted on the verge of the shaggy redbark forest, was a field of fireflowers flagging the passing breeze. Without thought, he did what he had done since he was a boy: he squinted his eyes almost shut until the orange-red flowers looked like wavering flames indeed. Was it a cloud passing over the sun that threw darkness over the fiery field? Or was it something else?

He had to be called twice by Kern before he moved out. Where the fireflowers grew marked the border of Forché. Beyond the trees, beyond the red-carpeted verge, lay the gorse covered hills of Corronheld Crown. Whatever was beyond the light-pierced denseness of the forest waited for him in that portion of land that wasn't a province, but the sovereign center that held all the provinces together—a circle of royal land encompassing the capitol city of CorronKeep. Though the duke's allegiance to the reigning monarch was complete, today for some reason his path across the boundary of home held an especial weight. In his bones he felt the stirring of change. Yet he resolutely put one foot in front of the other, his eyes set straight ahead in the direction of the court city. Behind him, fireflowers waved in agitation, looking more and more like flames.

Chapter Three:
CATHRYN

FIRST IT WAS the bad tasting dryness in her mouth. Then it was the pounding headache. Finally it was the wedge of dimming light that made her climb into groggy consciousness.

How very odd, she thought, and how wonderful. It was the sleeve on her own arm under her cheek. And so it must be the buttons on the cuff she was seeing. So intricate. Not like buttons back home, machine stamped and plain. These buttons were tiny and yet covered with what looked like intricate wrought iron filigree. Each was unique. One had a sliver of moon and a dozen stars delicately etched behind a latticework that looked like roses climbing a trellis. Another had boughs of tiny birds with a background of cloud wisps. Each button was set on the sleeve with careful stitches that continued all around the cuff in a stem-and-leaf pattern that, until she looked this closely, might never have been seen.

What kind of world was this that decorated buttons, cuffs

and language with such care—and yet tore her from everything she could call home? She'd been drugged, that much was for certain. By the jouncing and creaking, she knew she was in a wagon. The wedge of light pushing its way under the hood over her face made her believe it was daylight. Carefully, not knowing what watchers there might be, she painstakingly squirmed until the hood slid off. The fresh air began to revive her.

She lay under a thin canvas tarp covering a wagon bed lined with straw, her hands and feet tightly tied. The last effects of the drug fell to building anger. First torn from home, then manipulated by that duke person who clearly knew much more than he let on, then kidnapped by somebody for some unknown reason. It was too much. Even if these were the good guys (and how could she tell?), their methods made her furious.

Looking out the back of the wagon bed she could see dense brush and rolling hills spread out beside the narrow band of road. If she could get loose, it should be easy enough to get out and get hidden. But how? Cautiously she wriggled through the straw, feeling for anything useful. The more she moved, the more the straw itched and the more the heat of the sun made her sweat. She still ached all over, now more ever, and the jolting ride wasn't helping.

Suddenly, a pothole grabbed one wheel and the wagon tilted hard, throwing her against the boards and metal rib of the wagon's side. Banging around like that didn't do her body any good, but it did bring a wonderful discovery: the metal posts along the cart's side were sharp. Not very sharp, but good enough.

When the rope around her wrists finally snapped, her arms were almost useless with fatigue. But she pushed herself to untie the knots at her ankles and slid down toward the opening at the end of the wagon. Trying not to rustle too loudly, she picked straw off her clothes and pushed the loose stuff back from the end of the wagon. It would do no good to drop off the cart and leave a pile of straw to mark her exit spot.

As she worked, the sky grew paler, the light dimmer. Dusk was sliding quickly into place, another aid to escape she hoped. Finally, with some strength returned to her arms and the straw as out of the way as it could be, she lowered her legs over the edge of the wagon and at the next bump, slid off to land lightly on the road. City smarts told her to move away quickly, but another instinct made more sense and she listened to it and stayed crouched, motionless, where she'd landed. The cart turned with the curve in the road and lumbered out of sight. Free.

Now to stay free. Keeping to the edge of the road, she began to run in the direction the cart had taken until she could hear its creaking just ahead. In this world, she didn't know who to trust or where to go. Her only plan was to follow the cart to its destination and find out who was doing this to her. It might be crazy not to put as much distance between herself and the kidnappers as possible, but frustration at the lack of unfiltered information was even worse than the anxiety of recapture right now.

Eventually, it was the smell of smoke that drove her deeper into the roadside shadows. Sure enough, an inn of some sort squinted its lamp lit eyes out toward the darkening night. In the orange light spilt from open windows, she could see the slowly swinging sign outside and the hulk of a barn behind. Already the cart was pulling past the main building and into the stables. Her absence would be noticed soon.

Quickly, before the inevitable hue and cry, she sprinted for a huge broad-leafed tree that grew between the inn and stable buildings. With a running leap, she just managed to grab the lowest branch and, with an effort made harder by years of desk jobs, swung her legs up and over as well. By the time she maneuvered herself upright on the branch and climbed higher into the dense leafiness, she was panting and hot. The stable doors banged open with a sound like a shot. Then she froze and the hair on the nape of her neck prickled in alarm. She couldn't see through the leaves, but she could hear the kidnappers coming her way.

"We are dead men, brother! They will blame us and we will be dead!"

"They cannot blame us for their own mistake. They promised she would sleep the whole time. The fault is not ours. But if we do not report this, our lives will be forfeit, little brother. Besides, she has the worm. They can find her anywhere. When they do, we have our lives back. But only then." There was that creaking, shifting sound of someone climbing into a saddle. "Stay here and wait for me to return with the Takers."

"But…"

"Just get inside and see what you can learn. Maybe she'll be stupid enough to wander in." The horse and rider moved away in a rush. Mumbling angrily and, she thought, fearfully, the brother-kidnapper left behind reluctantly started toward the inn. When he opened the back door of the place, sound tumbled out and then was shut back up again.

What more information she might hope to learn here didn't seem worth the risk after hearing the brother's talk. There was little time. Down she scrambled, out of the tree and into the barn. A small glowlantern hung near the door. She grabbed it and started her search. There were tools pegged up along one wall. She took a knife, a small pail, an empty grain sack, some rope. Stroking the glowlantern downward as Lucette had shown her, the light went out and she tucked it and the rest of her supplies into the sack. Horses, belonging no doubt to the inn and its guests, stamped fretfully in stalls along the back wall. Not a one was saddled and, for all her vacationing in the woods, city-bred Cathryn had no idea of how a saddle got put on—or, at least put on to stay. She knew she could move faster along the roads on a horse, but how to accomplish it quickly and in quiet was beyond her. Scratch that idea. Better to just leave. Fast.

Outside she went and then noticed sheets and towels hanging on a line to dry. Thanking whatever lazy worker had neglected to take them in before nightfall, she pulled a few dishtowels off the line and stuffed them into the sack, making sure to wrap the metal items so they wouldn't rattle as she moved.

As well as she could in the gathering darkness of night, she slipped out through the inn-yard and back down the road the way she and the cart had come. Keeping to the edge of the road seemed the only possibility in the darkness. And it would be the only way she could hope to find the smaller road that branched off several miles back. She'd noticed it before she'd jumped out of the wagon and thought she might backtrack to follow it since it didn't look to be going toward either the kidnappers or the duke and his secrets.

Now she really missed her watch. Taking it off for the whole vacation had seemed a happy thought. But without it she couldn't tell how long these alien days and nights really were, and certainly could not tell how long she'd been running along the roadside. Besides, it would have been a comforting companion from home. As it was, the only item other than clothes and her silver ring that came through was half a package of trail mix and a book of matches. She patted her pocket. Still there.

She would have missed the branch road completely if the moon had not come up and laid a path of peachglow on the old, canted flagstones.

"It's not quite the yellow brick road, Dorothy, but it'll have to do." She startled herself by speaking out loud. "And shut up, why don't you, and move." Ignoring the stitch that was building in her side, she turned down the gleaming ribbon of side-road, careful to leave no marks of her turning.

This road soon narrowed and, though it didn't ever completely disappear, it wound and rambled in a disorienting way. Even trying to keep the moon as a sighting line didn't help. Eventually, the underbrush and land formations began to change. Trees clumped together, leaving more of the hills uncovered. More rocks clotted the hillsides. And every now and again there was an odd smell. A smell she tried to place. What was it?

Sulphur.

Another, stronger whiff came and she was sure. Sulphur—or this world's equivalent. The moonlight was bright enough to show up small straggles of steam appearing here and there among the rocks. The road looked to be safe enough. She tried to remember her childhood trip to Yellowstone. There were boardwalks and roads laid out so you could move in safety. Hopefully it was the same here. No sense surviving so far only to fall through a brittle crust and get parboiled.

Then she smiled. This might be just the place for the thing she had to do. The steam and stench might cover the smoke and smell. Now if she could only find fresh water that didn't smell like matchheads.

Half a mile down-road she found a clear stream and followed it away from the road. She could find her way back, she was sure, but it would be safer to do this thing in a more remote spot. At a clearing along the riverbank, she unslung her sack and emptied it out beside her. There were plenty of dry branches and twigs within easy reach and they, with the help of her very welcome matches, soon became a small fire. At least she had camping skills good enough to be able to fill the pail with water and set up forked sticks to hold it over the flames.

She cut up the towels and put the pieces in the now boiling water. When they'd simmered for a while, she speared them out with the knife and draped each piece on an overhanging branch. Finally, she tied one strip of cloth around the knife's handle and it went into the boiling water, too. After she waited what she hoped was long enough, she cleaned her hands in the stream, wiped them on one of the warm, wet strips of cloth, and pulled up the knife to cool. She set the pail to one side to cool as well. While it gave off its steam, she rolled up her sleeve.

There it was. No longer a bruise or a ridge. No longer painful, either. But almost too revolting to look at. The worm in her arm twitched and wriggled, roiling under her skin. Her kidnappers had said she could be tracked because of this worm. It had to go. But more than that, it had to go because it was wrong, uninvited, an unasked for invasion, an ugly mercenary in the service of others.

She took one piece of towel and twisted it around her upper arm, tying it snugly. She took another bit of cloth, twisted it and clamped it between her teeth. Before thought could forestall action, she took the knife, extended her arm over the river and raised the blade to where the worm slid, oblivious, under her skin. Breathe in. Blade point through her skin near the elbow and down along the worm's side. Down. Across, trying to avoid the veins and arteries that lay all too close. Start back up the other side of the ridgy body. With one end cut loose, the worm's freed tail flopped loose and began a horrible, bloody slapping by her wrist. Hurry. The knife continued its red trail up and then across again. That should be it. Blood ran like a fountain, dripping a dark tributary into the little stream.

Chewing down even harder on the rag in her mouth, she dropped the knife and reached with her other hand to pull the beast off. Slimy with her own blood, the worm wiggled frantically. With a muffled howl she couldn't help, Cathryn threw the thing on the fire where it snapped and spattered and twisted and then burned into stillness. She couldn't look away until she was sure.

When she did turn away, it surprised her to feel tears running down her face. It surprised her to feel the small pinpricks of pain on top of pain. She spit out the cloth.

"Salt water...stings. No kidding."

She reached for the now-cooler water and washed down the wound, bandaging it with the clean cloths and fashioning a makeshift sling. Almost in a trance, for the pain was hot and cold and much too intimate, she cleaned the knife, drowned the fire and washed its nauseating ashes into the river. When she had stuffed all back into the sack, she stood up, very carefully, very gingerly.

"Stay with me, woman. Don't fade now." She took a first step back toward the road. "This foot and then that foot. You know the drill."

By sheer will, the two feet were kept at their task. She reached the road and once again turned toward what she thought was the direction of freedom. Each mile covered was a hard won victory. She didn't think about what lay ahead, only where the next foot was falling.

Somewhere in the night, the fever came on her. But she walked through it all, until dawn and the limits of her stamina came rushing toward her together. It seemed as though she fell slowly, that it took hours to reach the ground, hours between one fluttering breath and the next. So she could not say for sure when she noticed the feet in front of her face. She just knew that, as hands reached down, she saw a digital watch.

Screaming for air. Running...again...it's getting closer. Red air—blood red. Can't run fast enough. NO! It's closer. RUN. Trees in the dark clawing face, tripping feet. Run. Faster. Help me. There! A road—someone's there...with a car! Lights on—get

there. Run. Woman with the car door open—get inside backseat. Close the door—hurry, please, drive away, please hurry, it's coming. MOVE! The woman in the driver's seat turns. Can see her face. Opens her mouth...

"Can you hear me?"

Opens her mouth. no...No...NO! Blood pouring out, drowning...

"NO!"

The face blinked. Cathryn shook her head, trying to clear the dream away. But the face stayed where it was, gradually coming into focus.

"The fever must have given you some nightmare," the woman said as she leaned over, taking a cool cloth away from her forehead. The digital watch flashed past her face as the woman's hand went by. "You really worried me. When I found you, you looked completely wiped out. It's been two days."

She tried to speak but only managed a dry croak. The woman had a cup of water to her cracked lips immediately. At that moment, the liquid felt like heaven, though it tasted just slightly like sulphur.

"Where am I?" Trying to speak was a huge effort.

"If you can wait a little, there's some soup just about ready. I think we'd better get as much liquid and nourishment in you as possible. My guess is that you're next to completely dehydrated—what with the fever and not eating for a couple of days. I mean, I got some water down you, but not enough for sure." The woman bustled away, words trailing after her.

The effort to repeat her question was too much for Cathryn. She shut her eyes for just a moment, but knew she'd drifted away again when she heard the woman sit down next to her.

"This broth should do you good." She put the bowl down on the small table near the bed and moved to help her sit up. Both of them were breathing a bit faster when they were done. Now the woman picked up the bowl and began to feed her. The soup tasted salty but good. Each spoonful seemed to bring strength with it. When the bowl was empty, she felt much better. Still thirsty, she reached for the cup of water herself but ended up wincing and wishing she'd not moved so quickly.

"Your arm is still infected. I've got some medicine on it and made a pretty good go of bandaging it. But you'd better not move it too much. Why don't you just lie still for a bit and I'll get you some more water." Taking up the cup and bowl, the woman once again left in a trail of words.

This time, Cathryn could focus more easily on her surroundings. What she first thought were the four walls of the room, turned out to be long panels of cloth hanging from rods. She couldn't tell for sure, but both the ceiling and floor seemed to be made of stone. Where the diffused light that glowed through the cloth panels came from, she also could not tell. All of this made her increasingly, poignantly aware that the promise of the wristwatch might very well be an empty one.

"I'm not home, am I?" They were the first words she spoke to the returning woman.

The woman held up her arm so that the sleeve of her tunic fell and revealed the watch. Her lips pursed ruefully. "No. Neither one of us is. I'm sorry. At least we found each other. My name is Joan. Joan Conley-Foster—originally from San Diego, went to Washington State to go to school and just stayed on."

"I'm from Seattle."

"You're kidding? I live…lived…in Bellevue. I'm a real estate developer. You probably have heard of Haven Heights, right on the country club golf course? That's one of my developments."

"Everybody's heard of it—only this year they're selling houses in Haven Heights II." Cathryn paused, unwilling to hear the answer to the next question. "How long have you been here?"

Joan grabbed her own forearms and held on so tightly that the long sleeves of her tunic bunched under her white fingers. Her ears still rang a bit from the just passed fever, but she thought she heard Joan hiss.

"Ten years. Ten years I've been here." Even ringing ears could hear that bitterness. "It was an accident. He says he can't fix it. It better be fixed. It better be." Cathryn couldn't put a name to the feeling she heard behind the voice. Something in the bitterness had twisted. But something in her twisted as well, knotted up and tensed around the question she dreaded asking.

"Ten years? Isn't there any way to get back?"

"You think I haven't looked for a way to get home? I have looked. Every single waking hour of every single day. For ten years. There is a way back—I know it. I just haven't found it yet."

Suddenly Joan threw herself on the edge of the bed and grabbed Cathryn's hands.

"We've got to work together, Porter. We can figure it out. You want to get home; I need to get home. We can do it if we just help each other. No one else understands. They all lie. All of them. They hide things. But they're not that smart—you've seen them. Stupid. And we can use that. We'll take care of each other, won't we? We'll get back. Soon."

Spittle flew from the force of the pleading. She couldn't help but shrink back from the onslaught of Joan's intensity. But that withdrawal, as slight as it was, brought a violent response. Joan yanked at the bandage on Cathryn's arm, tearing it open and—how she could feel it—tearing open the wound.

"Look! Look at what they do to us!" Stunned, Cathryn dropped her eyes to her own arm. There, under skin freshly slathered with blood, was another worm. Horrified, she looked up at Joan only to see her ripping off her own shirt, buttons flying off and ricocheting like bullets.

"See what they do. SEE!"

Caught in this flashflood of rage, Cathryn's gaze was carried up to Joan's bare torso. Four worms rippled their crowded way under Joan's skin. Each arm had one. One slid around her stomach, its tail disappearing below the trouser waistband. One wrapped around the neck, its head cruelly visible on the swell of her left breast. These worms were huge, wider and longer than hers. And agitated, twitching as if they were electric.

The room became too small. Joan crowded closer, spitting out words in her ear.

"You can't cut them out. They leave parts inside that grow back."

Claustrophobic. Too close. Cathryn pulled away from the worm-riddled, hissing woman. Later, she could not be sure it was a trick of the light or the last vestiges of fever, but at that moment small strangenesses seemed to rush past her awareness. Each strand of Joan's quite obviously bleached hair wriggled in subtle rearrangements. The blotchy flush of the unnamable emotion drained away, swiftly replaced by peach on cream. And the digital watch, a small signal in a larger storm, lit up by itself for just a second and then resumed its relentless count of time as if nothing had happened. Dressed in a neat tunic, Joan folded her hands in front of her. All of it, whatever it had been, was over in a blink of an eye.

What was going on? She felt as if she were thinking through mush. Stalling for time to collect her thoughts, she reached for the cup and took slow sips of water. Oddly, her arm didn't hurt with the reach this time. It felt cool and tingled slightly under the bandages. A few sips. Wait. The bandages were back? Had they really been off? Tired. A few more sips. The face. Sleepy.

When she woke up, she could see the curtain walls had been removed. In the midday sunlight streaming in from outside, Cathryn discovered she was in a huge cavern of pale cream stone. The cavern's mouth yawned hugely—fifty feet high and just as wide. Beyond the stony edge stretched high, rolling hills and beyond the hills reached snow-peaked mountains.

She sat up and slid her legs over the edge of the bed. Not too bad. While she steadied the slight dizziness, she looked around the rest of the cave.

On the back wall a spring pushed its way out between old cracks and sprayed down into a dark pool. Out of the pool a small flow ran in a deep groove in the cave floor, down the middle of the room, outward to the cave edge and then over. Here and there above the groove were flagstones placed to make little bridges. But the most striking feature was a sort of large, stone table set over the groove so that the water ran under it. Made of red-flecked, deep brown rock, the table looked out of place, the wrong kind of stone shaped too awkwardly for any useful purpose. No chairs near it, either.

But there were chairs and a wooden table not too far from her bed with bread and fruit and something to drink set out. Gingerly, she stood up. The stone floor was surprisingly warm. So far so good. Her feet touched on something which turned out to be slippers that slid on with ease. Now the tricky part: walking to the table.

But it didn't turn out tricky. For all the trauma her body had been through, she felt stronger than she had thought she would. In fact, after ploughing through the food with almost frantic zest, she felt very good. Time to explore this place. First, to look over the cave edge and see what was there.

She wasn't stupidly brave, so she had no intention of teetering on the brink just for an adrenaline rush. Still, she wasn't as close to the edge as her caution would have allowed when she was stopped short by... Well, that was the question. Stopped by what? She could see nothing, but she could feel a barrier. Not hard, it gave a bit like dense foam rubber. But, though it was transparent, she could not put her hand through no matter how hard she pushed. Beyond the unseen wall, the cliff dropped hundreds of yards straight down.

"It's like a baby gate. You know, one of those things that keeps kids from falling downstairs and stuff." Sometime during her exploration, Joan had entered the room. "They have these kind of combination bat and bird things here that I, for one, don't want to share my house with. Plus, it lets in fresh air but keeps the temperature just right. From the outside, strangers see just a black hole with a spring gushing out. Saves us from prying eyes. Rather handy, really."

"Magic?"

"Yeah. They really do that here, you know. I didn't believe it at first, but proof just kind of built up over time. I guess that's one thing they can do here we can't do back home." Joan paused as she looked Cathryn up and down. "You seem better this morning."

"I feel pretty good, actually. Thanks. You look like you feel better, too."

"Yes, I guess I'd better apologize for yesterday. I get worked up about things sometimes. But you have to realize I have a husband and two children back home. They probably think I'm dead. Heidi was 10 when I left, Josh was 13."

"I am sorry. This must be so hard for you. My ex-husband was out of the picture long ago. No kids. I was on vacation when I got taken, so I don't think anyone even knows I'm gone yet. I can't imagine what it must be like for you."

"I could handle it a whole lot better if I could find someone, anyone, in this place I could trust. They all pretend to be noble types with that fancy talk, but every one of them is hiding something. You never know where to turn." Joan walked over to the empty bed and put down the bundle she'd brought with her. "Anyway, if you're feeling up to it I brought you some clothes. The stuff you were wearing was pretty much trashed."

"Thank you, Joan. I really appreciate what you've done."

"We Earth girls better stick together, don't you think?" They laughed a bit together, though the laughter was trimmed with stitches of sadness and touches of reserve.

"Well, I'll clean up the breakfast things while you get dressed and then," Joan shot her a sidelong glance, "we'll see about trying to find a way back home. Okay?"

"Sounds good to me."

She watched her hostess exit through a passageway hidden by a sheet of cloth hung over the opening. Immediately she threw on the fresh clothes and began to look behind the other wall-hangings for passageways. Of the ten or so panels hung around the edges of the cavern, three had passages behind them: the one Joan had taken, a second near the spring on the back wall and a third almost exactly opposite of the first. She had just found the last one when she heard a faint sound from across the room. Joan must be coming back.

Quickly she returned to the center of the room and bent down, as if just pulling on the boots she'd already donned. It wouldn't do to have her hostess find out she was spying out escape routes. Not until she got the answers to some nagging questions. Like why she'd fallen into such a stuporous sleep so quickly the day before in the middle of such an intense conversation. Like how this Joan knew her name when she'd never mentioned it; why Joan's hair was still bleached to the roots and her watch still worked after ten years. Like why this woman's face and the face in her nightmare were one and the same.

No, until those questions were answered, caution was her best—and only—friend.

The curtain moved. A hand pushed it aside. Joan Conley-Foster of Bellevue, Washington entered—followed by someone Cathryn knew.

"Lucette?"

Chapter Four:
BENEDIC

E TRIED TO settle into a more comfortable position, but the splintered bench yielded no such spot. Behind him the window leaked cold rain. Before him the sweaty rankness of drunken ostlers assaulted his nose.

In a gesture of defense, he pulled his hood farther over his face as if to filter out what the orange-red firelight revealed of the reveling. He didn't think any one of the inn's patrons would recognize him through his disguise. By this time of night, he doubted they could recognize their own faces in a brightly lit mirror.

From the corner table, he could make out, through the smoke and dimness, Kern's fretting hulk and Bayly's flash. What had seemed a workable plan on the ride to the capitol, felt like a wearisome prison after nearly three hours in this stew of smells and sounds. Bayly had been most persuasive: find where the ostlers spent their wages and they would find someone who could point a way to D'Brin. So here they were, mingling with the handlers of horses for most of the stables and inns of the city.

None of the three had put spells on themselves before coming in, just in case there were those sniffing for the magic of deception. He had laid on the right amount dirt and a foul enough cloak to pass as a stablemucker—for that particular smell and station would almost guarantee being shunned by one and all. Bayly had put on the flowing, hooded robes of a Linton horsetrader, Kern passing as her first-hand. From where he sat, Benedic could hear the story she gave out. Her usual trade was in stolid horses for the ploughs of Kilder province, but she longed for the excitement of trading with higher placed folk—sleek, fast people who wanted sleek, fast animals for the purposes of power.

Bayly's spilt ambition drew the mock of the tipsy ostlers who vied with one another to dissuade her of such notions. Sleek? Most courtiers were not sleek, they said. Some waddled through the corridors of power. The hardest of the courtiers had been roughened by the abuse of power over others. They were the dark ones never to be looked at in their stony eyes, only bowed to and avoided.

Fast? Yes, they were fast enough to climb the tightening circles of favor—and faster still to sink like a stone when jealous eyes turned on them. Horses the ostlers could understand— even the rogues. They did not understand those who licked and clawed to rise in the ranks. What joy was there to be friendless? For in superior hallways, no one trusted another. Even those who had been ruined there could not let go, but lived in hope they would be recalled again. That mad wizard, for one...

Benedic blessed Bayly's skill. He and Kern had perked their ears so noticeably that they would have tipped the game right then. But Bayly never twitched, only laughed in disbelief.

"Sure—a mad wizard. And there's a ghost in the hay barn,

too, you'll be saying." Really, Bayly's laugh could be infuriating. It did its work now on her tablemates.

"I don't think she believes us, T'Pooy." A particularly fragrant stableman poked his neighbor hard enough that ale spilled from the mugs of both of them. The lumpen, hairy stableman called T'Pooy frowned deeply, looking for all the world like an irate hedgehog.

"Believing it or no matters not to the truth of it." T'Pooy looked with regret at the spilled ale.

"No, but tell her the full of it, man. Our story alone could send her happily back to parlaying plough-horses."

"We've been paid well enough to suffer what is done and say nothing. Let it go."

"Yes, let it go," Bayly drawled, leaning back in her chair insolently. "Whatever trap you've let be sprung on yourselves, I know I could 'scape it. I know how to handle my horses. And myself."

"You may have got the better of a farmer or two, but a fool you are to lord it over those whose lives you have not lived." T'Pooy's knuckles whitened as he gripped his mug tighter.

"Can it be that bad, then? What possible harm comes from the straightaway hire of a horse?" Bayly leaned in toward her tablemates, all insolence gone. She seemed the picture of concerned disbelief. It worked.

"Harm? We'll tell you harm, but you'll hear the story odd-like from us. It is part of the wickedness of it, see." T'Pooy took a last sip to wet his lips, licked them as if they were still dry as dust and then, straining strangely on each word, began his part of the tale.

"My friend here works the stables of Keeney's Inn, a half day's no-sweating ride from here. He's been there for most of his life turning his trade, and mostly honest. Honest enough."

T'Pooy's friend nodded seriously and hard. "Sometimes the fast riders come through with messages for the court, or carriages come by in a hurry and he got 'em fresh horses just the way he should, charging what he could bargain for and neverminding the odd bit of coin slipped into his pocket that Keeney never missed. Just to do a favor for a lady or lord now and again. Not-ever saw the harm in it, nor I."

Another pull at his mug kept T'Pooy talking. "And he'd never have come to harm either, if things had been right. Started with that wizard..." It looked as though the man wanted to say a name, tried to say it, but winced instead. "He," T'Pooy spit out the 'he' as if it were poison, "came wanting a fresh mount. Always in a hurry, flipping coins like they was nothing. Most of ten years ago it was. Always came with a half tired horse. Always in a rush to make CorronKeep before dark.

"Then two, or is it three by now, three years past it was, I'm thinking, the wizard left off coming and sent this other one." T'Gruen and T'Pooy both shuddered, looking sidelong at each other with burnt eyes. "That one hurried, too, but not as often. Then the day came this new one took his time. Took time to talk with T'Gruen, talked and whispered and spelled when T'Gruen couldn't help it. Spelled a magic T'Gruen's never heard 'a, but knows the full of it now, eh? This magicking made my friend do whatever service this other one wants, but can never talk of it. I can talk of it, though."

But here T'Pooy stopped abruptly, clutching his head with a sharp cough. T'Gruen, whiter now under the dirt on his face, took up the tale.

"Aye, he can talk of me and I can talk of him. But not each of ourselves. Not since the curse, as it was, and that's the way of it. T'Pooy," T'Gruen shifted, increasingly uncomfortable on the bench, "he works at the Blue Goat, doing the same as me but here in the city. It was to the Blue Goat that the wizard and the one he sent came in town, the horses run tired and cruel-like every time. T'Pooy took the coins for years and when the wizard stopped and the other started, he took the spell and suffers from no will to resist the orders, and no ableness to tell about it. And no coins now, neither."

T'Gruen sunk his head lower over his mug. "And no coins for T'Gruen for these last years."

Then T'Pooy leaned in to Bayly, swiftly, as if he needed to speak at once before he could not. "But T'Gruen knows where the wizard hides himself. It's the mud gives it away. Each time, no matter the magic-grinder came from a different spoke-road to throw him off, there was that different mud under the hooves. T'Gruen knows. T'Gruen knows but he can't tell. That's the one part of his story I can't tell because I don't know it, haven't lived it myself. How can we take our revenge when I can't know because he can't tell?"

Kern's huge shadow covered most of the table. He'd moved in to stand behind Bayly and hung over the table like a redbark between sun and grass. Something in the movement of the shadow hand caught Benedic's eye. It caught Bayly's attention as well, it appeared, for she made a hidden gesture back and began to finish the conversation.

"My friend's friend has a friend at court. He says that there was an Esoteric master who hid on the edges. Said the wizard's name was D'Brin. Is that your wizard's name?" Bayly placed the name on the table like a dirty plate. T'Pooy and T'Gruen strained, tried to talk, tried to move, tried to nod. Anything. Nothing. Veins in foreheads stood out, ropy neck tendons bulged. But no sound. No yes or no nod.

"That you cannot answer is answer enough. From what my friend says, I'd be the greenest of fools to even say his name again, let alone try the trade with him or any of his. My thanks for your warnings. It can't have been easy to tell your story. Or live it." She put coins softly on the table between the two, tired ostlers. "Here, these are for your troubles. You know what they say: A good dinner never harms the healing."

T'Pooy closed his meaty fist over the coins, nodding. "You mind what we say, trader. Linton Stand may be plainer than our crown city, but it is a safer haven."

Kern interposed himself between Bayly and the direction of the inn's main bar, herding her toward the side door with a barely noticed touch. Not only had Benedic heard all the conversation, but he had seen what Kern had seen: a Taker at the bar asking questions of the 'keeper. Benedic slipped out the same side door with all discrete speed.

Outside, the three turned into the shadows, pausing only long enough to make a plan. The fighters would get their horses from the stables a few minutes' walk from the tavern. He would get Kell from his solitary and sordid lodgings at the end of the next alley (they had split up in town for safety's sake) and meet them at Keeney's Inn as soon as they could get there.

With the slightest pressure, hands touched and parted. In the smallest slide of time, the street was empty. Then, briefly, it was not. And then was not again.

As he had first begun this, so he was now: hidden, waiting, in the avoidance of a Taker. He had made his way out of CorronKeep well and swiftly enough. He didn't think he'd been tracked, having taken all the precautions he knew, from spells to alter the signature trace of himself to the basic backtracking and false side trails learned so long ago in his soldiering days.

Now he was hidden in a spot overlooking the place where two roads converged, only a small distance from Keeney's Inn. Waiting too long. His friends were overdue.

By his estimate, Kern and Bayly should have arrived hours ago. It was late in the day and nothing had moved since he hunkered down. He was a little stiff from too long riding, too long sitting, looking over the shoulder too many times. Once more he wondered, and was irritated with himself for wondering, how a piece of ground that had looked perfectly smooth before he sat down could have sprouted so many sharp rocks.

Then he heard it. A sound behind him, toward the deeper fastness of the forest. Thrashing of at least one horse, maybe two. And something else. Faster, with more agility than he thought he still possessed, he slid through the brush to meet the sounds.

Branches whipped and sawed frantically with the motion of the fight. Kern was still on his horse, red fingers clutching his shoulder. The horse bled as well, a knife still stuck in the wound. Both fighting pain, steed and man struggled to reach unhorsed, unarmed Bayly. For pushing toward her unprotected back was a black robed man whose raised hand held the wicked glint of a saw-toothed dagger.

Sight become nightmare: the knife point too swift, horse and husband too slow. Benedic, deafened by the pounding in his chest, strained to move. As from a distance, he saw his hand swing Truth out of its sheath, felt his own legs bring him over the rise that had hidden him, watched himself bring the blade up and then down in a whistling slice that sent the dagger, and what clutched it, glittering silver and red into the dirt. With a turn both slight and lethal, the stroke continued to its termination.

Almost before the Taker thudded, loose limbed, on the ground Bayly caught Kern as he tilted and fell from the saddle. Benedic, plunging his own gory blade into the dirt, grabbed the dirk jutting from the horse's rump and pulled hard. One scream, one teeth-bared try at biting and the horse moved away, trembling, from the blood-musty clearing.

Another yell, a baritone blend of pain and anger, rang in his ears.

"You didn't even try to do that gently."

"It wasn't a hangnail, brave husband." Tearing strips from the hem of her tunic, Bayly bound her husband's arm with movements that were less than soft, watching him with eyes more than tender. "Gentle isn't necessary with these little things."

"Little! Your heart is as hard…"

"If the both of you could stop bellowing, I think we'd all be safer. It's only a short way to Keeney's and I don't doubt they can hear you two all the way to CorronKeep." The blaze of battle that had come over Benedic was starting to fade, leaving a sense of relief with a residue of bitter reality. His friends must have felt the same way, going at each other so roughly to cover the closeness of a worse ending than the one that kept the three of them together.

"Reprimanded by a castle-coddled dukelet, Kern. See what comes of your complaining?"

"My complaining? It was your ham-handed tending did it, wife."

"Enough. We've horses to recover and…this…to dispose of before the daylight deserts us altogether." Benedic stood over the body, loosing a ragged sigh into the sudden silence.

Bayly and Kern looked at one another. Letting her husband rest, Bayly went to tend to another kind of wound.

"You remembered our lessons with the sword very well, cousin. But you cannot remember the feel of blade biting flesh because," she laid a gentle hand on her cousin's shoulder, "you have not done that before today. Have you?"

He couldn't look away from the body that sprawled before him, could not look away from the black-red puddle, the black robe, the black-bearded face turned into the reddened dirt, the grime-blackened nails of the fingers that curled unnaturally too many inches away from the arm that should have been their anchor.

"Listen to me, Benedic. If you are a good man, and I know this is deep-running true, then you never will forget. In time, there will be days pass without remembering—then longer between the night sweats and the smell of your own disgust. But it never leaves and never should. It's a hard thing to know, cousin, but smelling the blood again and seeing Death hag-riding the fallen is what keeps us from the light taking of life."

He willed himself to look away from the body, struggling to ignore the acrid sting of death-odors that threatened to turn his stomach inside out.

"It is too hard. I…" he held out his bloodied hands, "How do you live with this knowing?"

Kern's rumbly voice lifted itself in reply. "Ah, then, you know how we live with it. We live, and that is the answer. But for you, my wife, who is my life, would lie there. We did not begin this. We did not seek to pour life into the dirt. You chose our lives over his. Weigh that in the balance when the dark rememberings come."

"Is it enough?" He felt Kern's heavy gaze but heard no answer.

From the nearest tree one red-brown leaf fluttered through the halted breath of that moment and came to rest nestled in the bend of the lackhanded arm of the fallen Taker. Benedic, having followed the leaf to its end, knew it was time to finish what had been begun. Kern's pack held a soldier's field shovel. He rummaged until he found it and began to dig.

By the time the horses had been found and brought back, a

freshly turned mound of dirt was the only evidence of what had been. Bayly's strong arms helped her husband onto her horse and pulled herself up behind him, giving him the reins of his injured horse to handle with his good arm. Behind them, Benedic pulled himself away from the clearing that accused him. In moments the clearing was empty again. The first few drops of rain, cold and hard, dislodged three more leaves that slipped from a high branch and shivered through the fading light.

Keeney's Inn hunched behind a wall of water. The skies had lowered and let loose a flood. The inn's windows squinted through the dimming grayness of night and rain with a look of shelter and suspicion. On the front porch, under the eaves, a woman loaded firewood from a stack into her arms. Seeing three more guests, she kicked open the main door and waited for the travelers to dismount.

"Tire's up. Come on in and dry off." With a hitch of her hair, the woman nodded toward the dry interior.

"Thank you, hostess, we will." Bayly was the first to climb down from her soggy saddle perch. "If you would show my friends in, I have a horse that's some scratched up and needs tending."

"Go ahead round back if you need to. Afraid you're on your own, though. The stable-tender's away right now."

"Just heat up something good to eat. I'll be done soon enough." Bayly took all three horses and headed toward the back barn. As she passed Benedic, she murmured into his ear. "Get Kern dried off right away, will you? I don't think the old dog knows enough to come in out of the rain." He heard a chuckle over the slosh and mutter of mud.

The logs carried in by the hostess had already been added

to the blaze in the huge stone fireplace. Four other travelers sat steaming near the drying heat, making almost as much mist in the effort to dry inside as the rain made in its effort to dampen outside. Wet wool, burning sap and fragrant roast vied with one another for the attention of the noses present just as vigorously as the cold wet and damp heat jostled for supremacy.

The four seated before the blaze glared at the newcomers with a mix of self-interest and resolve. They had no intention of giving up fireside seats until they had dried out. As it turned out, the gray clad man and his hulking companion wanted nothing to do with the main room. Instead, they plied the hostess with just enough coin that suppers and firewood followed them to their room as quickly as, with the storm outside, thunder followed lightning.

Once safely in the room, with hot food inside them and fire-warmth round about, they could marginally relax. The bed, though endowed with a wealth of random lumps, was comfortable enough to tempt Kern into a pleasant doze. Benedic spread his sopping cloak next to the fire to dry and pulled the bent-branch chair near enough to the blaze to send steam rising from his tunic. So comfortable so fast was he that it was startling to be brought back to full alertness by the sound of a hacking cough.

"Kern? Bayly?" The room was dark. How long had he slept? The cough came again.

"Kern, are you well?" Benedic roused himself and went over to the bedside. Even in the gathering gloom, he could see the fever sweat on Kern's pale face and hear the raspy breath. Fearing the worst, he loosened his friend's clothes and pulled free the bandage only to see what he had feared: red and swollen flesh puffed all around the gash. For the sweats to come this quickly, the weapon must have been polluted, defiled.

He had to get Bayly. Where was she? Why wasn't she here

already? Concern and self-recrimination mounting, he charged out of the room and down the stairs. The only person in the main room was the hostess who was wiping down tables.

"Our friend who was tending the horse, has she come through here yet?" He could hear the edge in his voice and fought to sound calm.

"Not yet she hasn't." The woman rubbed her hands on her apron. "Must be a pretty scruffed up animal out there, you think?"

But he was already to the door and, in a blink of an eye, out. The rain had left behind muddy puddles and light-damping fog. Though it all he ran toward the stable entrance outlined by the faint glow of a glowlantern.

"Bayly?" Caught at the doorway by his own fear, he could barely breathe her name.

She was lying face down in the straw, unmoving, her loosened hair spread around her like a fan, fog nestling in the bend of her arm, the crook of her knee.

"Cousin."

He couldn't catch his breath. Kneeling down, he managed, as tenderly as his trembling hands allowed, to gently turn her over. That simple motion did two things; it showed him the garrote and loosened it enough that, when his fingers brushed it, it came away in his hand. For a long moment he stared at the thin rope. Then his hand, seemingly of its own mind, flung the twining bit away as if it were a snake.

Thus emptied, his hand sought better employment. He gently laid his cousin down, then reached out to gather her hands in his, to bring her arms to her sides, from akimbo to rest. But what was this? One hand had blood on it. He checked her belt sheath. The dagger was gone. Had she injured her killer? The other hand clutched something. Carefully he pried open the fist. Mud. Ocher-colored mud.

His mind took over and started the search. Grooves led away from her legs. She'd been dragged. He followed the marks backward to a stall. A still-trembling horse stood in the far corner of it, wet and shaky. A quick glance told him this horse wasn't splattered, yet the stall it stood in was littered with dried clods of the odd-colored dirt.

The conversation with the ostlers in the tavern…what had T'Pooy said? Yes, that was it, of course. The wizard's Taker left his muddied horse here when riding into the capitol.

Cold. Gray clad and cold. He knew. Takers hunt in pairs. Two must have been sent to CorronKeep to make sure no one found D'Brin's hiding place, a hiding place built on oddly tinted soil. We questioned in CorronKeep. They overheard and followed us. We stopped one. And did not remember there would be another.

An immense, rolling shudder shook him. He began to move, first one stride, then faster, longer ones. They took him to the inn, to the hostess who he pulled up the stairs behind him until they stood beside Kern's fevered form. In a voice hoarse with need, he poured out his demands.

"This is my friend who has taken a wound which is now infected. Amarisa leaves in a compress and salyk tea will cure, if you do it well. And in the barn," his voice faltered but carried on with its burden of words, "is this man's wife. Someone has killed her and I will be away in only a moment to find out who. You take these coins and tend him. And do what is right for her while I am gone hunting." The hostess shivered at his last words, in spite of the room's fire.

"Aye. He'll be well. And I'll care for her. Who shall I say…?"

But he had picked up his cloak and pack and was already through the door. He could not wait any more or risk losing the trail. Back to the barn he ran to get Kell who, tied at the farthest end of the stable, was troubled and skittish.

"We've seen too much tonight, you and I. Seen things we didn't stop." He rubbed the horse's neck to settle him down. "But we can hunt now. Stay with me, Kell. Stay with me."

The great black horse steadied and allowed himself to be led past the shell that had once been Bayly, though his nostrils flared and his eyes widened. Horse and man gripped what resolve they could find and stepped outside to pick up, through the bleary mist of fog and postponed loss, a trail of blood and vengeance.

It was easy enough to find the trail's beginning. Bayly must have wounded the Taker badly. He could see the spatters of blood leading away. But it would be hard to follow with the rain and night each thickening in clots. He bent every skill, every instinct to the tracking, brushing wet branches back, bending down to pick out the traces, straightening up to strain for sound, for motion, for the ambush of gloom-hidden, face-high tree limbs.

His entire being focused so completely in determined alliance that, what might have been missed, was noticed. Against the odds, he noticed the shift of color in the damp and dark soil, the odd fresh break of branch, the sharp aside of mortality, the faintest tendril of wood smoke winding through the deepening mists. He came on the house convinced he was undetected. A winded, mud-shinned horse in a back fenceyard shivered from cold, hard usage and the smell of the blood smeared on the saddle that still burdened it.

Smoke bent over as it climbed out of the chimney. A chill wind was rising, bringing the threat of more rain. Misted windows hid details, promised shadows. He crept closer—close enough to peer in, close enough to count only one shadow in motion. Was the Taker too wounded to move? Or was someone else making the shadow? He needed to know more. He edged warily along the wall toward a covered porchway.

Even as carefully as he was moving, he almost fell over the body as it lay covered in the darkness of night and a black cloak. His heartbeat in his ears, he knelt down for a closer look. From a tiny crack under the back door a sliver of yellow light sliced over the pale, cold face. Brown and gray hairs straggled beyond the black hood to soften the hard planes of her features, though they could not warm the frigid ice blue of her sightless eyes. Just below, on a beatless chest, her hand had stopped. Only the black and gray bands at her wrist struggled to move in the freshening storm. What futility to follow the darkly stained ribbons, to follow the hand still cupped to catch the relentless spill, follow them to the darkest place in the night, a spot slick with lost life.

I thought to kill this woman, wanted to kill her, planned, tracked, prayed to do it. He folded the stiffening hands under the cloak edge and stood up slowly. But the killer of my cousin is killed, at length, by my cousin's hand. And still this is not ended.

A sudden gust rattled the door and shot hard pellets of rain at the nearby window. It brought him back to the moment. In the wild buffets of the storm he stilled himself, whispered first one spell and then another. Finally, he reached to his sword, took hold of it and gasped. It tingled to the touch, both warm and cold to his hand. His hand, arm, eye and mind moved as one, drawing the length of metal out in a hiss of intention.

In the small nothingness between one storm blast and another, he slipped the latch and silently insinuated himself through the door.

Inside, the shadowmaker moved in strange spasms around the book-littered room, oblivious.

"Not much longer. Soon, soon. I must be there. I will be

there." The house's master absently fingered the thick black band circling his wrist.

Through the open door the storm reached in to turn pages on books in several sudden rustles. The man's bony shoulders shivered once and then he turned. Between one breath and the next, the worlds both men knew hung suspended.

"Benedic?"

"D'Brin."

Glimpsing a tiny movement of lip, Benedic kicked the door shut, covered the distance to D'Brin and brought the sword named Truth up in a blur to rest its point on the wizard's cheek. Though it rested lightly, a trickle of red began to slide downward. The lips stopped.

"You misjudge me, my lord." D'Brin's eyes snuck to the blade's hilt and the hand that held it, as if gauging their separate purposes.

"My judgment is still to be made, D'Brin. Only your story remains to be told and then sentence passed."

"You sound as if guilt is already decided. Is that what the much vaunted justice of Forché has come to, old friend?"

"Not friend. Never friend. Sliding your eyes from honesty, you brought my wife back to me in a box, leaving behind a regretful story of experiments gone wrong. Yet you fled that very night, found a hiding place and pulled obscurity over you like a shroud. And, with hired hands, you have this very night killed my cousin. Guilt? An apt word, indeed." Benedic burned with the same resonating ferocity as the blade he held.

D'Brin's eyes twitched toward the front door. There was noise out there suddenly—more than just the howling of the gale. With a gust of windborne rain, the door blew open and a messenger, caped and hooded against the elements, staggered into the shelter of the room. He stamped and shook and then saw. His eyes widened.

Benedic settled the blade closer to D'Brin's neck. "For a remote house, old man, this bears much traffic."

"I have associates here and there who send news now and again."

"Then let us hear this damp harbinger together, shall we?"

The messenger swallowed hard but preferring, it seemed, a quick and safe exit, immediately began his spell of recall. D'Brin shifted in agitation. But when the words began, all grew still.

"When this news finds you, the time will have drawn even closer. The signs of Passing showed themselves first but an hour ago. The King has been kept hidden to all but the ones who know. You were right about the chosen Heir. He would have been beckoned. But I have seen to it this messenger is the only one who leaves here. The woman will know by other means and be here hard on your heels. Your moment is at hand."

The messenger's eyes opened and focused. His news had been delivered.

"This message came without introduction and yet the voice you used sounded familiar. Before you go, tell us who sent it." Benedic's voice was so low that the young courier strained to hear it.

"I would tell you if I could, but it came third-hand to me. I have no idea who the author might be." The silence that greeted this pronouncement made the cold, wet courier break into a sweat.

Benedic frowned and reached toward his belt. Metal spun through the air toward the messenger who startled violently before he recognized the coins for what they were. He grabbed for them and, before he'd even touched payment to purse, was out the door and away.

Perhaps it was the slamming door, or the gale battering the chimney or just the fleeting humor of chance that made the fire blaze up in that moment. The white-red flames howled with heat and once again Benedic saw burning behind him. This time it was reflected in the length of the glittering blade he held to a white-red neck, and in the fever-like glitter of D'Brin's eyes.

"You heard as well as I did, Benedic. The King is dying. Now is the time of the Passing. The Heir has been summoned." Flames cracked, furious and wild. D'Brin's voice sank to a hoarse, hypnotic whisper.

"Did you think it would be you? Did you dream to feel the crown heavy on your head? Did you dream this room would hold a future king? Did you…"

Benedic's knees gave from under him. As he sank to the floor, he watched D'Brin reach down and retrieve a tiny dart. Though his body would not respond to his urgent commands to move, his ears were condemned to hear everything.

"Did you imagine that a wizard would resort to such mundane defenses? Or did you believe I would let you be king?"

The duke watched, unable to move, as the wizard reached for Truth as it fell from his nerveless hand. Darkness rushed in.

Chapter Five:
CATHRYN

LUCETTE STOOD, UNHEARING and mute, rooted to the cavern floor.

"She was found wandering like this." Joan made the information sound routine, unremarkable. "Isn't able to hear or talk; at least, I can't make any headway with her. She doesn't know me—and I only know who she is because she was pointed out to me once. Her father is a local squire someplace. But maybe you can help her since you know her."

Cathryn tried to mimic the disinterested tone. For the sake of the young woman. "I've barely met her myself. She was near where I was found when I—I don't know what to call it—when I came through."

"Really? You know, maybe if she was there when you came through, she might be able to help us find out what happened. Could be a step closer to a way back. Maybe all this rescuing will bring me luck after all." Joan chuckled. "I'll just go get some things, you know, for travel. A road trip rounds fun, doesn't it?"

The evidently amused woman pushed aside a cloth panel and disappeared into the corridor behind it.

Cathryn's caution whispered urgently in her ear. Something was fundamentally askew with this whole situation. The young woman showed signs of enormous strain. Sweat trickled obliquely from temple to neck. Neck cords bulged. Hands clenched and unclenched fitfully. This was someone trying to speak, trying to move—trying so hard her whole body burned with the effort.

"Lucette? Can you hear me?"

Nothing.

"Can you speak? Please, whatever it is, you can tell me. Tell me." There. What was that? The young woman's mouth twitched. Had she made a noise?

"I'm here. I'll take care of you. Can you hear me?" There it was again. Lucette turned as if to locate a sound in the dark. At the same time, Cathryn felt a twinge in her arm. When she realized what had made it, her stomach churned. Her worm, grown back a bit, was moving.

"Speak to me. Tell me what to do to help you. Tell me and I'll help you." Cathryn focused on her words, ignoring as best she could the movement increasing under her skin.

Lucette's mouth moved. She saw it. There had been a noise, she was sure. She leaned in closer to catch the words the girl struggled so painfully to utter. Closer.

"Unfortunately, we've run out of time for this kind of thing just now." Joan had come up from behind and grabbed Cathryn's arm tightly. Near one of the doors, two formidable looking servants held out long brown cloaks. "Put these on. We have to leave. Now."

"But Lucette isn't well. Shouldn't we try to…?"

"Any other time I'd be the first one to try to help; but this is an emergency. We have to go." It was easy to see that frustration and urgency were building in Joan. But why? Cathryn took both wraps, helped Lucette on with hers and then donned her own. Oddly, when the cloak had settled over her shoulders, the worm in her arm once again began to move. This time it felt as if it were trying, somehow, to get out.

But she shoved that feeling down   Right now she was determined to move along with this irritating woman because she had decided to get away and take Lucette with her. Leaving this strange cave was the first step.

"We're coming." But Joan was already moving through a far door. The two prisoners, for Cathryn knew beyond doubt now that's what they were, followed. Behind them came the pair of silent guards.

Glimmerlights spaced along the rock walls showed a long hallway. Joan turned and shouted to them to hurry up. When the words were still in the air, the worm once again twitched. She's using magic. That's what makes the… that's what makes it move.

Her own thoughts were so engrossing that she almost missed the first stair. As it was, Lucette stumbled. Step by step, she led her young friend down and down, seemingly forever stepping downward into darkness. Even concentrating as hard as she could on being a guide, it was hard to miss the rush of water coming closer. A final twist of the stairway brought them to a large cavern and the source of the sound—a narrow underground river. Joan was already in the front seat of a long, narrow boat that bobbed at the end of the steps.

"Let's go. Get in."

"I think we're due a little explanation, Joan."

"If there were time, I'd explain everything, but there is no time. Get IN." What her shouting couldn't do, Joan's two minions accomplished. Picking Lucette up as if she were a damp rag, they slammed her into the barque with enough force that water slobbered over the sides. Not wanting to experience that treatment, Cathryn stepped carefully into the center of the wobbling craft. She lifted the girl out of the slopping bottom-water, and settled her firmly on the boat's middle seat. It seemed hopeless for, whatever stability she gained, Joan threatened to undo by standing in the bow muttering and wildly waving her arms. At first Cathryn noticed nothing, being more intent on trying to keep the gunwales level. But when her fingers touched off a static spark as she brushed the sides, she looked up. The cavern, like an electrified globe, burst into light with shoots and scrags of power. In the center of it all, Joan, crackles of lightning coruscating from the ends of her arms and the center of her chest, ranted on in words Cathryn could not hear over the shattering din. The pair of goons covered their ears and beat a hasty retreat back up the way they had come.

Then the boat began to move, slowly at first, but gradually faster and faster until foam began to fleck the prow. Now it was hurtling down the tunnel's black and narrow throat with such monstrous swiftness that she could not look up without being dizzy—or horrified. Her lightshow played out, Joan slumped onto the front seat. It didn't seem possible, but from the regular rise and fall of her chest she looked to be asleep. And still the barque churned, foamed, hurtled down the cold, stone gullet.

Unable to bear the sight or the thought of the speed, she crouched over Lucette, trying to comfort the girl.

"We're all right. We're all right." She smoothed back a damp lock from the girl's eyes. "It's not exactly the way I would have chosen to get you out of here, but you have to admit it is fast." She tried a small laugh but it died before it lived.

"If only I knew some way to get you talking and hearing again." The waves hissed as they were split by the craft's speed. The sound made her shudder. As if to comfort her, Lucette squeezed her arm. But where the worm had grown back, it hurt to be touched.

"No, don't." She tried to reach over and pull Lucette's hand away, but her other arm was occupied with holding on. "Don't—Listen—Damn it, look at me." Something lurched in her stomach. Lucette's head swung up violently; her free hand shot up to touch her ear.

"Did you hear that? It almost seemed like it, you looked up so fast."

Lucette nodded. Over her face came a dawning smile.

"You can hear again?" The girl nodded vigorously. "I don't know what did it, but I'm so glad. Can you talk?"

But Lucette had started a series of motions, trying to communicate what she still could not say. She pointed to Cathryn, then opened and closed her fingers, then pointed at herself and with that same finger reached to touch, once again, her friend's wrist.

"That can't be. Why would that…" She stumbled, unready to acknowledge to herself, let alone another, the evidence of her invader, "…make any difference?"

But Lucette was gesturing again. It was clear what she wanted as she touched the tunic sleeve where, underneath, a tail slithered. She looked up with an expression so open and so needy it was impossible to refuse.

"I'll try, but…" She looked up. Joan was still huddled in the prow as this endless gullet swallowed them whole. Despite the boat's speed, it had stabilized somewhat, so Cathryn cautiously pried her other hand loose from its white-knuckled grip. Quietly, so it wouldn't attract attention, she spoke.

"Lucette, I want you to be able to speak." She hissed. The worm knotted up violently. "Talk to me, please talk to me." The pain worsened.

"It is enough." Lucette's voice sounded rusted but useable. She pulled her fingers away to touch her own throat in relief.

In a sudden ebb, the throb in Cathryn's arm faded. But the joy she should have felt hearing the girl's voice again dimmed against the sickening twist of the beast in her body. Under cover of her own skin, it wound its way higher and deeper. When it reached the top of her arm, it seemed to sink in and clamp on to the shoulder socket, causing such agony that she flung her head over the side and retched once and then again and again into the waters rocketing past. At some point, she righted herself, with Lucette's help.

"Don't worry, lady. This sometimes happens when first you use the larger magicks. It will pass, I swear."

She wiped her mouth in mute misery. It was clearer than her besieged self wanted it to be: She had performed magic. The healer who first examined her was positive she registered no signature of magic. She had assumed it was because she was of another world where magic did not exist. But Joan could perform huge spells—and now she had done—something. What made the difference? Of course. Tears of frustration and anger welled. The worms. They must do much more than react to magic being used or allow others to track her. She could… It was almost too much to comprehend.

"You have to listen to me now, please." Lucette's voice was low and intense. "What D'Joan told, I do not know. This I do know: she caused me to be taken from the Keep at Forché and brought by force. She claims a need for me and for you, though for what purpose is not clear. And there is more. I must find my father. Please, tell me where he is."

"I don't know. Last time I saw him was at your house."

"But he went looking for you after you disappeared. Have you seen no sign of him all this time?"

"No. Nothing." There was a hanging pause as if the air had

quieted all on its own. "He came after me?" She turned the question over in her mind.

There was a sudden jerk and tilt. Ahead of them the passageway turned and then spilled into a huge opening. At the far end, water lapped irritably at a stone pier and the beginnings of a twisted stairway. Four figures in ornate uniforms of some sort waited motionlessly as Joan stirred to action once again, mumbling a few words that brought the unsettling voyage to a gliding stop.

"Get up here, you two." The witch (for that is how she thought of Joan now) wasted no time in clambering out and was already halfway to the first bend in the stairs. The watchers began to move toward them. But Cathryn had had enough of that kind of assistance. She stood up to disembark. In the process she moved close to Lucette as if to help her alight, managing to get in a few whispered words: "Pretend you're still deaf and mute. Maybe we can take advantage of it somehow."

"As you will. But take care, those are palace guards. They shouldn't be here. Something is very wrong." That was all she had time to say before the guards surrounded and then herded them up the stone steps.

They climbed, up and up, twisting up and around, past glowlanterns and small landings until the character of the cavern walls changed and became stone slabs enclosing a spiral staircase. Still higher they climbed and turned, upward until their calves ached. Gradually windows and doors appeared here and there beside a broad step or on a landing.

Just when Cathryn thought she could go no farther, Joan came to a stop on a wide landing where two figures waited: One who stood motionless, wrapped so completely in a long gray cloak as to be unrecognizable; the other a spindly, shrew-faced man who waited impatiently for a somewhat winded Joan to catch her breath.

"How close is he?" She puffed the words out between gulps of air.

"Close enough."

"Is he alone in there?"

"I have made it so." The tall man's right eye began to twitch.

Joan turned away from her anxious conspirator and his silent captive and toward Cathryn.

"We don't have a lot of time, so listen up, Porter, because this is our way home. The king of this place is dying." Cathryn could hear Lucette gasp. "But before he does, he goes into a kind of suspension that keeps him alive until his successor arrives. When that person comes, the sight of him triggers something called the Passing. The heir gets all sorts of information passed on to him and a bunch of state secrets and decoder ring stuff. Bottom line is, if we sort of eavesdrop during this little business, we can learn what we need to know to get home. You still want to go home, I assume?"

She drew a breath to answer, but Joan trampled right over the pause.

"So, here's the deal. My colleague is also rather interested in learning a few of the secrets royalty hoards. We help him get that information and D'Brin, with a little cooperation from Lucette here, will use what we learn about a passageway between worlds to hold it open so we can go through."

"But I thought you said you needed the heir to trigger this—whatever it is?"

Joan took her by the arm and pulled her toward the far door. "No sweat. I've got it all under control. As they say back home, don't worry your pretty little head."

D'Brin was already at the door, his silent companion following behind as if on a leash. The two of them entered a hallway that turned and turned again. She tried to keep track of the lefts and rights, hoping to be able to get out again, although with the guards still behind them and Joan's wild magic beside her, it looked unlikely. The odd sounds echoing in the high vaulted ceilings and the green and rose marble maze of passages in this place just increased her despair.

One more left turn and suddenly there were two more guards who made no salutes or challenges but opened the door before which they were standing without a word. As the bizarre parade entered the large room, it shed all the guards it had accumulated. They remained outside, closing the massive door with unexpected speed and no sound except for the chilling, metallic scrape of a lock being turned.

She looked around, trying to get her bearings. Taking up most of one wall was a huge fireplace, its heart blazing. One wall was all windows that looked down on rocky hills sinking into twilight. A huge canopied bed, rich in maroon and night-blue hangings, commanded the center of the room. Almost lost in the brocade and silk was a sleeping man. No matter that the room was opulent and the firelight shimmered, no matter that he was frail and quite clearly near death, still there was something about this person that demanded a response.

Responses came. The unknown, muffled-up cloakwalker bowed deeply, rising slowly. From the rustling beside her, Cathryn knew Lucette was doing the same. D'Brin made no obeisance, but, with a jarring, calculated coldness, moved over to grab the wrist so motionless on the covers to check for a pulse. Joan spit her response into Cathryn's ear.

"Errol Flynn stuff, huh? These guys are a joke. Watch this. Hey, D'Brin, is that any way to treat your King?"

D'Brin's muscles twitched spasmodically, almost executing the bow his body demanded but which his mind refused. Clutching the edge of the bed, the wizard forced himself to straighten up.

"They can't help it. Authority turns every one of them turns weak-kneed."

"He nears the end, D'Joan. We must do this now." D'Brin's urgency cut through Joan's amusement.

"This might take a bit, Porter. Why don't you and your girlfriend move out of the way and relax. All the doors are locked and the guards are, well, associates of ours. No one's coming in or going out for a while."

Joan and D'Brin turned their attention to unwrapping their shrouded captive. When the voluminous cloak was removed, there was a masked prisoner underneath. His hands were tied in front, his face hidden in a hood, and around his ankles were leather loops joined by a length of stout rope just long enough that the man could, with care, walk but not run. D'Brin pulled another piece of rope from his pocket and lashed one end to the massive crosspiece of the stead at the foot of the huge bed and the other to the hapless captive.

With the others otherwise occupied, Lucette drew close to Cathryn and chanced a whisper.

"They are planning to harm our King and the heir. We must do something. I am no match for her magic and they are armed. I've seen weapons on them." Lucette's distress came through loud and clear. "Can you not use your magic? It has broken through D'Joan's before."

"I want to help, really, but I don't know what to do. What if I screw up and they decide we're too much trouble alive? And this may be my only way back home."

"But—"

D'Brin moved to the far side of the bed and roughly shook the sleeping King until the invalid's eyes reluctantly opened. That small, pale motion brought a ragged and terrible smile to the wizard's face. He raised his voice in the cadences of ritual.

"The King has called. The Heir awaits. With Passing, release." He signaled Joan who pulled off the prisoner's mask. Free of his hood, the fettered man struggled furiously against his bonds. Cathryn and Lucette watched in mute sympathy as the fellow jerked and writhed, trying to break free and trying, it looked, to keep his face turned away from the bed-ridden monarch. In his twistings, the struggling convict faced, for a brief instant, the other two prisoners.

"Father!" His daughter's cry drove the duke to even more frantic exertions. But Joan's wrath exploded into a stream of words brutal with power. Then, with both hands, she grabbed Benedic's hair and yanked hard. The magic and the pain forced him to face forward.

"No." The duke's fear and anger moaned in the word.

"Yes." Joan tightened her grip. "The King will see you. D'Brin, why don't you help his majesty get a good look?"

Once again the wizard hesitated as the restraints of tradition fought with personal ambition. Once again, respect lost to desire. D'Brin flung back the covers, reached under the frail monarch and lifted him up from the bed. The body he carried was so wasted, it looked more like an old toy wrapped in white cloth, ready for storage. It surprised everyone in the room when the emaciated form spoke.

"I must…" Lungs labored to suck in air. "…stand." Remnants of authority still clung to the King's words; enough that D'Brin reluctantly obeyed. Carefully, the wizard maneuvered his burden until the King was propped upright a few feet beyond the end of Benedic's tether.

"We will stand on our own. It will not proceed otherwise." Even in his weakness, Reyfen sounded so determined, the wizard gave way and let go of the King's shoulders and stepped back.

How could someone so ill stand at all? Cathryn moved closer, sure the invalid would topple at any moment. Instead, he spoke in a voice surprising in its strength.

"The Heir is near, called by the First Servants of Corronheld in an unbroken line. The Passing is upon us." With each ceremonial word King Reyfen seemed to grow stronger. His hands, hidden in sleeves which were so voluminous because he was so diminished, began to rise as if to impart a blessing. Over his face, flickers of red light began to flare and blaze.

"He's ready, D'Brin. Get around to the front of him and get him to touch you." Joan's impatience was electric. "Move. MOVE."

In her frustration, Joan loosened her grip on Benedic. Instantly he pulled free of the bedstead rope and whirled toward her with hands clenched in fists that knocked her down and left her breathless.

D'Brin howled with rage, drew his dagger and went for Benedic. Lucette ran at the wizard, trying to block his arm as it stroked downward toward her father.

It was then the King, in his strange state, stumbled the slightest bit. In the midst of the confusion, Cathryn saw the stumble and reached out, by reflex, to support an old and dying man. In that moment, in that touch, all that was or had been collided. The burning light that blazed on the King's face blazed in her eyes. The strength that held him up, passed to her. And more passed, so dizzyingly fast she reeled from it. Then, in the center of the whirlwind, in the midst of the onslaught, two beacons pulled her to a calm place. His eyes. The King's. In them, she saw all that he had ever seen. In them, she saw what he saw now—his own ending. He had released what he possessed to her, now his release waited.

Slowly, as in a dream, the King and Cathryn, Reyfen and the Queen, sank to the floor. What light had blazed before now dimmed. All light dimmed. Death held the hand that held hers, and the darkness came.

Chapter Six:
BENEDIC

A N IMMENSE AND terrible magic was building. The air bulged with fury. Benedic brought his clenched fist swinging up and this time connected with the howling face of rage. The blow threw D'Joan backward, careening off the massive bedpost, senseless before the floor met her face.

A cry of pain. He whirled around to see the wizard struggling to pull a knife from Lucette's arm. Horrified, he pushed himself to cover the small and endless distance to his daughter's side. Suddenly, D'Brin's fingers slipped from the red-slick handle. Before the duke could reach her, Lucette yanked the dagger from her flesh, yelled in anguish and then turned the wicked blade back toward her assailant. In that moment, the room warped and twisted. He fought to keep his balance. Light shattered.

Even before he could see again through the purple after-images, the duke knew both wizards were gone. Place-shifting magic smelled exactly the same as the odor lightning leaves behind, except that the results of a natural storm seemed much less frightening. And never before, in all of Corronheld's history, had place-shifting magic transported living beings. So radical was this development, it felt to him as if his whole life had shifted as well—and not for the better.

His hands began to shake so badly he could barely pick up the dagger from where it lay, darkened with his daughter's blood. He sliced through the remains of his bonds so that his trembling hands could cut strips of his shirt for Lucette's arm. He forced himself to hurry. How long before the guards broke in?

"That's tight enough, father. It's only a shallow cut." It gave him more joy to hear his daughter's voice at this moment than ever before. "Just help me rise. The King."

She was right. The blood spilled on the floor, family blood, did not mean another loss. He had other matters to which he must attend.

He knelt beside the fallen monarch and, though he knew already it was a futile gesture, gently pressed his fingers against the King's throat. It was not a man that lay there, diminished and brittle, but only the empty vessel that had once held Reyfen: mentor, liege lord, friend. No matter the imminence of danger from outside the chamber, the duke took up in his arms the once-King and carried him gently to the bed, laid him on it and straightened the disarrayed coverings. It was little enough to do, but it was right.

From behind him came rustling and he knew he must tend to the demands of the living. He turned to see Cathryn struggling to stand with Lucette's help. Anxiety pushed him into speech.

"What privacy spell the wizards cast is fading. I fear we will never make it past these traitor guards."

"The walls are set stone, father. I can try collapsing the ones surrounding the doors. It might bring us time to think."

"I'm not certain we can risk even that much time. D'Brin has used place-shifting defensively. Should he think to return and use it as a weapon…"

"We'll get out through here." The Earth woman's voice rode over his words. Her head was tilted and eyes narrowed, as if listening for a dim and distant sound. Then she moved with certainty to a large tapestry, pulled aside one corner and touched, in a series of deft motions, several wall tiles. A black rectangle widened in the wall. Without a backward glance, she stepped into the dark and disappeared.

For a beat, no one spoke. Then Lucette started for the bolt-hole.

He retrieved the cloak he'd arrived in, entered the escape route and closed the door behind him. With the light from the chamber gone, it was absolutely black. He could hear footsteps ahead of him, leading away. His back prickled with the thought of pursuit. Carefully feeling his way step by step, he started forward. The first turn in the hall was tentatively managed, the first stair cautiously found. The next and the next managed somehow until he realized he could begin to see his hand before him. Though grateful for the light, it was the sound and the chill that drew him on until it became a force in itself, nearly overwhelming him. The damp, cramping cold penetrated his hastily wrapped cloak, daggered into his chest with every breath. And the noise. It shook him with its force, battered sense until the mind begged for respite.

He knew where he must be. CorronKeep had been built on the edge of a rocky cliff. At the Keep's far wall, the land fell away, plunging to a lake below, its rock face broken part way down by a huge cataract created by the exit of an underground river. Somehow, the descending twists and turns had brought them from the King's Chamber to caverns directly behind Madagar Falls.

The air was so heavily laden with water vapor, seeing was difficult. There, ahead, was a blur of colors. It must be Lucette and Cathryn waiting for him. Again carefully, for now the way was slimy with moss and mist, he aimed for the bright hues. When he got close enough, he could see they had found a glow-lantern and several lengths of rope. Some beleaguered monarch from times past must have planned for trouble.

As another lantern was stroked into light, he could see that his daughter was shaking with cold. The small store of supplies that long ago had been tucked away in a crevice had no clothes, so he once again used the hard-won, despised dagger to cut his voluminous cloak into three sections. One he wrapped around Lucette, who gave him a wan smile of thanks. One he settled back on his shoulders. With the third, he approached Cathryn. This close to the falls, nothing but its pounding thunder could be heard. She was making some preparations with rope and light, but was so preoccupied that he had to tug on her arm to get her attention. She looked at him with surprise and some-thing else. Was it fear?

He held out the promise of warmth. She looked at the offer in his hands and then looked at him. Her face was impossible to read as she raised her hands in front of her, palms out. She was refusing the cloak. Was she so stubborn? Did she mistrust him that much? Or, bent on some unknown scheme of her own, would she refuse any help from him?

Something of his confusion and anger must have shown, for the Earth woman reacted to what she saw. Abruptly changing her mind, she snatched the ragged length of wool from him. To his amazement, she turned and draped the cloak piece firmly around Lucette. Cathryn had to have been as cold as he was and yet she gave away an equal chance of warmth. Did she intend to humiliate him in the eyes of his daughter by this gesture? Then let her shiver if that's what she wanted.

Once more, Cathryn stopped and bent her head to listen to some distant voice and then led off again. This time she went slowly, picking each footfall precisely. The mist grew denser and the roar even more intense as the three of them made their precarious way closer to the water hurtling down ahead of them at the opening of the cavern. At the last possible moment, when it seemed they must step into the white death, she turned to the left and disappeared. Then his daughter did, as well.

When he arrived at the spot, he saw that a recessed ledge led off to the side. On his left were handholds chipped into the stone. At his feet was an uneven, narrow, vapor and moss slicked trail. To his right, beyond the too slight sanctuary of the indented shelf, tons of water plummeted past.

It was torturous progress they made. The falls had never looked as wide from above as it did from behind. Apprehension sank into his bones with the cold. His fingers were going numb and he feared it would make him miss a grip. The white torrents at his side seemed to tug and mock at him. What relief to see the trail pass the far edge of the water and widen out on a ledge that led away from the roar and cold and into the weak, but welcome, light of dawn.

Once past the falls, it was quite clear that the immediate danger was far from past. Cathryn had tied one end of a rope around herself and waited with the other end held out for him. Lucette sat slumped against the cliff, holding her wounded arm. When he got close, Cathryn began to mouth words. At least he thought she was making no sound. But the roar of the falls had deafened him so, he wasn't sure she was soundless or he just could not hear yet. He rubbed his ears, as if that might help. Before he could object, she put her hands over his ears.

To his shock, her hands were warm, almost hot. And dry. She took them away.

"Can you hear me now?"

"Yes." He looked at her in amazement. And concern. What had just happened?

"We have to help Lucette up the cliff. The wound doesn't look too bad, but it hurts and she's in shock." She began to tie one of the ropes around his daughter, fashioning a kind of sling from it. The other end she tied to her own waist. "None of your rulers had the healer's talent, so I don't have that to draw on. You and I will have to rope together and then…"

"Wait. What are you saying? You are able to work magic…" He started to say 'because of the Passing' but the words stuck in his throat. He could only manage a faint "…now?"

The Earther slipped a length of rope around his chest and began to tie intricate knots. It took him aback, this intimate indication of leadership, and left him motionless as she went about her task.

"I've been able to for a while. Even before…" She left the sentence unfinished. He realized he wasn't the only one having trouble coming to grips with the strange and swift turn of events. "I mean, when I really need a bit of information it kind of comes rushing at me. There's so much—" her hands trembled for a moment and she had to stop working with the knots. He could not see her face. "—I can't manage all of it at once."

She gave a tug on the last knot tied. It held.

"It isn't too far to the top, but it wouldn't be safe for Lucette to try. When we get there we'll hoist her up." She had already turned toward the rock face, searching for the first indentation that would serve. "There are holds cut into the rock and some rings to tie off on. You remember a queen called Tyree? That was one prepared woman." She found handholds and pulled herself up. And found more and pushed up farther. Words floated down from above him. She must be talking to herself, something about 'practice' and a thing called an 'ahreeyai climbing wall.' It made no sense to him, but the rope was beginning to tug him into action.

Once again, he had no choice. It was too late to tell her he had never climbed before and strongly disliked heights. Nor would his pride let him confess such a vulnerability to this Earther, so he suppressed any thought of 'down' and put his hands and feet to the rock.

Although it seemed to take forever, once at the top of the cliff he knew it had not been a long or even particularly difficult climb. Still, he was breathing hard and shaking just a bit. On the way up, he had learned that even the best mental effort cannot erase the concept of falling. The ascent hadn't had any effect on Cathryn. He disliked that quite a bit. He disliked it even more when she sat back from the edge and let him rest a moment before they started to haul Lucette up. So, when they did begin to pull, he put his back into it. Hard. In almost no time, his daughter was resting, safely hidden under the cover of a tangled brush pile, a comfortable distance from the edge.

From the undergrowth where he had found temporary shelter, he watched Cathryn finish coiling all the ropes and hiding them under nearby bushes. When she was done, she slipped through the branches and sank down to rest next to him. It looked as if she were going to ask him a question. Then she withdrew a bit, drawing her knees up under her chin and wrapping her arms around them. She began to rock just a bit, back and forth. It made him uneasy.

She stopped rocking.

"I can be tracked."

He didn't know what to make of her statement.

"I can be tracked. We can be found because of me."

"What makes you think this is true?" He struggled to make sense of this sudden admission. If it was true, they were in even more trouble. There were two very angry wizards and an unknown quantity of well-trained but traitorous guards who were by now combing the Keep, and perhaps the city, for them.

"I was told that…" She hesitate visibly. Then, with that small sound hope makes as it leaves, she yanked up the sleeve of her tunic. "I was told that these make me traceable."

It turned his stomach. He had read of the worms but never seen them. Until now. A dark ridge slithered slightly under the skin near her wrist. Disgust made his heart pound too loudly and he could not hear what she was saying.

"…can't get rid of them." She pulled her sleeve back down. He drew a breath. And then another.

"No, I have never read of any way to be rid of the bloodworms. But then, I have never heard of anyone living past a few hours with the worms in them."

"Well, you have now. Two of us. Joan has had them for years. And these things," her voice betrayed her own disgust at what had invaded her body, "give us another little gift, too."

"Magic, where there had been none?"

"Right."

Under the leafy camouflage the two of them sat side by side, stiff and awkward. He could tell she resented every word she felt compelled to say.

"Are you asking for help, or are you warning me of your powers? I cannot see where this confession takes us."

She actually snorted and it irritated him. It was crude and discourteous, a very Earth-like response.

"You can't see? Well, figure it out, duke. If we can't solve this little tracking problem, we'll all be caught. I don't think that would be a very good idea right now. Do you?" Anger pushed her voice to a deeper and louder place. "Why don't you ask your daughter if she wants to be captured again? I mean, I've rescued her twice, but if you don't think…"

He boiled over.

"If *I* don't think—? What would you know of it? Is thinking even practiced on Earth? I cannot believe it is. Lest you forget, I have seen your home." He glanced over at Lucette, who was stirring in her resting spot several yards away. When he turned back, he grabbed Cathryn's arm and lowered his voice until he practically hissed in her ear.

"It was your world killed my wife and murdered my cousin. I will not let it touch my daughter. Or my son. Or anyone else in my care. That you saved Lucette, I thank you. That she was ever in danger, I blame you."

"Blame me!" She threw off his grip, scrambled up and burst out of the hiding place, heedless of the danger of being seen. "I was dragged to this place by someone from your world—and with your daughter's help. Or did you forget that part? I didn't ask to come, but here I am, trying very hard to get back home and not hurt anyone in the process—and you blame me?"

"Yes. Your world. D'Joan. And you. You bring the smell of Earth; part cunning, part dementia, and part death. And I fear it. More, I hate it." He could not sit still, either. He stood up and, since she was pacing, took a stance of defiance as she lobbed more words at him.

"Is it Earth you fear; or is it how your people react to Earth that you hate? Are you afraid of what you'll find under this thin layer of pretty words and bowing and traditions? I never asked to be here. Someone—from here—forced me. I never wanted anyone to die, but there have been killings. I never asked to be infected with these—" she held out the evidence of her arms, "—but I have them. You wave that sword Truth around and sound pretty grandiose when you're talking about someone else. But look inside. Look inside."

She wheeled around and headed away from him. It was too much. First her hideous accusations, and then this stupid lack of judgment. Surely she would get all three of them killed with her recklessness. He must save his daughter first. And the only chance of success he had was to lose Cathryn. Wild and unpredictable, she was a danger. And she could be tracked.

He turned to get Lucette, but found her already at his side, ready to go again.

"She leads us once more. I will be able to follow again. I'm feeling some better." His daughter was watching his face. He didn't think she had heard the argument. It was time to tell her they were going to strike out on their own. He tried to frame a suitable explanation, but before the first word could be uttered, Lucette spoke again.

"Come father, we should not keep the queen waiting."

It undid him completely. Since that moment in the king's chambers until now, he had managed to suppress the enormity of what had happened. Now his daughter's straightforward loyalty broke through his fear and rage. She was right. He could not wrap his mind around the concept altogether. That would take time. But here and now he knew what must be done.

They would follow the regent and protect her. It was the choice he despaired to make, and it was the only choice.

Holding Lucette's unwounded arm in support, he started in the same direction Cathryn had taken. He could still see her, striding upwards though the trees ahead of them. She was lost from sight just before she reached the crest of the hill, but he had a bearing and could catch up. Lucette was making good progress, all things considered.

A pair of hands reached out from a dark, leaf-covered place and grabbed him and his daughter into the copse.

"Shhhh. Look. There." Under cover of the dense growth, Cathryn pulled him up beside her to peer past branches toward the far side of the ravine they would have crossed next. Four guards approached, two looking away as they walked, two looking in their direction. But it was the fifth person, the black-hooded leader, that made him turn cold. Another Taker.

In the deep shadows, the Earth woman's eyes were two glittering shards. She leaned so close to him that her lips grazed his ear as she whispered.

"I'm going to try that direction." She nodded slightly toward the west. "Stay hidden for a little while, then take Lucette into town."

While he would have welcomed the chance to be rid of her just moments ago, now they had to survive together. There was no time to explain. He felt the oneband of the Servant Guild on his wrist. Would this idea of his serve them well? The guards were moving nearer in their sweep of the ravine.

"Watch closely. Do as I do, say what I say." Even as he drew Lucette nearer to him, mustered his concentration and began the first words of the spell, he could see the Earth woman weigh his refusal to commit to her plan against her own sacrifice. Would she do this thing he asked of her? When she did not repeat the first line after him, his heart quailed.

Closer than before, the sound of the search came to them. Suddenly, Cathryn ran through the first words and motions of the spell. He could feel relief and anxiety both rise up over him. As quickly and quietly as possible, he completed the spell and she followed in every movement and word. Now would come the test. All three held their positions, motionless, silent.

The guard who had been approaching them had disappeared. He could see the others still searching the other side of the ravine. Where was the fourth officer?

Nearby, branches moved. The guard was moving into the thicket behind them. He couldn't risk even the smallest movement of his head to find out if they had really been discovered. The spell that he had laid on himself and Lucette and, with divine help, the one Cathryn had put on herself, would keep them unnoticed only if they did not move.

His back, right between his shoulders, twitched with imagined wounds from soon-to-be struck blows. This mad plan would not work. They would be found out. The Earth woman's magic couldn't cover the powerful signature of the bloodworms.

A twig snapped. It was very close. A branch flipped back into place. It was a bit farther away. A boot scraped on a rock. Farther still. He opened his eyes, surprised they had been closed, and looked out through the leaves. The fourth guard was emerging down the way and joining the others once again. The Taker that led them stopped, scanned the landscape and then moved on.

Beside him, Lucette let out a long breath. He realized he, too, had been holding his breath. He turned to Cathryn. There she was, head down, muttering the spell over and over. In her determination and with the raw, unbridled power of the bloodworms, she was becoming transparent, invisible. Already she was more a misty outline, fading rapidly.

While he could still see her at all, he covered her mouth with one hand and brought her near him.

"They're leaving." He poured hurried words into her ear. "We just have to sit still a little while longer. The spell worked." Her lips stopped moving under his palm. "It worked."

Slowly, still aware of the need for silence, he brought his hand away from her mouth. He was so close to her now, he could feel her heart beating, fast and hard. She was afraid. It was a revelation to him. Through all the strange and hostile events of the last few days she had seemed focused, taking things almost unnaturally in stride. But there was fear underneath, real and potent. That she had come this far in spite of it, brought him to the edge of admiration.

"I think it's clear, father. Shall we try for the city?" Lucette's words broke into the duke's thoughts.

He let go his hold of Cathryn and dropped his gaze. Suddenly he felt awkward.

"I know a few in the city that would help us no matter the circumstance. But the decision is yours." He looked up into the Earth woman's eyes. And found surprise there.

"I don't know. The information I get from the memories comes in bits and pieces. Right now I'm not getting anything."

"I can offer this suggestion: While the spell still works, we can seek out allies and get help for Lucette. It will bring us enough time, I hope, to make a better plan for what will come after today."

Cathryn looked at Lucette and then at him. She shifted nervously on her feet.

"Okay."

There was a pause. The duke was puzzled.

"The meaning of the letters 'O' and 'K' would be...?"

The Earther smiled and rubbed her forehead in chagrin.

"Okay means yes. Yes, we'll try the town and your friends."

As they set off toward the city, Lucette tried the new word several times. "Okay. Okay. Okay." And very quietly laughed. The laughter troubled him.

He should feel safer. Several times as the three of them

slipped through the city, parties of guards or paired Takers had ignored or missed them. Cathryn's spell seemed to have masked not only the signal traces of the bloodworms, but his and Lucette's presence, as well. In fact, he had to thump T'Tolyan on the arm twice just to get him to focus and really see them when they knocked at his back door begging for sanctuary.

T'Tolyan's house had more than a few hiding places. In his other visits, Benedic had been shown one secret room. This time he was shown two different ones. He figured there must be more, though how the extra rooms fit into a seemingly normally proportioned house mystified him. It must be bred into the blood and bones of every person born under the huge skies of Linton Province, the delight in being able to disappear and the satisfaction of keeping so many things private while appearing so wide-handed.

He had known T'Tolyan years before the plainsrider even mentioned he had a house in Corronheld's capitol. An ally that parsimonious with secrets should have made him feel more secure. But it did not. He had been pacing through most of the strategy meeting, but he knew it made others anxious so he sat down again and, this time, tried to stay still.

T'Tolyan's dark, hardened hands smoothed down the map that covered most of the table top. "The trip is already planned and known. If we cover your guild bands and that Forché-pale face, you can hide among the outriders taking horses upcountry, Lucette." He traced a route that ran from CorronKeep to the farms and fields of Chymion; a route that, of necessity, passed along the edge of Forché Province.

As she leaned over the map and reached out to trace for herself the proposed route, Lucette winced slightly. They had not taken the risk of seeking a guild healer for her arm, a choice Benedic disliked. But T'Tolyan's household boasted a sun-creased horsehealer who had been recruited to help. His daughter had borne the less-than-gentle ministrations graciously and seemed to actually heal well from them, though the salve that was slathered on the wound smelled suspiciously like the lineament used on T'Tolyan's racing stock.

"If I read your markings right, the place where I would part from the caravan is only a long day's travel to home." Lucette straightened up, satisfied. "How soon do we leave?"

"Tomorrow at first light. T'Gault is gathering the stock at our stables north and east of the city even now." With a crooked smile, the plainsrider glanced at Lucette from under the maelstrom of his untamed eyebrows. Benedic read the look and despaired in a very fatherly way: T'Tolyan's son and his daughter had seldom seen one another since they were children. It was obvious from this meeting, however, that they each warmly approved of what the other had become over the years. Though T'Gault was a fine person, and both young people were of an age to feel the pull of the heart, father Benedic had mixed feelings that Duke Benedic would have scorned.

"Then, by your leave, I will complete my preparations." Lucette moved away from the table.

"I can't believe you're sending her back by herself." Cathryn's voice startled the three of them. Though her overwrought magicking had subsided enough she was no longer translucent, she still tended to be overlooked in a matter of minutes when she stayed silent.

Lucette paused at the doorway.

"For your care of me, I thank you, majesty. If, as you suspect, our castellan inflicted you with the bloodworms, then we must know the truth of it. Should Arilon be innocent, coming alone will be of no harm to me. Should he be in league with enemies unknown, coming in numbers would only cause the truth to be more deeply buried, or my brother to become an unwilling shield." They all had gone over the plan several times already; the Earth woman had voiced her reservation more than once.

"Benedic?"

The duke sighed inwardly as Cathryn sought to enlist him in her fears. He shared them. Fully. But the events of these last few days had made it all too clear that whatever changes life held would come whether he was easy with them or not.

"The plan is as sound as circumstances allow. Lucette is, though my father's heart wants to deny it, the right and only one to do what needs be done at this moment." He watched Cathryn's eyes. She did not blink or turn from him as he spoke. Would she see his reluctance to let his daughter face this alone? Would she see his pride? Or Lucette's?

"Well, that's it, then. Come on, Lucette, I'll help you pack." To his surprise, Cathryn pulled aside the vividly-colored material hung across the archway leading to the main house and motioned Lucette through. Their exit caused the cloth suspended in front of the wall to billow restlessly, floating out over the darkly patterned rug and back again.

"If you never choose a horse, how will the journey begin, eh?" T'Tolyan leaned back in his chair and folded his arms across his chest, assuming the plainsrider position that signaled the start of a discussion or, most usually, an argument.

"I am almost reconciled to Lucette's mission. It is as close as a father can come."

T'Tolyan chuckled in a manner he found most irritating.

"Your daughter found her own journey, walking brother. Her father's approval was a sweet, not the meat." T'Tolyan's sharp eyes pierced his attempt at composure.

"If not Lucette, then what *do* you mean, riding brother. Your outrider riddles hide more meaning than they uncover."

"I mean that the Keep bells have knelled the death of a

monarch. Of those who know the Passing went to another, only you, the most courteous and just Benedic, have not used one title of state, one word of respect, given the slightest of honors to she who received the Passing. The question I ask you, walking brother, is why?" T'Tolyan huffed through the bristles of his substantial mustache. "If this opposition is from petulance at being called as heir but not chosen, it ill becomes you."

"Do you think so poorly of me that you believe this doubt of mine is based on nothing more than a bilious temperament? Forget I ever asked you to speak your mind plainly. Go back to your convoluted horse metaphors." He could feel the anger sting up and down his arms. T'Tolyan ever and always knew how to goad him into hot words.

"If you have good reason to withhold due allegiance, would it not be right to make that reason known?" The plainsrider shifted slightly in his chair, though the motion looked so much like settling back on a saddle that Benedic could almost hear leather creak. "After all, you have asked much of us. No sooner than the death bells sounded came word that a new king had been chosen by Passing. But no public ceremony for this one. No, he must stay barricaded in the Keep as his life was and is threatened by assassins who attempted to take, by force and magic, what was rightfully his. Guardians comb the city for the traitors. Takers, which we thought were gone for all time into fables to scare unruly children, are seen in their deadly pairs. And whom do they seek? Benedic. The same Benedic who comes in the night with the woman he says has taken the Passing.

"For the years I have known you and the love I bear you, walking brother, I did not hesitate, but pledged myself and my clan to a fealty that carries exile or death should it be revealed. We gave our pledge full and unqualified. It appears you have not. If there are reasons to consider, are not our lives and honor worth the telling of them?"

Benedic had a sudden picture of Bayly lying motionless on a stable floor. She and Kern had also committed themselves to action on his word alone. Now she was dead, and Kern sweated in a poison fever. For that, he had spent hours locked inside himself debating the right and wrong of what he had done. Were his allies owed the whole truth? Or would the whole truth bring with it the seeds of an even greater disaster?

He had always believed in his talent for leadership and bore with grave awareness the burden of responsibility it brought. But now the foundations of all he held true, those beliefs that translated into the actions of his life, were under siege. Were those ideals he had always believed worth living for, also worth dying for?

"When we patrolled the far-borders those many years ago, T'Tolyan, you used to spend a great deal of time in the night-camps poking at the fire with a stick. I should have realized then what all that practice stirring up hot coals would mean later on."

T'Tolyan's arms, while still crossed on his chest, relaxed the smallest bit. But he kept quiet, making a silence Benedic was obliged to fill.

"You are right. I have come to think my secrets in this matter have been kept more out of arrogance and fear than prudence. The only other person, beside myself, who has heard the entire tale is the King."

"Unless you have lied to us, the king is dead." T'Tolyan stirred restlessly. "So, in truth, the only other person who knows this tale is…the queen. Yes?"

Why hadn't he thought of that? Reyfen's memories of his report after D'Shaar's death, his fears about Earth and the meddling of certain Esoterics, had most certainly been a part of the Passing. If those memories had not surfaced already, it was only a matter of time before Cathryn knew his feelings and suspicions.

"Most of the time, T'Tolyan, this penchant of yours to say what others are too politic to discuss is maddening. But today you have done a valuable service with your prodding."

"I doubt it not. I am, by all accounts, a very wise and hugely adorable person."

"Well, I pray your wisdom, adorable one, and your humility will hear me out." With that, he proceeded to tell the plainsrider about D'Brin's experiments with time and place of ten years ago and how other worlds had been glimpsed, among them Earth. He repeated what his wife had told him of that place and why, therefore, he feared its influence, or worse, its intrusion so greatly.

T'Tolyan listened intently, breaking his silence only once when Benedic came to the part where D'Shaar had been returned to him in a coffin. At that point, he said those words which mean little of themselves but speak comfort to a friend. It took a moment before Benedic could resume his tale.

"This Earth seems to have the power to attract the obsession of those who view it. Other than the King, who was by right owed the knowledge, I did not feel I could reveal the existence or, most especially, the nature of that other place to anyone. All who see it become tainted by it."

"Even you, my friend?"

"Aye. Even me. I have stood as judge a hundred times and even when justice was hardest, I thought I could see where right ended and wrong began." He rubbed his eyes, as if doing so would clear his confusion. "Now matters are murky. I cannot deal with the Earth woman evenly. Trying to find the right, and then do it, has become like finding a trail through a field of serpents in the dark. How can I decide whether or not to trust her if I cannot decide whether or not to trust myself?"

T'Tolyan shook his head in disbelief.

"Who would have believed that I would someday have the honor to lecture the Gray Duke on his duty? That's a horse I had not thought to ride. Still, how could I live with myself if I missed the chance?"

T'Tolyan struggled, very obviously, to keep a wry smile from taking over his face. He almost succeeded.

"I believe the Passing happened as you said. That the Queen comes from another land, even another world, counts not at all. Over the years others have taken the Passing, by design or by accident, from the beckoned heir. Each one, without fail, has sickened and died within a few short months because interlopers, no matter their guilt or innocence in the matter, bear that curse. But each one, equally without fail, has been accorded all the due respect and allegiance of any other regent in what time they live to fill the office. It is both our law and our practice. There is no confusion, my friend."

Benedic got up from his chair and began to pace once again.

"You are right. Of course. When you say it, it sounds so clear. Why do I struggle so hard to resist the truth of it, then?"

"There are reasons for that, walking brother; but I am much too gentle and sweet a man to tell them to you."

The outrageousness of T'Tolyan's statement stopped him in his tracks.

"Sweet? You smarmy horsetrader. That word shouldn't be used even in the same province where you ride."

"Benedic, dear friend, because you are exhausted from wrestling philosophical phantoms, I will overlook your regrettable lapse in courtesy. Besides, if we are to be ready to leave the city before daylight tomorrow, much needs to be done. Come on. We will eat and drink and tell humiliating stories about one another in front of friends. It will be a good night."

Brooking no argument, the plainsrider stood up and swept to the archway in a flurry of color and attitude. It was obvious he was done talking. From long experience, Benedic knew he had no choice but to follow his friend. Tomorrow would be dangerous enough without bickering amongst themselves. For now it was enough to be here, as safe as the night allowed.

Chapter Seven:
CATHRYN

S HE FELT LIKE a fifth wheel. Lucette and Bushbin, T'Toly-an's round, red-cheeked and capable house-manager, bustled about the kitchen and pantry with good-natured efficiency. At first she tried to help, but had only gotten in the way. When Bushbin politely asked whether she might not want to lay the fire for use the next morning, she knew he'd thrown her a token task.

The hearth bench was wide. After she had finished arranging the firewood, she pushed aside a few pots of herbs and bins of beans and sat down. Idly, she picked up one of the beans and sniffed at it. The smell made her think of the backyard garden of her childhood: tomatoes warm and juicy in whatever heat the Seattle summer sun could manage, carrots cool from being buried in the dirt, a riot of berry bushes always threatening to overwhelm the well-behaved rows of vegetables. Little saucers of beer to drown the slugs. Nets on poles to foil the birds. And the bean poles with…

Fuller's beans.

No, wait. The kind her mother planted weren't called that. Where did that name come from?

In her mind, she saw bean plants climbing up a wooden trellis built along the back wall of a sod house. A sturdy little boy picked beans and put them in a bag slung over his shoulder. To reach the top of the trellis, he stood on a five-legged stool. The boy's name was Wennt. Her name was…

She clenched her teeth and shook her head. The visions were coming more often. It wasn't only Reyfen's memories that struggled up into her awareness, it was memories of the ruler before him, and the one before that and on and on, backward through time. The most recent ones were clearest, the older visions were cloudy, fading, vague feelings more than sharp pictures.

Some of the recollections were small: the name of a flower, a sense of familiarity with a place, the pleasure of tasting a favorite food she had never tried. Others were huge, overwhelming. She had awakened from sleep last night with one of those, her dreams violated by a paralyzing vision of Reyfen's last moments. She had felt death's hand reaching for him/her. Layered on that horror were the death-throes of generations of kings and queens, each one vivid and personal, each one belonging to someone else and now completely her own.

The vision had made her cry out. Lucette, from her bed across the room, had tried to reassure her. But even with cups of kaffe and a glowing nightlight, she couldn't bring herself to talk about it or calm down enough to go back to sleep. So they had stayed up most of the night chatting about little nothings. 'Whiling away the willies' her mother used to call it.

Lucette was good at it. She had rambled on with stories of her childhood, recounting tales illustrating her sisterly belief that Corry was a rascal, albeit one she loved. She told about travel to other provinces with her parents and brother, how she learned which magic talent she had, who had been her best friends during learningyears, told family jokes. It was a generous and gracious thing to do. Though they had taken to one another from their very first meeting, this act of the heart had endeared her to Cathryn completely.

And now her only friend in this place was going away, in large part due to Cathryn's admission that she suspected Arilon of infecting her with the bloodworms. It was odd the way she had realized it. During the last few days of hiding, information gathering and strategy meetings, she had been having some success in repressing the alien memories by sheer mental effort. But the exhaustion that followed the Passing and the escape from the Keep had taken its toll, and it was difficult to keep her guard up all the time.

While changing clothes one night, the sight of the hated worms in her arms caused a bubble of information to pop and it left a residue of remembering. A past ruler, a woman from the farm province of Chymion, knew that bloodworms entered the skin in a moment of pain and began to grow almost immediately. Like all farmers working the irrigation ditches, she wore high leather wading boots to prevent infection by the parasite that co-existed with fish but was fatal to most other living things of this world.

Remembering that Arilon's touch the first day at Forché had set off a brief but agonizing burst of pain, it all fell into place. When she had heard the duke planned to send word to his castellan that she had been found, she shared her suspicions. At first he dismissed the idea, refusing to believe that the family's righthand would do such a thing. But his daughter had reasoned with him. Eventually, he admitted he had sensed a great deal of unresolved guilt in Arilon and began to be concerned with the well-being of the province, not to mention his son, under his castellan's care.

It was hard to watch Benedic's affection for his children war with his sense of duty. She knew he wanted desperately to take Lucette home and make sure she and Corry were out of harm's way. But his job was to get Cathryn to a safe place, bring allies together and regain the throne for the rightful regent.

For me.

She pulled her legs up under her and moved farther back on the hearth, trying to get comfortable. But nothing was going to make her comfortable with this weird situation. Struggle as she might, she couldn't get her mind around the concept that she was actually queen of a place that, until a few days ago, she never knew existed. The thought constantly threatened to overwhelm her. In self-defense, she ruthlessly repressed thinking about it too much, trying to buy time to get her balance.

Even as she pushed the troubling thoughts deeper down and away, she realized how often in her life she'd done just that kind of thing. When a company she had once worked for was sold, she didn't start job hunting right away; instead she continued to work with frantic loyalty, believing that, with extra effort, the chaos of change could be controlled. No one was more distressed or unprepared for being laid off than she.

And she had been the classic blind wife with David. For a long time she couldn't bring herself to acknowledge his infidelities. But he'd been out with someone else the night she miscarried and there was no choice but to see and to know. The grief over that death was magnified by the grief she felt over the betrayal. It was so hideous that, in defense of her sanity, she pushed the feelings down into the dark corners.

The answer to the chaos of life, she had decided, was control. The answer to betrayal, withdrawal. She knew her solutions weren't perfect, but she was tired of being hurt, ached from the anguish that left her bruised and alone. Her life had grown smaller and smaller and colder. Lately, she had begun to be afraid the price she was paying for control and safety was too high.

"You looked far away, lady. If you prefer to be undisturbed, I can leave and give you some privacy."

She tossed the Fuller's bean back into the hearth basket. She must have been out of it for quite a while because only Lucette remained in the kitchen, and she was coming over with two mugs of steaming kaffe.

"No, no. I could use the company, actually." She pushed a couple of baskets further over and made room for her friend. "That kaffe smells pretty good. You know, where I come from, we have something called coffee. The city I live in is actually sort of famous for it."

"Does it taste like this?" Lucette settled down next to her, leaning back against the hearth.

"Pretty close. Which was a big relief to me because I drink a lot of the stuff."

For a while, the two of them sat and sipped in quiet. Some of the best times Cathryn ever had with friends back home had been spent in comfortable, companionable silence just like this.

"Would it ease your mind with my leaving if you had proof my father could be trusted?"

Her friend's question took her by surprise.

"Well, Lucette, it's not that I don't trust your father, it's just…" She stumbled as she tried to find a politic way of saying she made it a practice not to trust anyone.

But it appeared the duke's daughter had enough of her father's leadership talent to realize she'd hit a key sticking point.

"How can we blame you for holding us all away from yourself? Brought against your will from a faraway place, unfamiliar with our ways, sorrowing for home, touched by the Passing. This place has not been kind. Were I you, I would also be very cautious where I placed my faith."

Not knowing where the conversation was leading, she took another sip of kaffe and gave Lucette the chance to continue.

"You know, you have the means to judge my father's character. Reyfen and my father were more than ruler and subject. In our land, when children reach the last few of the learningyears we send them for half-cycle stays with family friends who live far enough away to require the adventure of travel. My father-parents sent their son to a small mountainhold deep in Quarel Province. Over the length of the stay, Holder Reyfen and my father grew to know and admire one another. It was to be so from that day on."

Lucette paused to put down her mug.

"You can beckon the memories you need to be sure of Reyfen's character. If you find him a person of discernment and honor, then his judgment of my father should be of some value. Do you not think so?"

"Maybe." Cathryn tried not to sound too skeptical. "But it's not that easy. At least not for me. It isn't just having other lives crowded into my head, it's having lives that are so alien. I don't know names for things, or your history or values or even stuff like bedtime stories. I get lulled into thinking we're the same, and then some strange custom pops up in a memory and I realize I have no idea what I've just seen, don't understand at all."

Her throat was raw and her eyes burned. Just as she feared, talking about this was uncovering the very things she was trying hard to keep buried.

"And the magic." One tear started a hot, stinging path down her cheek. "Everybody seems to have a—" she searched for a word "—gentle talent. You do constructive things with it. Every time I use whatever it is these worms have given me, it goes crazy. I'm afraid I won't be able to control it and I'll hurt someone, or worse.

"All I ever wanted was to stay alive long enough to get home. Now I can't even…" Her voice fled under the strain. The first tear was joined by many.

Lucette carefully took her mug away and set it down. She gently folded her friend's hands in hers.

"When did you find out?"

Cathryn took a deep breath, but it was too raggedy for speech. Within Lucette's clasp, she clenched her hands and tried again.

"It was part of what Reyfen was thinking at the last, that the wrong person had gotten the Passing but how it wouldn't matter in a few months because—" she could hardly finish "—because by then I would be dead."

The last of what little composure she had left was eroding. In a desperate effort to salvage some self-control, she drew on the power that lurked under her skin to steady herself. It was all she could think to do. Immediately, a measure of calm flowed into and cushioned her distress. It was a cool and oily sensation. Though her next words should have been terrible to utter, the false peace of the worms made her glib.

"I know it's true. This Passing doesn't allow mistakes…even innocent ones. I experienced the last moments of those few souls who, like me, wrongfully got the Passing. Every one of them dead within a month or two. Not easy deaths, either." Even with the shield of magicked tranquility, the remembrance made her shudder violently.

"Your father was the beckoned heir. He only needs to keep me in his reach and wait. If I don't make it, no big deal. I just have to be sure to die within touching distance."

"How can you speak that way of my father?" Lucette pulled back her hands with a jerk.

"Because where I come from we understand what the promise of power does to a person. Everybody here seems blind to that."

Lucette was practically sputtering. "We do not misapprehend how greed for power twists the soul. Not at all. But you impugn my father who would never—"

"Never what?" She stopped the duke's daughter short. "Never lie for his own benefit? Then tell me this: Just when did you think your father was going to tell me about this curse, about my death sentence? Or doesn't he consider hiding the truth a form of lying?"

"Had I told you, would you have believed me?" Benedic's voice splashed on her anger like cold saltwater on a wound. From the shadow of the kitchen's doorway, the duke emerged.

"It is late, daughter, and your journey of the morrow will begin early. It is time to rest."

"I am not an infant to put to bed whenever—"

"Now." When Benedic commanded, Cathryn could feel the words buzz against her bones. Lucette was up and moving toward the doorway before the sound of the dismissal had faded from the air.

"Falling back on your child-control tricks again?" She knew her guess had hit the mark when he visibly drew back. "Does your daughter know you still do that?"

Even with the worms providing a buffer to fear, the fire that ignited behind Benedic's eyes was intimidating.

"It appears you have complaints to make of me. Will you not grant me the honor of making them to my face? In our world, that is the custom." Each word was clipped and sharp as it left him and hurled toward her. Truth was, indeed, a two-edged sword; both of them were feeling its sting. The words she was obliged to speak now were hard and bitter in her mouth.

"I should have come to you first, I guess. I've offended you and I'm sorry." She couldn't resist adding more. "But you must admit, you haven't been a fountain of information. I think that someone who has just been given a death sentence by no fault of her own deserves a better way of finding out about it. I would have preferred the sound of another voice, maybe even a kind word, to the nightmares I got instead."

He shifted uneasily where he stood. "You are not the first person today to remind me of how much I have neglected to do. Where my silence has caused you pain, I beg the gift of your pardon."

His abrupt change from impervious to vulnerable played havoc with her. From white-hot anger she spun into confusion. To hide her bewilderment and the residue of anger that was still making her hands shake, she got up from the hearth and went over to the cooking stove and the kettle that had been left simmering on it. With her back to him, she began the universal and comforting ritual motions of making something hot to drink.

"I'm trying very hard not to do any harm to you or your family or this place, but help seems pretty hard to come by here. So far, Lucette has been my only friend; and I can't even tell her the whole truth because of my promise to you." Taking a towel from a hook by the stove, she wrapped the handle of the kettle and poured hot water over kaffe leaves laid on a piece of cloth. While she watched the water filter through, she continued.

"You've got a terrific daughter, you know. I can't imagine what I would have done without her. She loves you very much and believes in you, not just as a father, but as a person and a leader. She thinks that, if I look deeply enough into Reyfen's memories, I'll come to trust you, too." The brewing was done. She twisted the rest of the liquid from the scrap of cloth into the mug. Someone else's memories of kaffe brewing were making these motions familiar, reassuring.

"Here," she turned and held out the steaming mug to him "tuck into this. It will do you good." As she said the words, emotions flew across his face like the shadows of dark birds. Before she could even guess what it meant or what she had done to set him off, he wheeled around and left without a word.

For a few endless moments she stood alone, the offering still in her outstretched hand. The futility of her gesture eventually made itself felt, and she set the mug down. The gritty sound of pottery on tile set her teeth on edge. She was too tired to handle anything well.

The morning had been the perfect definition of controlled chaos. First T'Gault came thundering through the courtyard gates at the crack of dawn with a string of thirty horses, three other outriders and a supply wagon. T'Tolyan's son had all the exuberance of youth plus an obvious desire to impress a certain duke's daughter.

Lucette was almost as bad. Though she was practically submerged in a huge traveling cloak as part of her disguise, a pronounced jauntiness of bearing was all too evident, even in the earliest hours of the day.

Add to all of that the frantic last-minute preparations and the difficulty of doing it while keeping identities and intentions secret under the oppressive watchfulness of the city guards who roamed the streets and questioned everyone they saw. Viewing the whole process was like watching a circus with a hidden agenda.

She had made her good-byes to Lucette before dawn had softened the sky. Though both were well aware dangers were ahead, they kept their farewells cheerful and casual. But the closer departure came, the harder it was. As Lucette reined her mount through the courtyard and the gates shut behind the horses, wagon and riders, Cathryn could only bring herself to watch from a window.

As she turned away from the window, something caught her eye. Down below, in the corner of the yard, motionless in the settling dust, stood Benedic, staring at the closed gate. She felt some sympathy for the man. It must be very hard for a father to realize he was going to lose his daughter, if not to the dangers of this mission, then most likely to someone like the young plainsrider.

There was a brisk rapping at the door to the room.

"Come in."

At first, she couldn't see Bushbin's perpetually flushed face behind the mound of clothes he carried. Even his voice was muffled until he put the pile of brightly colored garments down on the bed.

"…leaving in an hour, he says. These are for you." The house-manager sorted through and laid out the clothes tidily. "When you have everything on but the sash and cloak, bring them out and I will help you settle them. Properly settle them, I mean. Important to do that." He shook a pleasantly plump finger at her in a genial way. "Playing at being a 'rider depends on getting the little things right."

"Thank you. I won't take long." She glanced down at the tunic she was wearing, the one she'd been given by Joan several days ago. "I'll need something to pack these in, I suppose."

"No, no. It won't do to take the things you're wearing. Might be recognized, you know. When you've gone, I've orders to burn them. Quick and all." As Bushbin headed for the door, she heard, for the first time in her life, a sound she'd only read about: "Tsk-tsk." It really did sound just like that. Strange, funny man. Quite nice, really.

The clothes were a riot of textures and hues. There was a pair of loose fitting pants of deep purple that tucked into calf-high forest green suede boots. Over that went a tunic of midnight blue embroidered on shoulders and cuffs with silver stars and copper moons. Two wide leather bracelets, one dyed a deep red and the other a rich brown, were also provided. She figured they must be guild bands: red for Begotten Guild, brown for Animal Circle, if she remembered Lucette's lecture on that first day correctly.

Once dressed, she felt like a gaudy package waiting for a blazingly dull ribbon. Self-consciously she carried the understated fringed black belt and drab-colored cloak out into the hallway and down to the kitchen. Bushbin, who was putting finishing touches on a huge hamper of comestibles, clapped his hands together with satisfaction when he saw her.

"Now, don't you look better?" His compliment made her smile. Could someone dressed entirely in various and lurid shades of red and yellow be qualified to judge if she looked better or not?

"Well, thank you; but I think I'm going to stick out like a sore thumb in these clothes."

"Sore thumb? What an expression. Though I can see it. Yes, and well." Bushbin chuckled as he reached for the belt she had brought down with her. Quickly and expertly he wrapped it around her waist, fastening it with a peculiar knot that he took great pains to teach her, warning her she must tie it just that way every time since the knots of a plainsrider sash were coded messages. He neglected to tell her what that message was, however, because he immediately became involved in draping the dun-colored cloak over her shoulders and fastening it with a large coppery circle and pin arrangement which, he said, indicated the wearer was part of T'Tolyan's clan.

When he was done, Bushbin stepped back to admire his work. "Now you're a regular 'rider, just like…"

"Just like me." T'Tolyan's huge frame filled the kitchen doorway. His rumbling voice rattled the dishes. "Almost we're ready to ride, but I've a stomach and a head need pacifying first."

Cathryn thought her host looked a bit under the weather. If she had to wager, she'd have bet a hangover as the probable cause. Bushbin had a concoction waiting for his employer, as if this request had been expected. She wondered what she had missed the night before.

T'Tolyan downed the drink, wheezed, coughed twice and stamped his feet.

"'Shoenails! You put dirt in this potion to spite me, Bushface.'"

Bushbin said nothing, but stood with his hands folded placidly over his barrel-sized stomach.

Little beads of sweat started to trickle down T'Tolyan's face. His unruly eyebrows raised themselves to new heights. She began to worry about the man's health, though the house-manager seemed calmed enough.

Suddenly, the massive plainsrider huffed, then huffed again, grabbed a kitchen towel from a nearby tabletop, covered his face and let go a single, explosive sneeze.

"Every time I drink that evil brew I swear my eyeballs will expel themselves." T'Tolyan used the towel to wipe his nose and then held it out for Bushbin to take. But the expression on the house-manager's face, a mixture of disgust and amiable resolution, made it clear he wasn't going to touch the defiled towel. T'Tolyan waded up the cloth and looked for a place to toss it, but Bushbin cleared his throat meaningfully.

T'Tolyan stuffed the offending towel under his cloak and made for the doorway.

"We should away, my lady, before we are hanged at home for trifles."

She followed her host out to the courtyard. Bushbin trailed behind with the hamper of food which he placed in the horse-drawn conveyance pulled up to the door. The vehicle reminded her of pictures she'd seen of Basque sheepherder's wagons. It had high walls, a peaked roof, little windows on each side, a small door in the back and a driver's bench high in the front. It was painted, from front to back and top to bottom, in the color of almost-ripe wheat and was drawn by two gray and white horses.

T'Tolyan clambered up on the driver's bench and reached out a helping hand to her. One of the horses stamped and pulled abruptly at the traces. Her face must have registered her skepticism because her host began to chuckle.

"Your attire speaks rider, but your face shouts walker. There is a need to keep this conversation of disguise in the one language only." T'Tolyan kept his huge, callused hand stolidly outstretched, both an offer of help and a challenge.

"I know. It's just that—" She eyed the draft animals with caution "—I've never really been around horses and they look so big and…well…unpredictable."

"The same, dear lady, has been said of me; but I am, as you can plainly observe, completely harmless. You only need to become more closely acquainted with horses to like them. I would think it a high honor if you permit me to introduce you to the pleasures of the ride." His hand was still waiting, large and capable; but by now he had pasted a good-natured leer on his face.

"Don't you think your wife might object to this riding lesson, dear friend?" Benedic had arrived at the wagon in time to hear which way the conversation was heading.

The plainsrider broke into a loud laugh that came close to spooking the horses. "My wife," T'Tolyan bridged the remaining inches between her hand and his, caught hold and hauled her up to the bench beside him, "is a better rider than even I, dear friend, and I am, by all I hear, a veritable legend. Who better to share the mysteries of horselore?"

Benedic looked up at them, squinting into the pale glare of the late morning sun.

"That is the first time I've heard what you are doing labeled as 'horselore.' I fear, Cathryn, you face a long and windy trip. My deepest apologies I could not spare you this ordeal."

"Apology? I don't know what you mean." She couldn't help but join in the good-natured teasing. "I plan to spend the entire trip helping this meek man overcome his painful shyness."

The meek man beside her huffed mightily through his remarkable mustache. Benedic looked surprised at the remark, a reaction she discovered she enjoyed eliciting from the usually unflappable duke.

"Besides, it will be much nicer riding with this bag of wind than being downwind of you."

"She's right, you know. You're completely disgusting." T'Tolyan leaned over Cathryn in order to speak directly to his friend as he delivered this helpful comment.

On the theory that a lone worker of dubious cleanliness would escape examination more easily, Benedic was once again masquerading as a dirty, down-on-his-luck stablemucker. His disguise was complete, from the ratty clothes to the pungent odor that kept friends and foe alike at a distance.

"Jealousy ill becomes you, rider. Here I am so well disguised that danger will not even glance at me; while you are cleverly disguised as what, pray tell? A plainsrider named T'Tolyan trying to leave town? The mind is staggered by your genius."

The plainsrider gathered up the reins and signaled for the gate to be opened. "We will see who 'scapes danger best and who arrives soonest at the inn." At the last moment, he retrieved the towel from under his cloak and tossed it to Benedic. "Just be sure to clean off that disguise before you meet us. The lady and I are too refined to countenance such filth."

When they were out in the street, she glanced behind and saw Benedic heading the other direction on foot, just as they had planned. Suddenly, the enormity of the danger—his, hers and anyone connected with them—threatened to push her into panic.

Settle down. Don't look guilty. Try to fit in. Her inner dialog came faster and faster, until it become more a litany of fear than a reassurance. Before she could muster up the appearance of calm, the wagon turned a corner and there it was: the first roadblock. A makeshift barrier and five guards had created a long line of people and conveyances waiting to be searched and questioned. T'Tolyan pulled the wagon up at the end of the queue.

Incladium sorten. Meelus fel. Incladium sor...

She stopped herself before she overdid the spell for being overlooked once again. All she had to do was be inconspicuous and keep renewing the spell that masked the worm traces. That was the sum total of her role in this part of the escape. Still, her hands were shaking.

"You will ruin my reputation, lady, with these apprehensive looks." How the plainsrider managed to keep his booming voice low enough to reach only her ears was a mystery. "I have it on good account and from many sources that most women are noticeably eager to travel with me."

"Don't you think you should take this more seriously?" She let a little warmth creep into her question. It didn't seem like a good time or place for T'Tolyan to amuse himself with this ridiculous flirting.

"You would have me serious?" T'Tolyan took one of her shaking hands in one of his mammoth ones and raised it slowly toward his lips. "Nay, let us instead trust the poets who call laughter a dread antidote to fear…and a dear companion to affection."

Just as his lips might have brushed her fingers, two guards reached the wagon.

"Ho, Horse Lord."

"Ho, Captain Pistel. I see someone's booted your great buttocks out of the barracks for a wonder."

The guard captain flushed angrily.

"Best you watch your step, sirrah. Our new king doesn't like insolence."

"Have you given him some that you learned so quickly?" The plainsrider leaned back against the wagon-side with a great deal of his own insolence evident. She couldn't believe he was stirring up trouble when all she wanted was to sink out of sight. She was having a hard time breathing right.

"You and your companion better get down while we search your shantycart."

T'Tolyan suddenly dropped her now sweating hand and looked guilty.

"Aye, Captain. I mean—" It was the first time she had seen T'Tolyan at a loss for words. That it should happen right now was terrifying. "—it's just that I can get down and you can search the wagon well enough. In fact, please, I urge you to do so. But you must understand, there is no one else on this cart." The huge man's wild eyebrows went up and down as he jerked his head toward Cathryn and laid his finger aside his nose. "You can see that, surely?"

The guard standing on her side snorted. "Does he think we're blind, then, Cap'n?"

"Not blind, Private. Stupid."

She could feel her heart slam into her ribs. By now, T'Tolyan was sweating, too.

"Now, now good Captain Pistel," the plainsrider looked ready to jump off the wagon and run for the hills, "would I impugn your daunting intellect? Surely I would not, for you easily comprehend the most complex of matters." T'Tolyan wiped his forehead with his sleeve. "You would grasp right away the plight of, say, a Linton horsetrader who had, let us assume for sake of argument, been forbidden by the Duchess of Linton herself to take ladies for rides to the quite beautiful but, uh, more remote hills of Corronheld. Why, your mind would immediately see how that trader would never, and I can say this without fear of contradiction—at least I trust I can—never have a lady riding with him on such a trip."

Captain Pistel's expression had, during this rambling, panicky speech, changed from a scowl to a stare to a smirk.

"Yea, milord, I would understand that much. And more. Very much more." Pistel rammed his hand into his tunic pocket and jingled the few coins that resided in it.

"Ah. Yes. Well." T'Tolyan jumped down from the wagon bench. "Allow me to open the door so you can search my rollinghome personally."

While the private stood stolidly beside the horses, the plainsrider and the captain went around back of what she couldn't help but call 'the camper.' The whole wagon jiggled and swayed as the two men went in. She could hear thumps, then clanks, then a sour, smug laugh.

When the two emerged, T'Tolyan slunk to the front of the wagon and pulled himself onto the bench once more. He was clutching a length of yellow cord that had several large knots along its length. The guard captain shouted at his aide.

"Open the gate and let them…let him through. I've searched his wagon."

The private, slack jawed at his commander's change of attitude, nevertheless jumped to obey the order. Suddenly, they were past the barricade and heading toward the open road.

Before the towers of CorronKeep sank completely behind the hills, they passed through two more roadblocks. Each time, T'Tolyan, now patient and respectful, produced the knotted cord and was let through without question. Every inch of the way she feared discovery so deeply, she felt as if a target had been painted between her shoulder blades.

The horses had put several miles between themselves and the last of the guard stations before the tension in her back subsided somewhat. The small farms that dotted the capitol's outer edges were left farther and farther behind. But it wasn't until the road entered the wooded hills that she judged it safe to ask the question foremost in her mind.

"What in blue blazes were you doing back there?"

T'Tolyan began to chuckle.

"Blue blazes. A doughty phrase. I must add that to my already exquisite repertoire of curses. Blue blazes, indeed."

"T'Tolyan!"

"You bellowed, your grace?" He looked over at her as he snapped the horses into an even more energetic trot. "Ah, you wish to hear how I bravely but cunningly managed our escape. It was blindingly easy, really. I know the captain of old. He is lazy but ambitious. In the uneven politics of late at the Keep, he has been promoted by seizing every advantage mischief can create. I only thought to play that same game as well, so I first made him angry enough that, rather than his brain, his blood ruled."

"You accomplished that with the buttocks remark, I assume." She felt her heart begin to resume its normal pace.

"Aye. And then followed with the intimation that, should your presence be known, I would be in dire trouble. You feigned guilt and apprehension most convincingly, too, I might add. We only had to wait a very short while until Pistel's greed got the better of his clouded judgment and the victory was ours." T'Tolyan looked inordinately pleased with himself.

"So, you really won't be in trouble with the Duchess of your province for taking ladies for rides?"

T'Tolyan laughed loud and long. As if in response, the horses picked up the pace so that the wagon jounced along alarmingly.

"You are a most droll sovereign, I do confess. The question is well targeted, though I think you shot that bolt in the dark. The Duchess of Linton has, indeed, issued a statement to me regarding ladies and travel. And well she might, for she is my most puissant and well-beloved lady wife. Did no one tell you that?"

"No. That little fact seems to have escaped mention." She could feel a flush spring up to her face. "So, let me get this straight: The captain of the guards thinks you're taking me out for immoral purposes and, because your wife rules your home province, he assumes he can now blackmail you?"

"A tidy summary of the situation, my liege."

"How can you be so casual about this? From what I've heard and seen, you probably could be blackmailed by a hundred people. And you let that guard person think I'm some sleazy accomplice to adultery. Thank you so very much."

T'Tolyan made a great, visible effort to restrain his good humor.

"Ah, but the opinion of Pistel is of no matter. When we have gathered allies and taken back the throne, then you may graciously rip the chevrons from his sleeve and send him to the scullery where, doubt it not, he does belong. As for my lady wife," here the huge man loosed a gusty sigh "as I delight in women, so she delights in men; though it is my opinion that she flirts a thousand times worse than ever I do. Perfectly shameless, is T'Meara. But all who know us agree: she is the only one for me and I am, by the Creator's good grace and my own excellent nature, the only one for her."

Cathryn was slack jawed with disbelief. How could T'Tolyan make this passionate declaration of fidelity in the face of his endless supply of lewd innuendos?

"Oh, come on. You can't mean to tell me your wife believes you're completely faithful to her?"

Now the plainsrider looked offended.

"But I am, so why would she not believe so?" He shook his head. "Ah, you do not know me or T'Meara well enough. That is the crux of the matter. Had you trusted to my word time upon time and never been betrayed, you would not accuse me so. It is the same for T'Meara. Her pledged word is all I need."

"You'd understand my doubts if…" In the intimacy of this conversation, she had almost said 'if you knew my world.' But even as the words were forming, the oath made to Benedic so recently kept her from voicing them. How ironic it was that her word of honor prevented her from revealing how little that kind of honor meant on Earth.

Glancing over at T'Tolyan, she found him studying her with a sidelong scrutiny that made her feel she was being judged against some hidden knowledge. Was everyone in this blasted place hiding information?

Without warning, T'Tolyan reined the horses to such a sudden stop that she was nearly tossed from her seat. Leaping down, the plainsrider headed back down the road at a run. He returned holding a piece of white cloth that she was amazed to recognize as the offensive kitchen towel foisted off on Benedic earlier in the day.

"Isn't that the…"

"The poorest of manners? Yea, lady. Befouling the common roads shows a distinct lack of good breeding." T'Tolyan gave her a sharp glance. It threw her off guard until she realized he was trying to tell her they were being overheard.

"Still, as we are stopped, perhaps you wish to…" he cleared his throat discreetly, or what passed as discreetly for him, "… attend to personal matters. I believe I will as well. Since we are stopped. By your leave."

T'Tolyan glanced toward the thicket that encroached almost to the edge of the road on her right and then, without another word, executed a hasty bow and headed off to the trees along the left side of the road.

Deserted and uncertain, she climbed down from the wagon's bench. She was fairly sure she'd read T'Tolyan's unspoken message correctly: head into the thicket. She hesitated, eyeing the verge dubiously; but, realizing delay might make watchers suspicious, she headed into the brush. Small, sharp branches poked and scraped her face and pulled at the bulky folds of the cloak. Roots grabbed at her ankles. Then, with a last thrashing, she was through the worst of it. Ahead was a small clearing.

Now what? She looked around. Nothing. Was she supposed to stay here until T'Tolyan came to get her? Or was she supposed to wait an appropriate amount of time and then head back to the wagon? Or had she read the whole thing wrong and this really was just a pit stop?

From somewhere behind came a low whisper.

"She's here."

She whirled around. Two hooded figures stepped out into the light and began to move toward her. She took up a defensive crouch and frantically tried to summon up some alien memory that might help her survive.

There. A spell burst into her head. It might work. The worms in her arms twitched violently as her lips began to move with the first words of an abruptly familiar invocation. Deep within her chest, an immense and horrible pressure began to build.

Chapter Eight:
BENEDIC

THOUGHTS GATHERED IN his mind until, heavy with foreboding, they condensed into cold drops of fear and fell into his heart. His comrade of old had helped for a while. He could always count on T'Tolyan to inject as much levity as impudence would dare. And the plainsrider hid a shrewd mind behind his unruly eyebrows. It always paid to listen to that rumbling voice, even if it meant enduring excesses of extravagant metaphors to get to the pithy bits.

But the pleasure of T'Tolyan's company and the sanctuary of his home, even Cathryn's unexpected good humor, faded with every step he took through the city. The streets were filled with comings and goings. The death of King Reyfen, the unsettling talk of assassins and the new regent who had yet to show his face had stirred up the populace. No street corner was spared a group of gossips. The door of every inn swung in with each new rumor from the palace and out with each fresh worry that emerged when it was heard.

At least the crowded roads made it easier to stay inconspicuous. Dressed as he was, walking alone as if to his job, he managed to avoid the main streets with their blockades or the notice of roaming squads of guards. He made it to the stables connected to a small inn just outside the city in plenty of time to meet his contact. One of T'Tolyan's clan, a woman picked for her resemblance to Cathryn, waited to join him. She also had a great gift for him: Kell. When Benedic had been brought by force to the capitol, Kell had been left in the palace stables. One of the best things about befriending a plainsrider was that they had ways to horses no one else did—even under the watchful eyes of royal guards.

In keeping with his stablemucker disguise, he had not entered the inn but had gone straight to the stables. Kell recognized him happily, in spite of the fragrant clothes he was wearing. The plainswoman, T'Orah by name, smirked when she saw him.

"There was no need to wear your robes of state just to meet me." T'Orah had the same flippancy everyone in her clan seemed to possess.

"Since I expected to meet you in one of the horse clan's castles," he gestured widely to include all of the ramshackle outbuilding, "I spared no ceremony."

T'Orah chuckled as she got up from the hay bale she'd been using as a resting place. He knew her from his days of being stationed in Linton province. She was a third cousin to T'Tolyan and, while she looked not at all like her relative, she was much the same in temperament.

From her pack, T'Orah drew out a parcel of clean clothes which she threw at him.

"The water barrel's out back, walker. Make use of it before we take to the roads or I shall not enjoy this ride as much as I have planned." The plainswoman winked at him. Great mercies, did all the clan flirt so terribly?

"Not yet." He felt obliged to put a stop to this foolishness. "I have a horse to tend to first, if you will pardon me." He scavenged a battered brush from a tilting shelf and gave Kell a short, but sincere, welcome-back grooming. Though Kell's coat already shone from T'Orah's good care, she still looked on approvingly at this evidence of his priorities. Take care of the horse first, the clan saying went, and it will care for you to the last.

Soon enough he visited the water barrel and donned his donated plainsrider garb. But T'Orah stopped him just as he started to lead Kell outside to start their journey.

"A good job you've made on that knot, walker. But my far-cousin has bid me wind a different message on your belt." She came close to him. "If you will allow me?"

Almost he thought this might be more foolishness, but her expression was serious. Knowing that the wrong code could mean death, he nodded his permission and made to watch carefully the knots she had been bidden to weave.

Of the seven leather strips on the left edge of the belt, T'Orah only undid three. Of the seven on the right edge, she undid two. Most plainsriders did their knots so quickly, it looked to outsiders as if they used magic to go so fast. But this time she worked slowly, with a frown of concentration. At the very end, she pulled from her pocket a thin red string as long as her forearm, twisted it around the final strip and wove both around all the rest in a complicated design.

"I've never seen that before. What does it mean?" He took hold of the red string where it hung free from the knot.

T'Orah stepped back to assess her handiwork.

"I've no wonder you've never seen the like of this. It's called the oathbond sign." She paused and looked away from him. "Once in a long while, a plainsrider will take on a quest or a burden of repayment for a debt beyond compensation. The rider is pledged to the debtholder for a period of time: sometimes a lifetime, sometimes less. He is treated as an extension of the other, as if the one to whom he is bonded had grown a new arm. He serves his bondholder in any way required, without question or limit."

"Why would T'Tolyan bid you tie this sign on me?"

"I asked him the very same question." T'Orah looked up at him and smiled a bit. "He gave me, you will not be surprised to hear, a very long story involving horses and the way children learn to walk. I could not make out the moral of it, nor how it spoke to my puzzlement."

Both of them shook their heads.

"But at the end," she moved out of the stable as she spoke, "he reminded me that oathbonders are protected. Never will a plainsrider, no matter what the circumstance, harm an oathbonder until he has fulfilled his pledge. It is our way."

Benedic, too, led his horse outside. "Then T'Tolyan was ensuring my safety with this, think you?"

The plainsrider mounted her nut-brown horse with all the ease of a Linton province native. "Safety? Yes, I am sure that must have been one reason."

With that enigmatic answer, she urged her mount into motion and all he could do was follow.

The riding was in too much haste and needed too much watchfulness for a great deal of thinking. Twice they were forced to take side trails to avoid squads of guards searching along the main roadway. Once, T'Orah led the duke to a deeply hidden spot while a pair of Takers passed by. The nearer they got to the inn that would be their rendezvous site, the more anxious he became.

"Hold by, rider." He drew Kell up next to the plainswoman for a word. "I begin to think it will be too great a risk for T'Tolyan to take his passenger straight to the inn. Is there some more hidden way we could accomplish this switching of you and…" Once again he stumbled over what to call Cathryn. He felt awkward and under pressure. "…this switching we must do?"

"Aye, my lord. We could stop the rollinghome this side of the inn so it would miss the place altogether." She slowed her horse's pace as she answered his question.

"If we can do that, then only I alone must enter the inn to check on a friend before I travel onward." He felt a sharp stab of pity and care for Kern. By now, his friend was either dead from the Taker's poison or recovering health and but newly informed of Bayly's death. Either way, it would be a sad, and now dangerous, foray to this ill-fated waystation.

T'Orah scanned the roadside for a bit and then reined to a halt at a place she declared had good cover. She dismounted and checked both sides of the road for the best spots in which to hide. When she was satisfied, she approached him with a request.

"If you have something T'Tolyan would recognize, we must drop it in the roadway. Between riders it is a sign that there may be watchers, but a meeting is needed. He will know what to do."

In the midst of his anxiety, he found something to smile about.

"Aye, lady, I do have something that good man might recognize." He reached under his borrowed cloak and retrieved the towel T'Tolyan had so graciously bestowed on him that morning. "Will this do?"

She looked puzzled but accepted the cloth and dropped it in the center of the roadway.

"Good enough. Now we take ourselves into hiding a few paces up the way." She led him into the tangled brush on one side of the road. They hid the horses even farther from the road, then returned to a spot behind a thorn bush that provided them a view of any travelers. Pulling the hoods of their dust colored cloaks over them, they blended into the surrounding scenery and waited. But not for long.

Soon, the rumble of a wagon announced itself. From behind the wall of brambles, he watched T'Tolyan and Cathryn come into sight, engaged in what appeared to be a lively conversation. On impulse, he glanced at the red cord wound in his plainsrider knot. He felt the onrush of an emotion he could not name nor restrain. The sensation that he was teetering on the edge of a precipice was so great, he reached out to grab a nearby branch to keep from falling. His hand had closed on a thorn branch and the pain from the several prickings was so sharp and swift it cleared his head and he could return his attention to the road.

T'Tolyan found the towel immediately. It was clear the huge plainsrider had gotten the message and was being cautious. Even from their hiding place, Benedic could hear the man's thundering voice direct Cathryn to the side of the road, playing out the charade of a stop for personal reasons. Where T'Tolyan entered the trees on the far side of the road, the sound of underbrush thrashing around was lavish and unmistakable. Thankfully, Cathryn was heading in their direction. The exchange was going to be easy. He realized T'Orah was talking to him.

"She's here."

The plainswoman began to move to the small clearing Cathryn had entered. He followed. Together they slipped through the leafy cover that had hidden them and stepped into plain sight.

But Cathryn apparently did not recognize them, for she began to back away and before they could reveal who they were, he was paralyzed by a surge of magic strong beyond anything in his experience. Voiceless and without hearing, he could not counterspell, could not even move.

Before his eyes, a strange tableau played out. T'Orah drew her sword and stepped forward as if to protect him. But as Cathryn finished casting her wild magic, the last broad gesture she used pulled back her cloak enough that the knot in her plainsrider belt was revealed. The reaction this elicited from T'Orah was remarkable.

First she stared at the knot code, then looked at him. After the briefest of pauses, the plainswoman knelt before Cathryn, offering her sword, hilt-first. It looked as though the Earther did not know what to do next; but then her eyes snapped into focus and she took the offered sword, reversed her hold of it and offered the hilt back again while urging T'Orah to stand. It was an accurate playing of the traditional ceremony of fealty.

With a swiftness that showed T'Orah was still very aware of his plight, she drew his hood back so that his face could be seen. The two women began a long discussion that ended in frowns and headshaking. Just as he began to fear he might never be released, Cathryn came forward and touched his forehead.

"...do it, I think. Can you hear again?"

He could. He tried speech.

"Aye. Thank you." His expression of gratitude touched her but little, and T'Orah was clearly uneasy. It did not take Servants Guild magic to see that they were looking at him with suspicion. He could not imagine why they did so, especially since he was the one that had suffered the effects of a hasty and poorly thrown spell. But there was no time and this was no place to find out.

"Farewell, T'Orah. Thank your far-cousin for his help. Tell T'Tolyan to stay out of trouble's way when he returns to town and wait for word."

The plainswoman received his words with concern. She turned to Cathryn and opened her mouth as if to ask a question.

But Cathryn held up her hand and spoke first.

"Don't worry. Give T'Tolyan my thanks as well. He put himself on the line to sneak me out of the city. And you, too. I really appreciate it."

"We would do no other, majesty." T'Orah bowed and then turned away toward the road. In moments, they were alone in the clearing.

"We need to keep moving, lady." He still felt the remnants of Cathryn's coolness toward him as well as his own anxieties. Perhaps action was the best remedy. "The horses are this way."

"Horses? I must have blocked this part of the escape plan out of my mind." The Earther not only unbent from the stiffness she had been showing him, but actually flushed a bit. "It's stupid, I know, to be afraid of them, but there you are."

For some reason, which he decided not to examine too closely, this admission on her part made him feel more at ease.

"I do not have T'Tolyan's talent or…enthusiasm…for teaching the riding skills, but we will be working with a very well behaved animal." He led the way through the dense foliage, speaking in low tones as they walked. "Paudge is quite an intelligent steed and you can be assured T'Orah spoke with him at length before she allowed him to carry you."

"I suppose." But she sounded dubious.

When they had retrieved both horses, he introduced

Paudge to his new rider. True to his prediction, T'Orah must have instructed the horse in the proper behavior. No sudden shakes of the head or unexpected snorts. He was decorum itself, as horses went.

Gingerly, Cathryn climbed into the saddle. At first he rode alongside, demonstrating and encouraging. But the terrain and the need for caution and quiet didn't allow for much of that. Fortunately, she seemed to be mastering her fear. In no time, they neared the inn.

"Let us stop here." Though they had avoided any searchers between their meeting place with T'Tolyan and the inn, he did not want to expose her to any dangers that might be hidden there. "If you stay with the horses, I will get to the inn and be back here long before nightfall. If, by some ill chance, you or I are discovered, let Paudge have his head and he will take you to Linton. Ask for..."

"I know the plan, Benedic. But I also have no intention of..." she hesitated briefly before she chose the next words, "... no desire to stay alone."

"You meant to say you had no intention of letting me out of your sight." This was too much distrust in times these treacherous. It would have to be addressed before they went any further. He tried to maintain a neutral expression while waiting for her reply.

Once again her expression became unfocused for a moment. It was clear she was searching for some piece of knowledge in the vast mental repository in her head. When she finally spoke, her voice had a different, but vaguely familiar, tone. The effect was eerie.

"You and T'Orah were so well hooded and so unexpected it startled me, and I panicked. From somewhere in here," she gestured in the general direction of her head and then vaguely toward her heart, "a spell presented itself that I knew would only do harm to those who would harm me. Friends would be unaffected. Enemies would be affected in the same degree they had intentions of harm toward me. If they planned to kill me, they would die. If they planned to hurt me, they would be hurt."

She paused. Her scrutiny of him was disturbing.

"Do you know this spell that came to me?"

"I cannot use it, if that is what you are asking; but, yes, I have heard of it."

"Then you can see why T'Orah and I had doubts about you. She was unaffected by the magic, but you…"

He felt anger rise like a flood.

"I would never harm you, Cathryn. I have given you my word. This spell was ill spoken and misdirected." He stopped himself before he went too far.

"You're not going to wound me or kill me. I believe that, Benedic. But the spell found only what was really there. It left you the way you would have me: unable to interact with your world or impact it at all. No hearing, no voice, no motion."

This accusation set his teeth on edge.

"You know nothing of me or my concerns or what this world requires. If no one else will tell you, I will: It was evil intentions brought you here and a mistake that made you queen. The least you can do, until those who really care can untangle this terrible knot, is to stay silent and do what you are asked. Otherwise you are a danger to yourself and everyone else around you."

The Earther's face had turned red, her lips were pressed together in a thin, furious line.

"Your daughter demanded I listen to Reyfen's memories. She said I would come to trust you if I did. Only because I did am I with you right now. Especially after the spell. I will go with you to the inn. We will go to Linton. You and I will do what needs to be done for all the right reasons. Because we, and people we love, are in peril. Because your world and mine must be kept separate and safe. And because, whether you like it or not, damn it, I am the Queen of Corronheld and you are my oathbonded."

She opened her cloak and showed him the knot on her ridersbelt. There, wound into the intricate lengths of leather were two strands of color twisted together: purple and red. T'Tolyan had identified her as the holder of his oathbond. It could mean nothing else.

Duty, fear and wrath fought, wrestled for his will.

"I never purposed that oath. You cannot hold me to this. T'Tolyan had no right."

"Maybe your friend was just trying to get you to declare yourself. I didn't ask for the Passing, and when I get rid of it—probably to you—you can do what you want. But for right now, we need to see how your friend is and get moving again."

The most horrible part of her brutal speech was that she was absolutely correct. It did not comfort him at all. He balked and fretted at the truth of it, and swore at himself for doing so. These strong reactions were making him a stranger to himself. In an effort to regain some control of the disintegrating situation, he laid a spell over his next words.

"Be easy. Stay here with the horses. I will find Kern and then we will go."

"Don't play games with me. It may work with your children, but not with me. The longer I carry these worms in my arms and the crowd of kings and queens in my head, the more I recognize things. Including compulsion magicks."

Gathering her cloak around her as if gathering darkness to hide within, she started toward the inn. He had been put down and his mood was bitter. It so distracted him, he almost ran into her as she stopped in the shadows at the very edge of the inn's yard.

"I wonder that you stop, lady. Will you wait here for my return after all?" He could not prevent a broad touch of disdain from coloring his tone to her. He heard it and was, at the same time, perversely pleased and horrified with himself.

She did not answer him. Instead she moved aside so that he could see what she was seeing.

At a small remove from the waystation's buildings there was a long, narrow mound of newly turned soil. On the mound were a few, wilting flowers. Near it, on a large, flat rock, sat a hooded hulk of a man. In regular sweeps, as inevitable as time, he brought a sharpening stone down the length of a longsword. Each time the stone traveled the weapon's length, it gave forth a gritty, rasping, merciless sound that made him shiver.

Kern lived. He lived, and he knew that his wife did not. Almost Benedic felt he must mourn that his friend had survived if it was only to learn such news. Nothing he could do would lessen the pain Kern must endure. He remembered that deep lesson all too well. Still, what gestures could be made, should be made. He started for his friend but was halted by Cathryn's sudden grip on his arm.

"Your friend is waiting for us. I don't think he wants us to be seen." Her voice was low, intended for his hearing alone. "Look. He has a pack next to him. Is there some way you can get his attention without attracting the notice of anyone else?"

She was right. He hadn't noticed until she had commented on it, but Kern's pack was lumped up next to him, close at hand. Once again, she was right. Once again, he was almost wrong. To rectify the near-mistake, he gave a three-noted whistle which he hoped he remembered well enough from his soldiering days.

At first, he feared he had not given the right signal. But Kern was only being cautious. And rightly so. Only a few heartbeats after the whistle, two men came round the corner of the station, walking casually but glancing at Kern and the forest's edge with purpose. When nothing happened but birdsong and the passage of the sunlit afternoon, the men returned to what Benedic imagined must be their posts in front of the inn.

Even when the watchers were no longer in sight, Kern did not immediately raise his head, but ceased sharpening the blade, put his stone away, then stood and stretched. He looked the picture of boredom as he slung his pack over one shoulder and walked toward where they hid, as if he were aimlessly ambling on a lazy afternoon.

But the semblance of casualness disappeared with the first close look at Kern's face. It was stone, set hard in a darkness no sunlight could ease. This warrior of a man, always before a huge and stable presence, was now somehow compressed, tightly wound.

"I will be missed soon. There is a way through." Kern's voice was inanimate, empty. Without waiting to see if they followed, he led away, moving between the trees and bushes without stirring a leaf. A specter walking.

For a wonder, Cathryn did not argue. Instead, she started after Kern, silent for a change.

It did not surprise him when Kern led them to their horses. It did not surprise him when Kern led them to where he had concealed a horse for himself. What did surprise him was the horse Kern had chosen. The soldier's own had been wounded in the Taker's attack and was evidently not recovered as fully as his master. But Bayly's horse had been unhurt and it was Towter that waited impatiently in the hidden glen. It was painful to see Kern had put his own saddle on the animal that his wife had ridden, taking up the reins she had so lately touched. Benedic could be silent no longer.

"Kern. Friend. This lady and I must go to Linton. Too much

has happened and what plans we had…before…have changed. There is no need for you to go with us. Let me tell you where things stand so you may then go home and grieve for Bayly in peace."

"Home?" The soldier's huge hands stroked Towter's neck slowly, mechanically. "There is no such place. If Linton is where you need to go, I will see you safely there." He swung himself onto his saddle and reached for the reins with a hesitation that was, at once, both slight and poignant. "And then I will be hunting."

There could be nothing more to say. Benedic turned to motion Cathryn forward as well, but she was already giving Paudge a nudge in the ribs. That she was ready to travel was not so odd; it was the silver trace of tears on her cheek that caught him so.

In ruffling billows, the grasslands of the Linton plains spread out before them like a dancer's hair. Tall grasses rippled as the wind dipped and rose in gentle, fragrant pirouettes. Each time he came upon this sight, it moved him so strongly he could not speak.

Yet speaking had not been the rule of this trip; it was the awkward, empty exception. Two days of travel punctuated only by the creak of leather, the soughing of the horses, breezes muttering now and again, the evensong of tree frogs and, too often, the tension of listening for danger. Kern's wall of grief was impenetrable. Cathryn seemed lost in her own thoughts. Whether she was consulting the lives she carried with her, or had just shut herself away, he did not know.

Now they had crossed the pass separating the hills and trees that led from the capitol into the first sweeps of the Linton grasslands. It should have been a moment of beauty shared; it was bleak.

"We have places much like this at home." Cathryn's quiet comment settled tentatively into the void the three of them had created. "In the very middle of my country are huge prairies. At least there used to be."

He could not join in her reverie. No mention of Earth sat well with him. His irritation made him pick up the reins again to resume travel. But unexpectedly Kern spoke.

"What happened to them?"

"My country has a lot of people. More every day. Much of the prairies were ploughed into farms, built into towns or paved over with roads. What's left of the open spaces and the parts that are farmed we call the heartlands."

Kern nodded. "Heartland. Prairie. Good sounding words."

"They *are* good places. My mother's people settled in the heartlands, right on the edge of one of the last prairies in a tiny town with so many uncles and aunts and cousins that almost everyone was related somehow."

"T'Tolyan's people are like that." Kern shifted in his saddle as he considered the panorama before him. "Perhaps it's the only natural response to spaces as wide as these. There must be some comfort in holding a large family close when one lives in such vastness."

For the first time, Benedic heard sorrow warm the stoniness that was Kern's voice. He looked over at his friend just as Cathryn spoke again.

"When my parents died, I had to take them back to the hometown cemetery. Do you have that word? Graveyard it means. It was just outside town where two huge fields of wheat converged on a dirt road. All the time I stood there, reading the same few last names over and over on all the markers, I felt surrounded by family, like they were watching over me, wanting me to be well.

"Maybe I just needed that assurance so badly I imagined it. By that time I no longer had a husband, I had no children. Only me, alone. Still, when the wind brushed the wheat and it rustled the way it did…"

He could only watch in silence. Kern and Cathryn each were staring at some private sadness far beyond where the grass met the sky. It had transfigured them, softening the hard planes, brightening their eyes with soon to be shed tears. What he had hoped and prayed he could do for his friend, an utter stranger had done with such seeming ease. She had opened her own grief and regrets, like tender gifts, to someone she had met but days ago. It spoke well of her. What did it say about him?

"…no, there. That hill." Sometime during his reverie, Kern had begun to point out the trail he was proposing. He tried to focus on his friend's instructions. "See where the grasses part near the foot of the slope? That's the trail we'll take. That low on the rise, we won't be seen against the sky and the shadows of morning and afternoon will help to hide us."

"I never would have thought of that." Cathryn shook her head and smiled. "I'm glad you're our guide."

"Thank you. Shall we go, then?"

"Lead away, Kern. We'll follow." She clucked at Paudge to move on.

The openness of the grasslands made him feel uneasy this trip. During his soldiering days, he and Kern and T'Tolyan had ridden Linton's borders days on end without this sense of vulnerability, even when the Ganish wilders had threatened to invade and, in their inexplicably destructive way, burn and pillage the border encampments.

The farther they traveled across the plain, the more uneasy he became. His shoulder blades twitched with the feeling that some unseen assailant was following, awaiting the right moment. So strong was this feeling that, when the plainsrider caravan appeared far in front of them, he was taken by surprise.

Kern stopped them to discuss what should be done. If they kept at their current rate of travel, they would overtake the caravan by evening. Was that wise, given the need for secrecy? Cathryn thought not, but Benedic argued that there would be more safety with plainsriders who knew the land and might be persuaded to take them to T'Tolyan's wife, the duchess of the province. Much to his relief, Kern sided with him. Eventually, Cathryn agreed as well.

Each time he saw a plainsrider caravan settle in for a night, Benedic admired the efficiency of the process. By day, their wagons were covered with dust-colored tarpaulins and long poles stretched from the wagon sides to teams of horses. At night, the horses were freed to forage and those same, dull tarps and poles formed long, wide tents. The caravaners were so skilled at this transformation, it was all done in a blink of an eye.

So it was that, by the time dusk had washed the plain in reds and pinks, the three of them rode into a pitched camp. The smell of supper was already drifting tantalizingly throughout. As they dismounted, silent outriders appeared like a billow of dust behind them. In front of them, several plainsfolk stood waiting expectantly, cautiously, while a few came over to take their horses. He glanced over the groups, searching for a face familiar from his earlier days of soldiering along the Linton borders. He found no one he knew and tried to resign himself to the long introductions that would be necessary.

But before he could begin the first of his greetings, a wave of murmurs swept through the camp, beginning near them and swelling to the farthest edges of the wagon circle. Whatever was being said drew out the entire caravan, from youngest to eldest. In moments, they all had gathered in a half-moon round the three of them.

The leader, distinguished from the rest by a length of yellow leather twined in his rider's knot, stepped forward and made a long, low bow. Since plainspeople weren't generally noted for conforming to the ceremonies of the rest of Corronheld, this gesture seemed extravagant. Then Benedic realized everyone else was staring at the knotted code in Cathryn's belt.

"Greetings, pledges and safety from the Shaundry Clancircle to our lawful and chosen sovereign. We welcome you, your guide and your oathbonded. What is ours, is yours, beyond the obligations of hosting, even to our lives."

The headrider said no more but waited on the Earther's response. She hesitated. He tensed. Plainsriders were notoriously touchy and private when on their own land. A wrong word and there could be great difficulties.

"Greetings, pledges and regard from Cathryn, Queen of Corronheld, to the Shaundry Clancircle. We thank you for the offer of rest, but there are those searching for us who would take our lives and those of any who shelter us. I would not ask this of you. I am in the care of Kern, soldier and guide, and Benedic, Duke of Forché and my oathbonded. Their hands hold my life by their own choice and mine. A moment's rest and food before we ride again would content me well."

He could see the crowd was impressed. She was saying all the right things in the right ways. But 'oathbonded' rankled him immensely.

As darkness settled over the hills, torches appeared and were handed toward the circle's center. In the flickering glare, the headrider spoke again.

"The names of Kern and Benedic are known to us. We could offer no better care than what you already have; yet, what we can do, we will. You could not demand our lives, no matter your throne. Plainsriders do not suffer such things. But we will host you, by our own choice, though it cost us more than a night's supper. This is the choosing of the whole of Shaundry Clancircle, if it so pleases you."

Cathryn inclined her head toward the caravan leader.

"You do us great honor at what may be a great cost. Nothing would content us more." She hesitated. "Except, of course, a bit of whatever that is I smell. What is that stuff? It's driving me crazy."

The sudden shift from formal to personal took him by surprise. It delighted the camp, which erupted in some laughter and much motion. T'Anders, for that was the name the headrider used in introducing himself, led Cathryn through the boisterous crowd. Others came to Kern and Benedic, leading them with much enthusiasm and curiosity to what was clearly the largest of all the tents.

No matter how many times he entered a plainsrider tent, he was always struck by the change from drab to extravagant. In the same way that they wore drab cloaks over brightly colored clothes, their dusty tarps hid a riot of hues inside. Rugs of red and orange and yellow and black were liberally thrown about. Curtains dyed in every shade of every color divided the larger tents into rooms. Decorated pillows and table scarves tumbled and swept in gorgeous and extravagant designs. Through it all drifted the smell of exotic spices and the sound of companionship. Plainsriders decorated as they lived, cautious and canny when they might be at risk, but slightly dangerous and lavishly exuberant underneath it all. He envied them now, more than ever.

"Come, sit. She calls for you." A young boy, no more than ten, tugged on his arm. From the way the boy spoke the word 'she', there could be no doubt who was meant, even though the youngster's open face and wide grin softened the sting of such a summons.

Cathryn had been settled on a wealth of pillows near a long, low table. Already bowls and platters full of consumables were appearing near her. Kern sat at her right, a large and somber contrast to the general hubbub. The place at her left was empty and, after taking his trail-soiled cloak, it was to that emptiness the boy led Benedic.

With as much grace as he could muster, he sank into the cushions that marked his place. The table was crowded and it was hard to find room for elbows and knees. With so many people so near, the steam rising from food and hot drinks, the layers of riotously colored clothes, the heat and closeness were almost overwhelming. Next to him Cathryn was pale, and her responses to the servers and table companions were increasingly terse. When the uproar that was Linton table talk fell briefly to a manageable din, she leaned near him and spoke rapidly and quietly.

"I don't know how to get out of here without offending these people, but I have to. Something's going wrong," she took a deep breath, "inside my head. I need your help."

So far, he had avoided looking directly at her face. But this plea made him do so, and he was startled at what he saw. Her eyes were wild, her lips pinched shut, bloodless with strain. Something was very wrong.

"I'll see to it right now." He rose quickly from his place and sought out T'Anders at the headrider's place at the end of the table. He leaned down and tapped the caravaner's shoulder to get his attention.

"The Queen is fatigued from the sorrow of the Passing and the rigors of the trail. She would not leave this feast, for she would honor you and your clancircle, but I am concerned." He could see the man was disappointed his honored guest would not be staying for the inevitable drinking and toasting that would follow the food. The duke watched him struggle with his duty as a host and his pleasure in the feast. Hosting won.

"Aye, milord. Even I can see she is worn, and the message T'Tolyan sent ahead of you talked of problems." T'Anders did not explain what he or T'Tolyan might mean by 'problems' but, instead, signaled for his eldest daughter to approach. She was a stout, pleasant featured young woman who looked to have laughed during a great portion of her life.

"T'Ertha, the Queen tires. I will stay here to be feastleader. You show the Queen and her oathbonded to their guestplace."

The daughter nodded earnestly and followed Benedic as he returned to Cathryn's side. Just as he reached her, T'Anders stood and bellowed over the din for attention. All eyes turned to him and, under cover of a long and convoluted speech and toast, the duke and the headrider's daughter managed to lead Cathyrn and Kern out of the noise and into the quiet night.

But the Earther could barely navigate the short distance across camp. Whatever was bothering her must be severe. At first she refused his arm, but when she began to stumble he ignored her resistance and lent his aid. In the space of a few steps, his arm was around her shoulder and she was leaning heavily on him just to keep moving. This would not do. It was not politic for a monarch to show such weakness, especially in front of such sturdy folk.

They were led to a tent which had been set somewhat apart from the rest and guarded by several stalwart sentries. T'Tolyan's message must have convinced the headrider of the need for extra precautions even before the three of them had arrived.

T'Ertha opened wide the outer door flap and tried to execute a formal bow at the same time. It was evident to Benedic that her plainsrider training had not dwelt on that particular skill.

"If I can get or do anything for you, majesty, only call and it will be done. These guards will stay near all night and there are others patrolling the perimeter as well. I trust this will help to give you a restful night."

"My thanks." Cathryn's words were clipped and strained, her voice so low it was almost inaudible.

"Are you ill, majesty? Shall I fetch a healer?" T'Ertha frowned at what she saw in the flickering torchlight. Worry creased her forehead deeply.

"No." Even that small reply must have cost Cathryn because she nearly collapsed. He caught her in his arms, struggling to stay upright himself as her sudden weakness pulled him off balance. He had to get her out of sight and find out what was wrong.

"If she needs anything, we will call." These were all the words he could spare as he worked to get Cathryn inside. He heard Kern's rumbling voice soothing and dismissing the young plainswoman and hoped it would deflect any intrusions.

As he attempted to get Cathryn as far as the sleeping pallet, she jerked her arms away and began to flail at the air. It was only with great effort he got her seated on the bed, though by then her whole body was shaking.

"Make. Them. Stop." Each word she uttered came out in a different voice. "Too. MANY."

Though the words sounded of other's voices, the plea in them was all hers. If he could put her to sleep, render her unconscious somehow, her struggles would stop; but would the lives inside her continue to assault her sleeping self? What or who would she be when she woke? If she woke.

Was this the first sign that she was dying? Those of Corronheld who took the Passing in error didn't show signs of their inevitable death at first. Perhaps her alien nature was so incompatible it was killing her faster than any native. Would she soon be calling for an heir? Calling for him?

That thought staggered him. Against all his Servants Guild training, against all his resolution of will and the disciplines of the noble heart he worked so hard to practice, the desire for power overwhelmed his reason. The taste of command was pungent on his tongue. All the voices impelled him to want, seduced him to desire the rule of Corronheld. They sang through his blood, pounded in his brain, coaxed, demanded. Promised.

His hands moved toward her neck, though he could not recall the moment of decision. Through the red haze of need, he saw them, dark upon the whiteness of an unprotected throat. The heat of his palms sought the coolness of that fragile column. Nearer.

Other hands grabbed his wrists and pulled.

"NO. STOP."

Stop what? Stop wanting this? Yes, that was it. I must, I do want something else. Ah, more than power I want—home. The very word stabbed so poignantly he could barely stand. He was entirely alone, so alone. If only he could get back. To see the deep forest, to be dressed in wool walking in the rain, catch again the aroma of coffee, know the reassurance of the cemetery in Nebraska.

Benedic wept. He tried to wipe the tears from his cheeks but his arms were imprisoned in an implacable grip. A face blurred into his awareness. Kern. Why was his friend dragging him across the room? He should struggle, but the farther Kern took him, the less he wanted to do so. And now there were words coming at him. He tried to focus.

"What is the matter with you?" Kern kept hold of his arms.

"I…I don't know what happened." His wrists were beginning to ache. "Why are you restraining me?"

"You had your hands around the Queen's neck. What else should I do?"

"Why should I…? I would never…" The enormity of what he had almost done fell on him like a stone. He looked across the room at Cathryn. She was sitting on the sleeping pallet. Behind her the heavy cloth walls of the tent swayed in an unseen wind. Her face was pale, her arms now still. Her eyes… He could not bear the accusation or, what was worse, the forgiveness he saw there.

"I was not myself, Kern. I swear." He sought for some vindication, some explanation that might bring light and a measure of comfort to the darkness of this thing.

"That is true." Cathryn spoke in her own voice, though it was thin and frayed. "It was my fault."

He could hear Kern take in a breath. The admission took them both by surprise.

"But how could that be?" Kern was obviously struggling to understand this unexpected turn.

"I don't fully understand it myself." Bewilderment laced her reply. "Benedic can help me, I think, if you will let me speak to him in private."

Kern had not yet released his arms. The tension still coiled in his friend's grip spoke all too eloquently of Kern's reluctance.

"My lady, is it wise, considering…?"

But she seemed to have reached the end of her ability to be civil.

"Leave, Kern. Now."

Benedic watched his cousin-in-law struggle with his soldier's training to obey. Training and duty finally moved him and Kern left the tent in a backdraft of uneasiness.

Before the door flap had completely settled back into place, Cathryn began ripping the cuffs and sleeves of her tunic. So great was her frenzy, the material tore like paper and fell to the red and black carpet in shreds. What was uncovered made him stare in horror.

There, on her arms, under the thinnest layer of skin, writhed worms grown so quick and large that her forearms were swollen and distorted.

She tried to stand, but her legs gave way and she dropped to her knees. She threw one hand in front of her to break her fall and in doing so hit one of her arms where the creatures squirmed. A wordless, soundless cry of agony assaulted him— not in his ears, but in his mind. He knelt next to her, intending to help her up and relieve her suffering and his, but at the last moment he could not. He could not touch the arms that held those abominations.

"I hate them, too." She could not have missed his revulsion. "They've grown and they're changing things. You have to help me. The Passing is trying to make me want to rule. The voices in my head are talking to me, more and more, louder and louder. I can't control them."

"I don't know what to do for you, lady. I'm sorry, but perhaps someone else…?"

"Damn it. I'm trying to keep my promise to you. No one else can help because you don't want anyone else to know about Earth." She was speaking too quickly, edging toward panic. "And no one else can help because these people," she pointed to her head, "have connected us. I don't understand it—maybe because you were the Called Heir—or will be. Whatever the reason, you're so tied up in this that, when we touch or I am in pain, you can feel what I feel, hear what I hear."

He shivered. Was it true? Was it the voices of the past and not his own greed for the throne that had overwhelmed him? He clutched that explanation to himself like a life rope.

"What you describe mostly sounds like an extreme form of the Passing sickness. There is nothing I can do for that."

"You can get me back to Earth. I can't control the magic that's starting to build up and I don't belong on your throne. Just find a way to let me go home before I lose myself completely. Please."

He suddenly felt claustrophobic. He wanted to back away, leave the tent, get out of this whole impossible mess. But duty, hard and merciless, lashed at his conscience. He had to tell her.

"Lady. Cathryn. Let us be honest with one another. Now that you've taken the Passing, even though it was not your fault, you're not going to last very much longer. Not long enough to discover how to return to your home. Even if I were able to send you home this moment, I would not. Corronheld cannot lose its Queen, or the wealth of knowledge that the Passing provides each true sovereign. The Passing chooses and educates, comforts and sustains. It cannot leave."

He tried to pick softer words for what he must say next. There were no other words.

"I am sorry, more than you know, but you must stay here until the Passing claims you."

She grabbed his arm. Immediately the clamor of the lives she carried with her reverberated inside him. He pulled back, but she held him too tightly. And then he could not move. The voices called to him, sang to him siren songs. Beneath and above and through all of the whispers that mesmerized him, he could still hear her, feel her fear and anger.

"You don't understand. I'm fighting the voices as hard as I can because I don't want to be lost in them. But they won't kill me. This worm magic has changed that, has twisted the Passing." Her voice was low and hoarse and filled with the imminence of tears. "Oh God, I didn't want any of this. Help me."

The promised tears began their sad rain. Her grief flowed like a gray shroud over the tent's spirited colors, wrapping Benedic in it as well. Most of what had been a cold, hard kernel of rancor in his heart warmed, softened and reshaped itself into compassion. He put his arms around the most profoundly alone Cathryn and held her, gently stroking her hair in a gesture of comfort, ignoring the cacophony their contact brought him as best he could. And hoped, prayed, begged his Lord Creator, her God, to keep his hands from any work that was not mercy.

The small remainder of the stony place in his heart stayed hard and treacherous. Like a sharp rock under a saddle, it goaded him. He thought: So the worms keep her alive. She will not die from the Passing. He thought: She is alone and afraid. She hates us, wants to go home.

Then it spiked a seditious question deep into his mind, through his soul and out toward his hands. It whispered to him: In all of this, what is mercy?

Chapter Nine:
LUCETTE

FROM BEHIND HER came a soft whuffle, reminding her there was a bright spot to be found in this. If she had not been kidnapped by D'Joan, she might never have seen T'Tolyan's son, and T'Gault would not have loaned her Weskit, the exceptional horse that had brought her thus far. Nor would there have been that wonderful, if brief, time she and T'Gault spent riding together from Corronheld City to where the road divided and took the horsetrader caravan toward the farmland of Chymion province and Lucette toward home.

But the farther she had traveled, alone and away from the lively and welcoming group of plainsriders, the more anxious she became. When, at last, from a hidden glen known to her brother and herself from childhood, she looked out on the homes of Forché, suspicion was too much with her. Daylight had abandoned all but the spire tops and tallest trees. Already she could see window lights begin their night vigil. Every time before, those lights beckoned warmly. Tonight they seemed to squint at her with a trace of malevolence, as if they knew she was hiding and why.

Weskit shifted restlessly and nudged her back. She turned away from her watching and gave the horse a pat.

"I know. It's cold and wet and we aren't moving. But if you stay here nicely, I've got one apple left. You like those, don't you?"

Whether it was the promise of an apple or just the soothing effect of the words, Weskit settled down so promptly it made her smile. T'Gault had promised that, if left unattended for more than two days, the horse would head for the Lintonese stables in Corronheld. She hoped it would not come to that.

Home. It was time.

She stepped through the dense wall of foliage that hid the little glen and began to wind upward to the keep. It did amuse her to know that she could do this only because she had done the inevitable adolescent sneaking in and out. If the guards still kept the regular schedule, the watch was due to change soon and that would be her chance.

The trail was rocky and steep as it rose from the forest road to the back gate. Not many used this way. She counted on that. The front entrance was much too busy, with sharp-eyed people who knew her face.

Two pairs of guards paced the wall. Even with the circles of orange light from the glowlanterns spaced along the sentryway, it was impossible to see who the guards were in the gathering darkness.

A rectangle of light wedged open. The small pass-through door, inset in the wall next to the huge gate wings, permitted the new watch to emerge. She knew the traditional greetings and recognition signs by heart. Though she was too far away to understand the words themselves, she could hear the cadences and rhythms and that was enough.

The retiring pair of guards turned and entered the keep. If all went according to protocol, the guards just coming on shift would now begin the first walkby of their watch. They would go all the way to the west edge of the back wall, giving her time to scramble up the stony incline to the shadows just beneath the sentryway. Then they would turn back, pass the door and go all the way to the east edge, giving her time to slip through the door.

The sentries turned—to the east. That wasn't the way it should be! She tried to think what this change meant to her plan.

The east edge was closer to the door. It took less time to reach. The guards would be turning back before she could get close enough to hide again. Or would they? She had never timed this part before. Should she chance it? Or did she even have a choice?

Taking a deep breath and making a decision she hoped she would have the luxury to regret, she began a mad scramble upward. Rocks jammed her ribs, scraped her fingers, bruised her ankles—and still she climbed, faster and faster. She tried to be careful, to be quiet and not dislodge a noisy avalanche of pebbles but it was difficult to gauge how silent she was against the sound of her heart pounding in her ears.

She spared a hurried look eastward. The guards were almost at the corner. She still had one last overhang to climb, a rock face close enough to the wall to be caught in the light of the glowlanterns. She tried to estimate if she could scale the rock and make the shadows in time. The crevice she was hiding in now was scant cover. The sentries turned and started back. She was stuck. The forced climb had winded her and she struggled to catch her breath.

"…and I don't care who they are, either. All I know is, they make me nervous."

She clung to her precarious hold, willing herself to be unseen

"Missing a meal makes you nervous, Winnigrue. New boots make you nervous. In fact, name something that doesn't."

"What're you trying to say, Skayler? Don't tell me there's nothing funny going on."

"Well, if something is going on, it is not funny and it surely isn't our business, mister nose-in-the soup. Besides, even if you did figure out what to report, who'd you report it to? I mean, what with…"

Her fingers ached from clamping them on the slippery, narrow handhold. At least the watch had passed by and was headed, with their backs turned once again, toward the west corner. She moved carefully up the last rock, then over the sentryway and to the door. It creaked as she opened it and for a moment she froze in panic.

Nothing. No sound of discovery.

One last pull at the door and she squeezed through. Keeping to where the returning guards had left their own wet footprints, she ran down the corridor and into the keep. Knowing each turn, every deep shadow or hidden alcove, she easily avoided being seen by the few staff about in the late night. But as she took the back stairs upward, she had three close calls with sentries. She avoided the first one by ducking into a deserted storage room, the second by hiding in a little known niche behind a huge tapestry. The third was going up the stairs she needed to climb, so she followed at a discreet distance until he turned down a corridor and she could keep going alone.

When she finally saw the entrance to the living quarters just ahead, she sighed in relief and hurried toward it.

"No, I don't think it's a good idea. What about the boy?"

Just beyond the doors, which were slightly ajar, someone she did not know had spoken.

"I will see he is kept out of trouble. But no harm must come to him. I have been promised."

That voice she did recognize. Arilon. What was the castellan talking about?

"You do not realize how delicate a position you are in, Arilon." The unknown speaker held a note of threat in his tone. "What may have been discussed before, might now be changed if circumstances require. We deal with matters larger and more significant than the domestic affairs of a minor dukedom."

"I understand." The castellan could scarcely be heard.

"Do you really?" There was a sound of movement, a whisper of long robes. "We shall see. Indeed."

The door began to swing open. She scrambled for the tiny alcove across the hallway and dove into its meager shadow. She forced herself to take quiet, shallow breaths.

Arilon stepped into the corridor, his head down, muttering to himself. When he reached the alcove, he turned and looked back at the doorway.

"Yes, we shall see." His voice was sullen and heavy with resentment. She had never heard such a tone from him in her life. It was as if he were a stranger.

When Arilon finally disappeared down the main stairs, she slid out from her hiding place. The door to the family living quarters had been left open and, after checking the salon carefully for the unknown speaker, she entered.

Rain and night pressed against the great windows. No fire warmed the dark hearth. The only light came from far down the passage leading to the smaller rooms. It was a cold, unsettling way to return to her own home.

More than ever, she needed to see her brother. Her father and Cathryn had given strict instructions before she left: talk to no one, not even friends whose loyalty would never be questioned. Go directly and secretly to Corry first. Their advice made better and better sense the closer she got.

She crept across the great room and down the hallway. The door to her room was wide open. The urge to dive into bed and pull the covers over her head was strong—but she kept going. The door to the library was opened slightly. A wedge of flickering light fell out into the hall. She felt the crackle of resentment. Who was this invading her home, making her sneak through it like a thief? She leaned toward the crack and peeked through.

The room was a mess. Books and papers were in disarray. Maps had been torn down from the walls and the venerable collection of ancient manuscripts lay carelessly strewn everywhere. In the midst of the chaos, with his back to the door, stood a man in long, dark robes. He held one of the old parchments up to catch light from a cluster of candles set in the middle of the main reading table.

How odd. The library was full of glowlamps ready to produce a steadier, brighter light for any reader. Why candles? Abruptly the man tossed the paper he held to the floor and grabbed for another box of scrolls. She could not help but be angry at the wanton and callous way the library had been violated. Every page, every scroll in the room was a friend of her youth, a reminder of her father's voice reading stories to his children, quiet times playing on the floor while her mother studied.

She could not watch any longer. She needed to see Corry. Quietly she crept past the library door toward where the hall turned a corner and peeked around the edge of the wall. No guards. She tried her brother's door. Not locked. Soundlessly, she stepped through the doorway.

It was dark. He must be asleep. Hoping against hope he had been keeping the floor of his room clear of clothes and boots for once, she felt her way to his bed. Nothing. He wasn't here. It was late. Why wasn't he here, sleeping?

"Oh my true love's a jumpcat, she's always on fire. If you don't like her scratchclaws, her husband's for hire." Down the hallway came the noise of someone raucously singing one of the most loathsome ditties she knew. From the sounds of a body hitting the wall, the singer was staggeringly drunk.

"Oh my true love's a flitter, if only you knew. When she's done flitting me, then she'll likely flit you."

The rowdy stopped bawling out his song for a moment to yell out, "And no young girls in there, D'Goran. Don't want you disturbing my sleep."

It was Corry's voice, almost unrecognizable as it slurred and bellowed through very inappropriate words. He must have made that last rude comment to the stranger in the library. She was stunned at the idea that her own brother was drunk and unruly. What was happening here?

The door banged opened and Corry reeled into the room and slammed the door shut behind him. She could hear him take a big breath and begin another verse of that bawdy song.

"Oh my true love's a..." Corry stroked up the light. As he saw her, taking what she felt was a properly disapproving stance, his voice wavered.

"...is something or other...I guess." His eyes lit up and a huge smile broke across his face. "If I'm sick in my room," he let his voice drop to a minor bellow that could only be heard a mile or so, "then it will be a big mess."

She started to speak, but Corry stopped her with a gesture. He then proceeded to throw a boot against the wall, knock over several very large books which made a huge thump on the floor, moan loudly several times and swear once as he flopped noisily onto his bed.

Into the quiet that filled in behind Corry's remarkable performance came the sound of a key turning in a lock. Someone had locked him—them—in.

Like a snowcat stalking a trybbird, her brother slid off his bed and padded over to the door. He listened for a long moment and then returned to stand by the side of the bed, took a breath and produced a throaty snore. Smiling at her all the while, he let loose a series of liquidy snorts until finally, from outside the door, came the faint rustle of robes and shushshush of houseboots moving away.

"I am so happy to see you well." Corry threw his arms around her and gave her a tremendous hug.

"And you, little brother. You cannot know."

He pulled away and searched her face.

"You are well, aren't you? When you disappeared, I feared some wickedness. Arilon sent out search parties—at least that is what he told me, and I did see troops of searchers leaving—but there was never any word."

"Yes, I am well, but so many things have happened and they are of such import, we must discuss them—and in a place where none may intrude. Do not forget I am sought after as a traitor. My life is forfeit if I am caught."

He nodded and began to stuff pillows under the covers of his bed. When he had created the likeness of a sleeping form, he opened the doors of his closet and from the high shelf drew out a small glowlantern.

"Come on, then. I know a little sanctuary where we will be undisturbed through the night. Hold this lantern for a moment."

She couldn't imagine where he could be going since the

door to his room was locked from the outside, but she took the light anyway. Corry turned back toward the closet and, to her amazement, stepped inside and disappeared among the clothes.

"Corry?"

An arm thrust out between two cloaks and beckoned. A muffled voice could be heard saying, "This way. This way."

She put one foot into the closet and pushed aside the clothes. The back of the cabinet was not there. Instead, it opened into the next room. The conservatory.

Her brother began to chuckle.

"Did you think you were the only one who sneaked in and out, older-sister-know-it-all?"

"I never..."

"Of course you did. How else did you find a way to come home and still not be seen?"

"All right, then. Perhaps I did once or twice. But you're much too young..."

He rolled his eyes as he pulled her through the cabinet and shut the outer and inner panels behind them and then let down the tapestry that hid the bolt hole from the conservatory side.

"You may think I am too young for this, but if I had not already found this escape, we might not have had a chance to get much older."

They crossed the room and slipped out through the glass doors to the roof garden. He kept their path among the shadows, avoiding notice by the guards who walked the parapets. In a matter of moments, they reached the gardener's shed. He undid the lock so quickly she knew he came this way often.

Inside, after the lantern had been coaxed into light, they settled into summer chairs stored here with the coming of the rain. No windows would give them away and no one came here on a rainy night.

She spent a long time telling Corry what had happened, starting with her own kidnapping by D'Joan. When she had to relate that Bayly had been killed, her brother turned pale. He had always had a special fondness for their father's cousin. She and Kern had been more like aunt and uncle to them.

By the time the whole tale was told, Corry, far from being speechless as she had thought he would be, was excited. This was not helpful. She knew she must caution her brother about the dangers of the situation. Even the guild to which he was apprenticed was rife with traitors.

"You must understand, D'Joan and Cathryn were both brought from their own far land by the meddling of the Unseen Circle. How deep their treachery and whether it taints more of the Esoteric Guild, we do not yet know. At the least, it has surely reached Corronheld and the throne that D'Brin killed the king to falsely claim."

A gust of wind caught the shed and rattled it. It gave her a sudden sense of exposure, as if the little building might collapse and show her to the gaze of a violent world.

"Corry, please believe me. This is no play-adventure, no bard's tale where death is only a word and heroes always prevail."

Her brother frowned, tugging on his bands, the black of the Esoterics and gray of his chosen Spirit circle.

"I know I am young, Lucette, but do not mistake high spirits for a lack of understanding. From the moment you disappeared, I have put my wits to use."

"I know you wish to help, Corry, but..." He cut her off with a gesture, stood up and began to pace the short distance of the shed's interior.

"My plan has been to pass myself off as a young and useless boy." He smiled at her and she recognized the touch of irony in his plan and his words. "Not being a bard's apprentice for naught, I wove a tale around myself about an adorable but rather dissolute student home for an unexpected holiday. I refused to have anything to do with the responsibilities of the province, slept late and caroused openly with equally disreputable companions."

"Yes, I saw—or rather heard—some of that story tonight." Against her will, she chuckled. He had put on quite an act.

"Mock me if you will, but this ruse encourages others to let down their guard. I see more and am told more than would be revealed to a sober and thoughtful man."

His use of the term 'man' made her grow more serious. He was of an age where being taken for a frivolous child was especially humiliating. To purposefully cultivate that persona must be very hard for him.

"Mock you I do not. In fact, I begin to believe you, no-longer-little brother. That you are still free at home while your father and sister are labeled assassins means your ruse is working. But for how long? Corry, this is real and dangerous. Father would see you safe among the plainsriders at T'Meara's hold."

The wind had picked up again. The small building shook and rattled as gusts battered against it. Corry stood in the center of the lantern's circle of light, his face pale but set in stubborn planes.

"I wish you and father were safely here. But since you cannot be, I must stay. You fear Arilon is allied with the traitors. I know it is true. I see messengers coming and going in the night to him. It makes me all the more determined to stay. We cannot abandon the province, and there are those here who are loyal, who are biding their time and waiting for some sign to show themselves on the side of the true sovereign. How could I not stay?"

She recognized and sympathized with Corry's bid to take

on his adult role. He was of the age and the temperament to want to do it. But in such a perilous time? Visions of her brother in the hands of a Taker made her shudder.

"It is hard for me, Corry, to let you stay. My plan was that we would both leave in secret: You to Linton for safety and me to Kilder to gather more allies. Now..."

Impatience and a great yearning to be of value were written clearly in her brother's every gesture, every word. Breaking from their accustomed light-hearted treatment of one another, Corry knelt beside her and took her hands in his.

"Believe me, sister, I have thought long and hard about this. No other choice is possible. Even if you would take me from here by force, I would resist. I know what I have to do. No one else can do it. I am staying—but..."

He looked directly into her eyes, all traces of humor banished.

"...but I would rather stay with yours and father's blessing."

If anything wicked happened to her brother, she knew she would sink under the guilt of it. Yet she could not, at this moment, refuse him.

"Aye, little brother, stay. If you see the right of this so strongly, neither father nor I would keep you from the doing of it."

Corry leaped up as if released on a coil.

"It will be well. You will see." He nearly whirled completely around in his excitement. Then, perhaps recalling his plea for adulthood, he gathered his cloak to him and went toward the shed door.

"You will be safe here for the while. I'll come back within the hour with food for your trip. Then I can show you a way to sneak out of the Keep that will bypass the sentries."

Before she could say another word, he was back into the night once again, shutting the blustering gale out when he shut the door behind him. But now, even though the shed still clattered in the storm, it seemed to her that a swirling blackness had settled into the space where Corry had been. Foreboding pressed against her so closely, so intimately, she could not catch her breath.

Chapter Ten:
CORRY

H E KNEW HE was being followed, and it made him fiercely glad. It meant that someone thought him important enough to be considered a threat. And since he knew he was being shadowed, it proved he was cunning enough to deal with it. Briefly he considered taking a short cut to the Green Branch, but whoever was tracking him might get lost and that was the last thing he wanted.

Corry threaded his way through the streets that led to the tavern, eager to begin the night's business but trying to maintain a casual, swaggering pace. With all the news his sister had brought and the work that would need to be done now, it was hard not to run. When he finally arrived at the inn, he had to stop in front of its green-painted door and draw a deep, calming breath while he shifted his lute from one hand to the other. He also checked to make sure whoever was shadowing him had arrived as well. He had. Confident that all the pieces were in place, he stepped inside.

"Corry!" His name was shouted out by several people seated at a large table near the far wall.

To those who had hailed him, he returned loud greetings.

"Ho, Aldred, Elinay. Have you started the merriment without me? You have, Jacq. I can see it by your glowing nose." He swerved around tables and unwary patrons on his way across the room. "Fortenlee! Are you hiding behind the bar again, host? Stir yourself and bring refreshment for me and my companions."

Like a wake, the tavern keeper arrived just behind Corry with a tray of mugs balanced high on one hand. But unlike previous evenings, the mugs did not get put down on the table.

"Here you are, young sir. Six coppers, if you please." Fortenlee held out his free hand, beefy palm up.

"Tally our night's bill and send it to the Keep. It will be paid." Corry waved his arm grandly through the air.

Ducking the expansive gesture, the innkeeper stood his ground.

"I think it will not, little dukelet. The last bill I took they paid, but said there would be no more coins flowing out. Not for you. So, I'll take my six coppers now, before you drink, if you please."

The rosy-nosed Jacq tried to stand and deliver some money from his pocket. But drink, it seemed, had the better of him and he ended up in a desperate struggle with his chair. The sight of this wrestling match was so comical, all the nearby patrons burst into laughter.

Elinay stood up, tossing her wild red hair defiantly while fishing through her belt pouch.

"Allow me to pay tonight. It is only fair."

"Fair?" Corry let his voice get louder. As he expected, the rest of the room quieted in order to catch this to-do. "Nay, it would not be fair. I must take it up with…" he poked Fortenlee's massive belly with his finger. "Tell me, who was it at the Keep denied me money?" The demand echoed through a now silent inn.

"It was your own castellan. Trying to see you stay out of trouble, I warrant."

"How dare Arilon do such a thing? Who is he to take that upon himself? You go back and tell him, from me…"

Aldred got up from his chair and moved to interpose himself between his shouting friend and the stubborn 'keeper.

"There is no need for dispute. Let us settle the bill now and deal with the tight-purses up the hill later." Aldred's tall, thin frame made a less than significant barrier. "After all, there is ale for our table. Why waste it?"

In plain sight of all, Elinay counted six coins into Fortenlee's hand while Corry took up his complaint again.

"Nevertheless, Arilon will hear from me, I tell you. No one sixteen winters old should be so humiliated in public. I will not tolerate it." He gestured to his friends. "Bring those mugs upstairs. We'll take one of the private rooms for our revelry, tavern-man," he put as much arrogance into the epithet as his upbringing allowed him, "unless you need more coins for that, too."

The innkeeper flushed under the insult.

"No more coins, apprentice boy. In fact, please do go upstairs. It will save the rest of these good folk from having to hear your caterwauling. Creator knows we've suffered enough the last sevennights to last forever." From somewhere near the fireplace there came a snort of badly suppressed laughter.

Trying to put as much high dudgeon into his exit as possible, Corry clutched his defamed lute and pointed his friends toward the stairs. Aldred led with the tray of mugs while Elinay demanded that the 'keeper send up any of their friends who might arrive later—especially if they came with coin. Then she put an arm around Jacq's shoulders to help him manage the steps. Corry brought up the end of the ludicrous parade, herding the whole group upward to the last chamber at the end of the second floor hallway.

When everyone was inside and the door had been shut, Jacq gave Elinay a great hug.

"I do so enjoy this charade, sweet Elinay. I believe you will have to help me stagger up more stairs very soon."

The lady so addressed pushed Jacq away gently, but with determination.

"Behave yourself, you randy pig. Darkness and devils, there's serious work to be done, if you remember."

Aldred set the tray of mugs on the round table in the center of the room and then flung his bony limbs on a long bench. "Be a little merry, Elinay. For a few hours we are out of our parents' ever vigilant care. And engaged in employment that will curl your crimson locks before we are done, I wager."

"All too true. I thought good, old Fortenlee was going to take forever to make us come up here." Corry chuckled as he turned his lute over the table. After much shaking, a thin, folded piece of paper fell out.

Suddenly, there was the sound of footsteps in the outer hallway. He slid the paper back through the strings of the lute and leaned the instrument against a wall in a dark corner. Each of the four grabbed a mug, struck a casual pose and began to chatter noisily.

The door to the room flew open. He breathed a sigh of relief. The Fiste sisters had arrived.

"Had to pay for these drinks myself. Who's the dunce mucked up the credit here?" Sotal strode in, one hand on the hilt of her sword and the other clutching another tray of drinks which she slapped down on the table.

Right behind her came Peer who, as usual, followed behind soothing any hurt feelings and making sure no one felt neglected. "Not that we minded paying, of course. It's really the only equitable arrangement. Unless there is a different plan...?"

It never failed to make him smile at how twins could look so much alike and yet be so different.

"Shut the door, Sotal, and let's get started."

"Sorry to hear your arms and legs are broken, Corry." Sotal found the chair farthest from the doorway and plunked herself on it.

Before he could frame a reply, Peer carefully stepped in.

"I'm closest to the door. I'll shut it. Did you want to get started now, or...?"

Jacq sat down at the table and then pulled out the chair next to him. "Come on, Peer. Sit next to me."

"Why thank you. Of course, if Corry thinks I should be somewhere else...?"

"Sit here, little dove," Jacq grinned as he motioned the hesitant twin to her destination, "and maybe tonight you will bless us with a complete sentence."

"No chance. Hopeless. Never happen." Sotal snorted derisively from the other side of the table.

Jacq turned his attention to the other sister.

"Or mayhaps we'll hear the blesséd silence of our militant-mouth not saying everything that comes into her head."

Sotal's face reddened and she started up from her chair, her hand once again on her sword.

"Fight each other and we will never get around to fighting the enemy." Elinay set down her still mostly-full mug of ale and took a seat at the table. "Sotal bridles at the slightest jest, Peer spends hours working toward agreement without caring what is being agreed upon, Jacq never addresses issues except in asides. And Aldred? Who but he could eat so constantly, move so little and still stay the laziest skinny-stick in Forché?"

Not for the first time Corry wished he had listened more closely to his father's lectures on leadership. What had sounded to his younger ears like another pointless ramble by an adult, now appeared to have had value. He had always been the un-official leader of this unruly group, but it had never been easy. Now it was never more important. He'd be certain to listen carefully if father got back.

If. That one, tiny word made his heart lurch painfully. Steel-ing himself to be the leader he must be, he looked up from his uneasy thoughts. And found, where there had so recently been foolish pestering, a circle of concern.

"Your father and sister will be well." Elinay put her hand on his arm with unexpected gentleness.

Aldred was no longer sprawled lazily on the bench. "We are yours to direct." He tapped his long fingers together, a sign recognized by all that he was now engaged at whatever needed to be done. "Not one of us has as much at stake as you. We will not fail you."

"You all…" He searched for words that might tell these brave few how much this commitment meant to him.

"Just tell us what news there is and what we must do." Sotal shifted in her chair. Clearly this intimacy of friendship both pleased and embarrassed her.

It was the same for him. To avoid blushing and stammering like a small child reciting for the first time, Corry focused hard on what he must say and they must do. The lives and well-being of a great many people, in this room and elsewhere, depended on their actions.

"I have received news about my father and sister." Even to this group he did not say Lucette had visited him. No one knew who might be subjected to pressure they could not resist. "They are safe for now, hidden as well as times and Takers allow. And, as we knew all along, D'Brin's claim to the throne is false. Father was the Called Heir but the stranger took the Passing by ill chance. She, too, is accused of being an assassin. D'Brin and his conspirators are holding the capitol city and control the palace militia, so proving all this will be next to impossible."

"I knew it. It's the rumors mother's been hearing." Like each of the others, Sotal was keeping her ears open at home. Her mother was a guard captain at the Keep who had military gossip sources at the Servants Guild and at the palace. It was one of the reasons the Fiste sisters were part of his network.

"There is much discussion at my home as well." Jacq, for once, was serious. His father was provincial guildleader for the Makers, his mother for the Begottens. If they were talking about something, it must be significant. "Orders are coming from the capitol for supplies and personnel to support the militia. Father says the requests are so large and so urgent it can only mean a military action is planned." Jacq had the good grace to blush a little when he added, "At least that's what I heard through the keyhole."

"That's what the Duke fears, isn't it?" Aldred had stopped tapping his fingers and had laced them together. "That's why you called us here."

One part of Corry leaped in anticipation of battle and the adventure that legends intimated it would be; the other side of him heard his father's voice warning him to be calm and remember that wars were especially cruel to the young. Trying to be balanced and responsible, he begged Aldred's question just a bit.

"In a way. Through your parents and friends and their families we can seek out in secret those who are loyal to the true Queen and to father. We can tell them to ready themselves for what may come and stay watchful." He looked around the circle of faces, gauging each in turn. "And we can find out carefully, without attracting any notice, who is not loyal and who is intending harm."

"I am for you, and for the Queen." Elinay's eyes lit with the fire of her determination. "Who else is with us?"

"Wait, Elinay." This kind of bravado was just what Lucette had warned him against. Quickly he went to the corner and retrieved his lute. Once again he shook the instrument over the table until the folded paper dropped out. "This is no summer's-night game. See this," he unfolded the message and laid in the center of the table. "The message comes from a friend in the capitol to tell us that troops are gathering there. But look here."

For a moment there was silence. Each of the six stared at the note. The written words had one message. The red-brown stain on the corner of the paper had another, just as serious and very immediate.

"You had better tell us, in more detail, what we will be asked to do." Peer's statement was straightforward and precise. "I, for one, would be hard put to swear to a plan I know nothing about."

He was grateful to hear sensible caution from such an unexpected source. "Father asks little of us but to watch, listen and stay safe. He means to lose never a one from our province. And that includes us. But, if a battle should come, preparations must be made. So here is what I propose."

The mugs of ale went untouched as he explained his idea. Each of those at the table had connections through family and acquaintances with sources of information. And each of them could feel out the loyalties of those they knew, creating a list of allies to call upon and enemies to avoid. It would take aggressive eavesdropping and carefully worded conversations that discovered much but gave away nothing.

It was the method of communicating their findings one to another that had the flavor of fun. Being seen talking together too often would be unwise, so Aldred came up with secret hiding places for passing messages.

Notes for Corry would be slipped between the strings of his lute. Given his current cultivated reputation for dissolution and drunken amnesia, his lute could be at any number of places, day or night, with or without his presence. Notes for the Fiste sisters were to be left behind a loose brick in the entry wall to the armory. Jacq could find messages tucked in a hollow awning pole at the market. Aldred had a hidden place near his mother's apothecary shop, Elinay just around the corner from her father's bakery.

"We are set, then." He sat back and, for the first time, took a small sip of ale. "All that remains is to watch and listen."

"Aye, and play the parts of debauched youth." Jacq slid his chair closer to Peer's. "For Queen and country, little dove?"

From across the table Sotal expelled a short, sharp laugh.

"Just try it, idiot-boy. You take my sister's politeness for accommodation. But she's more stubborn than you can even imagine."

Jacq sighed loudly and shifted his gaze to Elinay, who just shook her head and gathered her cloak around her. He must have deduced he was out of luck for the evening for he stood and moved toward the door.

"If that is how the night has declined, then I am heading for home. At least there someone wants me."

"Aye, and she probably wanted you safely home drinking hot milk about two hours ago." Corry couldn't resist teasing his friend just a bit. "Greet your mother for us, won't you?"

Jacq undid several buttons on his shirt, pulled one pant leg out from the boot and tugged at his cloak until it looked as tipsy as any souse.

"At least I will appear as though I've had a good time. And when I've single-handedly saved the Queen and led our troops to victory, you'll be sorry you weren't nicer to me." For all his brave humor, Jacq still hesitated a moment before pulling on the latch and letting himself out into whatever waited for him— for them all—in their new and dangerous undertaking. Corry searched for some bit of wisdom to offer but could think of none. Into the suspended moment advice was given, however.

"Reason like one who acts, and act like one who reasons." Aldred raised his eyebrows, as if surprised to hear himself say such a thing. "Well…anyway…I mean my father says that all the time. Seems right." He raised his bony frame from the chair and made his lanky way to the door. "Since I've been so grandiose, guess I'll do penance and walk idiot-boy home."

In unison, all three females grinned and said, "Thank you."

Looking somewhat chagrined, Aldred and Jacq left, pulling the door shut behind them.

Corry began sprinkling ale liberally over his tunic.

"I suppose it's time for me to stagger home." He flicked a bit of the brew at Sotal.

"Watch yourself, mash-for-brains. This is a new cloak." She stood up so abruptly her chair fell over backwards.

"I just want you to look and smell the part as you go home, duckling. After all, who will believe you unbent enough to have a wild time if you don't give them clues?"

"Clues? Humph." Sotal gathered her new cloak and old dignity. "Come on Elinay, Peer and I will walk you home."

"Wait just a minute." He moved to the door and blocked the

way. "You and Elinay may go home, but I need Peer to walk to the Keep with me. There is a—"

"No. Peer won't become a 'clue' to the disreputable time you've supposedly had tonight." Sotal moved in front of her sister.

"I was only going to ask Peer to translate part of a message I found written in the margins of a book. I couldn't very well bring it with me and she's the only one I know who can decipher Lakecrosser symbols." Dealing with the mercurial Fiste sisters made his head ache. No matter what he said, no matter how careful he was, he always managed to end up offending one or both of them. Even now, Peer looked crestfallen, as if a request for translation skills was a cruel disappointment and a reputation for loose behavior was exactly what she had earnestly desired all along.

"Come on, Sotal." Elinay tugged at her friend's sleeve. "Corry will take good care of Peer and I wouldn't mind having your good sword arm with me this late in the night."

That appeal to her vanity seemed to turn the tide for Fiste-the-Protector.

"Well, if you think you'll be safe, sister?"

Peer nodded.

"All right, then, Elinay. We are off." Sotal jerked open the door and stomped out into the hallway.

In a low voice and with a wink, Elinay commented on her way out, "Some of us are, indeed, off. Good luck, you two."

When the door closed again, Corry discovered that the silence suddenly was a bit awkward. Being alone with Peer's amazing dark eyes and soft smile was probably the reason for his difficulty. It wasn't the first time this had happened.

"Well, then." He looked down at his feet to avoid those distracting eyes. "We had better go. It is already late and, despite your sister's suspicions, I would not bring you trouble by keeping you out too long."

"Do not concern yourself, my friend." She put her hand on his arm. That was an extremely pleasant experience which did a lot to take the sting out of being called only a friend. "Whatever must be done, we will do it. Lead on."

"That is the problem. To maintain the charade, I think it would be better if you had to lead me home." Supporting a smelly supposed-drunk would not be the most enjoyable way to spend time together. Perhaps she would consider it too disgusting.

But she laughed, her black eyes glittering with good humor. Congratulating himself on his excellent taste in companions, he opened the door, checked for passersby and stepped into the hallway. Peer followed. When they reached the top of the stairs, she put her arm around him and gave him a nod. It was time to begin the charade, though how he was to concentrate under these conditions he did not know.

He began to sing a raucous ditty, making sure to keep it loud and slurry. By the time they had reached the first floor and crossed the main room of the tavern, Peer had rolled her eyes several times in an excellent approximation of a put-upon acquaintance too good in nature to leave a friend guttering for the night. Since this sight had become all too familiar of late, hardly a patron deigned to remark on the two of them.

When they reached the front door, Corry shifted his weight unobtrusively; just enough to be ready if they had to take flight, but not enough to draw notice. By way of warning, as they stepped into the street, he pretended to stumble a bit so that his face came close to hers. He ended his lurch with a low whisper.

"My follower is in the alleyway just across the street. When we reach the corner, I'll look back to make sure he's with us." Her ear was so close, he was certain he would not be overheard by the shadower. But there was the distraction of a slight but exquisite trace of scent that clung to Peer's neck. Not for the first time, he reminded himself sternly that not all obstacles to this mission of theirs would be thrown in by the enemy.

He pulled away a little, far enough to be able to focus on the task of getting home. At the corner, between stanzas of the awful song he had resumed, he snuck a backward glance. Their watcher was taking care to stay well hidden, but was still easily keeping up.

By the time they had reached the Keep, he was dragging his feet. The strain of maintaining the facade, the lateness of the hour, the long uphill climb through town and the tension inherent in this situation had taken its toll. He heard the clattering racket of a fast-approaching coach, but fatigue almost made him too slow to jump out of its path. If Peer hadn't yanked him back against the guardwall, he might have been run down. Instead, the speeding coach rounded the corner and turned up to the gates of the Keep without slowing one bit.

He stood for a moment, stunned by the sudden violence of the careening vehicle.

"Now that was enough to sober up anyone." Next to him, Peer was brushing away flecks of foam that had been spattered over them by the overdriven horses.

"There was a Corronheld crest on that carriage door." He could not imagine why someone from the capitol would be coming here in such a hurry. He was trying to puzzle an answer when Peer nudged him sharply in the ribs with her elbow.

"We're still being watched."

She was right. This was no time for their disguise to waver. It was also no time for Peer to be seen in the Keep.

Loudly, and with some trace of slurring, he spoke at her for the benefit of their shadow.

"Looks like I have company. Must be in a hurry to inspect the wine cellar." He leaned in toward her, plastering a lecherous leer on his face. "Care to come along with me and see what fun we can stir up with these unexpected guests?"

But instead of drawing away from him in a simulation of disgust, Peer frowned and stepped closer. The last thing he expected was an embrace, but it was happening. She leaned her cheek against his and murmured into his ear. At first he could not make out the words since his heart seemed to have relocated to his throat and was making breathing quite difficult. Knowing he sounded a fool, he still had to ask her to repeat what she had said.

"I would not leave you alone with whoever has arrived. It may not be safe."

He felt heat rise to his cheeks. She was concerned about his well-being, would even risk her own safety to ensure his. Their friends might tease Peer for seeming to vacillate and try to please everyone, but he knew how courageous and decisive she could be. And how caring.

"I thank you for your regard, but who and what awaits me at home I cannot tell. You must stay away so that, if the worst happens, someone on the outside knows. Go home, Peer, and call on me late tomorrow as if to inquire about my morning-after health. Please. Go now."

He pulled back slightly in order to see her eyes and discover her decision. Those eyes, dark and full in the lambency of the night, were a mystery to him. There was a sudden glint passed over them and she stuck her fist in his stomach. The force of her blow knocked most of his breath from him and caused him to bend forward. As he did so, his lips most unexpectedly met hers.

She wrenched herself free and slapped his face.

"How dare you. I care not what station your father holds. No one treats me this way."

Reeling from the kiss, he staggered a few paces after her as she ran away from him toward town. Then he stopped. She had created a perfect ploy. Just as he asked, she was going to watch and wait for him. As he turned and resumed his lurch to the Keep's entryway, he rubbed his reddening cheek. She had a good arm, that one. And she thought fast. And, from what precious little he now knew, she seemed to be someone who kissed very well.

With that thought in his mind, he entered the Keep. Inside the main entry hall it was curiously quiet. The arrival of some-one from the capitol should have roused most of the house staff. But the only movement was the flickering shadow of a late night fire in the foyer's hearth.

Wary of this unnatural inactivity, Corry stealthily climbed the long flights of stairs to the ducal apartments. He quietly pushed open the door to the main salon, hoping to find and eavesdrop on Arilon and whatever guest had arrived in the speeding coach. But the room looked empty. Uncertain, he started toward the library.

"So, the little carouser has returned?" The woman's voice caught him completely unaware. He whirled around, looking for the speaker. From a suddenly ominous shadow two hulking strangers stepped forward, came to him and, before he could open his mouth to object, gripped his arms in what was surely a prisoner's hold.

Something glittered from a pool of darkness near the huge fireplace. The glint resolved itself into a ring floating in the darkness. Then, in a flare of unworldly light, the hand that wore it was illumined. The hand was tracing malevolent signs in air.

He tried to free himself, tried to struggle, to move. But the air was thick with magic and he knew he was bespelled. The mage, whoever she was, moved closer to him, her cloak and her wizardry hiding all but her pale hands and the feral gleam of her eyes.

"We meet at last, Corry, my dear." She was near him now, near enough to draw one finger across his cheek and over his lower lip. "How I have wanted to make your acquaintance. The rest of your family has given me no end of trouble, but you and I are going to get along well. I know." She let her finger follow his jawline to his ear and then down his neck to his chest where the tunic did not cover it.

He shivered. Once. And again.

Her fingers were at his wrist, fumbling with the laces of his guildband. Where her skin touched his, heat bled into his flesh.

"Sweet boy." She said this in a soft tone, drawing the stolen leather guildband across his cheek. Slowly.

Then she turned away and crossed the room, evidently set upon going to the library that had been his intended destination. Over her shoulder she casually addressed the two thugs who so impassively held his arms.

"Take him to a cell. I won't need him until morning."

"As you command, Consort D'Joan."

Chapter Eleven:
KERN

FROM THE HILLTOP, Kern watched the caravan patiently breasting the waves of tall grass. Wagons and horses
headed slowly and inexorably southwestward. Where
they had been, the sun was falling into darkness. Where they
were going, the day's lambency nodded and deepened into evening.

He recognized Cathryn near the middle of the moving line.
Even from this distance, he could see she was tugging at the
sleeves of her tunic. There was no need, since the plainsrider
shirt was ideal for her need: full sleeves ending in snug, wide
cuffs. Perfect to hide the distortions of her arms and the tail-
ends that slipped across her wrists.

According to Cathryn, the infestation had multiplied within her, even in the few days they had traveled together. Her
arms showed signs of two worms each. And the beasts were
getting bigger. Not only did she fight intermittent pain as the
parasites grew, but Kern knew she battled an almost constant

revulsion at the appalling violation of her body. He saw revulsion in Benedic, except that in his friend the feeling was tied to a complex of other emotions the duke had not yet untangled.

Kern had no such conflicts, even though he had only discovered this strange secret the night before last. His fists knotted up as he felt the embarrassment of the moment again. He had thought Benedic was still in the Queen's tent, calming her after her agitation during the banquet. Unthinkingly, he had entered unannounced only to find the duke had gone and Cathryn had begun preparing for night, already attired only in a sleeveless undervest and thin sleep pants. His first response was to flush in chagrin at seeing his sovereign in such intimate apparel. Her first impulse had been to cover her arms. Too late.

In the awkward and halting conversation that followed, she made him aware that those of her country had no capacity for magic. The worms, that would have killed him, gave her access to a wizardry that was wild and immense.

The ability to work magic seemed of little consolation to her. Except for a newly tried spell Benedic had helped her construct to mute the clamoring of the Passing, she appeared to have small interest in taming the power.

Or, more likely, she was afraid to use it. From the first moment he met her, he could see fear in her, so strong that, at times, it had an almost palpable presence. He doubted anyone else knew how much effort it cost her to just keep functioning day after day. It was only years of watching recruits face their own vulnerabilities that had taught him to observe this so acutely.

At least she was conquering her aversion to horses. The plainsriders had noticed how wary she was with her mount. He thought they might mock such reluctance; instead, to a person, they gently and persistently offered advice, gave suggestions, rode alongside to give her confidence. It had all worked so well that she now sat the saddle with a more relaxed and assured air.

Caravan sounds drifted up to his hillside lookout. He watched the wagons jostle along the wheelroad; parallel to them in the narrow hooftrack were the all mounted riders. At this moment, there were no teachers beside her. In the dusk of the grassland day, even in the midst of the caravaners, she was alone.

Where was Benedic? Kern rose in his stirrups and scanned the trails, then the open lands, then the horizon. Below him, the nightcircling had begun. It would only be a matter of moments before cook fires flickered into life. And still no sign of his friend.

Distant thunder rumbled into Kern's awareness. He looked up. Though clouds sped upward from the horizon, the sky just above was clear. Already the Home Star, first of its company to appear each evening, gleamed above. So, if it was not a thunderstorm…

Behind him the sound grew louder. He turned in the saddle and saw two dust wraiths rising from the far side of the next hill. Riders raising that kind of dust must be moving swiftly. Even as he watched, a pair of racers burst over the hillcrest, heading for the camp at breakneck speed. The duke and a plainsrider scout were horseracing. Like boys tasting the first and dangerous days of spring. The two heedless, nay headless, rogues were not slowing down at camp's edge. Idiots.

He nudged his horse forward, winding down the hillside on a narrow, twisting game trail. The dust kicked up by the race still hadn't settled when he reached the encampment, though Benedic was already taking a blanketed Kell on a cool down walk. He caught up with them, dismounted and wordlessly took a place beside them.

Kell jerked his head and sidestepped often, each time getting a firm tug on the reins from his master. Kern watched the two of them irritate one another. But long experience with the Gray Duke had taught him to wait until whatever his friend carried as a burden surfaced.

"I had forgotten how immense and how empty the plains are." Benedic's words hung uneasily in the air.

"Mmm."

"T'Xey was but fair company today—rarely said a word, though his skill with a horse spoke volumes."

"Ah," Kern did not resist adding a comment. "So you lost the race?"

Benedic shrugged. "Yes. Why I imagined I could best a plainsrider…"

Kell chose that moment to toss his head and snort loudly. Oddly enough, the horse's derision seemed to lighten his master's mood.

"I intended no offense, good beast." The duke rubbed Kell's nose affectionately. "Any fault was entirely mine."

If his friend was ready to use the word 'fault', Kern decided it was time to do a little more prodding. "Not even the magnificent Kell and all the talents of a plainsrider could have won for you today. Not the race you were running."

Benedic glanced sharply at him. "That is a fairly enigmatic thing to say. Does it mean anything? Or have you just been too long with these metaphor-sotted Lintonese?"

"If it is straightforward you want, then here it is: I am frustrated—and angry—at having to watch you run from yourself. It cannot be done."

The duke stopped walking and turned, scowling, to face him.

"Your skills as an observer have failed you for once, Kern. Since this whole matter began I have done nothing but move toward events. To the quarry where Cathryn was found. To you for help, to D'Brin's lair, to Corronheld's throne, to T'Tolyan for aid, to these folks and these plains for safety and allies. All the time trying to reason through the welter of circumstance to find the right path. Running away? No. Quite the opposite."

"Oh?"

"Don't 'oh' me, Kern. No soldier-mentor attitude will work on me. I am no green recruit. You are mistaken and there's an end to it."

"Oh?"

Benedic yanked at his horse's reins, pulling the resisting beast behind him as he angrily started back toward camp. Kern followed, taking in the words that Benedic flung out over his shoulder.

"Leave it be. When the time is right and I have learned enough to make a good choice, then I will choose. But you, T'Tolyan, these gaudy-silked caravaners—and her, for that matter—can wait until then."

"Humph." Kern refused to let him go that easily. "All your Servants Guild training and you still forget the simplest precepts. It is the choices you make—or refuse to make—that shape tomorrow. You dare not ask Duchess T'Meara to commit Linton Province when you cannot even pledge yourself. You must be the Queen's man for as long as she lives, or set yourself against her and make your reasons known. But do not waver any longer. The stakes are too high to let the future be created by default."

The duke stopped abruptly and stood very still, outlined in the eerie phosphorescent afterglow of the sun's setting.

"Listen to me, Kern and hear the darkness I fear. Our rulers have always been of Corronheld born and bred, those who with every breath, in every fiber, understand in a most singular and intimate way who we are, what makes our dreams and forms our nightmares. We have paid a price for being so insular, so unwilling to upset the balance of our lives with exposure to the unknown. There may be wonders we will never know because our boundaries are so impenetrable.

"But look at what we have gained. It has been hundreds of years since the soldiery turned its hand to anything more than border skirmishes. Diseases which killed our grandparent's grandparents have fallen to the healer's arts. There is work for those who want it, food for those who need it. Our children learn, our citizens pursue their interests and talents, our elders are honored. Is there any better way for life to be lived? And now, like a castle of sand, a single malevolent wave can wipe it all away."

The wind had become intemperate, roiling the tall grasses in great waves of agitation. Dark clouds, heavy with the threat of storm, burgeoned across the blooming star fields. Both horses stamped uneasily. Kern braced himself against the buffeting.

"So you say, Benedic. But no full reason do you give why this particular Passing is one you cannot support. Though Cathryn is not of our place, in her now reside generations of leaders who give her Corronheld's thoughts and plans and passions. The Passing gives both the wisdom of the past and truly confers the title and power of sovereign. It does this, not to threaten our way of life, but to provide the very means of its continued existence."

As the gale whipped the duke's cloak about him, Kern had the unnerving impression he was seeing a wild, ghostly bird of prey. He shivered when Benedic spoke.

"I cannot tell you or anyone. I swore to King Reyfen my most solemn pledge I would not reveal the true name and nature of the place from which she comes, lest the doorway to it is found and opened again. But one thing I can admit that might give you a length of knowledge to measure this evil against: Our might-be queen and the witch D'Joan come from the same place."

Kern felt the revelation like a blow. "This is true? The same homeland bred them both? I cannot believe it. The witch is a malignancy, a wretched parasite. Not at all like Cathryn."

"Is she not?" Benedic leaned into the wind, his face hidden by the swirling darkness. "You have not seen the pit that formed them. Ten years here and D'Joan's true character has emerged. Given the power she already has, what will Cathryn become over time?"

"But your reasoning does not hold." Kern shouted to be heard. "Corronheld nurtures more good souls than bad. What wicked ones there are must be aberrations only. Surely—"

"Now who is running from the truth, Kern? You, among all, should know the evil that crouches in every soul, waiting to find meat fit for its hunger. It only takes the slightest temptation from an outsider who has breathed in depravity from birth to…it…unhhh." Benedic clutched his head, staggering so hard he nearly fell. Kern caught him and struggled to keep them both upright.

The duke cried out and pushed away. With a haste that bordered on panic, he began to climb into the saddle. Kern grabbed his friend's arm and kept him from mounting.

"What is wrong? What is happening?"

Benedic ripped away from him.

"She is dying. I must go—it is the Calling."

Lightning coruscated from sky to ground. A turbulence of thunder rolled toward them. By the time the sound peaked, Kern was mounted and racing toward the camp behind a frantic Benedic. Almost in unison they covered the distance to the circle of wagons and zigzagged headlong between tents and guy wires. They reached the queen's pavilion in the same moment, throwing themselves from the saddle, rushing into the storm-battered tent.

And stopped.

From the center pole hung a glowlantern. In the circle of its light they could see the appalling tableau. On the bright silks and soft furs of the bed, Cathryn lay motionless. Her eyes were open, she breathed, but her body was unnaturally still. Just beyond her a death-eyed Taker, whose black and gray guild bands showed starkly at his wrist, held a curved knife steady at her throat. Before they could manage a word, the assassin spoke in a tone devoid of nuance or warmth.

"She has been drugged. She knows what is happening but cannot take action either physical or magical. She believes, quite rightly, she is about to die. That conviction initiated the Calling. Now that the Heir is here, the Passing will be triggered. And lest you think of crying out, there is a spell of silence bound into the tent walls. No one outside will hear."

Kern tensed for an action he could not take as long as the Taker's dagger bound him to caution. There was a slight movement at the edge of his vision. Almost completely hidden in the shadows by the tent flap, just behind Benedic, was someone else. The other Taker of this pair, no doubt, with a weapon of some kind already aimed at the duke's back.

"Come forward, Heir." The assassin's only variation in tone came with the speaking of the last word. The change was not pleasant, for it spoke of foregone and unhappy conclusions.

Benedic looked over at Kern with an unreadable expression and then started forward into the brighter circle of lamplight. As he moved into the compassing brightness, Kern could see all too clearly the curved glare of a sword poised between the duke's shoulder blades. Prodded by the second Taker behind him, Benedic slowly came forward into Cathryn's direct line of sight. Her eyes widened as she caught sight of him. Her breathing quickened to a shallow, rapid fluttering. The Passing.

"Wait." The Taker whose blade hovered over the trembling Queen motioned the uncertain Heir to pause. "Before you touch her, my masters wish you to know one thing and remember it when you become king." From the folds of his cloak, he pulled out his clenched fist and then opened his hand.

There, on the outstretched palm of a killer, lay Corry's apprentice bands—the bands etched with the boy's name and made for him by Benedic, his loving father. Kern looked over at his friend. At this evidence of his son's danger, the duke's face had gone ashen.

"And, lest either of you contemplate some self-sacrificing rescue, think again. At the slightest sign of it, our blades will strike and those blows will kill more than a young boy, more than a duke and an undeserving monarch. When all are dead, so are the thoughts, desires, memories and knowledge of all the kings and queens of Corronheld who have ever lived. The Passing, all of it, will be gone. Forever."

Sweat trickled down Kern's back. The Taker was too horribly right: the deaths of both Cathryn and Benedic could not be chanced. Too much would be lost to the land and the people. His soldier's impulse to action beat itself in frustration against his will. He must do something—but he could not.

There. What was that? Cathryn had moved her arm. Or was it a trick of the light? No, she had not moved the position of her arm, it was the worms writhing underneath the tunic sleeve. He looked at her face. Her lips were moving. She was trying to talk.

The Taker's voice hatcheted into Kern's concentration.

"Now, king-to-be, take the Queen's hand. Time is running out."

Benedic stumbled slightly as he moved the last two paces

to Cathryn's bedside. Even as he reached down for her hand, the Taker raised his knife, readying for the downward plunge.

Suddenly Cathryn flung herself sideways, her whole body slamming lengthwise into the assassin. He staggered backward and the dagger flew from his hand. Kern took a running leap over the bed, diving headfirst into the Taker's chest. The three of them crashed to the floor, tumbling over Cathryn and wrestling toward the glittering blade that lay just beyond reach. He grappled frantically for some kind of hold, but the assassin was wiry and quick. They rolled over and over, so evenly matched neither could get a purchase on the other.

For an instant, his opponent was held down by something Kern could not see. He broke free and dove for the knife, closed his fist around it, scrambled to his feet and started to turn around. Something hit him from behind and he fell onto the bed. The Taker leaped on him, using the weight of his body to immobilize and force him face down into the blankets. Iron fingers closed around his throat. His nose and mouth began to prickle with inhaled fur and silk, his lungs burned and muscles screamed as he strained to move. The sound of his blood pounded in his ears. Darkness began to close in.

Suddenly he was free. He turned his head and sucked in huge gulps of air, then pushed himself up with his hands. His hands were empty. Where was the dagger? He looked up and saw Benedic pulling a sword from the body of his former captor. Only a few paces away the remaining Taker knelt over the Queen where she lay on the bright red and black rug, waging a battle to hold off the inexorably lowering weapon.

Kern shook his head, trying to clear it. But he knew he was not going to be fast enough to reach the Queen before she lost this last fight. Desperately he looked around for Benedic.

Bloody sword in hand, the duke stood over the corpse of his former captor a scant few paces from Cathryn. Stood and watched as the Taker's knife came closer and closer to carving life from flesh. Stood unmoving.

The Taker yelled and leaped up, slapping himself and gyrating like a dust wraith. Great gouts of smoke poured from him as he twisted and screamed, throwing himself at the tent wall, trying to get out. His whole body ignited. Hungry orange-red flames erupted from his limbs. The canvas wall behind him and the rug underneath him flared into flame as well. The sound of crackling skin and stench of flesh-consuming fire blasted through the pavilion.

Terror gave Kern new strength. He reached Cathryn just as she got to her feet. Her eyes were white-rimmed with horror.

"I didn't mean to. I didn't mean to. I just didn't want to die. I didn't know it would happen like that. I didn't mean to." A litany of self-loathing poured from her. He had to get her out of there. He pulled her arm roughly, but her body resisted. He pulled again, and still she did not move. By now the far wall of tent was completely ablaze. They had to get out.

Suddenly Benedic was at her side, taking her other arm. Between the two of them, they managed to pull her away.

Once outside, the storm's fury beat at them and they were drenched before they had walked a few steps. Then hands reached out. Through the driving rain, Kern saw plainsriders hurrying to help. A blanket was put over him and someone was supporting him. Others had surrounded Cathryn and Benedic, leading them toward safety. But just before Kern was led into the dry tent, he looked back at what had been the Queen's pavilion. Even in the downpour, it burned.

The council room hadn't stopped swaying since the meeting began. It made Kern queasy. Yesterday he blessed the wind for blowing away the rain and bringing him the smell of wet dirt and storm-crushed gaasha flowers on the ride to Linton Hold. Today he cursed it, vowing now as he had so long ago that he would never climb into the city again.

But the thought of climbing back down the maze of hanging footbridges, each one more perilous than the last, gave him pause. Benedic didn't seem to mind this place. Never had. But Kern, while understanding the plainsrider obsession with horses, could not fathom the insanity that made their ancestors build the provincial capitol along the monstrous branches of these ancient aiyden trees.

Still, it would much safer for Cathryn here than it had proved to be along the trail. Since the attempted assassination, the Queen's protection had become the caravan's only affair. That she had saved herself with a kind of magic none had seen before, was a relief. That she had come so close to death in their midst, was a cause of deep shame. Sleep, when it came to those few who tried it, had been filled with red and smoke nightmares.

All had agreed that speeding to Linton Hold as soon as possible was the only prudent course. It had been bruited about that the gray duke was the Called Heir. The rumor had only made everyone tenser. Surrounded by a guardian force of grim-faced plainsfolk, Cathryn and Benedic had ridden hard to make Duchess T'Meara's treehold before the next darkness.

The Duchess was rising to speak even now, outlined against a wall of breeze-tossed greenery. It took a great deal of determination not to let the undulating leaves distract him. And his suffering stomach. Kern forced himself to focus on the proceedings.

"The Shaundry Clancircle has done a great service bringing the new Queen to us safely and bringing news that the ancient evil of the Takers has spread upon the land once again. A threat uncovered is itself threatened." T'Meara paused. She looked at each of the seven clancircle leaders closely, one by one, before speaking again.

"But we are finished with telling what has come before. Now the tomorrow-making begins. We will conceive plans and contrive plots until a way to justice is secured. But hear me now, before a single strategy is spoken. You think you have hidden your desires behind noble words. But I see them. How you hunger for the heroic. How the taste of conflict sits like fire on your tongue. As great as your lust for war, so great is my fear. Because I see that, no matter what we choose, death will be riding with us."

Kern looked up at the massive sword that always hung suspended, point down, over the council table. A stray bit of lamplight slashed the weapon with streaks of glare. He shifted uneasily in his chair.

His motion caught T'Meara's eye. She skewered him with a sharp look. That he was allowed in this deliberation at all was a tribute to the respect the clans had for her, and the usefulness of past services he and Benedic had performed while stationed here in their younger days. Nevertheless, it would not do to stretch the sufferance of the council any further.

"I understand your caution, sister-leader, and the wisdom of it." T'Ahlla, clan leader and sister to the duchess, had a thick voice that seemed to come from the depths of her very ample belly. "But death keeps close no matter which road is taken. Who knows this any better than a rider? Better a short, hard trip on the right trail than a long, easy journey to dishonor."

Several of the clan leaders nodded. T'Ahlla folded her arms across her mountainous bosom, as if trapping the council's agreement against herself for safekeeping.

"But we do not decide for ourselves alone." The duchess leaned back in her chair. A stray shadow enveloped her face so that her words came from a dark place. "Does not Gandrake Clancircle have family serving in the palace guards?"

T'Ahlla frowned.

"Aye. You know we do, sister. Among them my own son, your nephew. But he will fight with us when he knows the truth. So it is and has ever been with the clans. Bloodlines are battle lines."

"So has the saying been." T'Meara stood, pushing back her chair and leaning forward, her hands palm down on the table. "But though you listened, I do not think you heard all that Kern told you. The palace militia, every one, are said to be loyal to D'Brin. The usurper and his dogsbody have fooled some of the guards, threatened others and magicked still more. How do you know which your sons or daughters or brothers or sisters will be? If among those bespelled, no amount of talk will convince them of the rightness of our cause. And then what will happen?"

For a moment the council chamber was silent except for the rhythmic creak of the ropes that bound the room to the branches above. The duchess rubbed her temples with her fingers. When she spoke again, there was both sadness and anger in her voice.

"Before the clan signs are counted, I ask you to consider carefully not only if this cause is worth the dying, but if it is worth the killing. Always before bloodlines have truly drawn the battle lines; province against province, country against foreign invaders. But this time we face the spilling of family blood by our own hand. Of all the evil D'Brin has done, pitting us against our own is surely the most horrible."

A great shudder wracked T'Meara's frame. He saw it mirrored in the responses of the clancircle leaders as, one by one, the terrible consequences of the decision they must make came fully to them.

T'Anders, leader of the Shaundry clan, rose slowly to his feet. He stood with that peculiar bent-knee stance plainsfolk took in this wind-rocked city. From his belt he took a knife, one worn with use and care. He seemed drawn to the sight of it. But when he finally looked up, his gaze came to rest on Kern. T'Anders took a long breath and then spoke.

"We thank you for your praise of the Shaundry clan. But we do not deserve it. Though the Queen and the Heir are safely here, it is in spite of us. We had heard of the Passing, we knew the usurper had hidden spies and assassins. Even so we stared into the comforting nightfires and were blinded to what moved behind us in the dark."

The headrider shifted uneasily, clutching his dagger so tightly his knuckles shone pearl white in the lamp's glow.

"And no one from our clan serves in the palace guards. Any vote we cast will seem hollow when placed next to those who have such treasures to lose in a conflict. Even Kern, our brother by knot, has already given what was most precious to him. Can we do any less? The whole of Shaundry clancircle says, with one voice, we are the Queen's. We serve her and will do what must be done to see the true sovereign on the throne of Corronheld again."

T'Anders laid down his dagger and then rolled up the sleeve of his tunic. He held his bare arm out over the council table and once again picked up his knife. With the deliberateness of occasion, the headrider slowly drew the point of the weapon across the flesh of his forearm until a line of red welled up and sent drops to splatter below on the table top.

"I show our clan's willingness to shed our blood, if it comes to that, by taking the first wound. And if there is a line to be held or a need for sacrifice, we beg the doing of it that our disgrace may be covered by our valor."

Kern held his breath, waiting to see what the rest of the council would do.

As if silent thunder were rolling beneath it, the meeting chamber began to sway more and more. Ropes and bindings creaked and groaned.

But it wasn't a storm that rocked the room, it was the moving bulk of the duchess' sister. With the odd grace so often given to the large, T'Ahlla had risen and walked over to take a place next to the Shaundry clanleader. Everyone else braced themselves against the pitch and yaw. T'Ahlla, alone, seemed able to effortlessly balance, shifting with each undulation like a barefoot sailor. It only was when she spoke that Kern could detect a trace of unsteadiness.

"We none of us saw the scope of this until now, headrider. At least Shaundry clan recognized the truth when Benedic and Kern told it. And the truth is this: We have a Queen and Benedic is her Called Heir. He who has stolen the crown of Corronheld is a deceiver. Nothing good can come from serving a liar, no matter that he wears robes of state."

With a roll of her wrist, T'Ahlla turned up the sleeve of her tunic and reached for the dagger in her sash.

"Gandrake Clancircle pledges to the good of all Corronheld. If we cannot take back the throne with words, then," she drug the knife point across her arm, "we will take it with swords. In pledge of that, I take our clan's first wound." Looking up, the great-bodied woman threw sharp glances at each council member.

"And lest you think we have not considered this matter in its fullness," a trickle of her blood fell to the Council table, "then let me add what I alone can offer—the pledge of one palace guard. My son.

"If he is acting in ignorance, hearing the truth will bring him to us. If he is bespelled," the resonant voice failed for just a moment, "then I know he would rather live...and die...for what is right. Knowing that, on his behalf, I pledge his life."

Slowly, T'Ahlla drew the weapon across her arm a second time. Two red chevrons marked her flesh, each weeping the stuff of life.

One by one, each of the remaining clanleaders rose and cast their bloody votes. Though these self-imposed wounds were another Linton metaphor, this time it made perfect sense to Kern. As knot brother to the clans, it would only be right for him to stand with them in this way. When the last headrider had stood, he rose to do just that.

"I know I have the least right to speak here, but we have shared nightfires and hard trails. Having brought this trouble to your wagons, I offer my own commitment."

He began to roll up his sleeve, but T'Meara came over to him and put her hand on his arm.

"Nay, soldier-brother. There is no need to draw blood among us. Already the first loss of this strife was yours. Bayly gave her life. You give your grief. It is much more than enough to seal your pledge."

From the moment he had been told of his wife's murder at the hands of a Taker, Kern had swung between grim determination and the appearance of acceptance. Now, in the face of such compassion, the grief that had been attributed to him escaped from the prison in which he confined it and overwhelmed him. Unbidden but unchecked, tears slipped down his cheeks and tapped softly as they fell on the leather of his vest.

The Duchess T'Meara reached out and caught some of his tears on her finger, then placed them on her own cheek.

"I weep with you, soldier-brother. And know also that T'Tolyan, my husband, your friend, weeps with you as well."

Even though he could not stop the tears, the release he felt at that moment astonished him. But T'Meara had two more gifts for him: time and a task to do.

"Our council is done, Kern. Give yourself this night to rest, then take word of our decision to the Queen and to Benedic. Tell them that the clans are gathering and we will soon be ready to ride."

Morning came, slipping through the leaves, pale green and tender. From somewhere beneath his room, the smell of kaffe and yeasty bread drifted upward. Above and trunkward, sounds of laughter splashed down, a child and father playing at some morning silliness. Kern pulled the deliciousness of it around him like a blanket and turned to share it with Bayly.

Ah.

Gone. And yet, in delight, she was his first thought. Though the tears of last night had done much good, still the strange mathematics of love made the sum of his joy less because it could not be divided.

It would be better to get to work.

Kern made short work of his morning ablutions and headed cautiously along the network of suspended footbridges that spiderwebbed T'Meara's hold. Thank the Creator there was no wind today. Even so, he did not trust himself to cross a hanging pathway when another person was on it, too. And he did not look down. Ever.

He found the dining hall easily enough and even managed to put food in his stomach, more to anchor it than for nourishment. When he had drunk the last of his kaffe, he was as ready as possible to bring the news to Cathryn and Benedic. Getting there would be a challenge, though. Where they were in this maze that stretched the height and length of the mammoth grove, he did not know. Their arrival had been a mixture of confusion and fatigue, and since then the Queen and Heir had retreated for much needed rest while Linton Province plunged into deliberations.

But he spotted a bright looking youngster happily scavenging bits of sweet rolls. She looked as if she might make a usefully informed guide.

"You, there. Young lady." It was hard to keep his command voice under control, but he made an effort. The girl glanced his way, curious but uncertain.

"Might I persuade you to abandon the breakfast leavings for just a bit? I am in need of a guide and you look like a person who knows where things are."

At the mention of food, the child self-consciously brushed the few errant crumbs from her mouth, then wiped her hands on her tunic. She cocked her head and, like a curious squirrel, alternately scurried and paused to appraise him as she came closer to where he sat.

"I am Kern, a guest of the Duchess T'Meara. What is your name?"

"Jilli." The child smiled shyly.

"Well, Jilli, my friends, Cathryn and Benedic, have rooms someplace but I don't where. Do you know where they are staying?"

"Uh-huh." She nodded with young assurance.

"Could you lead me there, do you think?" Kern felt in his belt pouch until his fingers found a copper piece. He brought it out and held it toward the girl whose eyes widened at the sight. "I try to pay fair wages to those who work for me."

"I know where they are." Her voice was light and high in the way of children.

"Excellent." Kern rose, ready to be guided. But Jilli remained motionless, standing directly in his way. Her immobility puzzled him.

"I am ready to go. Can you take me there now?"

"Uh-huh." Once more she nodded, but still did not move.

By this time, several plainsriders who had been finishing their meals nearby were watching with amusement. He began to feel a little uncomfortable. Was he missing some bit of etiquette, or had he approached this inappropriately?

In a voice he hoped expressed confidence to the spectators but was still not threatening to the child, he tried to salvage the conversation.

"Well, then, Jilli. Is there something else that needs to be discussed before we shake hands on this employment?"

Jilli frowned just a little.

"Uh-huh."

By now he was convinced he was being viewed as a monster who was scaring an impressionable youngster with his rough soldier's ways. He tried to put reassurance in his tone.

"Well, then, tell me what I should do to rightfully hire your guide services."

"Five." She said the word with some emphasis.

"Five?"

"Uh-huh." Jilli put her hands in her pockets and rocked back and forth on her heels, evidently waiting for him to say something.

And then it dawned on him what was happening.

"Two." When he said it, he put his hands in his pockets and took a waiting stance.

"Four."

"Three."

"Done." The child stuck out her hand and he shook it in

amazement. Horse traders were horse traders from birth it seemed.

Chapter Twelve:
CATHRYN

OW ODD IT was that a place so often in motion could feel so stable. It was both marvelously ingenious and gently beautiful. As she had the previous morning, she allowed herself to awaken slowly and become aware of each part of the room that pleased her so much.

First, the sleeping basket—a large wicker platform with curving sides stuffed with what might be called a mattress on Earth but here was more like a thick, downy-soft comforter. There were many pillows, round and plump with padding.

Topping off the bed was a huge coverlet. The underneath of it was a fuzzy, velvety sort of material she could not identify but thoroughly enjoyed. The other side was a kind of woven brocade, white and cream colored, soft but warm. Over the whole basket, layers of ivory tinted fabric, sheer and gauzy, were draped to create a private and elegant enclosure. Not only did this little retreat look and feel good but, from the sweet smell permeating the bedding, it was obvious all the linens had been hung in the sun.

The bedroom itself was crossed at the top by a huge branch from which the sleeping basket was hung. From that sturdy limb a table and, on either side of it, wicker chairs were also attached. Best of all, a breakfast tray had been left on the suspended table. It was the smell of hot kaffe and something made with yeast and butter that finally drew her out of her warm cocoon. Throwing a blanket over her nightdress, she hurried across the cold plank floor to one of the chairs and nestled into it. What a luxury it would be to have nothing to do for the moment but enjoy the quiet.

But when the bridgeway outside began to creak, she knew her privacy was about to end. It was selfish to wish the intruder was only someone anonymous bringing more kaffe. She wished it just the same.

Since the rooms here were canvas-sided, no one could knock. Instead, small bells were placed outside entryways, each with a distinctive sound. The bell outside her room sounded like a crystal chime.

"Come in."

A tiny hand reached through and tugged open the entry flap. In stepped a little girl with wide eyes and an infectious grin. With more confidence than Cathryn thought possible in one so young, the child crossed the room with the bent-knee, rolling gait so useful in this suspended city. When the girl was but two feet away, she stopped and seemed about ready to speak.

Nothing.

Cathryn waited.

"Are you...?" As the child's words sputtered out, a light, sweet flush slipped across her cheeks.

"Am I what?" She tried to speak gently.

The girl tilted her head and peered up at her face.

"Are you really a Queen?"

The question took her aback.

"Am I really a…? Well…"

"Because my mother says you are and I have never seen one before."

"Jilli?" From outside, Kern's voice boomed as the floor began to reverberate with his approach.

"Are you Jilli?"

"Yes, ma'am." The girl looked over her shoulder toward the entryway. "I brought your friend to see you. He takes a great deal of time to get anywhere."

At that moment, Kern stepped through the doorflap, wiping his face with a damp handkerchief.

"There you are, girl. You scampered away so quickly I could barely keep up."

Jilli just kept smiling and held out her hand. A variety of expressions crossed Kern's face, the most predominant one, as far as Cathryn could tell, being chagrin. He dug in his belt pouch and produced several coins.

"There. Your fee, on arrival, as promised."

With a giggle, Jilli pocketed the money then, suddenly serious, she glanced up to search Cathryn's face for something. When the moment had stretched just long enough to begin to be uncomfortable, the child took a strand of leather hanging from the small plainsrider belt at her tiny waist and made three knots along its length.

"My life in your hands." To hear such a solemn words given in a child's voice gave her heart a sudden wrench.

Jilli turned on her heel and, giving Kern a small, pert salute, scampered out through the door. The silence she left behind pressed against Cathryn hard.

"She is not the first." Kern's words startled her.

"What?"

"I am come to tell you that this same pledge was made last night by the plainsrider Council."

"But I thought the Council was deciding whether or not this Passing was legitimate. The little girl just said 'My life in your hands.' What does that mean?" As soon as the question was spoken, the voices inside her began a chorus of response so strong that the spell she used to keep the uproar abated was overcome.

Yes...yes. The first, but pray not the last. Confirmed. Many more are needed. Do not rest. They will follow the crown and it is yours. Take it up. Begin. Move. Move.

A march, a sea of faces, wave after wave of armed riders, martial horns and strands of leather, knotted thrice, held in bloody hands.

"Stop!" Had she said that out loud?

Kern was bending over her, gripping her shoulder.

"Are you unwell?" Underneath his words flowed a strong current of care. It steadied her enough she could re-impose control.

"I'm okay now. I mean, I will be well enough. If we could sit down, though..."

Willing her hands to work, she poured two cups of kaffe, refilling her own and beginning one for her visitor as he gingerly maneuvered himself into the other chair.

"Are *you* well, Kern? You look ill."

The red-faced soldier took a last swipe at his face with his handkerchief and then stuffed the sodden cloth in his belt pouch.

"I could say, as you just did, I will be well enough. Quite honestly, this city in the trees likes me not. When Benedic and I were posted in Linton on border duty, I stayed here once and thought that single visit plenty. My insides prefer more solid footing."

"I am sorry. I've never suffered from motion sickness, but my father did. He could barely even step on a plane without getting ill."

Kern frowned and shook his head. "Your father must be incredibly sensitive to detect motion on a plain."

"What? Oh, I see….no. You think I meant plain…as in flatlands. I meant a…well…a machine used to travel. The words sound the same, but the spelling and meaning are different."

"Ah." Kern looked anything but enlightened.

"Never mind. It doesn't matter. They're just words. What I really wanted to know—"

"But it does matter. Until the battle is joined, words are all we have. They are our only arsenal for understanding, for waging peace. No one knows this better than a soldier. Most of us are poor speakers, for our profession is not required until words have already failed. If our rulers cannot make themselves understood, then there is more for us to fear than the swords of our enemy."

A faint heat rose to her cheeks. Kern sounded so right, in his stolid, homely way, that his rationality was almost an accusation.

"You think I don't know that? Why else would I ask all these questions, trying to get more information, enough to make better decisions? But given one thing and another, I seem to have very few sources for help."

The soldier looked at her sharply. Lines formed at the corners of his eyes.

"Few sources for help? Forgive the contradiction, majesty, but you have ample assistance. Within you resides the wisdom of our queens and kings of old. At your beck and call are their memories, decisions, knowledge, fears, hopes. All their words, all our words, are yours."

Once again, she felt touched by guilt and bristled at it.

"You don't understand, Kern. All these voices…it's like drowning. If I give in and let them take over, where will I go? I'll be lost, submerged, a mindless puppet moved by the strings of the dead."

Kern flattened himself back in the chair, his eyes wide.

"Majesty, please. I understand." There was both comprehension and real alarm in his voice. Only then did she realize that her arms burned slightly with the residue of magic. In her need for compassion, she must have been sending her feelings at him.

"I'm sorry. As much as I want to control this, it is still difficult."

She watched Kern consider her anew.

"It may well be I owe you an apology, Cathryn. Even among those of us Corronheld-born, words can go astray. And, remember," a smile creased his veteran's face, "I did admit no great skill in speech."

"You do very well, no matter what you say." She took the offer of friendship his tone carried and returned it to him warmly.

"You are kind to say so, but if I had done better, you would have heard by now why this Passing was begun. We are taught this story during our apprenticeships. By the time we are admitted to full guild status, we have heard it so many times most of us could recite it in our sleep.

"But each time this story is shared, we are also reminded what it teaches us: That there is but a faint and tenuous line between the good that we would do and the evil we could do. That the true fight is not found upon bloody fields, but is waged within. Mayhaps the telling of this tale will be of some benefit now."

She reached for her cup and settled back in the chair. Perhaps she would get some useful information at last.

"Well, we won't know until you've told it. Have at it."

Kern took a quick sip of kaffe, squinted as he consulted his memory and then began.

"Hundreds of years ago our provinces were divided by boundaries more severe than lines drawn upon a map. Every valley, tree, rock and stream was fought over by clan leaders who ruled by the raging force of their ambitions and the destructive power of their spells. In pursuit of a few measures of dirt, crops were left to rot, houses fell into disrepair and the only music to fill the night was the sad wail of children newly orphaned."

It was obvious that Kern was reciting from a deeply etched memory. The rhythm of his speech had taken on the lilt of mythos.

"Into this darkness came a child called Lisska. For the first twenty-seven years of her life, she neither spoke nor evidenced any signs of magic. Her parents were poor, as were most in those times, supporting themselves by making wooden weapons: cudgels, war staves, horse-killing stakes. No regular army would take their primitive wares, so they made a meager living selling to the less savory of the mercenary companies.

"It happened that, during the last, sere days of autumn, one of those companies came to winter over in Lisska's valley. As the night air grew more chill, their leader, Red Tayzier, grew bolder. On the morning after the first frost, he and his troop took over Lisska's home, forcing her and her parents to scrabble for shelter in a nearby cave.

"But from that day, a strange and terrible sickness took hold of Red Tayzier. At first he was only tired, exhausted by the smallest tasks. But worse happened and quickly. He began to suffer running sores inside his mouth, then bloody boils infected the bottoms of his feet. In desperation, when he could no longer walk nor eat nor endure the pain, he had Lisska found and brought to him, for she was known to have healing ways.

"Upon seeing the mercenary captain's condition, Lisska cried out the first two words of her twenty-seven seasons: Forgive me. Provoked to anger by the treatment of her family, her magic talent had awakened but, in her rage, she had twisted it into a weapon. She was horrified at the suffering she had wrought, and at the knowledge that such savagery lived within her.

"When the members of the company learned what happened, they wanted to kill her. But Red Tayzier held them back, for he knew only she could undo what had been so terribly done.

"In the grip of deep repentance, Lisska conjured up a healing spell so strong and true that, not only was the captain cured of his physical afflictions, but that cold lockbox which had been his heart was healed as well and he turned from his killing ways. All that winter, the two of them worked the same kind of healing on the rest of the company until, as spring greened the valley, no single mercenary remained unregenerate.

"In time other war bands came, as they had before, to buy weapons. And, while not all warriors responded to the spirit of the place, many did. As time passed, more saw the wisdom of Lisska's vision. Where magicks had been used for battle, they were redirected into commerce and care. Where parcels of land drew the lust of would-be conquerors, provinces were created and maintained by vigilant and thoughtful leaders."

"But how did the Passing get started from this?" She felt

her impatience to know, to learn more, override her sociability. Kern shot a glance at her and chuckled.

"No more kaffe for you, my lady. Possess yourself, I'm almost done. A three hundred year old tale cannot be rushed."

Since there seemed to be no hope for it, she tamped down her fidgets and kept quiet.

"Where was I? Ah, yes…provinces had been made but still needed mediation from time to time. Because Lisska's valley was situated centrally, it was agreed by all that a capitol would be built there. It was named Corronheld, which, in the old language, means 'the place conscience is kept.'

"Eventually Lisska and Red Tayzier married and were blessed with one child, a son they named Quillian. As he grew, he incorporated the leadership of his father and the vision of his mother. When, at last, the provinces were stable and the magic guilds well under way, Quillian was chosen by a council of leaders to be the first monarch.

"Though the council believed in Quillian, they feared that the lessons of this hard-won peace might be lost or weakened with each succeeding ruler. So it was decided that the most powerful of the wizards would work together on a spell that would help Quillian and all future rulers find the most worthy successor and pass to that Heir their accumulated wisdom and experience. After great trials and effort, the spell and certain safeguards were completed and placed on the new king. And so they have been from that day forward."

Having ended his recitation, the soldier sat quietly staring beyond her at some unseen worry.

"I begin to see at least two important lessons from your story, Kern. The first one is obvious: you are trying to tell me that the lives I have been given aren't trying to possess me. That, if I can find a way to sort through all the voices, I can use them like a reference book to avoid making the same old mistakes. Have I got that right?"

Kern nodded, though she could see him trying to stifle a smile in the process. She certainly wasn't going to get any servile deference from anyone on this world. Respect, perhaps. Toadying—not a chance. Ah, well, maybe she could still surprise him with her second point.

"Secondly, if I understand what you probably think of as the hidden lesson of this story, there is a perspective to be gained on Benedic."

Kern looked up with an expression of anticipation and hope so clear, so unsubtle, that she had momentary misgivings. Would she disappoint him very much if her guess was wrong? Well, there was no getting around it now.

"What I gather is that Benedic thoroughly and seriously subscribes to the 'thin line' school of thought. He believes that it doesn't take much temptation to help someone move from light to dark. And he thinks I bring, knowingly or not, a type of darkness that could very well be contagious and he would do anything—*anything*—to prevent this world from lapsing again into chaos. Have I got that right?"

Kern nodded slowly.

"If you take that idea and deepen it tenfold, then you have it aright, majesty."

It must have been that a cloud passed over the sun just then, for darkness slithered, blind and hungry, across the room. She shivered and pulled the blanket around her more tightly, wishing for the safety of warmth as she asked the question that weighed so heavily on her heart.

"But what if Benedic is right? What if I am too great a threat? He's seen my world. He knows it can be…ugly. Violent. A place where unspeakable things are done. Every day. Not hundreds, but hundreds of thousands are killed by those who glory in the doing of it, or worse, care not one bit but kill just the same. You haven't seen it yourself, Kern. You don't know."

"Bah. You and he are too alike in the worst of ways." Kern stood up but the floor shifted under him and he clutched the ropes of his chair for balance. "Too much like this damn place. First one excuse and then another, never firmly settled. If I had a copper for each time either one of you spoke the words 'but what if' I should never know want."

"But, Kern—"

"There you go again. Will you two drive me mad?" Kern groped his way to the doorway, his face as red as it had been when he arrived. "There is no other choice to be made. You are queen. Benedic is the Called Heir. You are not required to decide whether these things should be. They just are."

At the entryway Kern paused, his hands balled into fists.

"You are correct, majesty, when you say I have not seen your world. Still, I believe what is true here is true there: That, before one commits, the chance of failure is greater. But the moment one pledges to a deed and acts, then providence itself moves on your behalf, providing companions, assistance and such unforeseen grace as you would have never believed would be yours."

She could feel the heat rise in her face as well.

"Assistance like the Passing?"

Kern sliced the air with his hand. "Obviously. Must I also mention the rest, those who aid you: The duke, Lucette and Corry, T'Meara and all of the Linton clans. And others who will pledge their aid in the days to come. And me."

At least here she felt on safer ground. He had become such a solid and comfortable friend in such a short time.

"You are right. You, most of all, have been so kind. I don't know how I can thank you enough."

"Thanks will not erase the pain I must endure without my wife." Kern's voice was thick with feeling. "Bayly had too brief a life, but she had a brave one for, when she met death, she was walking toward it. Straight and strong. No, gratitude is not what I want. A queen with enough courage to be one is what I need."

Though he set the bridgeway to her room to creaking with his exit, his stinging words stayed behind, sharp and convicting. She might have come to a strange, new world, but she had brought her old, same self.

Images of her past pushed mercilessly into her mind's eye: A particularly horrible day at the office, hearing that someone else had been promoted to a job she had wanted—and only because they had asked for it, grabbed the opportunity while she indulged in an endless internal debate on whether it would be wise to even apply. Marrying David, not so much for love but by default, because he asked and she could not decide on another course. So much more was at stake here, more than her own disappointments. A picture of the child, Jilli, came unbidden and powerful to her mind.

On impulse, she shrugged off the blanket and pulled up the sleeves of her sleeping gown. As if in response to her scrutiny, the worms stirred restlessly under her skin. There they were. Nothing could change that reality. Magic was there, as well, waiting to be used. Within her, also, were the experiences and wisdom of generations of monarchs past. And there were people of good will near her who, if they could not be called her own friends, at least had pledged themselves to the office she held. They, too, were waiting.

"I will try." Her voice sounded thin as a wire. "I will."

She began getting dressed for the day. There was much to do.

She couldn't figure out whether her head hurt from the din of the arguing or from trying to cautiously consult her indwelling encyclopedia so many times during the council meeting. Maybe this place was beginning to wear on her, too. The name 'Dramamine' had started to pop up in her consciousness.

"It is only right. We do not know other provinces will bring troops. If we face this alone, then better the commander be from Linton. Better it be me." T'Ahlla strode around the council table so forcefully it set the room to rocking, throwing everything and everyone off balance. It occurred to Cathryn that the intimidating woman was doing it on purpose, for Kern had quit objecting to T'Ahlla's proposal and sat clutching at the edge of the table.

Once again, a weary T'Meara tried to insert a reconciling word.

"This naming of a commander is the last matter before the council. Already the night watch takes to their posts. If we can find agreement, then all can rest for the rigors of the morrow. Come. Let us reach accord before the moon rises to chide us for being so late awake."

From around the table came mutterings of assent. The clan-leaders looked tired, obviously used to T'Ahlla's filibusters but ready to put an end to them. Only Benedic said nothing. But he had been silent most of the day, contributing only uneasiness to the meeting.

T'Anders rose wearily and started toward the doorway.

"If we must finish this business tonight, then let me send for hot kaffe. My eyelids have turned to lead."

"No." The strength of her own voice surprised Cathryn.

"There will be no need. There are actually two items to complete before we can adjourn, but they won't take long."

Faces turned to her with expressions of amazement. That she could so quickly command their attention should have pleased her, but it did not; she realized she had let this fruitless debate go on too long. These people were not filled with awe at her leadership, they were surprised she had spoken at all.

"The commander of this army, whether it eventually contain those of other provinces and guilds or only Lintonese, will be Kern." She heard T'Ahlla's sharp intact of breath.

"But—"

"It will be Kern." Cathryn cut off the complaint before it could be uttered. "It is my understanding that T'Ahlla is a brave and canny warrior, a respected leader. But our first objective is to negotiate with the pretenders who hold the capitol. We cannot, I will not, have our troops led by someone so eager for battle. Kern does not seek the commander's knot though he is trained and more than able to take it. I say he will be our battle chief."

Up and down her arms she could feel the slither and sting of approaching magic. She ignored the now quiet council members and looked at Benedic.

"The last remaining matter is the rescue of Benedic's son."

The duke's face went ashen.

"Begging your pardon, but that has already been discussed." Muscles along his jaw twitched with tension as he spoke. "I will travel with the army to the capital. It was hard enough to make this decision, knowing it might well mean the life of my son. You are cruel, heartlessly cruel, to stir up a father's anguish again."

His accusation brought a moment of stunned silence followed by the hiss of daggers being drawn. T'Meara stood up and motioned for calm.

"This is the Queen you so address, Benedic. We know you are distraught over Corry's capture and fatigued in this late hour. We will believe this is what makes you speak so unwisely." But even the duchess had trouble keeping her tone level and cool.

He drew breath to reply. She knew she must stop him before wrong words were irretrievably spoken. Pain lanced through her, from fingers to shoulder as she tapped into the raw power that was now hers. Abruptly she stood up.

"Enough." All motion in the room stopped. "Tomorrow, after the ceremony of blessing, Benedic will leave to seek the rescue of his son. I know the duke feels obligated to stay with us and advise us as we undertake this crucial mission. But I hope to lose no one in this cause, least of all young Corry."

She could see him struggle to speak, but she aimed even more magic toward him. Sweat broke out on his forehead, but he did not speak. Good.

"The war council is done. Benedic and I will stay behind for a bit to finalize his travel plans. I hope you all rest well tonight for we have much to do tomorrow."

No one, not even the bellicose T'Ahlla, missed the pointed dismissal in her words. Kern shot her a glance full of apprehension, hope and queasiness but still managed to stand and lead the way out. In a matter of moments, all had filed from of the council chamber except for T'Meara who briefly stayed for a last look at her new queen. It may have been the play of the glowlanterns, but it seemed to Cathryn that there was a change of expression on the duchess' face.

When the room of empty, Cathryn released Benedic from the spell of silence. As its power diminished, he drew in a sharp hiss of breath, left his chair, began pacing the room, but obstinately remained wordless. When she finally found the courage to face him directly, however, he was ready to speak.

"I remember you rebuked me, more than once, for using magically enhanced commands on my daughter, yet you have done more and worse tonight. There is a great difference between what you espouse and what you practice—though it is not surprising to find such hypocrisy in an Earther."

His anger had turned quiet and white-hot. She drew back from its intensity.

"I don't blame you for being upset. But I knew that you would argue with me and we can no longer afford that kind of divisiveness. I—"

"We?" The duke's voice turned harder and colder. "Who is this we that cannot afford divisiveness?"

This was not going well at all. Her reasons for sending him after his son were sound. If she could only find a good way to convince him, to overcome his fears about her.

"Please try to understand. When I say 'we' I mean both you and me. I have responsibilities that, although I did not get them in the usual way, must be met. This open antagonism dilutes the commitment of what few allies we have, and it is imperative that we are at full strength and power.

"And you need to ease up for your own sake. I know why I make you angry and suspicious, but these people don't. If you continue this public animosity without giving reasons, sooner or later the word treason will be heard and the Called Heir cannot suffer even the slightest accusation. Not now. Not when things are so troubled."

While she spoke, his gaze stayed on her, his full attention more an attempt at control than a mark of courtesy. It made her feel like a bug on a pin.

"You are ignorant of the nature of true friendship, then, if you believe these people will label me traitor. No matter my reasons for silence, they would never turn against me. It is you, the stranger, the unknown, who best beware. If you think I would even, for one moment, consider leaving you unwatched, you are gravely mistaken. My mistrust is so deep and the stakes are so enormous, I cannot leave. Even at the risk of Corry's…even if it means…" The duke's voice faltered and his gaze dropped. She followed his glance downward and saw that the knuckles of his hands were bloodless-white where he gripped the back of his chair.

The man's anguish made her chest ache. Almost she moved to touch him in sympathy, but as quickly pushed away the notion. He was too proud, his distress too intense, his distrust of her too strong. Instead, she stepped over to a long cabinet where pitchers of cool drinks had been placed for the council meeting. She filled a mug with fresh water and turned toward him again.

"Here, tuck into this. It will do you good."

He snapped his head up to glare at her.

"That is the second time you have used that particular expression. I would thank you never to use it a third."

"What is your problem?" All her impatience let loose. His unreasonable attitude was more than she could or would take any more. "I try to do the right things, keep my word, speak in the correct way and all I get from you is hostility. Your daughter once advised me to listen to Reyfen's memories of you so I would understand and appreciate you. Well, you may be interested to know I did check with the late king and he regarded you very highly. But nothing you're doing now remotely resembles the actions of the person he loved."

His eyes narrowed. "You cannot manipulate me in this way. Once in T'Tolyan's kitchen and here tonight you have usurped words made precious to me in the time I spent as a young man with Reyfen. Did you think it would sit well with me?"

"Well, yes, I actually did. I saw in Reyfen's memories how, after he had taken you to task or when you were ill or homesick, he would bring you some soothing drink and use the same words every time to build a bridge to your heart. I've watched him do it, Benedic. Time after time. In here." She tapped her forehead. "I hoped that, by using those phrases I, too, could build a bridge between us. That you would see I am trying to do what is best for Corronheld and for you."

Try as she might, she could not read his reaction to what she had said. His face was a cold, stony blank. Exhaustion rolled over her, exhaustion and hopelessness.

"I give up. It's late and I'm too tired to hash through this anymore." She sank down in one of the chairs again. The headache which had waited in the background all evening moved in with a vengeance. She began to rub her temples.

"All that remains to be said is this: You must leave tomorrow to rescue Corry. The reasons why this is the correct course of action are these: Only you know enough about D'Brin and Joan to find where they are keeping him. Only you, his father, have the strongest motivation to succeed. And, because you are, at least for now, the Called Heir, it is unwise for the enemy to hold Corry hostage. It gives them too much leverage."

The pain in her head had become so intense, it was making her sick. She closed her eyes, struggling to finish the night's business.

"You are oathbound to me, Benedic. You say you are not because T'Tolyan forced it on you for safety's sake. But I say you are because you are the Called Heir. Still, I would release you from any obligations if only you take on this one task. While you're gone you can take some comfort from knowing that, if you are killed on your mission and I am finally gotten by a Taker, whoever takes the Passing from me will get all of your knowledge and fears from my memories. It's not like you have to be right next to me for your paranoia to be carried on.

"Besides, you have to go if only so that it will never be said you sacrificed your son to your own stubbornness. Please, please. Go get him."

She did not know if the duke even replied, the throbbing of the headache was so excruciating. Vaguely she became aware of someone helping her walk, taking her over the hanging bridges and downward. With a jolt, her foot hit solid ground. Where was she?

Wearily, she tried to come up with a spell for the pain. It worked somewhat, enough that she could focus on the surroundings. Kern was on one side of her and Duchess T'Meara on the other, supporting her. They were down out of the tree city and at the edge of the huge encampment of plainsriders. Watchfires leaped and crackled all around the enormous circle of tents and wagons.

"Back with us a bit, majesty?" Kern's deep, steady voice was a comforting sound. "I think we'll both feel better after a good night's sleep on solid ground. Though I meant no offense, T'Meara."

The duchess gave a rich, throaty laugh.

"There is no offense taken, old man. I've grown rather weary of searching for you up there, anyway. Your face was getting so green I could not find you in all those leaves."

There was something in this woman's manner that immediately reminded Cathryn of T'Tolyan. A vivid image of the garishly-clad plainsrider sprang up in her imagination. He seemed to be reminding her that she was supposed to tell the duchess something. Straightening up and trying to walk unaided, she searched her memory. The three of them had almost reached the large tent quite clearly intended for her when she realized what she was supposed to say.

"I took a wagon ride with your husband, duchess, and T'Tolyan got me accused of adultery with him. I thought you'd better hear it from me, and know nothing happened, than hear such a thing from a gossip."

There was a momentary pause. Then both her escorts burst out laughing. Their obvious good humor carried itself infectiously to Cathryn and she smiled first and then chuckled. It made her feel better.

"Thank you, my queen, for telling this news about my husband." T'Meara's amusement could be heard underneath her words. "As for that unregenerate reprobate, I will deal with him when next I see him. Not, of course, that I mistrust the old goat, but it was dreadfully impolitic of him to compromise you so."

Kern cleared his throat mightily. Cathryn could not tell if he was trying to stifle more laughter or if he was not too subtly announcing that they had finally reached her tent.

The three of them stopped at the entryway to the immense pavilion. She realized she did not know what protocol was appropriate for this situation. But Kern, as always, tried in his own blunt manner to ease the way.

"I am bunked in that tent." He pointed to a nearby structure adorned by a number of flags which, though they stirred in the night breezes of the camp, could not be seen clearly in the darkness. "If you need anything, call for me." He touched her hand briefly, but even that swift contact was a reassurance.

T'Meara motioned toward the open door flap.

"I would give you any assistance you need, majesty. May I be of help?"

Cathryn quickly glanced into the tent. A comfortably ap-

pointed bed and other furnishings were already in place, awaiting her arrival.

"No, thank you." All she wanted to do was crawl in that
lovely bed and sleep. Attention was the last thing she desired.
"You've been more than kind. I...I could use some help tomorrow before the ceremony. I've never...well..."

"After you have broken your fast, I will come in to you and
will give you some few instructions that should make it go more
smoothly. The blessing ceremony is an ancient and revered tradition and much desired by soldiers when it is likely Death will
join their march."

Once again the duchess gave her a long look. Then slowly,
with the careful motions of ritual, she picked out a strand of
leather from her plainsrider belt and made three knots along
its length.

"My life in your hands," was all she said, then turned and
walked away into the maze of the camp.

In the early morning, fog had wound through the encampment, damping the dusky smell of horses and the acrid odor
of restlessness, concealing the caravans that had added themselves, one by one, all through the night. By the time T'Meara
had come to give her what scant instructions she could, the
mist had lifted, leaving only a few wisps fluffed around the
wagons like unspun wool.

Now it was almost time. On the ground, just at the outer
edge of the grove that supported Linton Hold, a high platform
had been erected. The dense shade and overarching leaves
formed a natural backdrop, while the sun had picked out and
lit the place where she would stand to speak. Already the crowd
filled the area around the stage. Mounted scouts, ready to move

out when the last words were spoken, ranged around the fringe of the camp, the horses stamping impatiently, the riders working to keep them in check. The shade, the sun, the horses and riders, the clans and their leaders, all waited. For her.

"It is time, majesty." Kern's voice cut through her musings.

"So soon?" She looked at him, hoping he would notice her stage fright and offer, as battle chief, to perform the ceremony in her place.

He only stared back at her, head tilted and eyebrows raised.

Linton's duchess arrived, making last minute adjustments to her riotously colored outfit. T'Meara had dressed for the occasion as only a plainsrider could.

"I only wish my husband were here. He does so love to put on his best finery. I swear the man is as vain as a mountain cat." She tugged the last loop of her belt knot tight and then held out her arms and smiled. "There. Do I not look amazing?"

The immoderate question made her laugh in spite of herself.

"You do, indeed, duchess. No one seeing your unique beauty could ever believe T'Tolyan would so much as look at another."

At her side, Kern chuckled.

"I see our queen is already learning the art of diplomacy."

T'Meara huffed in mock outrage.

"Diplomacy? Are you suggesting our monarch would tell me anything less than the beans-and-bread truth?"

The grinning soldier shook his head.

"Nay, good lady. She called you 'unique' and it is only too true."

T'Meara looked eager to spar with the redoubtable Kern indefinitely. But before she could utter whatever retort she had devised, they were interrupted by T'Anders, who wore such a serious expression that Cathryn was plunged back into the tension of the occasion.

"All have gathered for the ceremony. We wait upon you." The Shaundry clanleader motioned toward the rostrum.

Her mouth was dry, her legs weak. "Thank you. We will come directly." How was she going to get through this?

As she watched T'Anders walk away, Kern came close to her, whispering so only she could hear. "Remember, the platform has been spelled so your voice will carry throughout the camp. You only need speak in a conversational tone to be heard." With that last bit of advice and a reassuring touch to her shoulder, he took his place two paces in front of her.

T'Meara positioned herself the requisite distance behind her. The honor guard in place, it was time to meet her army.

What a strange concept. She suddenly felt an immense curiosity to see what this thing looked like—this army of hers. Almost before she knew it, she was at the top of the podium stairs. Ahead of her, Kern had stopped, taking his position slightly to one side of center. With the duchess close behind, she had no choice but to step forward, into the middle, into the light.

For a moment the glare of the late morning sun dazzled her and she could not see. Then, from the ground below came a noise unlike any she had ever heard. It was not loud, and yet it filled her ears. It was one note, yet it held within itself the deep sound of belief and the shrill counterpoint of need. It was the sound of the many, the sound of the crowd. And it pierced her like a sorrow.

She blinked. And to the sound was added sight. Before her, fanning to left and right, stretching from near to far, wagons, pennants, horses, tents, the glint of weapons and, throughout it all, the upturned faces of the plainsriders. Each one a blank, each one anonymous in the glare of daylight. Until she saw the child, hoist on the shoulders of her father. Jilli. And suddenly all the other faces sharpened, each into its own peculiarity.

Fear gripped her. Her mouth would not open. Words fled. The immensities of duty settled so heavily upon her she began to tremble. The crowd fell silent.

She cleared her throat. That horrible sound, magically enhanced, ricocheted from one end of the camp to the other. Heat rose to her face. Her palms began to sweat.

"I…Before we can go through with this blessing ceremony, before you decide for sure to march away from here, I believe I need to tell you some things about myself. No doubt you've heard a few facts and lots of rumors."

She paused at the sight of Jilli's upturned and solemn face. 'My life in your hands' the child had said. Surely the girl deserved the truth in exchange for such an inestimable gift.

"Well, you can tell right away I'm not from your country. That much is obvious. Where my land is in relation to yours, I really do not know. How I got here, I do not know except it was by a powerful magic that no one here so far has been able to understand. It is especially hard for me to comprehend because, where I come from, not a single person possesses magical abilities."

Murmurs swept through the crowd. More than one showed an expression of pity. It bothered her in a way she could not explain.

"After I arrived, however, someone infected me with these." She had unbuttoned her tunic cuffs and now raised her arms, letting the sleeves slide down to her elbows. Expressions of abhorrence swept away whatever pity there had been. "If I had been born here, I would have died. But I am just different enough that the bloodworms did not kill me. Instead, they gave me the capacity for undisciplined and powerful magic. Before I had time to master this new and strange ability, a terrible thing was done. King Reyfen was poisoned."

Many in the crowd shifted uneasily. A few stayed still, as if rooted in place.

"Benedic, duke of Forché and the Called Heir, his daughter Lucette and I were brought as prisoners to the king's chambers. You have heard it was D'Brin of the Unseen Circle and the witch Joan who did this, hoping to trigger the Passing so they might take the crown and all the knowledge that comes with it."

She knew she was telling the story poorly. The plainsriders had respected, even loved, Reyfen and they all knew how important this campaign would be. Yet, all she could sense from the crowd was a growing uneasiness.

In desperation, she looked deep inside, searching for Reyfen's memory of his last minutes of life. If she could see it vividly as it happened to him, maybe she could explain it better. There. The scene pushed to the surface of her mind. Immediately, the king's fear and helplessness, pain and anger blasted her.

"Ahhh." She heard his anguish and resolve in her cry. "Murdered. Poisoned slowly, in secret. No one to trust. Betrayed. But for pain, alone. I...he tried to stand by himself. To keep what shreds of dignity, of honor could be salvaged as the reins and traces of sovereignty were stripped away. Almost it was too much. He wavered."

She raised her hands as if to once again aid the king.

"I only wanted to help, to keep him from falling. He was light, no heavier than a breath. I didn't know. When the voices came, in a rush, in a storm, I was afraid. So afraid that I refused to listen, shut the lives away before I was imprisoned in a past I never lived in a place where I am, and always will be, a stranger."

Her last word fell into a vast silence. Keeping Jilli's ingenuous face before her like a beacon, Cathryn unloosened more of the Passing, tapping into its richness, letting it flow up into her mind and out in words.

"But even a stranger may serve. And so I serve you. I am sleepless with the fears of authority, besieged by doubts, wounded by the sorrows of those who love this land. For I recognize the evil that is slithering toward you. It delights in perverting good into the worst of abominations. Twisting a parent's love into abuse, devotion into obsession, beauty into idolatry, tolerance and a desire for peace into avoidance of truth.

"King Reyfen lost his life to the growing dark. But we have heard his warning and we will take the light of what we hold dear and march." The words of ceremony burst into her mouth, savory and satisfying. "March we will, with the blessing of the Creator and Sustainer, armed with the love of that which is right, desiring the good, promoting justice and remembering mercy."

With a roar that shook the camp, the whole crowd shouted, "For Corronheld."

But within her, like the eye of a storm, she had already heard the stillness of the future dead.

Chapter Thirteen:
CORRY

PART OF THE time Corry cursed that he was being held in the dungeons of Forché. If only his father had not made this place so escape-proof. But the rest of the time he was relieved and grateful that, if he had to be imprisoned, it was here. His cell was warm, well lit, amply supplied with books and writing materials and, though plainly furnished, comfortable.

Still, a dungeon was, when all was said and done, a dungeon. With a sigh of frustration, he shut the book he had been reading and got up to pace the length of the cell once again.

It had been two days since he'd been so unceremoniously dumped down here. Two days of waiting for whatever was going to happen. Though the witch frightened him, he was almost ready to face her just to end the suspense.

The sound of a key turning in a lock cut through his thoughts. He glanced over at the small table where a dinner tray still held a few, cold morsels. It wasn't time for a meal to be delivered. He stepped back from the door, his eagerness to confront his captor buried under a rush of apprehension.

"She wants you now." One of the witch's bodyguards filled the doorway, manacles clutched in his meaty fist. This did not look to be a pleasant outing.

"You don't have to use those on me, you know." He tried to sound harmless. "I have no intention of making any trouble— even if I could."

But the mound of determination in the doorway did not deign to reply, did not even change expression. He had probably been chosen for his post precisely because his brain was as much of a stone wall as his hulk of a body.

Corry held out his hands in resignation, wincing when the cold metal bit into his wrists, and again as the band snapped shut around his neck. He followed the guard quickly enough when the chains were jerked, but all the while, as they made their way up the stairs, he prayed fervently that no one he knew would see him until he was rid of the humiliating bonds.

To his relief, the Keep seemed to be almost deserted. Strangers in militia uniforms guarded the doors. None of the house staff was about, few of the lanterns lit, most of the fireplaces cold and cheerless. Yet the place did not feel empty. Something in the air was dark and pressing. It raised the hair on the back of his neck.

The guard pulled the chains harder as they reached the top of the main stairway and entered the corridor in front of the ducal apartments. The pair of militia guarding the doors to the main salon snickered as he was dragged past. Corry tried to summon up his facade of irresponsibility, but the unyielding metal collar and cuffs and the implacable disdain of his jailer made it very difficult.

Approaching the library, he could hear the witch's voice raised in anger.

"Tried? Well, if you tried so hard how come you didn't find anything? You're supposed to be this great miracle worker, but no. You had days to search this place and you turned up nothing. You're a fool, D'Goran. An idiot. I only hope you make a better messenger than you do a detective. Shut up and get out."

D'Goran, his face gone white save for a half-circle of dark gray under each eye, exited in a undignified hurry from the library. The guard hesitated before entering the room. Then, squaring his shoulders, the jailer tugged on the lead chain and the two of them stepped into the room.

Parchments and books, maps and containers had been pulled off shelves and flung in disarray. Pillows lay limp and flat, their stuffing bled through ragged tears. Candle stubs littered the desk top, some still guttering sour smoke into the odd, murky light that sneaked past a poorly drawn drapery.

"I brought him, like you said." The guard shifted uneasily as he made his announcement. D'Joan, who had been turned away from the doorway, whirled around. The witch's expression, unedited in that brief moment, made him shudder. Seeing his response, she quickly buried that flash under a coating of amiability.

"Ah, here you are. Dear Corry, where have you been keeping yourself?" She shook her finger at his jailer. "Now why would you put chains on this young man? Take them off this minute or I shall be very cross." Though it was said with all mildness, the guard's hands were shaking as he hurried to release the offending bonds.

D'Joan moved over and took his hands in hers.

"There, isn't that better? Now we can talk." She pulled him toward the window seat, glaring so fiercely at the guard as she did so that he backed out of the room and shut the door as fast as his great bulk permitted. Corry knew he should be glad to see the brute's back, yet the alternative—being alone with the witch—struck him as infinitely worse.

D'Joan sat down on the bench underneath the tall window and patted the cushion next to her. Though the seat was barely wide enough for one, she obviously expected him to join her. He lowered himself into the narrow space, trying to keep as much distance between himself and this discomfiting woman as possible.

"Quite frankly I had no choice but to keep you stashed away downstairs. You have no idea how concerned I've been for your safety. Your father's treachery has placed you in a most unfortunate position, young man."

This slur directed at his father made him angry. But he needed to maintain his pose as a green and thoughtless boy, so he pushed that reaction deep down and tried to keep his hands unclenched.

"My father's only trying to do what he thinks is right." It surprised him that his tone was so level. Perhaps he was going to get through this after all.

"Of course he is, my dear. We all are. Believe me, I understand how difficult it is for your family right now. I truly admire the way you, especially, are handling all this."

Her compliment made him shift uneasily. As he did so, D'Joan moved even closer to him. He could suddenly feel the warmth of her thigh through his clothes, the length of her arm against his shirt, pressing against his ribs. He had thought to make a comment, but it was lost in the distraction of unwanted touch.

"It's too bad we had to meet under such complicated circumstances." D'Joan's voice had gone soft and husky. "And just to show you how sorry I am about all this, I brought you a little present. I've kept it hidden until the right moment."

He meant to refuse the gift. The words formed on his tongue. But then the witch undid the first, second, third, fourth buttons of her tunic. Underneath her storm-gray shirt she was wearing a strange garment, one he had never seen before. It held her breasts in a confection of black lace and ribbon, making each swell into the most remarkable shape. She reached into one side of the garment and pulled out a delicate silver chain, letting it slid across the impossible whiteness of her skin as she drew it out.

She held up the necklace. Hanging from it was a tiny, green amulet worked over with silver filigree. It was beautiful.

No. It was ugly.

He blinked, afraid that his eyes had betrayed him. He blinked again and, for a moment, the necklace seemed hideous. Through it he saw D'Joan's face, the wide pores across her nose, the deep lines that pulled down at the edges of her mouth, the specks of sweat clotting on her forehead. And just below the sagging creases of her neck, where the creaminess of her bosom should be, there were lines. Moving lines. No, not lines.

His stomach rebelled and bile rose in his throat. Before he could move, the witch dropped the chain over his head. It circled his neck like cold fire.

He felt better. His stomach settled down.

"Are you all right, Corry?"

She was concerned about him. It made him feel much better.

"I thought I was going to be ill, but it passed."

He smiled at her, hoping she would forgive his momentary lapse. She studied his face for a long time and then she, too smiled. More than that, she reached out and stroked his cheek. He glanced away, fearing that once he looked at her fully he would not be able to stop. But she would have none of that.

"Look at me, Corry." She put her fingers under the line of his chin and urged him, by touch, to meet her eyes. "Look at me sweet, sweet boy. We have so much to talk about. And when we are done talking…well, we'll see."

Slowly, hardly daring to draw breath, he turned back until her face, soft, warm and perfect, filled his vision. She leaned toward him, began to whisper in his ear. The sensation was so remarkable that, at first, he could not understand a single word.

He had to keep reminding himself to eat breakfast. He was always ravenous, but this morning he found himself drifting into a languorous mood that made him neglect what had been served and admire, instead, the view across the table.

She was there, talking brightly, happy. He dared to think some of her pleasure might be due to his presence. Joan had asked only one thing of him last night, and he had complied. Once she had explained why she needed his mother's research notes, he had willingly retrieved them from the hiding place.

For a while last night it had been embarrassing to reveal, under her questioning, how little he knew of his mother's work. But he'd been too young, only six winters, when she died. Most of what he did know had been stitched together from bits and pieces of conversation heard over time.

Then he had taken Joan to the small, secret vault which was spelled to open only to the touch of a family member. How she praised his cleverness, his discretion and mature comprehension of complex matters. Just thinking about it now made his ears heat with pride, stirred him up inside, making him feel strangely powerful. He discovered he was stroking the amulet she had given him. It, too, was warm.

"A penny for your thoughts, Corry." His hostess (had he

called her witch but yesterday?) pushed away her empty breakfast plate and sat back.

"A penny, my lady?" Sometimes her figures of speech were
hard to understand.

"You look so—how should I say it—pleased. I was just wondering what brought on such a mood." She took a sip of kaffe,
looking at him over the edge of the cup.

"I was just…that is…" He sputtered to a halt. How could
he tell her what he felt when it was so wonderfully confusing
to him?

There was a knock at the door. He breathed a quick sigh of
relief. Some conversations were better left unspoken.

"Enter." Joan put down her cup and pushed back her chair.
Giving him a brief, enigmatic smile, she rose and moved to the
center of the room. Evidently whoever was waiting outside the
door was going to be received formally.

The click of a latch opening sounded unnaturally loud behind him. He turned in his chair to get a good look. A guard
pushed someone through the doorway.

It was Peer. Disheveled, pale and wide-eyed. What was she
doing here?

He got up from his chair and started toward his friend.

"Corry, dear. Come stand by me." Joan's voice stopped him
halfway between the two women.

"Corry?" This time Joan spoke almost too quietly and yet
the word, which he barely recognized as his name, sounded
like a discretely hidden blade. It made him shudder. For reassurance, he reached for the amulet. And hissed with pain when
it burned his fingers. It made him break eye contact with Peer.

"I assume this is one of your young friends, my dear?" The
consort's voice had returned to normal.

"Well, I do know her." As he spoke, he could see an unknown expression flicker across Peer's face. Joan straightened up just enough that he felt a sudden apprehension. "I mean, this town is not vast. There is no one I do not know."

"But you are not especially close to this girl? I only ask because she was caught sneaking into the Keep last night. It occurred to me she might be checking up on you. People don't usually show that much daring on behalf of casual acquaintances."

If only he could see Joan's face, find a clue as to the proper answer. Then he might shake the feeling that something very ominous was happening. But she did not turn. Instead, she stayed silent, awaiting his reply. Tiny lines of sweat began to creep down his back and erupt on his palms. Where he had burned his fingers on the amulet, the salt of his sweat stung. How was he supposed to reply?

"No. This girl means nothing to me. She is only one of many children in the town." He held his breath. Had he said the right thing?

The tension that had held Joan's back ramrod straight left. Her shoulders relaxed.

"Then there is no reason to keep the child here." She turned around and faced him. "Is there?"

"No reason. None at all." The chain on his neck felt cool, refreshing after such anxiety.

"Take her away, then. You know what to do." The consort did not face the guard to whom she was giving orders. Her tone was enough. "And send Arilon in to us. We have preparations to make for a trip."

He felt himself sinking into Joan's eyes once again. Yet he did catch Peer's last glance at him. It reminded him of a yearling he had once seen swept away by a spring flood. How odd.

❋

Parchment trees. In air thick with threatened frost, gold and russet leaves spinning, singing dried songs of falling slowly. Attenuated branches thinning into wizened fingers. Through the cracks of the peeling white bark a dead, glistening darkness curls. Under the smell of damp soil, decay. Under desiccated leaves crumbling in layers on the dirt, tiny, wicked undulations.

A brightness forms, pulling to it what light there is that is not unnatural. Forms a shimmer of cloud, a phantasm, a woman. Beyond color, beyond this life but scented with the next.

"Mother. Help me."

"Corry." Breathing his name more than speaking it.

Her eyes are sad and terrible. They are all that can be remembered. And all that must be forgotten. From them start tears of pale blood.

My hand, veined with molten silver, fired by green flame, reaches for her, reaches through her, to the four conjoined, tiny, boundless chambers of her crystalline heart. Closes around it. Pulls it out.

The wind screams, leaves tremble, trees quake. Without an anchor, she is twisted into shredded vapors by the blast. And still the hand, now red and steaming, holds its dreadful plunder.

"Mother?"

She is gone.

My hand is hot.

No. No. NO...

"Corry. Wake up. The carriage isn't big enough for you to be thrashing around like this."

Someone shook him. He tried to sit upright, but his arm was numb and would not support him. He fell hard against the side of the coach. The jolt made him open his eyes and what he saw made him flatten himself against the seatback. The witch. The one who…

No. It was Joan. The consort. The one who…

He knew he had been having a nightmare. He tried to remember the dream, but the effort made it splinter and disappear in a burst of small wounds. All that remained was a stomach-wrenching headache and the heavy-lidded lassitude that had plagued him since the trip started this morning. He could not seem to stay awake.

The red-orange of sunset seeping through the coach window lit Joan's face. She was frowning, the furrows between her brows deepened by shadow. He must have done something wrong again, though in this woolly-headed state it was hard to think what that might have been.

Trying to get some feeling back into his sleep-numbed arm, he clenched and unclenched his fist. Trying to put better feeling into the carriage ride, he puzzled together a start at some journey conversation.

"I have not been good company, milady. For that I apologize. Most journeys I am the one who entertains to pass the time. If I had my lute, I would be honored to sing for you."

With a snappish sigh, Joan clapped shut the book of papers on her lap. It was only as she did so that he realized the consort had been reading his mother's notes while he slept. Blood began to return to his arm. His fingers felt warm with it.

"I don't need entertainment. I need quiet." She shut her eyes, the blackened frown staying where it was.

"Then you are finding what you need in the notes?"

She half-opened her eyes. The deepening red of day's-end caught in them so strangely it seemed they were windows looking on fields of fire.

"Almost everything."

The carriage swayed heavily into a curve in the road. He braced himself so as not to fall again. Joan lifted her arm and stared at the odd, segmented metal bracelet on her wrist.

"We ought to be near the inn by now."

As if in response to her observation, the coach began to slow. Outside, the driver spoke, calming the stable-eager team. When all motion ceased, one of the inn's attendants stepped forward and pulled open the coach door and extended his hand to help down the first passenger. Corry leaned back into the seat and shifted his feet so they would not block Joan's exit. But she did not move, only looked at him strangely.

"After you, milady." He gestured toward the opening.

"Why?"

Her question and odd inaction puzzled him.

"Why what?"

"Why should I go first? Is it because I'm just the woman? Because if that's it, buddy, then you have a lot to learn about..."

Once again he had done something wrong without knowing how or why.

"No, no. Please milady. Whatever you are thinking, I had no disrespect in mind. I would not presume to precede the consort at any time."

He watched Joan's stiff shoulders ease a bit. That small release was such a relief that he rushed on, trying to banish the remaining tension.

"It is a matter of the respect in which I hold you, milady. You are a member of court, a wizard of great power and, of course, my elder."

From the dimness of the coach he heard a hiss.

"Get out. Get OUT."

In a panic, he stumbled out of the coach, hitting the ground so hard he nearly lost his balance. Frantic to be in her good graces again, he scrambled to right himself so he could turn back to help. But she took no assistance. Instead, grabbing his arm so hard he had to clamp his teeth together to avoid shouting with pain, she pushed him ahead of her into the inn.

"Greetings, Consort D'Joan. I am honored to see you again at my humble—"

"Just get me another room." She cut through the innkeeper's welcome speech with such spleen that the man's jaw dropped open.

"Huh?" The innkeeper's wits seemed to have deserted him in the presence of the woman's wrath.

"What are you? New? I reserved one room for myself, but now I need another room for the boy here. Something suitable for a child."

Corry felt his face flame. Something he had said had destroyed their growing intimacy. What a fool he was to so stupidly believe he had even the smallest hope of becoming close to such a woman.

When the innkeeper indicated he could provide another room and led the way upstairs, Joan shoved Corry ahead of her again. He willed himself to be invisible, wished the stairs would collapse and end his misery. But no disaster intervened. Once in the tiny room assigned to him, when the door had been locked from without, he flung himself on the narrow bed and beat his fists on the mattress in silent shame until his body gave out and the darkness won.

Something was wrong. Enough wrong that it pulled him from sleep. He held his breath and listened. Distant nighthowls. The rumble of a snoring sleeper in a nearby room. His own heartbeat. The random creaks of a timber and thatch inn shifting in the cold. No other sounds.

Yet the feeling of a presence was still strong. Of a sudden, he remembered Kern once telling him that night vision came best from the side of the eye. He turned his head slightly, peering off-center into the shadowed places of the room. He knew one corner's apparition was only his cloak thrown over a chair. But he didn't recognize what composed that other ink and moon-silver shape. He told himself it must be a blanket hanging on a peg, or a broom leaning against a wall hanging. But fear still scraped its nails on the inside of his skin.

There was no choice. He would have to move, have to find out for sure if he was not alone or if his mind was fashioning monsters from the mundane.

The best plan he could think of was to throw off the covers in one huge movement and quickly drop to the floor beside the bed. That way, if there was someone in the room, he'd have some protection. He tensed his muscles, preparing.

"Son?"

"Father?"

From a pool of midnight, his father emerged.

"Aye, son. I have come for you."

Corry sat upright.

"What have I done?" He heard the terror in his voice and it made him flatten himself against the backboard.

His father came closer, close enough to touch him. He tried to squirm even further back.

"We must be swift. Here." Something owl-sized flapped toward him. He flinched, then realized it was only his cloak his father had tossed.

"We need to ride far before the witch discovers you gone. Make haste."

But he could not move. He was paralyzed by the sight of his father's face glowing an unnerving green, green the color of decay. The ghastly luminescence seemed to be coming from—from the amulet.

"Is something wrong?" His father's voice was full of concern.

Before a reply could be made, an answer came. The door opened. Light spilled into the room. Two guards, weapons readied, stepped in. A third intruder also entered and, when she had smiled broadly, spoke.

"So, Benedic, you've decided to join us at last? Has your son given you a warm welcome?"

Joan's laugh carried no mirth in it.

Chapter Fourteen:
BENEDIC

THE JOURNEY FROM the inn had been a nightmare. But being in the dungeon of CorronKeep was even worse, for it was a nightmare from which he might never wake. How could he endure being brought to the city where the King had so often and so warmly received him, only to see the underside of it? To be reunited with his son, only to be betrayed. It was an anguish too intimate for bearing.

He blamed himself for leaving the boy. He blamed Cathryn for bringing the stench of Earth's corruption with her. And he blamed Earth. Vile, alien, damnable Earth.

Through the metal-bordered slot in the door of the cell came the sound of footsteps. The outer lock rattled. The door opened.

D'Brin stood in the doorway, staring with an unblinking intensity. The wizard's hawkish eyes were devoid of warmth, his stance predatory, his silence infuriating. Seeing the one he now knew to be his wife's murderer, Benedic ached with the need to loose his vengeance. But he resisted, planting his feet even more firmly on the cold stone.

"Good morrow, D'Brin. Playing errand boy for the witch?"

"Good morrow to you, my late cousin's husband."

The cruel reference made Benedic reach for his sword. When his hand closed on air only, a cry of rage burst from him and he sprang for his enemy.

The wizard made a slight pass with his fingers. A concussion of force hit Benedic, throwing him against the far wall of the cell. He crumpled to the floor, his arms useless to cushion the fall. He tried to rise. No part of him obeyed his desperate commands. Unable to move, and until he could regain his breath, the only channels for his wrath were his eyes. He poured his fury into and through them, willing his glance alone to ravage.

"Do you really expect to do me damage with hard looks, near-cousin?" D'Brin slowly stroked the thick velvet of his crimson robe. "It amazes me it has taken all these years for you to generate this feeble bit of outrage. Did D'Shaar mean so little to you?"

The duke panted with the exertion of recovering enough wind in his lungs to speak, and enough control to reach his enemy.

"Only of late have I learned it was you murdered her. Killed her, not by accident, but by design. What remains of your life is mine. What remains of your soul will be sent to the pit that spawned it." Mercilessly, he strained against the bondage of the wizard's magic, throwing every muscle and every spell of his own arsenal against it. In vain.

"How very droll. Your much vaunted sense of justice kept you from accusing me without proof, and now it is too late. Really, Benedic, that is so unfortunate."

"It is only too late for you. Now that I know—"

"Know? You know nothing." D'Brin crossed the frigid cell and grabbed Benedic's hair, pulling him to his knees and forcing his head painfully back. "Trust me when I tell you your life is over. I am king now. I hold your existence in my hand. Pray you continue to be useful to me, because if you are not…"

"Remove your spell of restraint and let me show you what use I could be."

"Yes, yes. Of a certainty you would gladly play my judge, even executioner." D'Brin pressed his lips together and stretched the edges of his mouth outward. It took a moment for Benedic to recognize that the man was trying to smile. With a start of amazement, he realized the wizard, too, was struggling for self-control. He gripped that thought with as much resolution as his hand would have gripped a dagger.

"Nay, once-cousin, you have no need of a judge. I have no doubt you know all too well what others think of you."

The expression that the wizard had offered as a smile hardened. He yanked Benedic's hair even harder.

"You have always despised me. That I know. But no longer are you the king's well-loved. For I am king and I hate you." D'Brin hissed his words so violently that spittle hit the duke's face in hot, explosive droplets.

The self-declared monarch abruptly let go and returned to the doorway. Once again he stared at Benedic a long, offensive moment before speaking.

"Your use to me is this: If Cathryn begins to die, you will be Called. The signs of that Calling will be unmistakable and they will allow me to intercept the Passing. Though the Takers failed, there are still those around her even now who will take the Passing for me, at the cost of their own lives if need be, if I am not close by."

"So," Benedic stabbed with his unseen weapon, "even you know you are not king. Now *that* is droll."

The wizard did not move, but only shut his eyes and drew in a long, raspy breath. He used that air to call out down the dank, ill-lit hallway.

"Bring the boy."

D'Brin's voice, flat and cold, fell into the cell like stones. Benedic tried to lurch to his feet, a parent's fear and stubborn pride pushing him to stand.

"You mistakenly called me a 'witch's errand boy.' But you will be among the first few who learn that she serves me. For me, she created the amulets that have given us such a large and willing militia. For me, she used such a bauble on your son and led him to so blithely betray his family and friends. And it was for me she read D'Shaar's notes and discovered that the boy will be of even more use to us than his fool of a father."

From the far end of the hallway came the dull thud of boots on stone, a hideous counterpoint to the beat of Benedic's dread. D'Brin opened his eyes and smiled, this time a true and appalling smile.

"Unfortunately, your wife's notes tell us that Corry can only be useful if he is not magically coerced. When the time comes, he must help of his own accord. Since I have no doubt that, as a worthy parent, you instilled in him your own naive brand of ethics, most likely he will not be willing to help if left unmagicked. It leaves me with no other choice, really, but to break the boy. Shall we begin now?"

The wizard waited for the guards to reach him. He turned toward them and spoke to the one they had brought.

"Corry. Dear boy. Come here. I have a surprise for you."

D'Brin turned his attention to Benedic once again, muttering to himself and gesturing wildly with his long fingers until they looked like pale, busy spiders.

With a jerk, Benedic felt his limbs released from their paralysis. One by one he tested his arms and legs, readying himself for any advantage, any opening.

D'Brin stood aside from the doorway a bit. Cautiously, tentatively, Corry stepped through the entry, looking lost and confused. The wizard kept close behind, speaking quietly into his ear.

"Look carefully, little man, and you will see that the person in this cell is your father." D'Brin reached for the chain that held a silver and green amulet on Corry's neck. "And when I take this from you, you will be able to remember. Everything."

With exaggerated care, D'Brin lifted the necklace and removed it. Corry looked startled and reached for it with a small cry of need. But the wizard raised the amulet out of reach. As he did so, its spectral green light dimmed into darkness. When only the feeble glow of the cell's tiny lantern remained, D'Brin sighed deeply, as if in profound satisfaction, and stepped into the hall, closing the heavy door behind him. There was a slight pause, then a small, cold rasp as someone turned a key in the lock.

Before Benedic could speak one welcoming, comforting word a terrible transformation brutalized his son. The color left his cheeks and he began to shake.

"My mother. My friend. The queen. You. I have betrayed them all. Oh, father. What have I done?"

The pain of those words nearly broke his heart. He rushed to put his arms around his anguished child.

But two paces from Corry's trembling body, he was stopped. Hard. Why could he not reach his son? He tried to call out his name, but no words would come.

D'Brin had laid another spell upon him and now, when Corry was sinking under brutal guilt, he could neither touch nor talk to him. Despair, pitiless and contaminated with grim revenge, filled him to overflowing.

At that moment, his son looked up, infinitely small vestiges of hope still in his suddenly older eyes. Horrified, Benedic knew that, at that instant, Corry would see only his black and terrible bitterness. He tried to change that expression, to reflect instead a father's love, to forgive without words and comfort without touch. But it was too late. His son recoiled, scrambled to the farthest corner of the cell and, covering his face with his arms, sank to the floor with a moan that should have wrung tears from the imprisoning walls.

Eventually Benedic could only sit quietly and watch his son descend into the kind of slumber that comes with complete exhaustion. He could lend no comforting touch when Corry cried out from nightmares. He could speak no easing word to soften the hard terrors that bled into the boy's sleep. D'Brin's spell was too thorough. Even when Benedic had torn open a cut on his hand and tried to write forgiveness on the cold stones in blood, his fingers could not trace the letters that were needed.

Now was the darkest, cruelest part of night. But for Corry's fitful breathing and the soft, seductive whisper of despair, it was immensely still. The guards, who earlier had sent their uneasy patrols echoing through the corridors, were silent now, perhaps dozing in the timelessness just before false dawn.

Remembering his own days and nights on patrol brought odd scraps of memory into his mind: Midnight duty with other cadets, struggling to keep eyes open; attending his own guard captain as she made surprise inspections of the night watch.

"Benedic?"

Suddenly, and most vividly, came a picture of the broad night skies of Linton Province and the wide grin of T'Tolyan as the two of them rode border patrol. It was so long ago, and yet he could almost smell the new sprouted moongrass and feel the workings of his eyes opening to a lavishness of stars.

"Benedic?"

Great Maker, he was truly under severe duress to imagine T'Tolyan's voice as well.

"If it is not too much trouble," a whisper that sounded much like a mudslide trying to be discrete came through the cell window, "could you get off your ducal buttocks and," the cell door swung open, "escape. It seems the least you could do seeing all the effort we've gone to."

There stood the imagined man, real and immediate. T'Tolyan and his clanswoman, T'Orah, slipped into the cell, bringing with them the sweet scent of free air. Though they came in quietly, the movement woke Corry, who tried to speak but was shushed into silence. T'Orah pulled the boy upright and wrapped him in a militia greatcloak. T'Tolyan gave Benedic a cloak and, without another word, led them out the cell door.

Sleeping guards littered the corridors, a sure sign that the rescuers had employed strong counter-magicks. As if to confirm that guess, just before the small, tense group left the prison gate, T'Orah motioned for a halt. She began a series of gestures and a mumbled litany. Clearly she was casting a spell, but it was unlike any he had seen before. The casting was taking a toll on the woman. She had gone pale and, from where he stood, he could see a vein pulsing at her temple.

"Corry, you must go first." T'Tolyan's hushed instructions interrupted Benedic's focus. "If my kinswoman's magicks hold, you will appear to be a member of the palace militia. Walk across the courtyard to the stable as if you had every reason to do so. Once inside, go to the last stall. The horse kept there is thought to be vicious so the palace types stay far away. But it will let you in. Wait there for us."

"I understand." Corry accepted his orders, setting his shoulders straight and scanning the courtyard. It hurt Benedic to see how much his son needed to be given this task, how much he ached to redeem himself.

"Must you send the boy out first?" Benedic meant for the question to demonstrate his concern for his son; but Corry winced and drew away.

"T'Orah will be nearly spent when the spell is finished." T'Tolyan continued with his plan, though puzzlement had crossed his face. "You must help her cross the yard; the two of you will look like a pair of drunkards, if you play it right. The captain of the guards is a fussy sort. Often sends over-indulged soldiers to sleep it off in the stables. Cannot abide the sound or smell, I'm told." The giant chuckled just a bit and for a moment the tension lessened. But his next words brought the fear right back.

"And I will cross last. In case."

T'Orah gave a long, rasping sigh and leaned against the wall. Though they were all hidden deep in shadows and silent as martyrs, there was no mistaking her exhaustion.

"You are too tired for this I know, cousin." The plainsrider's voice was gentle with regret but edged with apprehension. "But we must hurry before the alarum is sounded. How say you?"

T'Orah said nothing. Her answer was the great effort she exerted to stand upright. She was as ready as her iron will could make her, but Benedic could see she was shaking. He came close and put his arm around her.

"If drunkards we must be, rider, then I am game." His supporting grip tightened as he felt her tremble. "And this time, as you smuggle me out of the city, perhaps you will not plague me with teasing as you did before."

She rewarded him with a weak but real smile. He glanced up, ready to move out across the courtyard—in time to see Corry already heading out onto the torch-lit flagstones, a too young soldier walking to meet the night. His throat tightened with tears that could not now be shed. How must his son feel to see his father warm others with comfort but remain, as he believed, coldly unforgiven himself? Great Maker, keep my boy safe until we can touch and talk again.

When Corry crossed the last few paces of courtyard and slipped into the stable, Benedic sighed with relief. Now he must gain the safer shadows of the stable, too. He eased T'Orah forward into the open.

He could not imagine that they resembled late-night revelers. His tension and her exhaustion must give them away. Yet, when a pair of guards passed them, he could hear their mocking laughter and caught one saying something about soldiers in their cups.

By the time he maneuvered T'Orah through the stable door and back to the farthest stall, he was sweating and edgy. His hold on T'Orah slipped, but just as he made to shift his grip, she seemed to fly upward. It was only T'Tolyan who, just arrived from his gauntlet run across the courtyard, had put a huge hand under her arm and nearly lifted her off the floor.

The horse with the reputation snorted only once at the invasion of his quarters. T'Tolyan pried open a panel and motioned the small company through the low doorway that was revealed. Once through, he pulled the boards back into place behind them and gave a sharp whistle. From the other side of the wall came a fierce neighing and the sound of hooves on wood. No one would readily search that stall for escaped prisoners.

Light spread in the darkness, revealing a long, very narrow passageway. T'Tolyan held up a glowlantern and led them along the corridor toward the inky shadows that hunched at the far end of the beam of light. Carefully, Benedic resumed his support of T'Orah. Ahead of them, Corry hurried to keep up with T'Tolyan.

The cramped passage seemed to go on forever. From the shape and length of it, he surmised it must be hidden within the very outer walls of CorronKeep. Eventually, the plainsrider stopped to search a length of wall, running his hands over the blocks of stone until he found an almost unnoticeable indentation. When the depression was pushed, a doorway began to appear, accompanied by the sound of rock grinding on rock.

The door, which surely weighed more than a foothill, moved very slowly but with such ease that he marveled. Someone from Rock Circle had done a masterful job. But the thought of rock-working brought his daughter to mind—his other child in peril, trying to separate allies from enemies. He shivered.

"Too much walking in too much cold for the Gray Duke?" T'Orah stood upright, using the wall for support.

"You must be some recovered if you have strength enough to employ your wit at my expense once again." It surprised him how relieved he felt to say such a thing. The escape had been so unexpected and swift that the enormity of the risk his two friends had taken was only now becoming real.

The door slowly ground open with a screak of rock against metal that set his teeth on edge. The sound would also, he realized, announce their presence to anyone waiting outside the hidden corridor. But T'Tolyan motioned them through with no evidence of caution. Though Benedic was the last to come through the doorway, he was prepared by the unmistakable smell to emerge into another stable. He was, however, wholly unprepared for the sight that greeted him.

In shadows broken only by a few dim glowlanterns, from

one wall to the other, plainsriders stood shoulder to shoulder, each holding the reins of a saddle-readied horse. If that were not surprise enough, the usual maelstrom of noise that passed for Lintonese conversation was missing. Only the syncopated rustle of hooves on straw sifted through the crowded stable.

T'Tolyan addressed the group of riders. "It is good to find all who were left in town safely made this sanctuary. As you see, our rescue of the Called Heir was successful, so much so that it was possible, by sheer good fortune, to bring out the duke's beloved son as well."

At this, the riders finally made some noise—a murmur of satisfaction. Benedic looked for and found Corry, who had moved through the press of animals and people to the far corner and stood half-hidden in the crowd. He watched the boy as the words 'beloved son' came from T'Tolyan. When Corry turned his face into the shadows, Benedic closed his hand, yet again, on emptiness—this time the void where a son's shoulder should have been.

"Now we all must leave CorronKeep to join the Queen's army. It has not proved easy," T'Tolyan's eyes glittered, "even for such as we unassuming plainsriders to avoid capture."

The bit of laughter that followed that remark was well seasoned with rue.

"Still, we have the honor of escorting the Called Heir to safety. No others could do this perilous deed—not with such skill, such honor—" T'Tolyan pulled open his dusty cloak and revealed a brilliantly colored tunic, "—nor with such style."

The laughter that trailed that regal display was genuine. Even as tired and distracted as he was, Benedic felt cheered by the way T'Tolyan spoke. The Creator had indeed blessed him with friends of inestimable worth.

"So, this is the way we will cheat the guards and steal our prizes home: Three parties will ride out tonight. T'Gorn and my good Bushbin will lead two of the groups. I will take the third. Because I am like to be followed with more malice than any other rider, I cannot take Benedic with me. I will take my cousin, Bushbin will take Benedic and T'Gorn will take Corry."

"No." Corry's voice came from the back of the room. "I must…that is, I beg to be released to return to Forché."

Riders turned to look at the young man. Benedic felt a chill drive down into his bones.

"I want…I must go to Forché. A friend, a good companion," Corry's voice wavered and then grew stronger again, "has been imprisoned. May even be…dead…because of me. Please. If my friend is still alive, I beg the rescuing of her."

How he yearned to embrace his son, to speak to that wounded heart. Though he strained to form words, it was T'Tolyan who replied.

"I cannot commit the riders of your escort any farther than the city's edge. But, if your honor demands you part from them to do this thing, then I would not be the man stands in your way. But surely your father will speak to this. What say you, Benedic?"

Without waiting for a reply, Corry turned and stalked out through the stable door into the night. T'Tolyan looked to him for some explanation.

"I beg you to excuse Corry. He means no disrespect."

T'Tolyan huffed, his mustache bellowing with the force of it.

"That I would not believe if I did not know the boy from his naming day til now. Still, I have promised him an escort at least part way." T'Tolyan started to signal several riders. But Benedic pulled down his friend's arm before the sign could be given.

"Wait, rider-brother. One favor, please." He hurried, knowing that each moment put a greater distance between himself and his son. "While we were imprisoned, D'Brin revealed to Corry that the boy, under magical coercion, betrayed me and others he loves. Then, to lay evil on wickedness, the wizard bespelled me so that I could not…so that I cannot even now speak to him. Or even be near enough to touch him. Corry believes I hate his deeds, hate him. But you…"

He dug into his tunic pocket and drew out Corry's ruined guild band, then tore the red leather strand from his own belt.

"Give him these. Tell him to use the oathbond thong to tie on the band. Tell him he means that much to me. Tell him…"

Pain and need closed him throat and he could say no more.

T'Tolyan took the mangled pieces of leather.

"I will tell him, walker-brother." The huge man held the band gently in his fist. "And, with the Great Maker as my witness I swear, for each instant D'Brin laughed with triumph, I will repay him with an hundred-year of howling." He turned again to the company.

"T'Gorn. I must speak with you before you leave to overtake the duke's son. Bushbin, guard our Heir well. You all know what to do."

T'Tolyan closed his hand over the bits of leather and then raised his fist high.

"Let there be confusion and defeat in the camp of the enemy—"

"Confusion and defeat" came the response from the plainsriders, low enough that the noise would not leave the stable, but strong enough of heart.

"—and secrets and feasts in our tents of victory."

"Secrets and feasts." As one the company responded by slapping the ends of the reins they held hard against their leather-gloved hands. The sharp crack was the signal for the sentry to pull the stable door wide open. Riders began to lead their mounts quickly and quietly out into the darkness. Bushbin approached him, holding out the reins of one of the two horses he led.

"Now we go, and quickly, I'm for sure. Worry not at all, I am as amazing at cooking up a delicious escape as I ever am with venison pies and stickyrolls." The short, round man chuckled and pointed at his saddlebags. "Some few, by the by, have I packed for your lordship, though the nibbling will have to wait til we've found a safer place."

Benedic took the reins of the mount intended for him, but did not start toward the door. He searched the shadows of the stable for T'Tolyan and T'Gorn. He wanted to talk to the plainsrider who would be taking his message to Corry, to impress on him how crucial it was.

"Have you lost a something, milord?" Bushbin was at his side, a rare frown on his face. "It is not exactly or precisely safe to tarry."

"I wanted…" He could feel the man's anxiety. This lingering must be putting them into danger. It would have to be enough to put his trust in T'Tolyan and his clansman. For the time, his son was in other hands.

"No. I hope I have not lost anything. Lead on."

As it was, the two of them were the last to leave the safety of the stable for the vulnerability of the darkness. Once outside, he could see that their hiding place, while built against the keep's outer wall, was surrounded by the dense tree-fence of one of the town's large manor houses. Not only did the manor's perimeter walls hide the stable from passersby, but the trees hid it from guards looking down from the battlements.

He did not recognize this manor, nor know who owned it. Yet again, allies he had never met and might never be able to thank had put themselves and their households at risk for him.

The great wooden gate at the far end of the courtyard swung silently open. Without a word spoken or a signal given, the first of the rider groups urged their horses into a run and gained the street. Rising up on his stirrups, he searched for a glimpse of Corry. But it had all happened too quickly. He settled back into the saddle and laid the reins more carefully across his palm.

The second group was through the gate, turning a different direction and filling the night with hoof beats and flicks of leather against hide. When the last of those riders had gained the street, Bushbin snapped the end of his reins on his horse's rump. Before the echo could repeat itself, the entire group followed suit.

Benedic struggled to anticipate which streets they would take in their charge out of town. But he could not. And it soon became clear he did not have to; his horse seemed determined to keep him in the center of the escort and had none of his problems anticipating the twists and turns.

A sharp turn, a length of road run at full gallop, narrowly missing a surprised drunkard on his way home. All at break-neck speed. Then there were shouts behind them. One of the riders pulled back from the group. Another corner turned. Then another, and the slowing rider was lost from view. More shouts. The sound of metal on metal from nearby, then farther away.

Shouts from the left. A second rider broke away and headed left. In the space of a breath, she was lost to view. A warrior's battle cry. Screams. Then only the sound of horses being driven to the limit and the smell of sweat and fear.

Finally, ahead of them, the street ran past a guard station and then out of the city and into the free night. He strained to see how many guards would be blocking their way. Nearer and nearer they rode. Not a guard appeared. No hue and cry had been raised yet. Was everyone drunk or asleep? What stroke of luck was this?

As they passed the station, he glanced down at it. There were guards. Almost a dozen he could see on the ground on either side of the blockade, limbs akimbo, unmoving. And there was something else: five or six times he glimpsed the gaudy colors of plainsrider clothing. Beneath him, the horse had begun to labor for breath, lungs rasping like huge, rent bellows. As harsh as the noise was, he focused on it. It had the sound of life.

Around him closed the night and those who remained of his escort. They rode. And as his horse took him toward the armies of the queen, he saw before him the faces of the dead: his wife, cousin Bayly, plainsriders barely known. Each of them sorrowing for him, each of them speaking to his heart the same words: Evil is here, Benedic. It has always been here. We saw the right and we did it. What do you see?

Chapter Fifteen:
CATHRYN

BEFORE, IT WAS only in books she had experienced the idea of 'saddle-sore.' This intimate, and seemingly endless, acquaintance with the real thing was taking its toll. Last night she'd even had a dream in which aspirin and a sauna figured prominently. It certainly put an end to any sense of triumph that learning to stay on a horse had given her. After six, long days of travel she was constantly creating schemes to be on two legs only.

The dry, dusty days were filled with other schemes, as well. At first she wondered if she could add anything of value to this foray, or would simply be a logistical complication. But the wagons of the huge caravan had barely moved away from Linton Hold when the first delegation came to her. Could she settle a dispute as to whether one clan should be allowed to provide all the scouts? From the stubborn set of the Shaundry rider's mouth, and the expression on the face of the Border Guard captain, she could easily see how the debate had gone so far.

This time she had not resisted, but immediately reached into Passing memories to find a tack to take. In a matter of ten minutes or so, the rider and guard had ridden away, no longer in conflict. She had smiled to herself.

By the end of that day, she could not give a smile every time a question was settled or an order given. No mortal could keep each and every person in this growing vanguard happy with every decision. And the sheer number of requests for a moment of her time began to be overwhelming.

She shifted in the saddle, trying to find a portion of her anatomy that didn't hurt too badly. The movement brought on a fit of coughing as her disturbed lungs tried to expel at least one layer of trail dust. She unstrapped a leather water pouch from the back of the saddle and drank. Once again she was delighted by how cool and good the water was. No chemical aftertaste. This world had its pluses.

"We are making good progress today, majesty." Seery, the captain of the newly appointed Queen's Guard, brought her horse closer.

"Yes, I can tell." She jammed the plug back in the water skin. "I've been inhaling the evidence of that progress all morning."

A small frown skimmed across the captain's brow.

"If you would prefer to ride at the head of the column once again, I can call the vanguards and…"

With a sigh she could not help, she interrupted her escort.

"No, Seery. I took to heart your warning of last night. Dust or not, I'll stay safely in the middle of things where you can easily keep an eye on me. I was not planning on doing anything rash. Just making a comment."

"If it is the dust bothers you, we can send scouts ahead to damp down the trail."

"Good grief, Seery. Don't do anything of the sort. We're not going to put people out for such a minor thing." She smiled at the woman, trying to keep the conversation from any further escalation. "If it bothers me too much, I'll just..." she waved her arms in front of her, "...poof...you know."

The veteran border guard flinched. Cathryn pulled her tunic cuffs down hard over her wrists.

"Just kidding, Seery. Really. I'm sorry." It hadn't occurred to her that these soldiers would fear magic. Though it was likely only her magic they feared. She did, too.

The awkward moment was interrupted by the hard-riding arrival of one of the forward scouts, accompanied by Kern who had been circling the caravan all day looking for trouble spots. The scout and the battle chief were both let into the circle of guardians. They reined up hard, sending a new and bigger cloud of dust spiraling into the air.

"I bring the forward report, majesty." The scout was breathing hard. Cathryn loosed her own water skin once again and held it out to the man. He raised his eyebrows, glanced over at Kern who nodded very slightly, and then took the pouch and drank a small amount. When he was done, he looked down at his hands and clothes and back at the container. Confusion crossed his face.

"My thanks for the water, majesty. It was a most gracious gesture. I seem..."

As the scout's sentence hung, unfinished in the air, she realized the problem. He had wanted to wipe off the grime his dust-streaked hands and mouth had left on the water skin, but could find no clean inch of apparel or skin to do so.

"You seem in a hurry. I would wish your report is good news, but we will hear whatever you bring us."

She took the pouch from the man's uncertain grasp. He

looked relieved and Kern looked approving. Maybe she was starting to get the hang of this rulership thing.

"We have met groups of plainsriders coming this way from CorronKeep. The first of them should arrive in moments. They tell us that all Lintonese have been banned from the capitol. Any still in the city will be killed on sight. All who were able to escape are on their way here to join your army."

Kern's bass rumble joined in.

"We have places and duties for them. And most escaped with food enough for the time being. I will see they are brought into the caravan as they arrive." He hesitated the smallest of moments before adding, "If that is your will."

"Of course." She silently thanked Kern for giving her such obvious directions on how to deal with obstacles. Though this problem was not hard to solve. After the warmth and loyalty shown by those of Linton Province, she would have willingly taken any and all of them, no matter the cost.

But the thought of cost, brought her up sharply. There was a question the scout had not addressed.

"Why were all the Lintonese living in the capitol thrown out? Why at swordpoint? Did any of them tell you the reason?"

"Aye, majesty. When it was discovered by the Pretender that you and Duke Benedic had been sheltered by T'Tolyan at a clan town-manor, he was furious. Within the hour he learned of it, a warrant was issued for the arrest of T'Tolyan and his entire household. That same edict banished all other Lintonese on pain of death. It was also heard that the wizard had been told this army approaches. They say his rage is great."

"And these refugees…can they account for everyone? Did all make it out safely?" She winced at the need she felt to learn the answer to the next question. "And T'Tolyan?"

The scout scanned her face as he might have searched the

plains for signs of travelers. When he answered, it was clear he was choosing his words carefully.

"Almost all made it safely. Of the rest…there is no sign that the missing few have been taken. The lord T'Tolyan is one of those whose fate is yet unknown."

She looked away, out over the wind-blown grasses of the plains. Along her arms, small twitches pricked and skittered.

With a will, she pulled herself back to the matters at hand.

"Your name, scout, if you please."

"T'Faan, majesty."

"Thank you, T'Faan, for your swiftly brought and carefully given message. Kern, be sure this man gets rest and food. He has done us good service." She hoped the request would head off any feelings that she nursed a 'shoot the messenger' attitude. Dealing with people was damn complex.

"Aye, my queen." Kern nodded at her and waved the scout through the cordon of guards. The chief's approval once again slipped through and she felt the warmth of it.

"What should we do now, Kern? I'm guessing only a few of the refugees are trained soldiers. It can't be wise to have civilians in the caravan."

Kern reined over until he was riding beside her. "I have not heard the word 'civilians', though I believe I ken the meaning. Nay, it would not be prudent to have a great mass of folk attached to this force—though the majority of Lintonese are weapon-ready and most provincial militia would not care to face the youngest plainsrider unprepared."

"I don't doubt that. But still…and we've collected so many others on our way here. Those who joined us after we crossed the border do not have the look of warriors."

Kern squinted into the sun, scanning the forward wagons

as he replied. "We should encamp early this evening. Tomorrow we will reach the edge of CorronKeep. Tonight, we'll plan."

She shifted in the saddle with a twinge of pain. "Stopping early sounds good."

Kern chuckled. "I did think, majesty, that our strategies might be more easily considered were we seated, not mounted."

"You are truly a noble man, commander."

"I may miss most subtleties, but I can see a barn in broad daylight." With a long-perfected flick of leather, Kern guided his horse through the guard-circle and toward the head of the column.

But before she could revel in the brief moment of quiet and the prospect of walking, not riding, a trio of border wardens approached. Another dispute, no doubt. As the three came closer, she focused on her arms, drawing some physical strength from the power the invaders of her body had brought. Muscle cramps shot through her hands and she worked to massage them out even as a surge of energy brought her some relief from fatigue. It would be a long afternoon.

To catch any breeze that chanced the humid night, the sides of the meeting tent had been rolled up, leaving only gauzy curtains on all sides. But as far as she could tell, there had been no movement of the curtains to signal a freshening of the air. After the council had gone on for several hours, she could stand it no longer and reached again to the erratic magic within her and sought, by its force, to cool the tent.

But control was still an elusive quantity and the sudden chill that brought, for a cold moment, fogged breath and anxious silence was not what she had in mind. She decided it was better to sweat with her war council than worry them with temperature tantrums.

"It is not an ideal solution, I grant you." T'Meara's reasonable, calm tone showed no signs of strain even after the long debates of the night. "Nonetheless, those of my province can move quickly if need be. It is not necessary to deplete our force by more than a handful of warriors to escort those not of the army safely home."

Kern cut off further discussion with a curt, "Then so be it." Though T'Meara still sounded fresh, the battle chief was definitely near the end of his patience. One of the Begotten Guild masters who had arrived just hours before with a contingent of healers took a deep breath, obviously ready to debate further.

"We thank you, Master Sauter, for your concern." Cathryn spoke quickly, seeing that Kern was already flushed with temper. "You are right to be so careful with the refugees. But if the duchess vouches for the competence of the escort, who are we to argue? Better we spend our time marshaling what forces and plans we have just now."

Master Sauter looked anything but thoroughly convinced, though what he might have said was interrupted.

"In here are they?" From outside the tent came a familiar roar that made her heart beat so hard with relief it was almost painful. At her side, the usually tranquil T'Meara leaped from her chair, knocking it over in the process.

"T'Tolyan!" Before the name quite left the duchess' lips, the thin curtains were wrenched aside and the mountain of a plainsrider strode in, bringing with him a wash of fresh air and a noticeable lack of ceremony.

"Wife!" His laugh almost billowed the tent with its force. "You look council-weary. Come here and give me welcome."

T'Meara met her husband with a whoop of joy. The embrace that followed was so enthusiastic, Cathryn's ribs hurt just to watch it.

"Are you tired with your journey my lord?" T'Meara's question was so phrased that none in the tent mistook its meaning. Especially not T'Tolyan.

"Not so tired I cannot return your warm welcome with some invention when this meeting is done." T'Tolyan disengaged himself from his wife's arms and came toward Cathryn, grinning as he did so.

"Still put out with me, majesty?" He winked broadly. "Or am I enough forgiven you would ride my wagon again?"

Her jaw dropped. Snickers were heard from some of the council members and Kern was trying to cover a huge grin with his hand.

"Mind your impudence, husband." T'Meara's voice was stern with chiding, through her eyes crinkled with mirth.

"Nonsense." The rider-lord pounded Cathryn on the back so genially that she staggered. "This queen knows when friends should laugh. Besides, she will think me most wonderful, if indeed she does not already, when she sees the present I have brought her. It should be…where…?"

T'Tolyan went back to the tent's entrance and peered into the darkness.

"He was only a bit behind me," he muttered to himself in a rumble everyone heard. "Yes…there. Hurry up, man." With a flourish, T'Tolyan opened wide the entry, announcing, "See what I found."

The moment Benedic appeared in the doorway, a pale but smiling T'Orah and a red-cheeked Bushbin close behind him, the tent filled with exclamations. The council rose, almost in unison, and surrounded them, giving Benedic, in particular, the warm greetings and respectful salutations justly due a well-liked friend and a king-to-be.

She stood on the far side of the pavilion, alone and unremarked. The first, powerful onslaught of relief that had gripped her upon Benedic's entrance fled, leaving her hollow. She could feel no beat of a heart, no movement of blood warm and insistent, no electricity of nerve or synapse. Only a desolate quiet.

The thin tent walls breathed in and out with the press of the welcoming. The shiff-shiff of gauze in motion whispered the only words to pierce her silent void: He is beloved, you are tolerated. He belongs here, you are a mistake.

There was an interruption in the swirl of the councilors, the tone of the crowd modulated into upward ending notes, the sound of inquiry. From the circle, Benedic emerged, breaking through the ring of others. He made his way toward her. Everyone else fell into silence.

"Cathryn."

The sound of his voice touching her name rang like a bell.

He spoke again, standing before her and the whole of the company with eyes downcast.

"You bade me find my son and so I did. Then he and I both failed you. He gave his mother's notes to D'Brin—though the boy had no choice, being magically ensnared by the witch."

He took a deep breath. She could not breathe at all.

"I have no such excuse. Heedlessness and a stubborn spirit blinded me and I fell into D'Brin's trap. Corry and I would be imprisoned still but for T'Tolyan. He and his entire household risked all to rescue us."

A cascade of nervous energy reasserted itself the length of her spine. From its power, she found words to respond.

"There is not a plainsrider to whom we do not owe our lives and more." She could see the duchess of Linton and her husband bow slightly in recognition of the gratitude. "But you cannot have failed, Benedic, for Corry was safely brought out— and you as well. Though I do not see him with you."

"My son…" The catch in the duke's voice reduced the whole assembly to silence and sent a pang through her heart. "Corry has gone again—home and into danger. To rescue a friend and send to us those loyal of our province who will join this cause."

Of a sudden, she realized that he had come directly to her from his escape. The smell of hard-ridden horse and fatigue was on him and in the brightness of the room's lanterns, sweat drops sliding down his face caught the light. She took hold of the edge of her tunic sleeve and touched away the moisture.

His breath caught sharply in his throat. Never before had she seen this man startled. Dismayed, she realized how intimate and unexpected the gesture had been.

"I see you have ridden hard tonight. You should rest." The silence in the crowded tent now felt awkward and uneasy. "And there is no failure, my lord. You were sent to bring Corry from D'Brin's hand, and this is what happened. That you were helped in this by friends is no failing, but rather is a sign of how much you are loved."

Along her arms, the pricklings of magic stung and flickered. Approbation rose like a chorus from the host of rulers-past within her. And somewhere on the fringe of awareness, emotions she could not name, but dimly remembered, began to travel inward.

"Indeed, sir, that you accomplished your son's release and prevented D'Brin from having such a tender hostage fulfills the oathbonding so unexpectedly put upon you by someone else." She glanced at T'Tolyan, who showed no signs of shame over his past actions. "Give me the red cord of your bond and I will release you from it."

"I cannot, majesty. It is gone." Benedic finally brought his head up and met her eyes. "Because I could not speak the words of comfort I so desired to give my son, I gave him the cord of my bonding. It was all I could think to do."

From beyond them came rustlings and mutterings. It did not take a magically enhanced reading to see clearly that he had stirred up a tempest. Somewhere in the words that the council members spilled in their apprehension came the single word that sent a chill across her skin. Treason.

"Benedic, do you think this public forum is the place to discuss the matter?"

"Aye, majesty. This is the very place, before those who were loyal from the first, who, unlike myself, pledged themselves wholly and immediately. They, and you, should mete out justice for what I have done...and left undone."

The silence of uneasy anticipation spread throughout the tent. With no flourish, no warning, the duke knelt.

"I await your will."

In her mind, Cathryn saw the unrelieved gray of a Seattle winter sky. Saw herself lost in that grayness, hiding from conflict, ambition, need, life. Saw the moments when 'could have' became 'never will'. Heard the walls she built with words when others came too close. Felt the deadness of desire that has been tamped down, tied up, stored away, feared, forgotten. And because his dark hair was touched with gray, and because courage may be found in the smallest things, she found the words.

"Then this is my will which, as I speak with a hundred voices, is the will of the many. You are released from the oathbond because you have fulfilled it. You are not forgiven for giving away the bond cord," there was a collective intake of breath from the council members, "because there is no forgiveness needed. What you have done with a father's love, I affirm."

Reaching down, she took his arm, pressing upward until he

moved with her intent and rose to his feet. She pushed gently on his shoulder, turning him until, side by side, they faced the crowd.

"And this do I affirm as well: When the throne of Corronheld is taken back from D'Brin, whose evil I understand more than any other here, then willingly shall I yield the crown to its rightful heir. Though I should live a thousand lifetimes, never will I be other than what I am—one who has come to love you all well, but who is now, and always, a stranger. To the true and native prince do I give this, my oath."

Her fingers shook as she pulled the blue leather strand from her belt. When she held the cord out to him, it—and she— trembled. Yielding to that newly sprung courage that persisted even in the face of her fears, she turned to him until she could see his eyes.

And she knew that he knew. Knew that this oath could only be accomplished by her death. Knew that beyond her desire that peace return to Corronheld and her belief that he could bring it, was a desire she could not, would not, name but which would never leave.

His hand closed around hers.

"Not one of us would take this oath from you, my queen, least of all me."

He gently removed the piece of leather from her grip and bent to retie it on her belt. When he straightened up again, he signaled to T'Tolyan who started forward, digging in his tunic pocket as he came. He smiled as he held out his fist and then opened his fingers. There, crumpled on his palm was a red cord. Benedic took it from him.

"I have refused the truth until now. But now I see that evil has not come from other lands, but lies in wait wherever lives are lived. Believing that those of honest heart must trust each other and the greater good, I, with all the will my soul contains, bind myself to serve you." And he threaded the length of cord through the knots of his belt so thoroughly, it was not clear where the red leather began or ended.

The voices of the Passing and the wordless clamor of the worms rose in a suffocation of sound, driving her to speak ancient words of authority and power. But that part of her which was most herself fought, with all the stubborn and fearless courage that belongs to those newly loved, and won. She did not speak of duties and service, did not try enchantments. Speechless but strong, she turned and faced those who watched.

Kern pushed through the onlookers and raised his commander's voice.

"We are united. Dawn will see us come to the field of negotiation with the strength of oneness. The work of the council is done for the night. Tomorrow it begins."

"Tomorrow" echoed throughout the crowd. Then Bushbin opened the tent's entrance flap. Not a single council member misunderstood the signal. In moments, the room was almost empty. T'Tolyan glanced back at Benedic and nodded once before exiting, hand in hand with his duchess. Finally, only three were left: Cathryn, Benedic and Kern.

In the sudden intimacy of an almost empty room, she felt awkward. The strength of her silence began to ebb.

"Cathryn, I..." Benedic began.

Like a foghorn, Kern's voice cut through the tension. "It amazes me how such thin walls let in so little breeze." He grabbed a bit of gauzy curtain in his callused fingers and rubbed it thoughtfully. "I would believe that material so fine it allows those outside to see in would be...oh...airier, I suppose."

Benedic laughed and she relaxed at the sound. When the duke spoke again, it was in an easier tone.

"Do you suppose, old friend, that it might be more comfortable and less public if we were to, say…" Benedic arched one eyebrow and tilted his head toward Kern.

"…walk abroad in the night's coolness?" The battle chief managed somehow to retain a serious expression. "If you each cast a servant's spell, it might even render you nearly invisible to boot. Well, I have preparations to make. Good even to you both."

And with that, Kern left the council tent.

But his departure dropped her directly into confusion and a kind of embarrassment she had thought departed along with her younger years. What could she say to this man who, in the presence of witnesses, had just given his life to her? And she had offered hers to him.

As the tent settled back into place behind Kern's exit, Benedic turned to her once again and held out his hand. "Will you, then, walk with me?" He tried a hesitant smile. Much to her amazement, it made him look shy.

"I guess we must—or answer Kern for it." Her arm resisted her mind's order to raise—it seemed to take forever for her hand to finally come to rest on his. "And I suppose we ought to try the spell he suggested as well."

"I think not, for if you put as much power into your spell this night as you did when we first escaped CorronKeep, we may not be seen again until mid-summer."

She laughed with him, albeit tentatively, as they ducked through the entryway and stepped into the night.

Some quiet scent had crept into the night air of the camp, so subtle it had not the strength to enter the council tent. But as they moved past watch fires and sentries, it gently came, fragrant and cool, to her awareness. Because she wanted to know and, partly because any other subject was much more awkward to broach, she asked him what might be blooming at that time of night to produce such a delicate perfume.

"Ah, you have never seen our little folk." He changed the direction of their walk, heading toward the far north edge of camp.

"You have them here?" Her mind, the part that was one-quarter Irish, bumped against the phrase.

But he did not reply. Instead, he led her past the outermost fires and perimeter sentries until they reached the base of a hill.

"There." He pointed ahead of them into the night darkness. "Do you see them now?"

"See what?"

He turned to her.

"You have been lightblinded from the watch fires. Shut your eyes so they may open wide to take in the dark." He brought his fingers up to her face and gently brushed her eyes closed.

"There. Now. Open and see."

She slowly opened her eyes. Spreading out beyond them, all over the hill they stood by and the next, were low-growing flowers of the palest ivory. Each flower was so arrayed that the bloom looked, in the dimness and soft breeze, like the face of a child nodding in the moonlight.

"Little folk. I see now."

"Are they not wondrous?" He asked with words more sighed than spoken.

There was no other reply to make but to drink in the sight and smell of the night flowers. Long moments passed before she slowly became aware that the two of them were, for the first time, aligned. While flora-watching might not be the most crucial of activities, yet the pleasure and relief of being in one accord with this man was deeply satisfying.

"I wonder, my lady," he continued to gaze out over the dark

hills, "how you endure being so removed from your home? Were I in your place, I am not certain I could bear the pain of being separated from my world."

"It isn't so very much different here. Well, I suppose the magic and the lack of machines would seem huge to some. But it strikes me as a reasonable and constructive arrangement. And most of the other differences I've come to like—especially the people. Lucette and Corry, Kern, even that rascal T'Tolyan. It takes little work and no courage to feel affection for them— even for me, the cowardly queen of shutting away any but the mildest of feelings."

He turned toward her, the planes of his face catching as much of the moon's light as did the flowers dancing on the hillside.

"You are queen of a good deal, Cathryn, but not of being unfeeling or cowardly. Do you remember the first time we argued—late at night in front of the fire?"

She smiled. "I remember all too well—you were completely intimidating and I was totally overwhelmed. But I most certainly wasn't going to let you know that."

"I, intimidating? Nay, it was you commanded the conversation. Even then, though I despised the admission, I could not but admire your courage in the face of such enormous changes and wonders."

His confession made it difficult for her to catch her breath. Nor could she continue to look directly at him.

"I never thought...I mean, you have no idea how much your good opinion matters to me. And how much I need your help."

The duke looked down at the red cord knotted through his belt. "When I realized I had been so wrong, so blind to the true and resident nature of the evils stalking our land, I could not come to you quickly enough. You asked me, in the council tent, if I should have made my oath, asked my questions in a less public way. But I tell you this…"

He let go the leather cord and raised his eyes to hers.

"…I will no longer hide from that truth to which I paid such arrogant lip service. When my wife died, I sought to blame something, someone outside my world. I was wrong. In doing this wrong, I allowed the evil that was always here to grow and take other lives. My cousin Bayly. Reyfen, king and friend."

His voice cracked, yet he did not look away and she could not move, could not turn from him even had she wanted.

"It was my shame I waited too long to act. With all my heart, I believe you are the true choice for Corronheld. If you take up the crown for your lifetime, I will always be at your side. But, if you choose to lay down the power….if you…I will be there, as well. Never before you, never behind you. Beside you. I swear it."

A warm breeze stirred the rolling field of little ones so that they nodded in drowsy agreement. And his oathbonding had appeased the voices within her so that the darkness had become almost halcyon. But even in the embrace of the night's sweet perfume and the surety of the just-made pledge, disappointment weighed down a corner of the hope she had only tonight begun to nourish.

"Thank you." For a wonder, her words were steady. "I'm glad I don't have to go through the negotiations tomorrow without your help. If you could…"

Suddenly he turned toward camp. Almost in the same moment, she heard the noise as well. Just as she took the first step to return, a young herald came running, his long hair flying out around his head.

"Pardon the intrusion, but you will want to know what

awakens the camp." The boy struggled to catch his breath, whether from the running or from excitement it was impossible to tell. "Troops from Quarel and supplies from Chymion are even now arriving."

She saw Benedic begin a smile. He must be hoping this meant that one of his children was safe at least. She did not want him to wait on the answer.

"And pray, herald, who leads this welcome addition."

"Lucette of Forché, who bade me find you both with all speed."

Even before the sentence was finished, Benedic was moving toward camp with exuberant haste.

"Well." She smiled at the flustered messenger. "You must have a name, sir." The young man looked blank. "Do you?"

"Y-yes."

"And it is…?"

"I am Ladwin called. Majesty."

"You are a seasoned veteran at this heralding business, are you?"

"In truth, milady, I am but newly sworn into the office."

"Really. How 'newly'?"

"Three days ago."

"Well, Sir Herald, I would have never guessed." Ladwin puffed up enough that she ducked to avoid showing the smile that she could not stop. "And now it looks as if you will have to accompany me back to greet Lucette since the duke has father-business ahead of us. Shall we?"

The herald grinned back at her and, with the awkward sincerity of early adolescence, offered her his arm. She resisted the urge to decline this hesitant, unnecessary gallantry. Instead, she took his arm and, together, they managed the short walk back.

The place was astir because of the new arrivals. Arrangements for integrating the fresh troops were well underway. Kern passed by, a cluster of captains trailing in his wake catching the orders he tossed over his shoulder. Closer to the center of camp was a gathering of newcomers and veterans. It was toward this group that she steered. And, sure enough, as she neared, the circle opened and within it were father and daughter.

"Lucette." Cathryn could not restrain her relief and pleasure. At the sound of her name, the young woman broke free from the small assembly and came toward her. When but a few paces away, Lucette began a formal bow.

"Oh, no, my dear. Let's not have ceremony between us. Ever." Cathryn held out her arms and her friend stepped right in to a long, warm hug. It was when they disengaged from the welcoming embrace that she noticed the change in the girl's face and manner.

"What has happened to you, young lady?" She spoke in a low voice she hoped only Lucette could hear. The question seemed to have hit a target because the young woman did something Cathryn had read about but seen rarely on Earth— she blushed.

"I had some help gathering allies. It made the trip much more pleasant."

She glanced over Lucette's shoulder and saw that a fairly blissful T'Gault was part of the nearby group. It looked as though T'Tolyan's son and Benedic's daughter were seriously— no make that giddily—contemplating a union of provinces. So to speak.

"Does your father know that…" she polled her inner voices for a proper way of asking her question, "…that you and T'Gault have begun to make together-plans?"

A small frown creased the young woman's forehead.

"No. There has been no time to tell him. And will there

be a good time? Other matters, of much more import, must come first."

Cathryn sighed. "How well I know that. But don't worry, you and I will find a way you two can tell your parents. Right now, life is too uncertain to let any goodness be passed by."

Lucette gave her another hug, this one brief but very enthusiastic.

"Thank you, Cathryn."

At that moment, as Lucette moved back toward her father and the others, she noticed Benedic watching her. His eyebrows raised in question. She guessed he was very curious to know what she and Lucette had talked about so privately. But this was not the time or place for it, so she sent what she hoped was a reassuring smile to him and began checking with the leaders of the new arrivals on the state of their troops and how they might assist in tomorrow's affairs.

As she moved among her leaders, there came once again a faint aroma, this time not the fragrance of blossoms, but the scent of hope with a touch of joy and the dark spice of fear with a touch of death. An already long night was going to get much longer.

Chapter Sixteen:
BENEDIC

B Y THE TIME the members of the allied council finally returned to their tents for what little sleep could be snatched before daybreak, frost coated the camp. The abrupt, unnatural change from warm and humid to cold and icy caught him unprepared. Before he could settle into his cot with any chance of resting well, he had to rummage through his supplies for another blanket.

But even when he had warmed the bed with his own heat, sleep would not come. His mind would not shut down and it kept his weary body restless and disturbed. To pass the time usefully and perhaps to lull himself into a more relaxed state, he went over, again, the predicted votes of the Council of Corronheld on the morrow.

Of the five provinces, only Forché, Linton and Chymion were Cathryn's. And even then, Forché might still be under the control of D'Brin's puppet, Arilon. If so, his vote at the Council might be an empty one. Quarel and Kilder had not pledged to one side or the other, yet what information could gathered suggested they would both side with D'Brin. Still the provinces, at least, seemed tipped in Cathryn's favor.

The guildmasters were not so easy to predict. He pulled his blankets tighter around him and turned restively as he counted out their votes.

Esoteric Guild—completely D'Brin's. The more they heard of the wizard's influence in his own guild, the more it seemed that the heart of the rebellion, the darkest of the wickedness, lay with the Esoterics.

Makers Guild was a different story. The Soil Circle saw profit in supplying foodstuffs to both factions if war came, though they claimed a righteous neutrality now. Rock Circle, influenced strongly by Lucette, was for Cathryn. But Water Circle had lined up behind D'Brin for reasons no one had been able to discover. One circle for, one against, one abstaining. An uneasy stalemate.

It was straightforward with the Begotten Guild. All three circles had declared for Cathryn. And their Guildmaster, Morne, was the Council's current Mediator. That boded well.

Not so certain was the stance of his own Servants Guild. Almost without exception, the circle leaders and members stood behind Cathryn, to a great degree on his word. But the exception to that commitment was powerful and deeply influential. The Palace Militia.

He pulled up the blankets hard and then cursed himself for it. Now his feet were sticking up in the cold. Was there to be no comfort tonight? He threw back the covers and left the restless semi-warmth of the bed to search his pack once again—this time for another pair of socks and a thick sweater.

It was as he sat near the loosely-tied door flap of the tent, pulling on the second layer of wool, that he glanced outside and saw a faint light. If he had not been thrashing about in the dark for so long, his eyes would not have been adjusted and he would not have seen it. But there it was. Coming from so close by—from Cathryn's tent. At that moment, there came a muffled gasp.

He grabbed his dagger and ran out toward the queen's pavilion. As he reached her doorway, he took in a great breath, ready to call the alarum, and barged inside.

She sat, wrapped in a blanket, on the edge of her cot, a large unfinished banner laid across her lap. In one hand she held a threaded needle. The forefinger of the other hand was in her mouth. Her eyes were wide with surprise at his entrance.

"Majesty. My sincerest apologies for disturbing you." He tucked the now-unneeded dagger into his sweater pocket and tried to recover his sense of decorum. "I thought I heard you cry out. I thought you had been attacked again."

She took her finger out of her mouth.

"Damn it, I was attacked. See?" She held out the ailing appendage. In the light of the glowlantern, he could see blood welling from a tiny puncture. "It's this damn—excuse me—sewing. I wasn't born to it. I shouldn't have tried it again—I know better. It's just that I couldn't sleep and I've been told I need a personal banner for tomorrow and everyone in camp is busy with other things and I thought…"

She stopped and narrowed her eyes at him.

"You find this amusing, don't you Mr. Duke-Benedic-Whoever?"

The amusement within him threatened to erupt.

"Not I, milady. I understand. I, too, was having trouble sleeping. Though I had not thought to sew…it did not occur…" But he could go no further with words. The laughter began.

First she frowned, then she shook her wounded finger at him and opened her mouth to speak. But whatever imprecations she had wanted to pronounce were lost in her own laughter—the sound of which pierced him with a dagger's point of pleasure.

As her humor subsided to a smile, she set the banner and the needle down on the floor. "So now you know my darkest secrets. I hate sewing and I don't handle anxiety very well. I guess I won't be able to cross you ever again, now that you've got this kind of information to hold against me."

He went over, leaned down and picked up the green and white pile of materials and thread. Sitting cross-legged beside her, he began to sort out the wrinkled mess.

"Truly, you must be wary of me because I know these things—all the more so when you see that," he took a tiny, well-placed stitch, "I sew very well." He drove the needle through cloth again. "Very well, indeed."

She groaned. "Oh, that's even better. You're as competent at domestic skills as I am inept. Where I come from that would make you the perfect wife."

"Really? Sewing is such a common and rudimentary thing I cannot imagine it would set me apart for such high praise. Wife. Indeed."

He looked up at her and found, to his surprise, that she was showing some signs of being flustered.

"Oh. Well. It's just that…on Earth, mind you…we…well, not me in particular, but many others hold on to deeply stupid ideas about what kinds of jobs men and women do and how desirable certain of those skills are in a…um…prospective mate." She grimaced and shook her head. "Obnoxious, really."

He slipped the needle through a loop of thread and then bit off the tag end. He held up the pennon.

"There. Finished. Plus I've taken a couple of extra stitches where…well, where the—"

"Don't be coy. You redid the worst of my efforts. Right?"

He stood up and draped the large rectangle over one of the camp chests by the tent wall. "Actually, yes. But I did not mean to offend you. I was just fastening down one corner of this dark red cross-bar." Now he felt awkward and rushed to change the subject. "And wondering about the significance of the design."

She got up, wrapping the blanket more snugly around herself until only the lace-ends of her nightdress sleeves and her face showed. She moved over to where he stood and nodded at the banner.

"When I was told I needed a personal flag, I just put on stuff that meant something to me in this world. The green background represents Forché, where I was found. The white flower is the first truly unique plant I saw here—it was at the healer's lodge and Lucette brought some into my room. Seeker's Rose, I think they're called. The diagonal red bar…well, that's you. As it turns out."

She tucked her hand back inside the blanket. The gesture distanced her from him somehow.

"Me? How is that?"

She turned back toward the cot, away from him.

"Well, you came to see me that first day in a garnet-colored cloak. That's why I chose the color."

"And the bar slashed across the flag. How is that me?" He wanted to see her face when she answered. But she did not turn as she spoke.

"Actually the design was cut before you came back from getting Corry. So, the diagonal line runs across the flag because…because we crossed each other so much. It indicates impact—a negation. Sorry."

"Ah." The chill had crept into his bones and he pulled his

hands up into the sleeves of his sweater. "I understand. I had thought…well, it is late. Perhaps—"

She turned to face him.

"You had thought what?"

He shifted uncomfortably.

"Ah, well, I thought… Often now you consult the Passing voices, and I thought perhaps their memories had explained that a ribbon worn from shoulder to hip across the heart means that the person signified by the ribbon's color is dear to the wearer."

No wind stirred the tent, no sigh was made, no touch was taken. All hung, suddenly suspended in the smallest moment, waiting for the smallest word that, until he knew the yearning for it, he had not known he desired.

She opened her lips to speak, but before she could utter any word, his courage deserted him.

"Tomorrow will come all too soon for what must be done. I would not disturb you any further." He could not look her in the eyes; instead, he reached for her hand and, though there was some slight resistance, brought it out from where it lay, half-hidden in folds of wool, and lifted it to his lips.

He meant to give a farewell kiss, one that might be given to a queen by a subject. Until the moment he touched her, that was his only intent. But her hand was warm from the blanket and carried upon it the ever so gentle smell of sun-dried linen and the indefinable, unmistakable scent of her body. His senses beat against his reason so strongly he could not help but turn that hand over and kiss, instead, the tender place where palm met wrist.

"Benedic."

She breathed his name so softly, it was more sigh than sound. Yet nothing else could have made him lift his mouth from the touch it had of her. Nothing else could have given him the courage to dare her eyes. But even as he began to raise his head, an odd movement beneath his fingers made him take one more glance at the wrist he held. An arrow of darkness slid beneath his grip, under the skin he had just kissed. His arm jerked back and he caught his breath sharply.

She wrenched away her hand.

"Get out." The pain in her words opened a chasm between them and he fell into it where he stood.

"Cathryn, I—"

"Thank you very much for reminding me how repulsive— how… My own world always did a great job of that." She had begun to tremble violently. "How could you, of all people, forget that I must keep these horrors until all is set right. And when they do leave, I die. So. I can be disgusting, or I can be dead. You…" She took in a deep, ragged breath. "Get out." The air crackled with magic-to-be, wild and imminent. "Get out. Now."

He could not refuse. Her power compelled him. He knew, with a despair that drove the breath from his chest, he could offer no words that would undo what had just been done. Through the frenetically charged air, he left her pavilion for the less perilous darkness.

But as he neared his tent, his skin heated and his very self was battered with the waves of her distress. Damn the Passing and damn the worms for connecting them in such a fashion that, having hurt her, he must feel both her pain and his shame at provoking it.

He had to get farther away. Find some measure of comfort, some portion of wisdom, quiet. But where to go, whom to seek? By habit his steps turned toward Kern. But he changed course almost immediately. Kern was too recently bereft of his wife. Better to leave his friend to the distractions of battle preparations. T'Tolyan? No. He was too recently reunited with his wife.

This night should be theirs. Lucette? As grown as she might be, he could not be at ease seeking a daughter's advice in a matter so intimately his. He had no one to talk with about this, only the thin consolation of his own company. At least he knew a place where he might get a moment's peace.

He stopped at the supply tent and requisitioned a bedroll, stuffed with an extra blanket. It did not take long to find a hollow nestled beneath the hillside where the little folk nodded. He arranged the sleeping sack on the ground, hoping he had chosen a space where no stone or branch also made its bed. For the second time in one night, he set about warming cold blankets.

Yet, even when his feet were no longer cold, sleep proved elusive. In vain, he sought to find words he could have said, assurances he could have made. His heart would almost convince him that opening to the possibility of Cathryn should take second place to no other matter. Then his head would remind him that the welfare of Corronheld must be paramount. Almost his reason would persuade him that no physical manifestations should so affect him he would forgo the pleasure of her presence. Then his body, wincing even at the thought of the worms, would tell him she had the truth of it. He could never look on her with equanimity as long as the beasts remained. Not even her courage and wit, the nearness of her touch, the warmth of her hand, the allure of her stubborn heart could change that reality.

Surrounded by mute witnesses, he wept. For his wife, for cousin Bayly and friend-monarch Reyfen. For years wasted in hiding from hope and avoiding the truth of it, the needless walls he had built, his children who he now knew would leave him soon.

When the sun finally blushed the fragrant blossoms near

his makeshift bed, there was no rock or twig, no argument of soul or intellect with which he had not wrestled. And lost.

The wind blew bitter and erratic. Heat mages had run from place to place all morning trying to magick enough warmth to keep those who were waiting reasonably comfortable. What the spells couldn't do, bonfires and blankets struggled to produce as the councilors took their places in the circle of field chairs. Icy gusts whipped the four provincial and five guild banners that had been planted on pikes in the ground, circumscribing the meeting area.

He wanted to pace, but he did not. He wanted to move among the waiting guildmasters and provincial leaders, but he did not. He wanted to be at her side, but he could not. Instead, he sat upright, trying to look calm, beneath the rippling green and gray banner of Forché.

Already he had paid a high price for this theatre of calm; his stomach had refused to consider breakfast, his head ached from the strain of holding his face in pleasant planes and, though a spell of warmth had been placed on him only an hour earlier, his nose was cold. More than anything, he wanted the council to begin. More than anything, he dreaded the beginning of the council.

The last delegate, the Guildmaster of the Esoterics, took her place. Dressed in blackest furs, D'Clan seemed to suck in the light around her. Murmurs ran swiftly around the inner circle of council members and beyond, through the ranks of the opposing camps, as two attendants took places behind D'Clan. Attendants? Nay, bodyguards. It was obvious and unprecedented, a slap in the face of everyone else present.

He uncurled his fingers from the arm of his chair. Today he would not be provoked.

Into the space left at the north rim of the council circle stepped a lone trumpeter, who raised her horn and played the traditional strain that heralded truce talks. As the last notes were taken by the cold wind, movement began in the center of each outlying camp.

From the direction of CorronKeep came a glittering, sinuous procession. At its head walked D'Brin, dressed in the magnificent uniform of ceremony, robes of state which, even in themselves, carried the authority of tradition. At his back walked the witch D'Joan, accoutered in a costume of pageantry, a tunic and robe of midnight blue traced with goldthread and trimmed with deep, brown fur.

He shifted in his chair, determined not to stare at the finery coming toward them. Why was Cathryn not already here? He turned in the direction of their camp and saw that, from its center, a small movement had started. One figure, plainly cloaked, walked steadily toward the circle.

The Pretender arrived first, but not alone. Once again, the protocols had been broken. The other Earther hovered at D'Brin's side, whispering almost constantly in his ear. In a well-orchestrated move, two courtiers came forward to take the hooded robes of state from the self-proclaimed king and his consort. Gasps and murmurs rose from the assembled councilors and crowd. On his brow, D'Brin wore the circlet of Corronheld, and from his side swung the Regent's Sword, which was called Justice. From a gold cord around the witch's neck hung the Consort's Pearl.

That they should wear those signs of legitimacy before the council had even begun the debate...! His heart beat loudly in his ears. He almost missed seeing Cathryn arrive, quietly and without fanfare, and take her place in the circle opposite

D'Brin. She stood unmoving so that, gradually, like the ripples of a pebble dropped in a pond, her quiet spread to those nearby and then farther and farther out until all was silence.

From her seat near the trumpeter's space, Morne, master of the Makers Guild and mediator of the council, rose and faced the contenders. Benedic could no longer feel his fingers in his gloves.

"On this day is convened the Council of Corronheld under a flag of truce. The purpose of this unprecedented and most serious gathering is nothing less than mediating claims to the throne itself. All Corronheld holds this convention wholly and rightfully accountable for what is said and done here.

"Hear, then, all of you, the order that will bind the words, deeds and deliberations of this council." Mediator Morne paused, narrowed her eyes and scanned the circle, now unbroken. "Each of the Claimants may give three statements. The order of speakers will be decided by lot. Then, upon recognition of the mediator, councilors may rise to offer evidence and arguments. Should necessity warrant it, a councilor may call forth witnesses. When all have been heard, then each Claimant may make a final address to the assembly. At any time, judgments may be cast by the placing of a voting stone in the verdict circles."

A sweep of Morne's arm indicated the fist-sized whitewashed stone by each councilor's place and the two spots, outlined in ash, on the trampled turf. One verdict area had an Esoteric guild pennant staked in the middle of it. The other had the new banner: a white Seeker's Rose against a field of forest green with a slash of garnet.

Benedic discovered he had been holding his breath. He took in a deep draught of cold air that smelled of trampled grass and made him shiver.

Morne raised her arms and voice to include the onlookers ranged around the outside of the council circle.

"To each and to all present, our demand is plain and irrevocable: This assembly must hear without distraction, decide without coercion and dismiss without retaliation. The truce will hold. The verdict will hold." She lowered her arms and then, in the immense and icy silence that followed, announced, "Let the Claimants' lots be cast."

The herald entered the circle, holding a cylinder the size of a small cask. Stopping directly in middle of the circle, he shook the container and then tossed its contents over his shoulder. Turning, he walked to where the two metal discs landed.

An errant burst of wind tore the hood down on Cathryn's cloak, picked up her hair and tossed it wildly around her face. Her expression did not deviate from the patient, calm and attentive look she wore, though he thought he saw a minute tightening around the lips.

The herald bent to examine the lie of the cast plates. From outside and around the circle came the creak of leather and the rustle of cloth as the many also leaned forward to see what destiny had been tossed on the frost-beaten ground.

"The Great Seal lands on the Esoteric plot. He will speak first. The Sword of State lands on the Seeker's plot. She will speak second." So saying, the herald bent to retrieve the discs and then withdrew. A greater silence, broken only by the thin shrieks of wild wind and the crack of buffeted cloth, built itself around the field.

D'Brin stepped forward so calmly he seemed to glide. His stately movement was marred only by a tiny, abrupt jerk of his hand in D'Joan's direction. Benedic wondered if anyone else noticed how she had to be warned not to accompany the wizard. But there was no time to look around at the crowd, for D'Brin was ready to pronounce his three sentences and he wanted to hear every word, see every gesture.

"Because this day does not give us Reyfen as King and companion, we mourn. Because, though he is gone, he is not lost to us—" D'Brin tapped his chest with his finger, "—we rejoice. Because traitors, jealous of the Passing, seek to practice their wickedness on us, we bring our case before those who work justice so that peace may prevail."

He measured and admired D'Brin's presentation. The tone was serious, the voice well-modulated, the statements pointed but not overwrought. It was masterfully done and, judging from the faces of those who heard, well received. How had this usually reclusive wizard suddenly become so skillfully charismatic? Yes. There it was. The slightest tang of Servant magic, very well hidden, heavily masked and somehow both familiar and alien. He glanced at D'Joan, but the witch's face was unreadable.

Could Cathryn feel what was going on? He forced himself to release his tight grip on his chair. Too much was riding on the next few moments.

A stray gust of wind lifted Cathryn's cloak and whipped it so violently it cracked. The sound, loud and sudden, caught the attention of the entire company. All turned to hear the other Claimant.

Yet in that space of quiet, she did not speak, but moved. Carefully and slowly, she walked across the circle, approaching D'Brin. The gathered council members, onlookers and he leaned forward and suspended breathing. What was she doing?

She came very close to the wizard, began a slow bow, extending her arms toward him as she did so. This wasn't what they had planned. Was she conceding?

Suddenly, she twisted slightly, plunged one hand toward D'Brin's side and withdrew the Regent's Sword from the scabbard at his belt.

"Assassin! Assassin!" D'Joan screamed out the word. The crowd erupted in shouts and panic.

Guards ran toward the confrontation, but before they reached her, Cathryn quickly turned and took a position in the center of the circle, holding Justice high above her head. She closed her eyes and began to chant words that, though he could not decipher them, were plainly the makings of a spell. Guards, spectators and councilors alike stopped where they were and watched.

Slowly the tip of the sword sank downward until it pointed out at the council members, parallel with the ground. She began to turn, or rather it seemed the sword turned her, as if it were the needle of a compass seeking true north. Around and around it went, describing the equator of the council. Then it slowed. Then it stopped.

It was pointing directly at him. He could almost feel the cruelly sharp blade tip at his heart, a heart that pounded in his ears.

She opened her eyes and looked directly at him. He couldn't read her expression. He took a slow breath and rose until he was standing firmly and evenly, and waited.

She crouched just a bit and then, as she straightened up, she tossed the sword end over end up into the air. It flashed and turned, hung for a long moment at its zenith, then began its journey downward. As it descended, strange sparks and flares flew off the blade and hilt, hissing and spitting as they struck the ground. The sword fell and turned, fell and turned, coming down closer and closer to him. At the last moment, he caught it by the hilt.

It was all he could do not to cry out. Those close to him did cry out. Murmurs raced around the assembly. When he thought he could control his shaking hands, he raised the sword above his head so all could see the engraved letters which had been revealed: Truth.

Without uttering a sound, Cathryn had made her first statement.

The hilt of his province's sword was hot—almost to the point of being painful. But no almost-pain could make him let go of the long-absent, and now so triumphantly returned, weapon. He drew the borrowed sword from his scabbard and stuck it in the ground beside him. With profound relief, he settled Truth were it belonged and turned to see what Cathryn would do now. All eyes, even D'Brin's hooded ones, were upon her.

She threw back one side of her cloak, revealing an empty baldric and scabbard, then once again began to move. Round the inner edge of the council circle. Slowly. As if she were blind and must feel her way. Yet her eyes were open, seeking, searching.

When she reached the Esoteric Guild flag, she stopped. Benedic drew in a breath and forced down the awareness of his aching head and the knotted muscles across his back. He knew he was only one of many straining to see what would happen next.

Only D'Clan, the object of Cathryn's focus, remained markedly incurious. Wrapped in black, the guildmaster stayed as she was, leaning back in the field chair, hands concealed in the lush darkness of fur-covered sleeves.

Cathryn did not speak, only pointed at one of D'Clan's bodyguards and then motioned the man to come forward. The guard did not move. She gestured once again and then waited.

Though his eyes were gritty from staring so fixedly at the scene, Benedic could detect no movement from either the Esoteric guildmaster or his queen. Yet something was moving. He rubbed his eyes and looked harder.

There. Between the two women tiny motes of light and dark, just on the edge of sight, whirled and surged. The hair on the back of his hands stood on end as he felt and recognized the phenomenon. He had experienced it twice before—Cathryn's wild magic, born of anger and need. Underneath that swirled a darker tide. D'Clan.

For long moments the battle raged, undetectable by all else, but felt as a creeping uneasiness and evidenced in the watching crowd by rustlings, shifting and whispers. Cathryn had become pale. An unhealthy sheen covered D'Clan's face.

Then, just as he could no longer bear the tension, D'Clan's bodyguard jerked forward, step by contested step, until he stood a scant pace in front of Cathryn. His arms began to raise from his sides, certainly not of the man's accord, for his body was rigid with strain as he fought to resist what was happening to him. But inexorably his arms did rise, until they came parallel to the ground. It was then Cathryn slowly leaned forward and reached toward the guard's now unprotected scabbard.

From it she drew, so swiftly that it rang in the drawing, a sword. As she had done before, she threw it into the air above her. It turned over and over, a shower of sparks and molten metal flying from the blade. She caught the sword and, as he had just done before her, lifted it high for all to plainly see the word it carried: Justice. The Sword of the Crown. Disguised and hidden by Reyfen before his death, its location a mystery, revealed only to the true taker of the Passing.

The second statement had been made.

Now the crowd burst into shouts and calls. Those on the outer edges pushed and shoved, trying to get a closer look. Council members tried to make themselves heard over the din. Across the circle D'Brin had become as still as a stone. Suddenly, one of the guards near the wizard began to run toward the middle of the circle.

Benedic yelled a warning and started running, knowing, even as he did, he could not make it to Cathryn's side in time. Over her shoulder he saw the terrible glitter of a dagger blade descending.

Thunder. Falling. Smell of lightning. Taste of dirt.

He struggled to get up from the cold ground, stunned to discover he had been knocked down. Shaky from the suddenness of the battering, he finally managed to stand.

Cathryn was safe. She stood, untouched, in the center of the Council circle. Limping from welts he could feel forming even as he walked, he crossed to her.

Then he saw it. Delicate threads of smoke, twining in the shivering air, rose from the assassin's corpse, a charred ruin, anonymous but for a nightmarishly warped dagger still trapped in finger bones stripped of flesh.

He could not look on it. He sought her face. And found the horror he had not yet time to feel. She had done this. She knew she had done this. Though she had not planned it, this was now her third and final statement in all its terrifying finality.

He took off his cloak and laid it over the place where danger had once been and death now was. Even as he straightened up from the gruesome task, he caught sight of D'Clan moving. She picked up the Esoteric Guild's voting stone and walked toward the verdict circles.

"Hear me, all you who have witnessed this abomination." The guildmaster's voice carried to the farthest onlooker. "The woman who claims our throne is not of Corronheld. She has found us, intruded upon us, taken our magic, ripped it from its former uses and turned it into a weapon of such evil as cannot fully be fathomed by any who have even the smallest acquaintance with good." D'Clan reached the edge of the ash-marked circle where D'Brin's banner had been planted. "More than that, this usurper has stolen as well, with foul alien spells, a mirror-copy of the Passing."

The crowd stirred and moaned, a beast in pain. But the black-clad master forced her words down upon the sound.

"More. More has she done. Her perverted magic extends her life against the poison of the bloodworms. She will not die as she should, but unlawfully lives to wreak havoc and wickedness on us all. If..." Here D'Clan raised the whitewashed rock high above her head. "If we choose she who trespasses, then we choose death. But if we cast our lot with D'Brin, the true and native king, we embrace life."

D'Clan put her guild's voting stone in the space beneath D'Brin's pennon. That done, she gathered her robes so they did not touch the ground and made a meaningfully wide arc to avoid walking near what Benedic's cloak covered. All around, the crowd stirred and began a low and dissonant muttering that troubled his ear and affronted his fidelity.

The Esoteric vote needed a strong counterbalance. Cathryn looked too distraught by what had happened. She had not even moved from the now unfortunate center of the Council circle. It was time he cast his and Forché's lot before all. Summoning a speaker's spell to be heard and reaching deeply for clarity, he drew in a breath.

"So a guild's stone has been cast. Would that D'Clan had heard all evidence before so doing. To the rest who more wisely wait to be fully informed, listen to what D'Brin would keep from you."

As he took in another breath, the echoes of his just-spoken words registered with him. They sounded flat, uncertain. Beneath the echoes, he felt the current of the crowd sweep away from him. What was wrong? He quickly glanced at Cathryn and saw she was frowning. She closed her eyes, bent her head and crossed her arms tight against her chest.

He chanced a darting glimpse at D'Clan, but the guildmaster was listening distractedly to a courier whispering in her ear. What about D'Joan? Ah. Her head was thrown back, her eyes closed, her fists clenched at her side. Another unseen battle was raging—and this time he was the focus.

He tried to swallow, but his throat was dust. He had to go on.

"Reyfen was my king and my friend. When his life was near its ending, I felt the pull of the Calling. But I was not free to take the Passing, for D'Brin and his shadow witch held me captive. They brought me to Reyfen's deathbed. Why? Because D'Brin could not trigger the Passing. Only the true Heir could do so."

As he struggled to speak the right words rightly, Benedic could feel the opposing magicks strive against each other. Yet, with each phrase, he heard strength, volume and certainty return to his voice.

"As the Passing began, Reyfen's strength left him but a moment and he stumbled. Cathryn, who was also held captive by D'Brin, reached to help the dying king. It was a gesture sprung from natural compassion, but it brought her the burden of ultimate service. It brought her the Passing and, with it, the crown of Corronheld, which she has assumed with all good grace and care."

He turned and pointed at D'Brin.

"If Cathryn is not true queen and but stole a mirror-copy of the Passing, then ask this Pretender why he did not know where the Regent's Sword was hidden. Ask him why he carried a disguised sword of Forché and where he could obtain it if not from an unwilling prisoner. Ask him why, if our queen, whose heart and soul are now Corronheld's, must be hated only because she was born elsewhere and elsewhen, then why does D'Brin consort with an otherworlder himself? The witch, D'Joan, is from the very same place as Cathryn, brought here by the wizard for his own purposes—vile purposes he pursued beyond reason, even to the death, nay the murder, of my wife."

He paused to let his revelation be fully absorbed by the crowd. He heard a higher pitched murmuring and, though the acrid smell of confusion and fear remained strong, he knew he had hit the mark. Bless Cathryn for keeping the witch's spell at bay. He glanced at her and felt his elation desert him. She was pale and trembling. He must hurry to finish before she gave out.

"Many of you know me, have dealt with me, for years. I would not send assassins to silence competitors. I would not force those who oppose me to kill in defense of self." He took a quick glance at the mound covered by his cloak, knowing full well he was not the only one to do so. "You also know how much can be wagered on my word." He walked back to his chair and retrieved his province's voting stone. "I declare to you, upon the evidence I have witnessed and upon mine own honor, that Cathryn is the true Queen. Here is the decision of Forché Province." He placed the stone in the ash-marked circle under Cathryn's banner. "And so I do pledge my own allegiance, my service, my life."

Even as his last word echoed over the gathering, T'Meara stood up and brought Linton's stone. When it was settled firmly next to Forché's, she, too, spoke.

"We of Linton are among those who know Duke Benedic, his deeds, his life, his merit. He has not hidden himself and his purposes for these many years, but has been fully open to the scrutiny of those he serves. And he has been found worthy. Linton trusts the intentions of the Queen, for we have supped and ridden and shared water and the night sky with her. She is not stranger to us, but our sovereign."

The duchess raised her arms high and gave the long, loud trill which was the sound of victory among the plainsriders. It was picked up and returned by all the Lintonese throughout the crowd. Before their exultation was finished, Duchess Ekko of Chymion strode to the middle of the circle. She raised her voting stone and her voice.

"Chymion knows the truth. We spend our days with farmlands, orchards and vineyards. We are too close to life to mistake it." She placed her vote under Cathryn's green-backed banner. "So says the Province of Chymion."

Benedic felt hope return so strongly it gave new light to the day. He and the two duchesses returned to their places with more confidence than they had left them. It was now up to the rest of the guilds and provinces to follow their lead.

But he had only just sat down when Guildmaster Tylew rose and made his way to the center of the circle, a voting stone in one hand and a scroll in the other. In all the Servants Guild, Tylew was the most renowned as political strategist and the frown of disapproval featured on his brow made Benedic uneasy. He watched the master signal to four attendants who came into the Council circle and went straight to the body of the assassin. They tucked the cloak more firmly around the charred mass and, under the watchful eyes of all present, carried the remains away. The assembled crowd, once again a single entity, gave a troubled sigh and winced away from the sad parade. Cathryn, who had not yet moved from the place where she had been when the attack had come, finally turned and walked slowly back to her place in the outer circle.

Now that the attendants had left with their terrible burden, Tylew held out his hands and surveyed the scroll and stone they held. The man's utmost attention directed at the items drew in the attention of all, until a focused silence once again made itself apparent. Into that receptive quiet came the guildmaster's deep, smoky voice.

"This is a sad hour. For these hundreds of years our homes have been blessed with harmony, our hearts with the fruits of unity. In one day, in this hour, all is swept away. Our beloved King Reyfen is gone. The surety of the Passing, its heretofore unbreakable connection with the past and its powerful usefulness for the future, shaken. And the peace of centuries shattered, replaced with a terrifying schism which threatens to estrange guilds, provinces, friends, wives and husbands, parents and children."

Benedic closed his eyes. Tylew was right. What an unhappy day that should see them lose the life they had always known. His heart sank.

"And yet—" Tylew's voice held a note of hope. Benedic opened his eyes and looked to that note.

"And yet even in the shadow of this tragedy comes the possibility of a greater glory. D'Brin and his colleagues have not hidden away these last few years, but have immersed themselves in study, patiently and persistently testing the boundaries of the known, taking learning beyond the limits of convention. And when their studies revealed a vast, new vein of knowledge, one that will enlighten and enrich us all, what did they do?"

Tylew thrust the scroll he clutched up above his head, waving it for all to see like a treasure to be viewed. Benedic wanted to reach for it, read it. The need to know was a fire within him. From the crowd came cries of "tell us—tell us."

"These scholars petitioned the Servants Guild. Help us, they wrote in all humility, find a leader, for we are but explorers untrained in matters of rule. We have found the way to mine the riches of many worlds, to take from other places, other times, the brightest and most potent wisdoms but fear we cannot share it justly across Corronheld entire."

"Yes, yes," from the crowd.

"We, of the Servants Guild, asked ourselves: Where can we find one who possesses both the power of a great leader and the scholarship of a sage to judiciously steer the course of the state through these unknown waters? And even as we debated, such a one was raised up. Not from the Servants Guild, though the honor would have been great, but from the Esoterics themselves. As he lay dying, our beloved Reyfen named and touched D'Brin."

The guildmaster now raised his other hand high. The voting stone he held gleamed white like a well-picked bone.

"The Servants Guild pledges to the rightful king. May he open our minds and fill our purses. Hail D'Brin."

From the assembled throng came cries of affirmation. "Hail to the King. D'Brin. Long life to King D'Brin." Duchess Clayre of Quarel and Duke Parll of Kilder came forward and each laid their voting stones beneath the Esoteric banner. As the two returned to their places, they were accompanied by exclamations of support. Then Tylew began to stride along the inside of the circle, still holding the scroll and stone high. A swell of shouts rose as he rounded the circuit. Benedic rose from his chair as the master approached, excited, hopeful, ready to...

What was that? Something Tylew was wearing glinted and made him squint. It looked like...

He shifted slightly so that, as Tylew passed directly in front of him he got a swift look at where the purple robes gaped across the guildmaster's chest.

Yes. A medallion all too familiar and malevolent. The leader of all leaders, mentor to the Palace Militia, had been ensorcelled.

He swallowed hard. He, too, had almost been victim of Tylew's imposed magic and subverted charisma. The shouts of the crowd rose as the guildmaster completed his circuit and laid his stone in D'Brin's space.

What had this performance done to Cathryn? He looked across and saw that her eyes had become wide, troubled 'O's.

Yet, against the pallor of her face, her lips were still a vibrant red. No. It was blood that was so bright. She must have bitten through her lip. Creator protect her. And protect us all.

Then he could not see her, for Guildmaster Sauter blocked his vision. Standing within the Council circle, the head of the Begotten guild, attired in simple robes as white as his beard, his hands empty at his sides, patiently waited. Benedic found himself caught by the man's calm. When quiet once again descended, the master raised his left hand in an ages old gesture of benediction.

"From the guild of life, peace to you and health. Like the master of Servants, I, also, have two items that you must see." Sauter made a small gesture of beckoning. From the area near the Begotten's flag came a pair of healers who, between them, held a struggling prisoner covered completely in a gray winding sheet, as if the miscreant were already dead. Behind these three came a green and brown clad forester bearing the guild's voting stone. As this strange parade neared the guildmaster, he spoke again.

"We have not always been the guild of life. Long ago, led astray by our own arrogance, we used our inborn magicks not to heal body and spirit, but to persecute and kill. Of all the guilds, we alone once had four divisions. Three still survive today, the Plant, Animal and People circles. The fourth became so foul, so terrible, that it was disbanded forever. Or so we thought."

A freezing gust of wind pulled at Sauter's robes and ruffled his beard. Benedic clenched his jaw, willing his teeth to stop chattering so he could hear Sauter clearly.

"But terrible reports have come to us and now we know that our most foundational fear is realized." The guildmaster pulled away the sheet from the captive. Gasps and curses rose from the crowd at the sight of the black and gray clad man revealed to them.

"Takers are among us again." Sauter's voice turned hard, his face stern. "Those who have no business but death have stepped from the darkness. Who has brought this abomination on us? Who has made flesh this nightmare of old?" Sauter reached for the white rock held by the forester. "We have searched for the demon who unleashed the Takers and found him wrongfully wearing the crown of Corronheld. We condemn him and choose life."

Guildmaster Sauter laid his voting stone in Cathryn's decision circle and led his party from the field, forsaking even his Council chair, walking past it toward the healer's tent at the northernmost edge of the crowd. The number of stones in each contender's circle was now equal. A tie.

Only Morne of the Makers Guild had not indicated her guild's decision. Benedic sought for some clue in the woman's expression but found none. Slowly she rose from her chair, cleared her throat and found words.

"Of our guild, the three circles have decided thusly: Rock Circle names Cathryn and instructs me to say their choice is as solid as the medium in which they work."

Cries of approval came from here and there at that announcement.

"Water Circle names D'Brin and instructs me to say their choice is as inevitable as the tide."

Benedic nails dug into his palms so hard he hissed in pain.

"And Soil Circle." Morne paused, raising her empty hands in front of her. "Soil Circle abstains and instructs me to say they are as immovable as the deeps in which they practice their talent."

Swifter than startled birds, a flight of whispers lifted from the crowd. Benedic stood, reaching for the hilt of his sword as Morne fulfilled her final duty as mediator and delivered the verdict.

"Equal are the lots cast for the Claimants. Maker Circle cannot, will not, break the tie. By default, as is the law, the verdict is—"

But her last word was lost as council members and crowd erupted in chaos. Within him, the word left unheard, but so deeply feared, pierced him again and again as he struggled against the raging tide of onlookers who flooded the council circle.

War.

Chapter Seventeen:
CATHRYN

A FTER TWO DAYS of trying to untie logistical knots, inventorying and deploying weapons, planning and re-planning battle strategies, it was a toss-up as to whether she was more numb in the area used for thinking or the one used for sitting. To make matters worse, a dismal and cold rain had started a scant hour ago, falling mercilessly ever since. The entire camp was a chill, dreary swamp.

Inside the pavilion, it was not much better. This was the fifth group to meet since midday meal and, what with the weather and the strain, the tent smelled like wet dogs.

Cathryn sighed and tried to focus back on the discussion. Neevan was still holding forth. No surprise. It had been hard to get the sculptor talking but, once started, he seemed impossible to stop.

"...and that, as I'm sure you can now easily see, is the relationship of the fluid shape to the deployment of foot soldiers.

Now, historically, there have been two schools of thought as to—"

"Thank you, Master Artist Neevan." Kern's bass overrode what threatened to be another lengthy recitation. "Hearing you once again brings back very clearly your lectures to my recruit class so long ago."

Neevan puffed up a bit and smiled broadly. Kern plowed on.

"But you have not addressed the major problem: The wild magic we fear will be used by D'Brin's witch. She has already bespelled medallions which are being worn by most of the militia captains. And what information we have been able to get from the Pretender's camp suggests that D'Joan is planning to direct mighty spells over the entire battlefield. What we must know is what type of magic, of the Esoteric kind especially, will be used and how we might counter it?"

She watched Kern survey the painters, counselors, sculptors, writers and bards who had joined them at the meeting table. His frown told her he thought the situation grim. His downturned mouth eloquently gave his estimate of how much help he thought this particular group could provide. These were the only defectors from the Esoteric Guild they had been able to gather. All of them were from the Spirit Circle—which made her wonder anew what help a bunch of artistic types could possibly be in a war.

"Well," Neevan began, small wrinkles of frustration appearing around his eyes, "that is just what I was getting to, Battle Chief."

Kern leaned back in his chair and folded his arms, looking for all the world as if he were about to submit to the torturer's tools. Across the table, Linton's duchess repressed a grimace and T'Tolyan squirmed mightily in his overstrained camp-chair.

"You see, we who work in shapes know that once an item, a piece of jewelry for example, has been spelled, no other magic will work against it. Removing it from contact with the wearer will countermand the effects. However, there is sure to be some supplemental spell compelling the wearer to resist, rather actively, the item's removal. Though we have not tried it before, perhaps a counterspell aimed at the associated compulsion would be possible. "

T''Tolyan's hearty bass boomed his thought to the assembly.

"Is this not a matter for the strength of soldiers, rather than the cunning of wizards? Why can't the medallions simply be removed by force as the flow of battle allows?"

Neevan and Kern looked at him. The sculptor seemed to have no reply, but Kern ventured one.

"Aye. That would be simplest, I suppose. Using magic as an offensive weapon is still new to us. Perhaps looking for a complicated solution is not necessary."

"You are right, Kern." Cathryn smiled at her commander in chief. "A straightforward answer might be the best we can do. The laws of the Council gave each army two days to prepare for battle and that planning time is almost gone without finding an answer to the biggest obstacle: a whole battlefield blanketed by magic. How will Joan create it? I am too new to this power and this place to guess how it will be done. And if we don't know what she will do, how can we plan a defense?"

"I may have an idea."

At first she could not determine who had spoken, only that the voice was ripe, throaty and rang of authority. Then the very tiny and very elderly woman sitting directly across the table from her opened her eyes, raised one brow and rose from her chair with a surprising fluidity.

"I am Nimira, instructor/mentor at the Storyteller's Academy. I have been a bard and teacher for some little time." Even Cathryn could tell the 'some little time' was a massive understatement. "For the last few years I have noticed the increased activity and secrecy which has come to surround the Unseen Circle. It is to my shame that I did not understand what I was seeing."

Nimira leaned forward, bracing herself by placing her palms on the table.

"We who tell stories have neglected to tell the hard ones, the tragedies which convince our hearts that evil brings inevitable ruin; that, though dreams are reached by uncompromising paths, there are many shortcuts to every nightmare. In this, we have failed our people. Now we offer to become a line of defense."

Cathryn heard the words plainly enough, for the bard's voice still evidenced the carrying power and diction of one well trained to reach the public ear. But what was meant was not so clear. A quick glance at Kern, T'Meara and T'Tolyan told her they were nonplused as well.

"We are glad you are willing to help, Master Nimira." There seemed to be no way she could avoid sounding dubious. "But I'm unsure how storytelling might fit into battle plans."

Nimira straightened up into a teacher's stance.

"I do not expect you should know. Even were you not newly among us, even with the memories of the Passing, you could not know. What I propose has never before been attempted. Our proposition is this: The witch, as do you, possesses magic bound by no training, tradition or discipline. It is strong, and it can be deadly."

There was a twinge near Cathryn's wrist. Her lethal response to the attempted assassination at the truce council was still a fresh rawness of guilt.

"But D'Joan has been these ten years in contact only with members of the Unseen Circle. Because of this, and what we can discern about the nature of your imposed abilities, we who also deal with magicks that affect the unseen may be of great use. We propose to raise a mighty barrier over the battlefield that will prevent the use of any magic at all, by either side in the conflict."

Sputtering in alarm, Kern nearly started from his chair.

"Master Nimira—how…? You cannot be serious. It has never been done because it cannot be done. Should not be done. Think of all we will lose without access to military magicks? How can we function?" The battle chief looked to Cathryn, a wild plea for support evident in his dismay.

"It is an interesting idea." Ignoring Kern's agitation, she focused on the bard's concept. "It bothers me that soldiers rely so heavily on magic that could so easily go astray."

Nimira nodded. "True enough, majesty. I see you have the drift of it. Traditional military spells deal, on the whole, with communication, morale and the enhancement of weapons. It will not be difficult to substitute articulate heralds and determined runners for ensorcelled couriers and message boxes. As for morale, I believe having truth and an excellent group of epic-singers on our side will be more than enough. And, if our warriors know they cannot rely on a spell to cover up lack of attention to the use of a weapon, perhaps they will lean, instead, on skill and discipline." The bard looked over at the battle chief, who still had not been able to close his mouth. "Or are your troops so ill trained, commander, that this will be a problem?"

Kern's face turned red. She thought the poor man was going to explode. As it was, he could barely spit out his reply.

"Our troops, Master Bard Nimira, have trained as hard and fight as well as any in Corronheld. My life on it. But I, myself, and my wife when she still lived, also trained most of the Palace Militia. They, in turn, have drilled the troops that have joined

D'Brin's army. What could possibly be gained by taking away the advantage of spelled weapons?"

Nimira quirked an eyebrow at Cathryn. It was obviously a cue for her to provide the answer to Kern's question.

"Ah, yes. Well, commander." She poured all the confidence she could muster into her tone. "Your exceptions are well taken, but I believe I see what Nimira has in mind. D'Brin's troops, careless in their reliance on magic, will be unprepared for its loss. We will not be careless nor surprised. Thus, the advantage will be ours."

"Exactly." The bard master nodded again, adding a slight smile this time.

Kern had no such response. "But, reserve troops held off the field—they will not be covered. And the healers. When they go out upon the field of battle to care for the wounded, magicks are used. Any advantage found in surprise would be lost in needless and terrible deaths if our healers cannot do their work. Majesty, you cannot allow—"

"Hold, Kern." She raised her hand to stop him but nearly could not manage to lift her arm. The worms suddenly curled and lashed so frantically, it felt as if each and every muscle from shoulder to fingertips had been twisted into a knot and set on fire. She cried out and slammed her arms on the edge of the table, desperate to trade a known pain for the other, deeper one. Against the backdrop of that agony, the memories of those locked within erupted. In her mind's eye she saw scenes of carnage—long ago battles fought before the guilds had tamed the magic. Torn limbs, eye sockets flowing red, slashed legs, stomachs more outside than in. The smell of soldiers voiding in their death throes. The stink of blood and fear.

Then a stomach-wrenching shift and other, appallingly familiar horrors seared her mind's eye: Brick and stone ovens with tiny doors and rows of paper-thin women. Gouged out ditches choked with anonymous dead and the scurrying of scavengers. A billowing, ravening blast throwing the indelible shadows of irradiated corpses on concrete walls.

"No, Cathryn. Listen. Listen to us."

Dimly, beyond the screams of the wounded, beneath the shining whiteness of bones, beyond the terrible swiftness of loss came a low, sweeping current of sound. Not a song, and yet sung. No words, and yet meaning. No touch of hand, and yet the comfort of another's presence. Unbidden, but with the sweetness of release, tears came and fell like grace.

"Can you hear us, majesty?" Nimira was holding her wrists with tiny, capable hands.

"I can hear…something." Cathryn struggled to put down the terrible visions, clutching the lifeline of Nimira's voice and that other, noteless melody. Slowly, like an uncertain swimmer pulling for solid ground, she regained reality.

As the interior of the pavilion once again came into focus, she found that the elder bard supported her. Beside them were two singers just finishing a song. Or was it two poets reciting the final couplets of unfamiliar verses?

"What…what did I…?" She could not bring herself to ask what horrible thing she might have done this time while memories and fears had flowed over the power of the activated bloodworms.

"You did no harm, child." The steadfast gentleness in Nimira's voice nearly brought her to her knees with relief. "We are all safe. Though I must say the pictures you made us see will be the stuff of our nightmares forever."

The admission sent a wracking shudder through her, one so strong that it crossed over through the bard's supporting hands and shook the old woman with its force.

Kern stepped closer and took charge of the moment. He

put his arm around her waist and, disengaging her from Nimira, led her to a chair. As if that was a signal, the rest of those in the tent sat down in their places once again. But the battle chief remained standing at her side, one hand on the hilt of his sword and the other gently but firmly on her shoulder. When he spoke, she could feel the vibrations of his rumbling voice.

"Let me be the first to thank our queen for what she has done for us tonight. Our talk of war triggered memories—and warnings—from the Passing. We were allowed," Kern's voice broke for a moment on that word "by the power that resides within our Queen, to share those scenes."

What was the man doing? She tried to turn to him to ask, but his hand bore down on her shoulder.

"I did not understand all the images I saw, but I felt them. Too long have I been a soldier to plan war without knowing the grief that must be mine for purposing the death of so many. To the queen, therefore, I give thanks. She has brought my soul to its proper state for what must be done."

Many of the others nodded soberly. Linton's duchess seemed deep in thought. Beside her, T'Tolyan frowned. Kern more tightly clutched her shoulder.

"No plan that might open this war to such horrors should be considered. The lessons learned of old must not be forgotten. Even in war, let mercy be shown by the freedom of healers to practice their battlefield arts."

"The mercies of war?" Nimira's eyes were still shadowed by the violence of the visions. "There is great evil in D'Brin's heart—all the more so because the flaw of arrogant, self-referenced ambition, upon which this evil feeds, is so common and easily reached in others. He will not, the witch will not, practice restraint. If we do not take the ultimate stand against him, unmitigated by magicks, then the terrors which have just been shown us will occur more and more often and the temperate safety the guilds were founded to bring, will be gone."

"Aye, you have the right of it." A familiar voice, one that arrowed straight through Cathryn, came from the back of the tent near the doorway. Benedic had returned from helping Lucette drill the troops she had brought with her. "The bitter lesson war taught long ago has paled over time for most of us. Still others, who would obtain power by any means, have willfully put aside any moral restraint. To rescue the crown from such is a worthy goal. But we must remember this—"

He came forward into the pavilion, scanning the faces that were turned to him. "By choosing to die for this matter, we have, by default, chosen to kill for it—even to the killing of those who have been magicked or duped into complicity. Let us determine to do as little of it as possible. For when a question can only be answered in blood, then best we give the swiftest and clearest answer."

As she watched Benedic, it seemed to her he stood taller than before, as if a burden had been lifted from him. And, though he spoke of dire events to come, notes of hope were laced through his tone. There was only time to hear the change and not to discover a reason. She took up the reins of the meeting once more.

"Then, by all means, let us try Nimira's suggestion. If we are able to raise a negating spell over the battlefield, we will have an advantage. If we cannot, or if it is only partially successful, we will proceed as before and trust to the strength of our skill and our cause."

The elder bard stood and all those in the delegation rose as well. "Then give us leave, majesty, to withdraw and plan our songs and epics. The ones we used moments ago with you were of some help, but not strong or focused enough. We will work the night through and bring to the battle those notes, those verses that will serve."

"Of course, Bard Master. And thank you. No matter what happens, I want you to know how much I admire your willingness to help, the fearless way you reached into the untried and unknown for ideas. I believe you are the bards of whom bards to come will sing."

Nimira blinked several times, as if startled. Slowly she raised her fingers to touch her lips and then brought both hands down in front of her, palms up, one overlaid on the other. Having finished that odd, complex motion, she turned to leave the tent, drawing behind her the rest of the delegation.

"No." T'Meara rose from her seat. The guild members paused in mid-departure. A hard silence pressed against the tent walls. The duchess slowly gained the center of the pavilion.

"To this queen have I given the oath of my province and mine own bond. To the cause of right and to the battle it makes necessary, I have brought Linton flesh and blood. For those lives—and what deaths there may be—I am responsible. Though Cathryn has burned our hearts with the abominations of war, what greater darkness would I know if I denied healers the full means to work their battlefield mercies?"

T'Meara held out her open hands, a plea for understanding evident in that vulnerability.

"Beloved!" T'Tolyan's exclamation startled the assembly. "Do not let me hear that the duchess of Linton gives one traitorous moment of thought to breaking her oath. We have pledged ourselves and our people, not to our own expediencies, not to a mortal person wearing an ephemeral crown, but to the greater right, the greater justice, the greatest mercy. Let everyone who wars with or against us tomorrow live—and die—without blinders. It is the only way to ensure that the peace which follows will last." The huge man moved toward Cathryn, a lumbering bear with anguished eyes.

"Be assured, husband," T'Meara planted her feet more firmly where she stood. "my only desire for all Linton—including you, my heart—is that peace be bought with as little bloodshed as can be managed. Our queen carries the legacy of the Passing—but it is tainted by the wickedness of her native land. No one seeing the heinous nightmares she, herself, fears could deny that. For her sake—to keep her from making an error for which we all will pay too dearly—let us use our magicks in the morrow's battle."

Kern moved from her side so that he had a view of her face as he spoke.

"Cathryn…Majesty…do not despise this advice. It comes from the heart of Corronheld, a place—a state—you cannot know as we do."

There was distress in his eyes. His whole body was tense with the effort he was making to reach her with the argument and yet not offend her with the substance of it. But his evident concern could not lessen the way the core of her shrank from the truth of his words.

"It was the heart of Corronheld brought us to this pass. Or have you forgotten that?" Benedic stepped into the void where Kern had been standing. "It was a native son who first crossed the boundaries of wisdom and delved into forbidden arts. It was he murdered D'Shaar when she cautioned restraint. My wife's own cousin! He brought D'Joan here and nurtured the powerlust he was glad to find in her, compounding the guilt by implanting bloodworms in the kidnapped accomplice. In concert, the two uncurbed wizards brought Cathryn through and infected her without one shred of respect for her will in the matter."

The duke took in breath and scrutinized the face of each

person he held with his intensity. He found something disquieting, for he continued in a tone that did not allow equivocation.

"And, lest ignorance prompt us to say that D'Brin is a unique aberration, understand that it was the Esoteric Guild which allowed this wickedness to go unchecked—whether from indifference or by choice, it matters not, for the hideous outcome is the same in either case. Nor is anyone less guilty in all of this than I."

There was a rumble of disagreement from T'Tolyan which Benedic cut off instantly.

"No. I, too, bear the burden of the lives lost, the evil done. For I had heard my wife's fears, knew D'Brin's ruthlessness, hid from the enormity of his actions, was timid in informing my King. And when Cathryn was dragged into our domain, forced to take the Passing and then assume the burden of leadership, I refused to acknowledge it. Because my heart, which like yours is of Corronheld, was blinded with pride. And, worse, my hands yearned to take a crown that I had come to secretly believe was my own.

"Examine your own hearts, even to the darkest corners, and see where evil lies. Then ask yourselves if we have any right to accuse Cathryn's homeland of abominations worse than our own?"

The heat of his conviction, the fire of his defense, burned through her despair. With courage only another's bravery could inspire, she stood to address those whose lives hung in the balance of this debate: T'Meara with the stubborn and honest set to her mouth, Kern the battle chief caught between the impulse to be humane and the loyalty that threaded through the whole of his being, T'Tolyan who clenched his fists mightily as if to hold fast his beloved wife, Nimira and the other bards who stood silent as the winds of decision blew about them. And Benedic.

"No one knows more than I how much a stranger I am here. You are right to question the strategy proposed tonight. T'Meara's vision of a battlefield where friends are left untreated and in anguish is too appalling and too possible to ignore." In almost the same instant, she felt a long line of warmth along her left arm. Benedic had come to stand so close to her, she could feel the heat of him.

"But I beg you to consider this: There are not two but three reasons why we should negate the use of magic on the battlefield tomorrow. The first reason is that it will give us the advantage of surprise. The second is that all will see the full horrors of war and have that lesson seared upon their hearts so strongly that your children's children will feel the pain of it and put away even the imagining of war. But the third reason makes me most afraid—and you should fear it most. If Joan and D'Brin are allowed to use their magic as offensive weapons, the results will be more horrendous, more savage than the vilest of Corronheld can imagine. Trust me when I tell you that Joan understands the ways of both mass destruction and intimate torture. No healers, no defensive battle magicks could begin to counter the atrocities she can conjure. For this reason alone, please…please allow me to enlist the bards and overspell the armies."

The gathering in the tent was silent, each tensely in thought, trying to work through what they had been told.

Kern moved uneasily, shifting on his feet. "The thought that the wounded must be dragged from the field, out of the overspell, in order to be aided makes me so angry that it feels as if hot sand is pouring through my veins. But I have seen—more, I have felt—Cathryn's nightmares of home, and I believe her. What may be thrust upon the battlefolk may be so terrible that we should pay even this high price to ensure it will not happen." Looking at Benedic and then Cathryn, he concluded: "Let the bards sing. I will abide by your decision, majesty." He looked down again, suffering evident in the stoop of his shoulders. "And may the Creator save us all."

"Save us, indeed." T'Meara's voice was raw with tension. "I pledged myself and my province to this cause. We are pledged still. But in all good faith I cannot offer Linton lives so wantonly—no matter what alien magic may threaten. As we have pledged ourselves to you, Queen Cathryn, you have oathbonded to us. I call upon that bond and beg you to spare us from this waste of blood, this reckless squandering of lives."

"Beloved, please do not ask this." T'Tolyan's face was dark with anguish. He spoke to his wife as if they were alone in the pavilion. "She is our queen and she has the right to demand this of us. Can you not see that?"

His supplication nearly broke Cathryn's heart. T'Meara stared at the tent floor and drew in a shuddering breath. When she looked up again, silvery tracks traced her cheeks. "Linton will not fight tomorrow if the overspell is used. Our troops will wait near the battlefield. If the spell is broken, and our help is needed, we will come. That is all I can offer."

Nimira and the bards, Kern, Benedic, a despairing T'Tolyan—all, all turned to her, waiting on her response. The voices of the Passing were quiet, the bloodworms still. No whispered advice, no rush of power. Only silence, expectations and the knowledge that, no matter what decision she made, death would come for friends tomorrow.

"I understand your request, Duchess T'Meara. And I respect your reasoning." She felt the muscles in her face becoming rigid with strain. "But what I need is your support. If you cannot give that, then best you leave this war council. Go, talk with your troops. See if they wish to abandon their queen. Should you find they disagree with you, then you are welcome to join us in battle. If your troops agree with your desire to forsake me, then do not wait. Leave for Linton immediately, for I will not guarantee that loyal soldiers will refrain from lashing out in anger and we cannot afford to fight amongst ourselves."

T'Meara blanched deathly pale. Without another word, the duchess turned and went out of the tent, leaving behind a terrible void.

T'Tolyan staggered where he stood, as if he had been struck. She could not stand to see his distress. She went over and took his arm, pulling him toward her so he could see her through his grief.

"T'Tolyan, listen to me." She spoke firmly and he seemed to hear, though he shook his head back and forth like a great suffering giant. "Your wife is no traitor—nor are the troops of Linton. Even if they will not join us tomorrow morning, they will join us eventually and that is enough. I need their strength, so I spoke harshly. But you must know I would never punish them—they will punish themselves enough by the time the day is done. Know this and hope."

The plainsrider stopped shaking his head. Slowly, slowly he nodded.

"Go to her. Wait and see, my friend. And bring me word when words are ready."

Again T'Tolyan nodded. And then made his way out of the tent. Nimira and the bards followed him into the night. Only Kern and Benedic remained with her. And so there was just one more demand to make, one more cruel departure to watch.

"Benedic." The presence at her side shifted. She could not look directly at him, for she knew what pain that would bring. "Since Linton will probably not stand with us tomorrow, it is even more important that the troops on route from Forché arrive sooner and with full knowledge of our plans."

"Yes, Cathryn." The rough suede of his voice made her shiver. "I understand this well. The most recent couriers speak of a good-sized company from Forché that is getting close. I will ride out and bring them, informed, to the work of tomorrow."

"Thank you." Still she did not look him in the eyes. For he had left unsaid that Corry led the troops—and that his son would join the battle, too. And he had left unsaid more. But it was too late for many things.

And so he left.

Her eyes felt gritty. She heard a sentry call midnight rounds. So late, and yet so much still to be done. Across her tongue there came the faint and needy remembering of her favorite double tall mocha. A blend of sweet and heat. A taste of home. For a moment she should almost smell the tang of salt air and hear gulls crying as they circled, waiting for the inevitable biscotti crumbs. She saw the red neon of the public market sign glowing against gray Puget Sound, waters cut by white and green ferries with bellies full of commuters and tourists.

The yearning to be there again was heavy on her. To once more be in…be in…the name was lost in a flood of other places, other homes. She was almost too weary to pick out the right one. Linton Stand. Forché. Gansweald. Seattle.

Tears pushed themselves hotly to her eyes. Blinking furiously, she looked around to see if she was being observed. But the only person left in the tent was Kern, and he had his back to her, busy rolling up a map.

"There," he said. "I have what I need. Is there anything more you wish before I leave?"

She hastily wiped her face and cleared her throat. "No. Time is all I need, thank you."

He put the parchment cylinder down on the camp table and rubbed his lower back. "I believe I have had too much time. Hunched over battle plans, hours in the saddle herding this patchwork of armies." His tone was soft, sad and plaintively surprised. "It is in the midst of so many that I miss Bayly most."

Affinity and fondness for Kern impelled her across the tent. She touched his shoulder, meaning to give him some sign of respect, some small measure of comfort.

Her contact startled him. She could feel his muscles tense beneath her hand.

"I should not have said that." He turned toward her. "You need no complaints tonight, of all nights." He inclined his head, whether in apology or from sadness she could not tell—until he raised his eyes and she saw the honesty and sorrow that rested in the deepest part of him.

Guilt at his loss and the prospect of tomorrow's sacrifices gripped her painfully. The memories of the past rose in militant cacophony. Their sounds were myriad, sharp and, this time, edgy, as if a flock of ominous birds flapped restlessly within.

Instinctively, and futilely, she put her fingers in her ears. But Kern's callused hands caught her arms and pulled them down. His splayed thumb rubbed the ridge where one worm ended at her wrist.

"Use them." His voice was rough with conviction. "Let them bring peace, if only for an hour."

"Only if you let their comfort cover you for a while, too."

Kern released her hands and slowly shook his head.

"Nay. There are many voices from which you need respite. I have only one who speaks to me, and I would not have that quieted. Ever."

She could think of no good reply. No apology or expression of sympathy would be enough.

"Do not look so sad, majesty. Tomorrow I take my warrior wife into battle with me. No one had a nobler heart or better sense in a fight. We, two, will go in one soldier's body and do the fiercest good and glory in it. So you see, I am most blessed."

He took her wrists again and held them, vulnerable side up.

"Since you need not fret about me, take what peace you can find. Use the magic for gentle purposes and give yourself rest. The eve of your first battle is difficult enough. You don't need an old fighter's word for that."

"You're a dear man, Kern." As she spoke the words, his face reddened under its sun-browned toughness. "How could I have come so far without you?"

This time slowly, so as not to alarm him, she put her arms around him and hugged him, gingerly at first, then with all the warmth she felt for him. They clung to each other for a long moment, taking what comfort they could.

"Be careful tomorrow, Kern. I couldn't bear to lose you."

Kern pulled away to grip her by the shoulders.

"Bayly is with me and I am with you. We will not fail you."

He turned, grabbed the map tube and left the tent before she could speak a word. Only a tang of night air and the settling of the canvas door remained.

The enormity of what was to come and the unceasing static of the past threatened to overcome her. Before cowardice or remorse left her unstrung, she did as Kern suggested and began weaving words with desire until the voices sank into a far place. When that was done, she took up the large black cloak Guildmaster Sauter had left behind, pulled it on and tugged the hood low over her face. Now she would walk the night and find what peace could be had. She stepped out of the queen's pavilion and into anonymity.

Chapter Eighteen:
BENEDIC

H E LONGED TO sit with his back against the textured coolness of a redbark tree, to close his eyes and have the precious luxury of safety and the chance to remember and remember again the touch of Cathryn's heart in the night. But Benedic knew what he must do before all else. First, in to Lucette and another leave-taking. Then, out to find Corry and the aid he brought. Then, the work of the morrow.

He looked around, suddenly aware that, since leaving the queen's pavilion, he had been walking through camp without noticing his direction, simply going from one circle of torchlight to the next flare of glowlantern. He found himself surrounded by the dun-colored exteriors of the plainsrider wagontents. Just a few steps away was the largest of them—a wagon most familiar. Sentries walked the perimeter of it and from it came the sound of raised voices. Though he could not make out words, it was all too clear that T'Meara and the Linton battle captains were in hot debate.

Even as he watched, T'Ahlla appeared, her rolling gait bringing the sizable field commander of the plainsrider troops toward the meeting place. With her came T'Tolyan, the two of them arguing as they approached the tent.

"You know my sister has the right of it, man. Healers must be on the battlefield. Anything else is unthinkable."

"Unthinkable because you cannot—or will not—consider it?" T'Tolyan bent awkwardly as he trudged beside T'Ahlla, trying to see into her eyes as they walked. The unfortunate result was a sideways gait that made him look more like a supplicant than a persuader. "We none of us know what D'Brin and his witch may do. Best we should try to neutralize what evil they intend before it can be done. You are a great strategist—surely you see the wisdom of that plan?"

T'Ahlla merely grunted and kept striding toward her sister's wagon. T'Tolyan stopped just outside the tent's guarded perimeter.

"And will not one day's unmagicked battle—nay, one hour's unprotected fighting—be enough to teach us all again, D'Brin's troops and ours as well, that war is but a most horrible last choice?"

His friend's frustration made Benedic ache with sympathy. He had almost decided to step out of the nightshadows and into the conversation when T'Ahlla suddenly halted, spun on her heels and faced T'Tolyan.

"You have never understood." The commander pitched her voice low, the spite in it brutally clear. "You spend your time playing at secrets, taking friends outside the clans, humiliating your lady wife by propositioning every woman past her blood-age and yet you dare lecture me on what is or is not right?"

T'Tolyan's jaw dropped and he struggled to speak, but T'Ahlla pressed on, each word a weapon.

"There is no place for you in this gathering of fighters, no seat in the Linton Council. Neither your duchess nor I wish to hear from your compromised soul. Best you go back to your temporary queen and her nightmares, for you are not welcome here."

She made a military turn and disappeared into the wagon-tent, signaling to the sentries who stood at the entrance. The pair of guards closed ranks and blocked the entryway.

The plainsrider's humiliation had been witnessed—the sentries would surely spread word of the incident through the Linton contingent and from there it would flame throughout the camp. Benedic did not have birth brothers, but Kern and T'Tolyan were as close to him as any siblings could be. This could not go unaddressed.

"Ho, rider brother." He stepped into the light, speaking loudly enough that the guards and perhaps someone inside the tent could hear. "I have been looking everywhere for you." He reached the unmoving T'Tolyan and clapped him soundly on the shoulder. "Lucette begs your aid—she says the Chymion province cavalry is made of plough horses and farmhands and only a plainsrider can turn them into a fighting unit. Then you must have T'Tolyan, I told her. Only he will do. So I am sent for you, my friend—if you can spare the time."

He had to pull T'Tolyan along with him, for the man seemed unable to move of his own volition. He had just managed getting them both out of sight of the Linton guards when T'Gault came hurrying in their direction.

"Father. Duke Benedic. Well met—I wanted to ask…" T'Gault halted in mid-request. "What is wrong? What has happened? You have the look of the Dark Herald about you, father." The young man's eyes widened in alarm. "Is it mother… is she…?"

T'Tolyan reached for his son's arm. "Your mother is...she is not ill."

"Yet something is amiss, father. What...?"

It would not do to air this matter in the open night. Benedic knew they must find a more private place.

"Come along, T'Gault. You father and I are on our way to Lucette's tent for a conference. We will tell you all when we get there."

"I've just come from there." The young man smiled shyly in spite of his still evident worry. "It is she sent me to find you. But..."

"The duke is right, son. Come." T'Tolyan seemed to be emerging from the paralysis his sister-by-marriage had provoked in him, though the deep creases of sorrow in his face showed no signs of lessening.

The three of them made their way through the maze of tents and watch fires in a tense silence. When they entered Lucette's tent, she was bent over a camp table littered with maps. She looked up and saw them. The welcome and love in her eyes, while certainly meant for all three, most especially rested on T'Gault. There was no missing the intensity of it—nor the joy it produced in the young plainsrider.

But the light of her face dimmed as she caught sight of the shadows on their faces. Benedic sighed inwardly. Was tonight to be nothing but sadness and farewells?

"Ah, daughter, I have discovered these two gentlemen wandering about in search of strong kaffe and soft chairs. Might they find refuge here?"

She took his cue and motioned the riders toward stools arranged in front of a mage stove that boasted a steaming brew pot. "I cannot swear those chairs are soft, but by now that kaffe could animate a stone."

T'Gault poured out two cups of the fragrant brew and handed one to his father. The other he extended toward Benedic.

"Thank you, but no. I must leave to find my son and those he brings from Forché. They will be especially needed now that—"

T'Tolyan banged down his cup, kaffe slopping over the edges and splattering on the table.

"Now that Linton has turned traitor." He clenched his huge fists and began to pace the small tent, so agitated that the heavy cloth walls trembled with his angry tread.

The two young people stood silenced by the outburst. Silenced and unhappy, looking to one another for support—a gesture that wrenched Benedic's heart. He was losing his daughter, had been wrenched from closeness with his son, T'Meara and T'Tolyan were deprived of the intimacy and trust they once had, Kern grieved for Bayly. Despair, like a raptor, battered against that tender promise which had, of late, lived within him.

Yet from the edge of the dark descent he stepped back, for he saw near him those who loved him and looked to him, even in this moment. What might be belonged to tomorrow. What was belonged to this night.

Then, to this nearest sorrow first.

"Rider brother." Benedic placed himself in T'Tolyan's way to put a halt to the pacing. "I need a favor from you, my friend."

T'Tolyan stopped and glared, his hands still closed in mighty fists. "A favor? Was it not a favor to you started this chaos? I would be in my lady wife's arms this very night were it not for favors to Forché's duke."

"Father!" T'Gault's shock spilled into his voice. "Listen, please, to what I came to tell you before you speak more words that cannot be taken back."

Lucette came to Benedic's side and laid her hand on his

arm. He loved his daughter so dearly for that gesture, warmed that she sensed so immediately how much T'Tolyan's bitterness hurt him. It allowed him to hear T'Gault in spite of the pounding of pain and guilt in his ears.

"Father," the young man struggled to get T'Tolyan to look at him while he spoke. "As we readied the Chymion troops for the coming battle, we began to hear rumors that the queen had banned healers from the field and those who fell wounded would be left to die most horribly. Offers had been made to the leaders and warriors of the other provinces to join Linton and refuse to take the field tomorrow. We could not believe this, so Lucette and I sought out the spreaders-of-tales, working backward to the source of these things. It was not to the duchess, my mother, that we traced the rumors, but to our provincial field commander, T'Ahlla."

T'Tolyan's wind-darkened face flushed even darker. But the young man was not yet done.

"More there is, father. Best you hear it now. T'Ahlla never accepted Cathryn as queen, nor Kern's appointment as battle chief. She feels the reins of power already laid between her fingers and bends every effort, though in secret, to take from the queen and her commander what she already grasps in her heart."

Lucette's grip tightened on his arm as she added her portion of the report. "There is some evidence that T'Ahlla does not wish to take the title of duchess from her sister. It is as a leader of soldiers she sees herself. She sees no harm in keeping T'Tolyan's influence away from T'Meara."

T'Tolyan groaned. "No harm? Driving a wedge between the one flesh of wife and husband does no harm?"

Benedic's despair became an onrush of anger. "Of all the evil D'Brin has done, this—THIS—is by far the most abhorrent. Turning us one against the other—parent and child, husband

and wife, leader against leader. Never will I forgive him. I hate what has been done to us—hate that we let it be done—I hate *him*—beyond mercy, beyond the cutting cold of justice."

"Father…" There was a trace of fear in Lucette's tentativeness. "We all detest what D'Brin has done. But we have always allowed for differences of view, no matter how offensive. Surely hate is too strong, too destructive a word."

"No." Benedic knew now where this argument must go. "No—Linton and our Queen have a difference of view on the use of magic on the battlefield. Kern and T'Ahlla have a difference of view as to who should lead our forces. But D'Brin's difference is not of opinion, it is of intent. His actions fountain from the pool of his soul and that pool is rank, defiled and corrupted. There can be no tolerance for that. None."

T'Tolyan frowned deeply. "Strong words for a man who has no authority to judge outside the borders of Forché. Your stubborn insistence on making highhanded pronouncements has stampeded us each into our own disaster."

"Fie, T'Tolyan, fie. I would gladly argue philosophies and strategies with you—even take the blows for my mistakes which, Creator knows, are many. But you know me better than to think I would misuse rank or authority. I know you too well to believe I could ever force you, the most stubborn plainsman ever to draw breath, to choose the road you ride."

T'Tolyan opened his mouth as if to respond, but Benedic overrode him.

"And you should also know well enough your lady wife. Do you really believe T'Ahlla when she says her sister will not see you, does not want your words and comfort in this hour."

He felt his breath run out as the vigor of his wrath lessened with the telling of it. How could he find fault with his daughter and friends when he, himself, took so long and circuitous a path to finding the right of this? Was he but falling into D'Brin's wickedness by letting his anger cause this estrangement of those he loved?

A wisp of connection brushed his mind—a connection that had the imprint of Cathryn upon it. Somewhere in the camp she walked alone. And her thoughts were of him. And they were fragrant with concern, powerful with resolve, heated with longing. It turned the moment into a new thing. He took T'Tolyan by the shoulders and looked strong into his eyes.

"Friend. Brother. Listen to your heart. It tells you that your lady would never waver. Go to her now. Agree to disagree on policy—but reclaim that union which belongs to wife and husband. And in that accord find a victory over the evil that has drawn us all into battle."

Into T'Tolyan's eyes, through his very muscles, swept a change of mind. The plainsrider drew up until he was his usual huge and stalwart self. "I will go to her. Tis true she would never..." He pulled away and headed for the door of the tent. Then he paused and turned slowly back.

"Benedic...I should not...that is..."

"Peace, old man. I could not take an apology from you—the shock of it would surely undo me." He smiled as his friend raised a hand in salute and went into the night.

T'Gault made as if to follow his father, but Benedic gently restrained him.

"It might be best to let your father and mother find their own way through this. Besides, you and Lucette could lend most valuable aid tonight, if willing."

The two young people glanced at one another first and then nodded their assent.

"Good. Then here is the message needs taking: It is true that there will be, if all goes well, a dampening spell overcast upon the battlefield. No magic can be performed under its power.

Instead, Cathryn will battle the wizard and his witch above the spell, hoping to disable the creators of this war.

"Only we will know that magic will not function where the fighting will be. With all our hearts we hope it will release those of the Palace Militia and others D'Brin has ensorcelled, so that we do not have to fight friends and family. Still, it may come to that and, if so, our queen has not denied her soldiers or our enemy's warriors the services of healers."

"How can that be if no magic may be used on the field?" T'Gault's question was not disparaging, but laced with anticipation of a good answer. It put a small but sure smile on Lucette's face.

"Ay, well, that is the difficult part. The wounded will have to be brought off the battlefield, out from underneath the overspell so that the healers might practice their arts. That task is what I would ask of Linton. Since your mother's conscience will not allow her to spend soldiers tomorrow because healers cannot go to the wounded, will that same conscience permit her to bring wounded to the healers?"

Thoughts flew across T'Gault's countenance swiftly and in earnest. That kind of keen and rapid analysis was so like his mother, it was almost uncanny. When the plainsrider's eyes lit from within, Benedic saw that T'Tolyan's fire had truly been passed from father to son. A worried place in his father's heart, one with Lucette's well-being central to it, let go and opened.

"I think I see a way..." T'Gault was clearly still planning as he spoke. "All the clanleaders will be with T'Ahlla in my mother's tent. I would have little influence with them, but I am not unknown to the rest of our warriors. If I were to talk to the plainsfolk and Lucette explained to the Chymion troops—tell them what you have said and the queen intends—would that be of benefit?"

Benedic admired the young man's grasp of the matter.

"Aye, you have the gist of this. A true plainsrider you are to catch the cunning this will take."

"For a fact, he is well known and well regarded." Lucette's tone could not disguise her own appreciation of T'Gault.

He clapped T'Gault on the shoulder. "If it can be done, you can do it. Still, I could not let you go without acknowledging that you will be standing at odds with your mother in doing this."

"My mother is doing what she has reasoned to be just. Though she may dislike my decision, she would not deny my right to decide. But thank you for that honest warning." T'Gault looked over at Lucette. "I take my leave of you, lady, until later."

"Until later."

Hearing the tenderness laid under the words of this leave-taking pierced Benedic's heart with a painful sweetness. It took a moment, when the plainsrider had gone, to be able to speak.

"T'Gault is a good man. And a fine man for you."

A tear traced its way down Lucette's cheek. "That he is. But you need not have worried. I would love no other kind of man, having learned to desire goodness by first loving my father."

He took the few steps that brought him to his daughter and embraced her, and she him.

"Already I miss you, little one. How can I bear to let you go—but how could I bear to keep you from the chance for joy?"

He tangled the fingers of one hand in her hair, a gesture practiced so many times over the years that his heart both broke and healed. She buried her face in his shoulder and tightened her hug.

"I love you, papa." Her words were muffled in his cloak. He was grateful she could not see the trembling of his lips.

"I know, sweet-my-love. Just promise me you will be especially careful tomorrow. As hard as it is to see you leave home..." He could not finish the thought—could not say another word for the fullness of feeling within him. He kissed the crown of his daughter's head and loosened himself from the embrace. Before he could not, he forced himself to move toward the tent's door.

The night had turned cold. From watch fire to watch fire, he made his way across camp until he gained the horsetethers. Along the line he searched until he found Kell—or rather his horse found him. In the darkness, Benedic did not have the advantage of being able to smell apples in pockets from a great distance.

"I heard you, Kell. And, yes, the apple is yours—though I wager it is not a surprise. While I refrained from spoiling my children, I cannot say the same about you, beast." He wiped his hand where Kell left enthusiastic slobber. "I just hope you are well rested, for we have much ground to cover tonight."

It was short work to find his saddle and make Kell ready for the trail. The thought of reaching Corry, both across enemy-held terrain and across the gulf D'Brin had put between them, made Benedic eager for the ride and determined to be careful.

He weighed in his mind the routes he might take. In the end, he decided to walk along the narrow floor of a ravine that meandered in the direction he must go. Though an ambush might be possible in such cramped spaces, the combination of overhanging trees and darkness of night would provide the path mostly likely to keep him hidden from enemy patrols. With a last look at the firelights dotted across the camp, he stepped down into the ravine, pulling Kell after him.

In moments the two of them were buried deep in the chasm's shadows. Twisting, first one way then the other, down the dry stream bed, he began to feel uneasy. He could not reckon his direction without a view of the stars and, though the lush foliage dampened the noise of his passage, it also would not let through the warning sound of approaching footsteps. The farther they traveled, the more anxious he became. Kell, whether from his own or a borrowed apprehension, whuffed and jerked against the lead until neither could stand the blindness of their route any longer.

He draped Kell's reins loosely back over the saddle and, gathering his cloak tight against the cold and the brush, began to climb. It took some sweat and discretion of language to gain the upward edge. Once there, he found a hidden spot from which he could spy. But it was not his eyes that caught the danger—it was the faint, but now appallingly familiar, tang of Taker magic in his nostrils. Willing his heart to stop shouting his fear, he froze as he was and, hardly daring to breath, waited.

It was not long in coming. There, across the clearing, more shadow than substance, a Taker. On foot. More like a grim hound on scent than anything possessed of a soul. Sweat beaded and slid between his shoulder blades.

The seconds crawled by as the Taker slipped through the night, stopping all too often to test the air. Just when it seemed the way might never be free, the assassin moved beyond the clearing's edge and away. But because the lessons of these last days had been hard, Benedic stayed unmoving still longer. And as sure as breath follows breath, along the edge of the ravine came the other of the hunting pair. Closer with each silent step. Now pausing to listen. Then nearer. And nearer. Until the specter stopped just an arm's-length from his hiding place.

The drumming of his heart faded, no sound of inhale or exhale, the muted noises of night did not bother his ears. Only the whe-whe of a wool cloak in slight motion, the delicate sigh of metal being drawn from hardened leather, the faintest creak of a boot bending came to his ear. The Taker crouched and turned until there were three glints of moonlight: one in each cold, sharp eye, and one from the twisted length of dagger in his hand.

The world ceased to turn, for the barest moment, as hunter and hunted truly saw one another. Then, in a movement elegant in its speed and execution, the hand that held the dagger described a small arc that ended in Benedic's flesh with a terrible jerk and a long slash of pain.

For an instant, the surprise he felt was mirrored on his attacker's face. Then Benedic launched himself at the Taker, knocking him over even as the man tried to bring up the dagger for another blow.

Over and over they rolled, the slash in his side demanding in its pain, his arms grappling for a solid hold—any hold. Suddenly, the other broke free and scrambled to his feet. Desperate, he grabbed for the man's ankle and pulled hard. Down went the Taker, his fall seeming to last forever and no time at all. Down and down. Then a sound unlike any Benedic had ever heard. A crack of something brittle and wet. And all was still.

He struggled to his knees and crawled forward. The pale moonlight showed him that the enemy was dead, his skull broken against a stone. The blood fierceness that had come so swiftly fled before the realization that, if not for a chance-placed rock, it might have been himself meeting death in the night.

He pulled his cloak away and was surprised when the tunic underneath gaped open. A long slice had been made through the fabric and into the flesh across his ribs. One of the tunic's silver buckles was ruined. Now it was not just a rock but a silver buckle to which he owed his life.

Enough. The wound was shallow and, though it would pain him on the ride, he could endure. He struggled to his feet. He chose to trust providence and gave a short, low whistle. In moments he was rewarded with the presence of Kell. Now he must ride swiftly, letting speed be his safety.

Chapter Nineteen:
CATHRYN

IF SHE LOOKED out over the valley, she could pretend she was safely removed. The peak opposite, where Joan had positioned herself, was too shadowed in the pale dawn for clear sight. And the roiling storm clouds still hunkered down at the base of the sky.

Almost she could feel safely removed. But then, down below, red-orange light would glint from the weapon of a forward scout, the flare of a far hillside watch-fire would catch her eye or, even closer, one of the singers would murmur a fragment of lyric loudly enough that it brought her back to the ominous duties of the day.

At last she could no longer put off what must be attempted. Plumes of dust had begun to rise from either side of the valley. Soon the slaughter would begin.

"It is time, majesty." Nimira was beside her, having gotten there so quietly Cathryn was startled at the sound of the bard's voice.

"Yes. Thank you. I am coming." But she stayed one moment more. The fateful cadence of soldiers marching to battle rose from the valley, that muted thunder echoed by the faint rumblings of the approaching storm.

"Will this work?" The question spilled from her before she could catch it.

The elderly bard continued to stare at the movement below them before she spoke. "All night I wrestled with why I had failed to convince T'Meara that this plan will work. In the weak-lighted morn it came to me: I truly do not know myself if we will prevail. How, then, could I have swayed others? Now I see your determination, too, was less rock and more sand." Nimira sighed and straightened her robes. "Yet I have come to this: Should this venture fail, only we few will fall. Should it succeed, so much more will be gained that it is worth the risking of these our few, offered lives."

Cathryn drew her thick cloak even closer and looked over at the tiny woman next to her. The bard's hair, sparse and white, was tied back with a gray ribbon. Her green-gold eyes, undimmed by stress or the early hour, glinted in the dawn light.

"You are right." She turned toward the small group of singers arranged in a circle at the very summit of the hill. Steeling herself, she made her way into the center of the circle. When she stood at a place marked by three white stones and Nimira stood at her left, the bards, at some signal unseen, raised their voices in song.

At first, she heard melody only. It rose and fell on the air like a bird riding the zephyrs. Her heart, which, until now, had beat a counterpoint of fear, caught the music's flow, shifted, steadied and slowed. Behind her, she heard Nimira take in a deep breath and from the elder's tiny form came words that she laid upon the tune. Songs of courage…

Then 'cross the swift, unfeeling waters,
Mother Breesa brought them out.
Bright-cheeked sons and keen-eyed daughters
plucked she from the flooding rout.
When the last one safe she laid,
high upon the greening shore,
then she rested in the river,
resting peaceful evermore.

Ballads of purpose...

In the Winter of our need
...songs of wisdom, sounds of sorrow
Came a dove-and-serpent savior
...notes of life to us returned
Bought the Spring—with honor earned
...songs of wisdom, sounds of sorrow
Which he gifted to us freely
...notes of life to us returned.

History sung from the blood, to be heard in the bones.

She opened to the songs, letting them flow through her, taking from them the strength of every noble deed recounted, every goodness sung again. At first, the worms slid frantically, painfully beneath her skin. Then they, too, quieted, steadied and...

...either she lifted or the hill fell away and she drifted in a dark, hot void. Vague bits of lightness surrounded her, like smudged pearls. She felt, more than knew, it was the circle of bards that hung about her in the darkness, pierced, strung together by the bravery of music.

She saw the dissonance approaching before she heard it. The sound came writhing from a distant place with a blind, grasping malevolence, smelling like a clash of notes, sounding like the stench of oblivion.

She reached out her hand and almost dropped what it held. Delicate, cool, a transparent globe lay in her palm. Inside it were tiny hills covered with even tinier dots in two, moving lines. She brought the sphere close to her face. There was no doubt. The armies were closing one upon the other, there, within the fragile glass—glass that was the shield against magic she and the bards had somehow, it appeared, constructed.

Over her hand, over the globe—a shadow. From within her rose a howling, an anguished chorus afire with horror. *Wizards' wars cannot be won*, this from a king long dead who had fought his lust for dark magic and lost. *Withdraw—Protect*, was the litany of a queen gone when the crown of Corronheld was still warm from the forge. *Shun the magic that should not have been yours*, demanded Reyfen, his spirit still strong, his fear palpable. *A dozen musicians and one alien are no defense. Ruin is the only outcome. Ruin and death. Find Benedic. Complete the Passing.*

Benedic's name brought him to her vision, a specter wavering between her and the plain of otherwhere. The apparition did not speak nor indicate he noticed her. He only reached for the sword at his side, drew it out and, facing a foe he could see but she could not, parried a blow from a weapon limned by a ghastly, crawling luminescence. In the curve of his defensive swing, the word on the sword burned into her eyes. The same word carved into the ring she wore on her hand, the hand in which rested the battle for Corronheld.

As swiftly as it came, the vision of Benedic disappeared, taking with it her breath for the space of a moment. Then she built back, in a place beneath her heart, an image of his face as she knew it—a visage traced with character, set aflame by demanding eyes, only softened by a mouth acquainted with intimate compassion.

Get your bearings, Cathryn.

The whisper she spoke to herself hung like a blot just in front of her face. In this place, this plain of otherwhere, words must have weight and impact. Visibly so. She closed her mouth tight. No words until absolutely necessary.

She looked around, trying to orient herself in this hallucination-made-real. A glow of nimbus lights indicated the singers were still close around her, but the shadow was closer, too, streaming toward them like the dark heart of a hungry storm.

The memory of a childhood visit to the Midwest and a tornado scare brushed into her mind. Hiding in the cellar, wind dying to horrible nothingness and returning like a hundred, merciless freight trains. The safety of damp concrete. Which she felt under her feet and against one shoulder. How could that be? But there was a wall and a floor, seeming solid. And above her head timbers resolved into being. Stairs grew from the void and dim mounds of basement junk—trunks, bicycles, tools, furnace—spun into sight.

Did she only need to desire something for it to be made? Each beat of her heart told her to believe that. Each breath told her she was a fool to believe any of this. In her arms, distant pain. Through it all, fierce exultation.

Faster now she drew from her soul the framework of a safe place. Home. It grew in jutting strokes. Without hesitation she ran up the basement stairs, and there was the kitchen. Tucking the globe close, she pushed through a door and found her living room—a green jacket on the coat-tree and Sunday's newspaper folded on the coffee table. This is where she would be secure, out of harm's way. Each mundane furnishing seemed a talisman. She touched a table, a pot of ivy, a half-read book.

Then she saw what was outside the window.

Nightmare clouds the color of scabs boiled toward her. Black, red-orange and bile green, they pushed apart the air and made filth of the sky. As she watched, the graceful circle of aspen trees that ringed the house bent under the storm. Bent and groaned and sang.

The bards. Somehow, in this recreation of her home, they were translated as a grove of aspen, many trees making one organism, joined and rooted. Protecting. Her heart heard the wordless songs and gave back a soundless plea.

Hold. Please, you singers and sayers. Hold and live.

The miasma groped toward the outside curve of the tree circle, blowing at the parchment and black limbs so viciously that the soil around them undulated with the tearing of roots. One of the smallest trees was bashed so hard its limbs broke in wind-whipped air and battered against the house. As the slender trunk bent against the onslaught, long lines of darkness flowed down from cracks and rips in the delicate, pale bark. Flowing too fast, too red, for pitch.

She pulled the globe tighter to her. The pressure of the orb on the frantically active worms in her arms was so painful that spatters of light exploded across her eyes. Beneath her feet, the floor shuddered and trembled. Somewhere windows rattled and doors pounded in their frames. She ran from the living room, away from the window that looked out on hell, toward a calmer sanctuary.

Her bedroom.

She shut the door and sat down on the bed. Now she could make a plan, create a better strategy. She tried to remember the instructions Nimira had given her. Concentrate. Focus on a safe place and keep the battlefield covered by the overspell.

We will protect you while you shield the field of combat from magic. Trust. Concentrate.

Carefully, she placed the orb on the bed and pressed the quilt up around it so it wouldn't tip. There still were tiny movements, pinprick flashes of light as sun glinted off armor, small puffs and shimmers of dust raised by mounted troops, a narrow ribbon of blue where a river divided the battlefield. So little, so precise and delicate these tiny images. She gave a sigh of wonder.

Fool. Death is hunting down there. Already some whose faces and names she knew were gone in a bloody welter of fear and pain. How could she make this horror end with less loss and still maintain the shield as she had promised? Could her magic, wild as it seemed to be, stretch that far, do that much?

Cautiously, tentatively, still keeping the shield stubbornly intact, she sent a part of her mind questing outward. Far below the thin smoke of awareness, the cries of the many rose. For a moment her focus trembled. Those cries—were they from warriors on the field? She listened with what portion of her mind she could wrest from the shield spell. No. These were warnings from the rulers of the Passing. Whatever she was doing must be triggering a rush of remembrances.

The louder the Passing voices grew, the more the shield thinned. Fiercely she willed herself to ignore the babble and bear down on maintaining the overspell. Slowly the globe strengthened, more and more, until the glass was so thick it was almost opaque.

If the bards could hold out, she might be able to distract Joan and D'Brin, break their focus and disrupt the magicks.

Guerrilla warfare fought on an unreal plane. She smiled grimly. It was an insane concept and yet, if it worked it would stop the butchery on the battlefield and—she admitted it—present an opportunity to overcome the two who had brought her here and caused so much chaos and suffering. Vengeance ignited and became a hot, bright burning.

She deepened her determination and, willing the overspell to flow through her hands, sent her mind out like a floating eye. Out from the bedroom that fear had recreated, down the safety of a known hallway, through the living room that promised the protection of the familiar and out the front door in a sudden blur.

When focus returned again, she found that her awareness hung just under the lowest branches of the aspen tree that was Nimira. The Nimira-tree swayed and twisted in the cruel wind's blistering assault. The golden leaves that should have fluttered on a kind breeze, were wrenched and whipped so bitterly that the branches that bore them cracked and splintered like broken bones. Fearing for the elder woman, Cathryn sent her awareness closer until she felt her mind's-eye make contact with the paperwhite bark.

Pain. Agony. Stubborn fierceness. And a singing in the blood that held together a circle of lucid good. The music of faithfulness, integrity and honor resounded like an immense pipe organ or a congregation of orchestras. Each bard, each aspen, rang with a unique tone—from the soprano of innocence to the deep bass of conviction. Since she touched Nimira, it was the master's tone, a contralto of fidelity and resolve, that sounded most clear.

Yet, even as protection resonated through her, there came a sudden and violent rending so intimate in its anguish that it felt as if half her teeth had been ripped from her jaw, root and nerve. She forced the proxy awareness of her mind's-eye deeper into Nimira's perception.

And found heartbreak. Fearful sorrow.

The circle had been rent. Sweet Mikel, youngest of the singers, dead. His pure tenor forever silenced. Tears, tears, weeping and discord. Ah, Mikel. Precipitous anguish made cacophony of what had been harmony. Her whole body spasmed with grief.

With that wrench came a sharp slash that destroyed the sending of the mind's-eye, pulled her awareness back into her body. With real eyes, she looked down and saw that the globe had cracked and sliced open her palm. New blood, still bright from airless arteries, smeared over the damaged glass in dreadful whorls. The surface of the globe begin to craze and crackle. Tiny fault lines split off from the long fissure, first one and two, then a spider web of lacerations in the glass. The spell was failing.

With an urgency sprung from fear, Cathryn held her wounded palm above her head to slow the blood loss, and laid her good hand on the top of the globe.

Regain the overspell. Repair. Hold. Hold.

Outside, the sulfurous wind roared at the perilous construct of home walls and windows. Beating to get in. Raging to get in. The blast screamed at her, "*We are coming. Open up. Let us in. You cannot win. Let us in or we will kill them all. Save them. You know you must. Save them and save yourself.*"

In terror, her heart constricted; yet the spell still caught and held. Each pulse-beat mended a crack. She tried to concentrate on the thup-thup, to let it drown the howling that battered to invade. As if in answer, the worms that swam through her tissues jerked and twitched. With a pop of flesh, one—a tiny one—emerged just below the wrist of the wounded hand. It began snaking upward to the oozing slash on her palm. When it reached the bloody gash, the worm nudged its arrow-shaped head into the cut, slid its slender length into the wound, drawing the sliced edges of flesh with it, closing the laceration like a long, pale door.

Then the wind stopped. It was so quiet, so suddenly, it seemed as though the universe itself had stopped breathing.

Odd bits and pieces claimed attention in that hush. The rose and green pattern of the bedspread. A minute gleam on the silver-blue ribbon of river deep within the globe. The smell of green breaks, sap and fire.

She blinked. And when the brief darkness of that motion was done, the light in the bedroom had changed, shifted, dimmed. From the bottom up.

She looked down over the edge of the bed. Familiar wood floor. Mother's handmade rag rug. Door to the closet.

From under the closet door, from under the bed, from under the door to the hallway oozed a darkness too complete to be a color. The liquid corruption seeped into the room, first slowly, then more swiftly. First in flat, amoebic extrusions, then welling into thicker, animate wickedness.

No voices of dead kings, no slithering of worms, no visions of friends now missing or dead, no circle of mythmakers gave her wisdom, power, love or assistance. The depravity that Joan had embraced and D'Brin had succored was made immediate. They had found her. And she was alone.

In the moment of her greatest dread, a small picture came to mind. Cathryn saw, as clearly as if it were in front of her, on the third page of the family photo album, a snapshot of her father and herself. He is tall and thin, standing in front of a forsythia bush. A lock of dark hair has slipped over his forehead and light is reflecting on his wire-rimmed glasses. She is four years old, dressed in a sunsuit embroidered with the letters of the alphabet. Her father is leaning to one side, bent at an angle, so he can hold her hand. Their small, contented smiles are identical.

"I am," she whispered to herself against the encroaching darkness, "not alone. I bring with me my father as well as my enemy. What I am was shaped by those who have loved me and sharpened by those who have hated me. On two worlds.

I am not the Passing, or am I the beasts that swim under my skin. And yet they are a part of me. I am not Joan's victim or Benedic's betrayer because I, Cathryn Porter, I do not will it."

The darkness had pulled itself into an amorphous hulk. In only a moment it would shape itself into death and reach for her. She knew what to do. Putting the orb behind her, using her body as a shield, she turned to wait for what was forming. Waiting until destruction had arms, until pain took shape and moved to take her. It was close, closer, now close enough. She drew in a vast breath of force, gave the force form and purpose and then reached forward and embraced the enemy and detonated the power that was within her.

Chapter Twenty:
BENEDIC

THEY WERE ON him before he could strike a defense, dragging him from the saddle. He cried out as he hit the ground hard and the barely closed slash across his ribs broke open and loosed its hurt upon him.

"Wait, wait." Someone whose red hair was unmistakable, even in the wan light of the false dawn, pushed through the circle of scouts. When he saw the face of his son's friend, Benedic stopped the painful struggle with his captors.

"Elinay. It is I."

"Oh my goodness." A flush rose to Elinay's face so that her cheeks matched her hair. "Let go of him. It's Corry's father—I mean…" She took action, pulling on arms and pushing at shoulders until the three scouts released him. But when he tried to gain his feet he staggered, exhaustion and blood loss taking their toll.

Elinay winced. "You are wounded, my lord. Let me help

you." She offered him her arm. Though it did not lessen the pain of his rising, he took the help for her sake.

"Thank you. I must say you are one of the most effective lookouts I have ever encountered." He slowly straightened and glanced at the group ruefully. "Or should I say that has ever encountered itself all over me."

"I am so sorry, my lord duke. If we had known…" Elinay's eyes widened in distress.

"On the contrary. You could not know who I was. You did the right thing. It is a great relief to see Forché's camp is so well guarded."

Each of the small band grinned in relief and pride. But that response did not bring to him the pleasure he thought it would, for the scouts were too young, their faces unmarked by experience, too many of their joys still waiting to be tasted.

"But now I need to talk to your commander. It is most urgent."

"Of course." Elinay shook herself into action. "Hallen, Gryff, Meka—I leave you to guard the perimeter. I will take our duke into camp." She headed out, Benedic and Kell following with weary steps, even as the three remaining scouts melted once again into the night.

It was only a matter of moments and an exchange of pass-words before they reached camp. Already there was activity as the prospect of sunrise brought the day's march closer. A few tents were already billowing to the ground. The smell of break-fast cakes and kaffe reminded him how hungry he was—and how exhausted. But first things first.

Elinay stopped in front of the tent above which a com-mander's pennon flew.

"Captain? I bring a perimeter scout report. We found Duke Benedic and…"

Sortia Fiste, the martial captain of Forché's provincial guard, burst out through the canvas door.

"My lord Duke. At last. I hereby turn over command of the Forché contingent."

"Wait, Captain Fiste." His fatigue made it hard to interrupt fast enough. "I am not here to take command. I have brought information and a plea for our troops to travel even faster. But most willingly do I leave our province's soldiers in your capable hands."

"Ah, well. Yes. It would be my honor."

But the strain of his night ride must have been too plain writ on his countenance, for Captain Fiste said no more to him. Instead, she ordered Kell taken to the horselines and sent Elinay for food and kaffe while opening the tent flap so he might enter.

"The campstools are not comfortable enough, believe me. It would be better to sit on the folded bedroll," said the captain as she followed him in.

Though he eyed the pile of blankets longingly, he chose a stool instead and lowered himself onto it, favoring the wounded side.

"Aye, but we have no time to rest. The battle commences this day and—"

"But you are hurt. I will send for a healer." Sortia headed toward the tent door.

"No."

She stopped short.

"I mean, yes, a healer would be appreciated. But the information I bring is the most urgent."

Sortia nodded her understanding and immediately dispatched the two sentries outside; one to bring the sub-commanders to them, the other to get a healer.

"There." The captain-commander pulled over a map table

and her own chair. "You rest a moment while I share what I know, the first being that your son is well. He and his companions lead our scout teams. Corry is out with one right now—but the moment he returns he will be sent to you."

Because a father-ache lessened with that news, the fatigue that had been so crippling before seemed suddenly easier to bear. The relief was great enough that he did not trust his voice to carry the thanks due. But Sortia just leaned over and gently gripped his arm.

"We are both parents," she said quietly. "I, too, know the need to hear. Our children…" She faltered. "Such good friends…"

They were interrupted by the entrance of Elinay bringing in a tray that held a steaming bowl of porridge fragrant with honey and cream, fresh applebread, several thick slices of buttery-colored cheese and a large mug of kaffe. The sight and smell of the bounty made him a bit lightheaded. Courtesy took second to hunger and he had taken a few hasty bites before he even thought to thank Elinay. By then she was ducking out of the tent—just in time to allow Faela, the first of the unit commanders, to enter. Hard on her heels came Grainig, his wild hair in its usual disarray. And then came Laehl and Fennec, always the last to arrive at any gathering.

He looked with fondness at the small group, each known to the others since childhood. As the group leaders reported the numbers of their troops and what supplies had been brought, though, the first swallows of breakfast became leaden in his belly. With a reluctant heart, he began to tell those who had chosen to walk this journey with him what plans had been laid, and with what hope, for the coming battle.

❈

Once again, and too soon for this day, he took to the saddle. The sub-commanders had listened, understood and dispersed to hasten the breaking of camp. Captain Fiste left with the forward scouts. A healer had come and gone, taking most of the pain in his side with her. And a fresh horse had been brought to him for this forced march so that Kell might be relieved of a rider until their partnership would be required at the moment of battle.

All had been seen to, arranged, expedited. Nothing remained undone or unaddressed. Nothing—except the growing anxiety that built the longer Corry did not return. And now, with the last vestiges of the night's camp packed and gone, the clearing looked ominously empty. Though he knew the scouts would have no trouble locating the moving troops, still he found himself trailing behind, glancing over his shoulder too often, straining for some glimpse of returning scouts.

The vague brightness that was the sun rose higher in the clouded sky. From the heat of so many hooves and feet, mists rose from the much-trampled mud into the cold, biting air. Too soon Kell was brought forward and he exchanged mounts, trying not to think about the reason for it. But of his son, there was still no word.

And then, from ahead of the main body of troops, came shouts—cries of horror so terrible that dread of it stopped the soldiers around him in their tracks. He urged Kell forward, needing to see. Afraid to see.

What he found when he reined up at the knot of angry, shouting fighters was the stuff of nightmares. In the center of the crowd, Corry and two of his scouts were slashing at the legs of a maimed and blood-drenched soldier. Some of the newly arrived Forché troops wrestled with the young scouts, trying to keep them from their horrific task. Others screamed for Corry to stop, that the man he so wounded was known to them, a friend. The gory soldier at the center registered none of it, but kept on rhythmically, mercilessly, wordlessly attacking Corry and the scouts, swinging a red-dripping longsword so hard that crimson drops scattered in gruesome arcs.

"Hold him down." Corry shouted hoarsely to the threatening crowd. "He will not stop. You must hold him down." Benedic heard the mortal urgency in his son's voice. He pushed through the jostling ranks, shoving his way through to the front of the press. He grappled to break the grip of those who sought to drag down Corry, shouting, "Listen to him. Hold down your friend. There is magic here."

He wrenched Corry free from those around them. The two of them shouldered through to the crazed attacker and managed to grab his arms. The power of the fighter and his silent frenzy shocked him.

The other two scouts took advantage of the distraction and fell upon the attacker's legs. With all the strength of four men, the berserker was finally brought to the ground. At that moment, a healer broke through the throng and began a hasty examination of the man they fought so hard to restrain.

"Can you do aught for him?" As Benedic questioned the healer he felt the pressure of the crowd behind him, heard their loud murmurs of confused anger. His presence and authority would buy them only a few more moments.

The healer sat back on her heels, a deep frown on her face.

"By all I know, this man should be long past help. His ribs are splayed open, the pain should have taken him down." The woman flinched as the one being held on the cold ground strained against the hands that held him. "Yet still he still moves. I do not understand."

Corry labored to catch his breath and speak. "Then can you spell him motionless, or counteract whatever compulsion drives him to this?" The desperation of his hoarse-voiced plea was so intense that the healer, though she shook her head at the hopelessness of it, began a healing spell. Even as the first words were spoken, the agitation of the crazed soldier diminished. But a sulfurous, dank miasma rose from the terrible wounds, twining about the healer's head, choking her until she could barely finish reciting the words of power.

And when the last of the magic had been laid on the man, he stopped his insane struggle, shuddered and breathed out, becoming so very clearly and finally, only and terribly a body. The dark wound-haze dissipated, leaving behind the faint and troubling odor of death.

"Never have I felt such…" The healer, pale and spent, struggled to find words. "…such wrongness. It…" She could say no more but wrenched herself away from the body and, hunching over the trampled grass, retched violently.

Corry released his hold on the now motionless corpse. Benedic reached out and, taking his son by the arm, helped the boy to rise. No matter they were surrounded by a suspicious crowd, no matter that they were too close to a fallen one, the father in him could not refrain from embracing his child.

"Son." It was all he could say but he knew he had put his soul entire into the word.

"Father," from Corry and the barriers built between them by another's deceit melted into grace.

The all too brief reconciliation was interrupted by the hasty arrival of Captain-Commander Fiste. From her sweat-lathered horse she shouted for attention.

"Silence for news! We have seen the battlefield and it is just ahead. The overspell we were told would be attempted has been accomplished." Sortia continued with less hopeful words. "Though battlefield-generated magicks are negated, the wizard's troop still carry their compulsions onto the field. Thus the fighting continues. We are needed—and that quickly." This, too, elicited reaction from the troops, but it was expressed in a sudden silence. Into that tense quiet there came more news.

"It will not be hard to recognize the boundaries of the over-spell, but it will be hard to accept. The valley is edged with bat-tle-wounded being brought from the field by Linton's riders." That news gave him relief. T'Gault must have been successful in his persuasions.

"But..." Sortia's horse sidestepped in agitation. She reined him in roughly, the two of them mirroring each other's dis-tress. "...but the damned wizard has sent those of the Unseen Circle round the edges as well. When they find the wounded, they—they use them, bespell them into mindless, merciless killing weapons that do not feel the mortal pains that would take them down. The wizards use any injured they find, foes or friends, it matters not."

From near them came shouts.

"We have seen it." "Here is one."

Corry gripped his father's arm and murmured, "Those be-spelled are all but unstoppable, father. Yet there are at least two ways to meet them—true death by a healer's spell and, failing that, making movement impossible by..." But Corry faltered in his telling. Benedic's heart nearly broke, knowing what his son must have endured to discover this terrible information.

"You have done well in finding this, Corry. Let us put this hard lesson to use, yes?"

His son nodded with relief, though his eyes kept their haunted look. Benedic raised his arm in salute and called out.

"Commander, your scouts report ways to counteract this wickedness." He took a deep breath and brought all the leader's magic he could to the words he must say.

"The most compassionate solution, if available, is to have a healing spell done over the should-be dead. It is most difficult for the healer, but ends the desecration of the fallen in the best way. If a healer is not near, then forcing the magicked back into the overspell should release them into their true state. Though it appears for the most of them, that state will be death."

Distress swept through Forché's contingent, its passage audible as many voiced their aversion to what was being done. He braced himself to continue, for he knew how what he must say next would be received.

"If you are not near the field nor by a healer, then you must protect the living. If you have numbers enough to do it, capture the creature and bind it until a healer can be brought. If you do not, then the creature, though it bear the face of a friend, of family, of a comrade-in-arms, must be made immobile. It is done as the scouts just tried to do here—disabling the legs by…"

Cries of horror rose as understanding broke upon the troops. Corry still gripped his arm so the duke could feel his son shudder, recoiling at what he had found, had been forced to do, had been seen doing.

Though she, too, showed signs of abhorrence, Sortia sent her command voice over the furor.

"Silence for orders! Those near me hear what I say and carry the news. Each scout group find a healer. As you were assigned compass points to scout, so take those points and surround the field of battle. Seek out the plainsriders, for they will be closest to the wounded. Tell their healers what you know and show them. You know what you must do. The rest of us are for the fight. We are in the Creator's hands now. To the battle!"

As soldiers streamed around them, father and son made their farewells, though Benedic hardly knew what to say to this child so suddenly grown.

"You will take as much care as you can, son. Promise me." It was a foolish oath to ask, but his father's fear compelled him.

"You know I will." The boy turned to go, then looked back a last time. "I didn't get home in time." The words tumbled from him. "This spell to use the injured—the witch experimented with it when she was in our home. Peer was at hand because I...because she... But the spell failed and Peer just...just died." The tears that should have fallen from Corry's eyes scalded Benedic's heart. In that moment his resolve hardened to stone, even as he laid a gentle hand on his boy.

"I love you, son."

"I love you, too, papa." And Corry turned away, toward his scouts and their grim duty.

Benedic looked for Kell and found him in the care of an ostler nearby, the handler and the horse both restless to be away with all the others. It was the work of moments only to rejoin the main body of soldiers, over the first hill and then on the crest of the second.

Below them spread the battle, cut through by a river of blue touched now in red. Weapons were drawn. Breaths taken. Prayers made. Then, with one shout, they loosed themselves like bitter arrows. Down the slope. Into the valley. Into the battle.

Kell took over the ride, as he had been trained to do, pounding downhill, stretching into the flatland. Through the battle haze that was building over Benedic he heard his steed's deep-chested breathing, felt the powerful muscles that worked the legs that carried him. In the moments of that ride, horse and man blended into a single entity of war.

Flash of a weapon coming at him. Striking back, his arm and sword in an arc, catching the target, feeling the resistance of flesh, the jolt of blade against bone. He gave a great cry as he wrenched his weapon free, hating the pouring red, hating the sound of splintering and screams, wanting to live, needing to live.

Strike, parry. Turn into, wheel away. To the next and to the next. Pulling away. And again. And again. Hearing screams, shouts, terrible sounds of metal and bone. And again. And again. Making a dreadful progress toward the hill upon which the queen made her stand. Feeling, even in warrior delirium, a thin, bright connection to her—a connection that wavered but held when the sky was suddenly slashed with crimson.

And still he fought, urging Kell onward, weaving his way through carnage. At one turn, he came upon a cluster of soldiers on foot, fighting so hard that the clashing of sword upon sword itself was deafening. In the midst of that ruinous group he saw Lucette and T'Gault, back to back, weapons rising and falling in syncopated destruction. His daughter's tunic was stained black-red, her face spattered and grim. T'Gault, guarding her back as she did his, looked no worse but no better. Almost he could not go on, his father's fear bearing down until there was no breath for him to take. Yet, the woman his child had become, and the man who loved her, were winning their own way.

At the edge of his awareness, he saw plainsriders racing into the fray, lifting the wounded from the places of their falling, riding with them to help. Once he thought he saw T'Meara pluck a wounded foot solider before he had even touched the ground.

But the need to reach his queen, to keep her safe, drove him into battle yet again, wielding Truth relentlessly until his arm seemed a separate being, a perpetual motion beast of prey.

It was then, above the chaos, he saw Kern. The battle chief blocked the narrow, steep path that wound up to where Cathryn and the bards waged their own type of war from the mist-shrouded hilltop. Kern's broadsword flashed a deadly silver and red as he battled Palace Militia who came at him three abreast in furious attack.

Suddenly Kern stumbled and, for a breath, faltered. Then,

like a mighty beast, he raised himself and, with a terrible cry, began once more to dispense death. Yet as surely as he cut down one, another guard stepped into the breach.

Benedic kneed Kell into motion and man and mount cleaved through the deadly tangles of the field—past knots of the soon to be dead, past the falling and fallen, some who lay hideously still, some who cried out the anguish of their bloody end.

As they reached the base of the hill, Kell slammed his huge body against the outer circle of attackers. Two of them went down and a third howled as white shards of her own bone pierced through her arm. Benedic rammed the hilt end of Truth against the wounded one's skull and the fighter went down without a cry. Again the duke found a target, and again, until he drove into the wedge and could see Kern.

And then Kern went down.

"No!" Benedic hurled himself from the saddle, plunging, heedless, through the noose of fighters until he stood over his friend. In an instant he saw that Kern still drew breath but would not for long. So Benedic turned to the barrier of blades that once again hemmed them in and made Truth sing. His mind abandoned him and only his arm and his need knew the time.

Exploding, shattering blackness.

Disoriented. Benedic tried to shake his head and found he could not, for his cheek was pressed against the dirt. How…? It startled him to see light when he opened his eyes, for the darkness had slammed him down so hard it had the taste of an ending. Forcing his limbs to his will, he lurched to his feet and raised his head.

All around him, like wheat flattened in a storm, soldiers lay scattered—some never to rise, some trying to stand in proof to themselves that life was still theirs. Nowhere on the field was there the dreadful glitter of wielded swords or the fearful hum of unexpected arrows. The explosion, the concussion—whatever it had been—had been so immense it seemed to have halted the fighting.

Close at hand lay the squad of Palace Militia, too dazed yet to move. Then came a groan. He turned and there was Kern, half-sitting half-lying against the stony incline. Crouched behind him was the young herald, pale as snow, trembling.

"I tried to help..." The boy's voice was thin and hoarse. "But there were so many..."

The ragged edge of panic in the lad's tone was obvious, but Kern had need of the lad's service now, so Benedic poured a leaderspell into his words.

"Your name is Ladwin, yes?"

The boy nodded, mute in his misery.

"Our Battle Chief's job is to fight. It was not your time to be brave. Now it is. Take my horse and, here..." He drew his dagger and cut his own bloodied guildband from his wrist. "... take this. Ride as fast as ever you can to the top of the hill and find the queen. Show her my band and tell her to hurry, that he is dying. Can you do that?"

Ladwin's trembling lessened. He set his mouth in a steady line and struggled to his feet. Benedic whistled for Kell and, when the great horse had come, set the herald on the saddle and spoke both to the boy and the beast words of urgency and direction. As fast as thought, they left on their errand.

He sank to his knees beside Kern. Along his friend's chest and down to his stomach were curls and wisps of steam rising in the cold air. It took him a moment to realize why.

"Did you see her?" Kern's voice had no depth. It was not much more than a whisper, yet it was alive with rapture. His anguished heart told him who Kern had seen. He sought his friend's hand and gripped it.

"I saw you, great heart. You bought Cathryn time enough—the compulsions are dispelled. Can you feel it? Weapons are being laid down. Healing magicks are on the field again."

But he could go no further and he broke.

"Do not leave me, Kern. It is selfish to ask—forgive me for it—but live, I beg you."

Kern's hand tightened on his.

"Nay, it is my fault, my friend. I am not brave enough for life. The sorrow is too much. Bayly knew. That is why she came for me." His breath caught, held in the grip of agony and joy. "We will wait for you." As his breath left, he smiled. "Promise you will take your time…"

Benedic laughed and wept. Tears rained down on the empty shell that had been his friend. He drew his hand over the unseeing eyes and closed them.

Chapter Twenty-One:
CATHRYN

S HE KNEW SHE must wake up, but could not remember why. Then a chill wind blew across her, stealing warmth and bringing, instead, an odor so foul it nearly set her gagging. It was that acrid taste that finally made Cathryn open her eyes.

Open to vast gray, edged with dark. It was a moment before she understood what she was seeing: sky with storm clouds rising. What a temptation to simply lie there, letting what would be flow over her. Almost immediately something small, sharp and immovable began to make its presence known to her back.

Stones. She must be lying on a sharp one. She tried to find comfort by moving just a bit, but other lumps and poking things announced themselves. With a groan, she struggled to sit up, though her very bones protested the movement.

The effort made her lightheaded. For a little while her vision blurred. When it cleared again, she saw there were three white stones marked with charred streaks near her feet. She looked farther outward to a bare circle of ground, outward to a low, dark mound from which smoke curled upward in gray ribbons, outward to the edge of the hilltop where black thunderheads furiously piled higher and higher.

A storm-sent wind gusted at her, cuttingly cold and heavy with the promise of rain. It also brought the smoke smell, an odor so unsubtle, so unmistakable, that the memory of what had happened here lashed out at her.

"Oh, God, not all of them!" She staggered to her feet, afraid of what she would find. What she found was worse than fear had predicted. The nearest smoldering mass would have been unidentifiable but for the charred remnant of what had been a long, gray braid.

She had to avert her eyes, and then hated that she had, for into sight came another ruinous pyre…and another. A ragged oval of burnt bones and flesh.

Gone. All the bards—gone.

She staggered out of the appalling circle, outside the boundaries of such death, sank to her knees and jammed her fists against her eyes to blot out the traitorous light and vomited the taste of death until her throat was raw.

Into the blackness of grief and guilt a sound came—the hollow, labored breathing of a horse pushed near to exhaustion. She looked up and saw a rider cresting the hill. She did not immediately recognize the person, but the pounding, foaming horse was—Kell.

She jumped to her feet. Who rode Kell if Benedic did not? The rider came nearer and she saw it was the young herald.

"Ladwin?"

The boy was all disarray. Wild hair, torn clothes, dark smudges under his eyes and white-lined tension around his mouth.

"Yes, yes. You must come." The boy pulled something from his tunic pocket and tossed it at her. His aim was erratic and she barely snagged the object. "He said to come quick. He said hurry, he's dying."

She looked down at the bit of leather. A Servants Guild band, crumpled and slashed. The brown-red stains on the leather circlet stole her breath and stopped her heart. She knew whose band it was.

Thunder crashed so loud and sudden that the crack of it shook the hilltop. Ladwin cried out and Kell shuddered violently. She tried to throw a restraining magic at them, but there was no responding tug in her arms. Damn.

She needed that mount. And needed it now, so she grabbed for Kell's reins, caught them and pulled his head down hard. It made him stumble and that gave her the moment required to swing up behind Ladwin.

She beat Kell's neck with the reins. And kicked him. And tightened her hold on the trembling herald as the great horse dove headlong down the steep trail, slid on loose rocks, fought to stay upright and reached, in a time too violent and seeming endless, the valley floor, stopping in front of a group of people clustered around a wagon.

Lucette. T'Gault. Both of them were there. With a few others whose faces were hidden by the dark haze of her fear. They were lifting a body onto the wagon.

She half jumped, half fell from the saddle, careening off of Lucette's shoulder in her haste. Then the girl turned—her eyes were red, her cheeks pale and traced with tears. When she spoke, her voice was tight with sorrow.

"Oh, Cathryn, you are too late. He is gone."

"No. He's not dead. I would have felt it. Where is he?" But she could not wait for a reply. She pushed her way toward the wagon. The body had just been laid gently down and those who had helped to do so still bent over the wagon-bed. One of the group was garbed in gray, his wind-wild hair black and frosted white. Recognition nearly drove her to her knees.

"Benedic."

At the sound of his name he straightened up and turned. He lived—he lived. Then she saw his face, saw the anguish written across it.

"He's gone. I could not save him. I tried—."

"Tried? Who?" She struggled to work past the relief that sang in her ears.

In the dimming light of a storm-threatened evening, the streaks on Benedic's cheek shone like thin crystal streams.

"They all leave. Now Kern lost—and I...don't...can't..."

"Oh, Benedic. I didn't know...I thought..." Some brittle wall of self-protection broke inside her. She reached out and touched his tears.

He brought his hand up and covered hers where it stroked his cheek.

"Stay with me."

"Always. I will always."

The moment hung before them for a small, precious time. Then, in an agreement without words, it was wrapped carefully in hope and put away. There was duty before them, and grief, and neither would place themselves above what must be done.

Cathryn turned back to Lucette.

"Our young Ladwin has seen too much for one so young. Could you—?" Before she could finish the request, Lucette moved to take the pale and shaken herald down from Kell's back, speaking to the boy quietly. T'Gault retrieved Kell's reins and led him away.

"We will meet again in CorronKeep when you have

brought..." The young woman said no more, but with an expression both sad and fond, followed T'Gault.

From somewhere nearby came the rumble of turning wheels, cries of pain and the deep, musky smell of blood. The battle was over. But who, in any form of sanity, could call the result a victory? Yet word came from weary, somber messengers that no soldier raised a weapon, no caster sent a spell. From either side. The smoldering remains of D'Brin had been found, but searches were still being made for the witch.

The wagon before them was ready to make its sad journey as well. Though others around them offered mounts, Cathryn knew how she and Benedic would enter the capitol. They climbed up beside the forever still Kern and the three of them traveled together for the last time.

Long before the somber caravan had reached the walls of CorronKeep, the rain had begun to fall, heavy and cold. While the living tended to those who clung to life, the heavens themselves wept for the dead.

Chapter Twenty-Two:
BENEDIC

I T TOOK THREE brawny apprentices to pull Gormyn away and keep the healer from hurling himself through a tower window. His screams did not cease until much elixir of cellandore, brewed so strong it was almost deadly, had been poured down his throat. By the time Benedic arrived at the care station, the man had sunk into a forced sleep. Even then, he flinched and groaned and uttered pitiable cries while blood oozed from his ears.

Benedic stood in the doorway clenching and unclenching his fists in useless anger. This was the second healer in as many days to be lost to D'Joan's nightmares. How often since she had been found wandering not far from the field of ruin, bruised, scorched and completely mad, had he wished she had died in the wizard's battle.

"I came as fast as I could." Cathryn rushed into the room, breathless and worried. "What happened this time?"

He took her arm and turned her back into the hallway.

"A healer is down."

"No—not another one. Who?"

"Gormyn. But there is nothing we can do but let the others work their arts and skills on him."

She broke from his grip and ran back into the care room. He followed her, watching with pain as the healers parted to let the queen through—too quickly, as if the movement were prompted not by urgency or courtesy, but something darker. He had seen it often in the past few days: seasoned warriors avoiding audience with her, servitors flinching at a casual glance, children hiding behind parents when she passed by. Word of the wizard's battle had spread, and with it a deep fear of the wild magic the bloodworms gave.

She bent over the stricken patient, laying hands on him. She leaned close, as if listening. When she straightened up, Gormyn was in a quieter sleep, though beneath closed lids his eyes tracked things only he could see.

"That should help him be easier until the dreams can work themselves though." She turned to the others near the bed. "But how did this happen? We agreed that no one should attempt to enter Joan's mind again. Yes?"

The four healers glanced at one another, the eldest of the group finally answering.

"We did agree, majesty. It was the witch that somehow reached Gormyn. The nightmares she used during the battle still claim her sanity. But the parasites seem to be recovering all of their former strength. Perhaps even more. The combination of such madness and such immense power is fast approaching a point where we fear no one can keep the terrors she dreams from becoming real."

It seemed to Benedic that the light, which was Cathryn, diminished in that moment. She turned away from the others and looked toward him. He stepped into the room and took up the exchange.

"What, then, are the recommendations of the healers?" He stood by the queen, willing the bond between them to send her support.

Once again the group hesitated to answer, clearly ill at ease. Again the eldest spoke.

"I am so very sorry, my lord, but we have found no solutions. We considered asking the queen to work on D'Joan. It is true that the witch quiets when her majesty is in the chamber. But when she leaves, it is worse than ever. We even considered…" here the man cast down his gaze, "…briefly considered, though we would all bear the guilt of it, ending the life that so threatens ours. But as healers we cannot. Nor do the bloodworms allow it—they seem to repel any attempt to harm their host. We do not believe that anyone would be able to kill the host…D'Joan…even if…"

The healer trailed off, unable to finish what, to them all, must be a shameful confession.

He tried to frame a reply, but before he could, Cathryn spoke in a tone too calm to be reassuring.

"I see. Thank you for your honesty. I will take responsibility for this problem. By tomorrow, with Duke Benedic's help, I should be able to provide a solution."

Abruptly, she turned and walked out of the room. He left four confounded healers and went after her.

She did not wait, but hurried down the hallway, down the great stairs. He lengthened his stride and caught up, keeping pace though she kept silent. Turning here. Turning there. Until they burst through the outer door and reached the gardens that swept down from one end of the Keep outward, between the cliff edge on one side and the town wall on the other.

The air that brushed them now was clear and chilled, making each breath a visible sign. And still she walked, as if that alone would exorcise whatever drove her. He could no longer stand the silence of her tumult.

"Wait." He reached for her arm to stop her headlong rush. "Cathryn, wait. Tell me what plagues you."

In desperation, he pulled her to a stop, took her by the shoulders and turned her to face him. Her face was flushed, her eyes over bright.

"What plagues me? I plague me—and you, and this whole place. I have tried, again and again, tried as hard as I can." She wrenched herself from his grasp. "Before—before I came here—got brought here—I never even tried. Always kept quiet, waited to see. Never took a chance, because I was so sure I would just make things worse. And now—"

She could not stand still and began to pace the cold stone of the garden walk.

"Now, when more than anything I want to help, when there is so much...so many who..." Her voice cracked.

His hope began to break as well. "You have done no wrong in this. I will not have you say that again. It was not you introduced wickedness to us; it was born and bred here. If there is any blame, let it fall on me. I, who should have known better. I, who lost a wife but would not see her death for the murder it was. I, who asked too much of my good cousin and her husband and so lost Bayly to the damned Takers and Kern...and Kern..." Grief took his breath away. He could not go on.

Cathryn reached out past her own despair, took his hand and held his palm to her cheek, meaning to give him comfort even in her comfortless state.

Nothing could have prepared him for what that touch ignited. She was his. Her eyes spoke it, her deeds declared it. From the most hidden place within him there came a fierce pain and he understood that it was the sweet anguish of release—the release of a heart too long shut away.

For a space he could not breathe, his heart would not beat. And then, not because he must fill the void his losses had made, but because there was no future in which he did not see her, he spoke what had been waiting to be said.

"If what I see within you is not love, Cathryn, tell me now. I..."

A piercing wail cut through the air. Cathryn doubled over, clutching her ears and crying out. He reached for her, but staggered and nearly fell as the very ground beneath his feet shook. Now the wail became a high keening.

He saw her wrench herself upright and start back toward the Keep, first struggling to take a step, then faster and faster. Running.

With fear driving him, he followed as swiftly as he could. Into the Keep, up the stairway, past bodies of those who had collapsed from the assault of insanity, past courtiers screaming in derangement, past guards who clawed their own eyes bloody. Pushing himself upward until he reached the Tower Chamber where the mad woman screamed chaos and destruction, ripping apart the very fabric of the world.

Cathryn was there already, laying hands on the witch, speaking words of power, subduing, restraining, calming, controlling. Beads of sweat rolled from her forehead. Beneath the sleeves of her tunic, writhing. Red light, fierce as fire, streamed into the tower windows. Even as she fought to contain the madness, outside the sun set in a wreath of dark flame.

When night had fully come and there was quiet once again, he carried his drained, exhausted queen from the prisoner's room to her sleeping chamber. He dismissed those who would have tended to her and himself laid the coverlet over her and coaxed more warmth from the fire. He meant to stay until she fell asleep, even through the night, to guard her from such phantoms of the soul that might come. But she would not let him. In a voice too quiet, in a manner too calm, she bid him take to his own bed and sleep.

Because she had asked it of him, he tried. But sleep did not come to him for a very long time.

Benedic

The grip of a shadowed and ecstatic dream loosed in a heartbeat.

Benedic

It came again; not his name pronounced, but a beckoning most particular, most urgent. The tone, the chord of it was touched with command and need and something else that ignited yearning and fear.

Benedic

He threw off the cover, crossed the room to seize Truth and was out into the hallway, the cold stone floor assaulting his bare feet.

He ran. Past her sleeping room. The soulcry was not coming from there. Up stairs. Two or three at a time. Upward, fighting time and denial. It could not, must not be. There was no justice in this. No—

Where were the guards who should have been outside the Tower Chamber? He drew in a deep breath, shifted his grip on the sword to an attack hold, reached his free hand to the door and pushed.

It opened silently. Readily.

She was dressed in travel garb. The circle of the room flickered with shadowed candlelight. Behind her, in the center of the chamber, on a long table, lay the living but senseless body of the witch, covered to the shoulders by a red cloth.

The table, D'Joan's still form and Cathryn. That was all. No assassins. No weapons seeking a target. Yet the imminence of death was as overwhelming as the unmistakable pungency of incipient magic.

Immediately he knew that the threat in the chamber could not be fought with blades, though his hand refused to release the sword it held. He was driven to ask his heart's question.

"You are not wounded or threatened, yet I have been Called. Surely you have found a way, with your untamed magic, to make the Passing come without the specter of death to trigger it. It is so, is it not?" The question asked, the night, the stars, dread and hope waited for the answer.

She did not reply, only drew in a breath and spoke a word. One only. One he had never heard before. Dark, cruel, final.

She shivered. He started to speak, but a small motion of her hand stopped him. All around the chamber, faint images of trees and tendrils of mist were forming.

She kept her gaze steadily on him. He tried to keep that contact, but the growing miasma behind her compelled him to watch for, like a disturbing dream, what could be seen of D'Joan's body began to fade. First its colors seeped away, then it substance began to wane until only a spectral outline remained. There was a sound of boulders thrown by floods, then the witch was drawn away, pulled toward the ghost trees, the shadows of the other world. In a clap of thunder, she and the trees and the mist were gone. The red cloth sank slowly.

There was a scream then. From somewhere, somewhen else. The sound of it hit Cathryn like a blow and she stumbled, nearly falling. He reached out to catch her, steady her. But she drew back with a cry.

"Ah, no. You cannot touch me yet." Panic and something more intense broke through her guarded tone. But whatever she endured, whatever she intended, he could not tell. For that connection, first felt in the Calling on the plains of Linton Province, was gone. There was no thread between them, no spilling over of thoughts, emotions. On Linton plain the connection had seemed an intrusion; now its absence raked through his heart.

"Tell me what to do, then, to keep you here and safe."

The smile she gave him promised nothing.

"Here and safe isn't part of the plan, I'm afraid. So, please," she shivered again, "put down your sword. The truth you're going to get will likely be sharper even than that, and I think you'll need both hands to manage it."

Reluctantly, he bent down to lay the weapon on the stone floor.

"It is laid aside, Cathryn. You must tell me what you plan. For your heart is not touching me as once it did."

"It costs me more than you know to keep it that way." Lines of strain deepened across the planes of her face. "So, this needs to be finished. Quickly. While I am still able."

"No, wait. There must be another way. Only you see this as an ending. I do not. I can make no plans that do not include you. No tomorrows can be dreamt that do not have you in them." He conjured bravery but could ask one last question. "Why must you leave?"

She raised a hand, as if to touch his face; but drew back again, drawing back with her the last of his hope.

"To answer your question: I must leave because it is the right thing to do. I have grown to love this place, and so many of the people in it. I would not have harm come to any one of them. But every moment Joan is here, possessed of magic but not of a sound mind, she is a danger to everyone I now hold dear. I have tried to remove the magic, tried to find healing for her. For good or for ill, the worms protect us both. The only answer I know is to return her to Earth and to close the passageway between our worlds so that this will never happen again.

"But," once more she looked up at him, "only I can accomplish it, and to do so I must go with her. Since I would not leave Corronheld without a true and rightful ruler, there is no choice. All I have learned, and everything I know in my heart, tells me there is only one way to give the Passing. Surely you understand that."

"No. I do not understand. You promised me, on a field consecrated by the blood of the fallen, that you would not leave." He shook off restraint. A fierceness of spirit had begun to sing in his veins. "Stay. Remain here for the sake of those you love and who love you—Lucette and Corry. T'Tolyan. Stay for me."

She began to roll up the sleeves of her tunic.

"I cannot. And here are my final arguments." He could not avoid seeing the worms, writhing furiously beneath the skin of her arms. "I cannot live another day with these. It keeps even those who care distant." She looked full into his eyes and he saw the anguish there. Her words had sunk to a whisper. "I have killed with these. I have thought to kill again. I cannot control the power they give me and, if I do not rid myself of them soon, I will not be able to summon the strength to do it. For the sake of my soul, I must leave. Without these."

"How...?" A sudden remembrance of D'Joan's parting scream made him leave the question unfinished. But Cathryn answered anyway.

"Your wife's notes, Joan's experiments and the oldest memories in the Passing showed me how. At a triggering word, I will be sent back to my time and place. But it will send only me. No other living thing will be able to pass with me."

"So they...?" His gaze dropped again to her arms.

"When I go, they will stay. It is as simple as that." But tears had begun to swell in her eyes.

Fear propelled him toward the table. He flung away the red cloth. There, in a hideous confusion, lay a dozen worms. Dead. Bits of torn flesh floating in the unmistakable black-red of spilled blood. "They are torn out as you leave. Nothing else would make this…"

He looked up. Her face was as pale as the light before dawn, and on it was writ so clearly the greatest fear and the greatest courage. Even as he drew breath to speak, she uttered for the second and final time that one, implacable word.

Around them air took form, pulling to itself otherplace shapes, pulsing with otherworldly sounds. In the center, in the vortex, she reached for him. With the power of the Calling. With a hand held out to give the Passing.

He stepped past the boundary of her outstretched hand, closer than the clamor of the ancients demanded, nearer than breath to the soft resistance of her body and the heat of her flesh. He would say now what he had meant to tell her before.

"Cathryn…"

"No words, Benedic." So closely and so well she fit to him, her lips brushed his ear in speaking. "It would be too much to bear."

"In this you cannot stop my mouth. I…"

Passing contact sealed between them with a wrench so violent he nearly fell with the shock of it. Desperately, he tightened his embrace, holding to her as an unrelenting whirlwind of voices, memories of life and nightmares of death rushed into him through her. Most ancient days first. Sepia-colored, cracked with age but potent. Succeeding crowns, coronations, judgements, failures, triumphs, daughters and sons, consorts and traitors, the building of wisdom and the inescapable follies of living—all, all invading and possessing the chambers of his mind, the abyss that had opened in his heart.

Until the image of Reyfen emerged through the onslaught of the Passing. The once-king passed with a vividness that was too poignant, for Benedic could feel, undiluted by the misunderstandings of the living, how much his friend had cared for him. Felt the affection like a deep wound because Reyfen was dead and was caught, unnaturally, in this turbulence of memory, like a fly in amber.

Then all that was Cathryn Passed into him, the face of yesterdays hovering ghostly over the flesh and bone of this moment. In her he saw the way to push all the rest of the clamoring memories down into a quiet place. From her poured remembrances of home: a mother scented by lilacs and bread, father with capable and compassionate hands, a home without riches but not without richness. Wedding a dark-haired, dark-eyed husband. Betrayal. Solitude. A desk near a window. Walking among the trees, falling into stone.

Here. Awakening to Lucette's concern, a carriage ride through the redbarks, the pain of the worms, capture, escape. T'Tolyan's bear hugs, Kern's daily mercies to her, the battle fought upon and beyond the hilltop, killing, death, fire, fear. And through it all was a strand of desire, growing stronger, weaving itself into the essence that was and was becoming Cathryn. The strength of it, the depth of it, in all its unrepressed and vulnerable truth was overwhelming. For the name of that passion was his name.

Ruthlessly, he pushed down the crowding images of the Passing until his eyes cleared and he could see her again—so close—sweet sorrow, in his arms at last. Pale she was, but her eyes told him she knew that he knew. Her body yielded to his embrace and he cried out. But his arms closed tighter and tighter around less and less. Only her face, translucent, marked by tiny pearls which were tears, shone for the briefest of moments before she was gone.

Blood, dark and terrible, fell where she had been.

There was no scream from the otherwhen. There was a howl from the King.

EPILOGUE

...a beginning ends it...

WIND BLEW HIGH above the forest canopy, stirring the mighty cedars to drowsy wakefulness. The ancient trees did not consider time in hours. The warm, amber-colored autumn day belonged, not to their awareness, but to the more ephemeral beings. Yet, when to this intertwined complexity of rainforest there came one of those brief-lived creatures, the tang of memory was sharp.

She had been here before. The first time, a hill of stone had been shaken by a force that had no roots in the known, something that stank of darkness. And she was gone.

The second time, she brought another with her and there had been blood. The nearest cedars had tasted it, for a great deal sank into the earth. The other never walked away, her flesh and bones judiciously and respectfully reaped by the forest. But this one had left, albeit so slowly that the youngest saplings, perched on their nurse logs, approached impatience.

Three cycles of seasons passed without sight of her. Now she was here again. The elder trees, caught in the fitful and restless wind, cracked and groaned. Around them, the woman and the rocks, the late afternoon sunlight slanted down in shafts. The gold of the day and the deep green and brown shadows of the rainforest moved in dapples on the low, heavy moss and dotted ferns.

She ran her fingers over the rough face of the rock. Her arms, stretched out before her, were furrowed with ridged scars. Perhaps she had been cut with trail blazes. It seemed that way.

For one of her kind, she stayed a long time with her face upturned to the sun—long enough that a nub end of a mushroom fought free to button the soil near her feet.

At dusk, when all things white gleamed dimly like old bones, she turned to go. It was then that the stones began to sing and birds burst from the branches in an explosion of wings and astonishment. Light not of the sun outlined an archway, at first a pale cutout and then brighter and brighter. The woman stared at the doorway of air and light, seeing past its frame to the man who stood on the other side.

He said, "I have found you again."

She said, "How...?"

He laid one hand on his chest. "You gave me yourself and all you knew. The key was there all along."

"But I tried to close the way, to keep you safe."

"There is one who has kept the way possible. She..." here he took a tender moment's pause, "—she keeps it open for us even now, but at great cost and for a very short time."

The bright doorway wavered and then steadied.

The woman said, "So, then you have come to...?"

"To ask if you wish to come home."

"Home," she whispered, tasting the promise.

ACKNOWLEDGEMENTS

This book began long ago, spent some time in hiding and recently emerged to be completed. In the beginning, help took the form of Kay Kenyon's application of encouragement and sharp elbows, as well as Kay Morison's literate heart and Florid Sister support. In this last stretch, fellow fantasist James Macon graciously tendered his beta-reading analysis. But the story would have languished in a dark place if not for Jenny MacLeod helping me to clear away many boxes of baggage and get to this journey. Alex MacLeod, book designer to the stars, made the interior a thing of beauty and a joy forever. Liza Brown so got the whole thing that her cover art nailed it. The Pendragons deserve crowns of gold for their ongoing attention: Kay, CJ, Lisa and Jim— best of the best. Gratitude and the usual snark to Katie, Jeff, Duncan, Shannon and all the stupendous grandchicklets, without whom I would never have developed such a rich internal life or laughed nearly as often.

Bonus Material

Excerpt of a new series coming soon from K.E. MacLeod:
The Hours of Under,

first book in the *Underoveron* trilogy.

Chapter One

It took Andeved three hours to leave the ledge. So far from upinward, cool and quiet as it clung to the rock, the ledge held him as he tried to reach peace with the heated, glaring and noisome thoughts that had brought him there. He threw stones into the sea, aimed one or two at waterflyers, kicked at salt-rimmed puddles without aim. After three hours, the only conclusion he found was that avoidance was impossible.

Having come to that inevitability, the intimate safety of the retreat lost what consolation it formerly held. A last time he scanned the two bluenesses, air and water, stamped his boots on the cold, rough rock beneath and drew what strength could be gotten from the far reaches of stone that loomed above and inward from the narrow opening that looked out into the unknown.

When he re-entered the caverns and began, with a determination he tried to fully feel, to climb the first of the chilled, dark passageways that would take him on the return trip, the Fool was waiting. As always. Belwether heaved himself upright, his hulking presence almost entirely blocking the tunnel.

"I am ready, lordling." The Oni's voice rumbled in the echoing tunnel like a verbal rockslide.

"Of course." Andeved sighed, and once again rebuked himself for his tendency of late to show so little courtesy to his inevitable companion. They each were doing what hundreds of generations of tradition demanded. What could not be changed must be endured. But there was a prickle of irritation across his shoulder blades all the same.

As they made their way up through the lower tunnels, Belwether began the litany. "When we return, it will be the Hour of the First Turning.

> 'In the Hour of the First Turning,
> The Lord of the Under awakes
> And remembers that beneath the above and
> over the below,
> The lives of the people turn with the tide and
> the light.
> Turned, turning.
> Hour of the First Turning.'"

As he climbed the stone steps to the first of the Inferior Hallways, Andeved made the ritual reply:

> "The lives of the people.
> Turning. Turning."

But he was a little out of breath from the effort of having already scaled the 378 Steps to the Beginning of Below and the words came out like a half-realized whisper. Hearing himself, he did not need to glance at the Fool to know there was a frown on that too familiar face.

"That was quite a climb, eh, Belwether?"

As usual, his most constant companion said nothing. And said enough. For the Fool was not puffing one bit after the arduous climb, though he was certainly a double handful of seasons older. So Andeved tried to regulate each breath, to take in more air with less noise, knowing even as he did that this pride of his would make the long trek to the Superior Hallways even longer.

Indeed, the last few minutes of the Hour of Beginnings were running their course when the pair made the refectory. Today, of all days, it was inappropriate to be late for breakfast. The leftovers, usually remaindered on the wide serving shelf cut into the wall of the lengthy cavern, had been removed by the cadre of Foodists. Already they had taken off their masks of office and, with circles of sweat blossoming between torso and arm, had begun the scrubbing of the tables. Slap, brush, slap, brush – four to a table, two tens of tables. Slap, brush, move down.

"We'll not get fed here." Belwether's rumble overrode the Foodists' cadences. "And your mother will want to see you, certain. Shall we go, then?"

Andeved's stomach protested, a metaphor and a reality.

"I suppose it must be." The young man took one last look at the serving shelf just in case he had missed something. Nothing remained but the now fading smell of yeasty morning bread. He turned back toward the junction of tunnels leading to his home chambers. A hot scolding, a cold bath and a change into a formal tunic that chaffed more than just his neck were only the first of what awaited him. For today his older cousin, Lord

Paell of Under, would receive at court his bride-to-be, the Lady Arrant of Over. Ceremony on ceremony, insult on injury.

His mother sighed, her hands moving in aimless worry. "I don't suppose you remember where you put the sash for your dress tunic?"

Andeved pulled the sash out of his clothes chest without a reply. It did no good to defend himself, to tell her he knew very well where it was and had just been in the act of retrieving it. It did no good at all. Though he believed his mother loved him, she had developed notions about him that no amount of time and proof could shake. In fourteen seasons of life he felt he had amply demonstrated competence, knowledge of ceremony, a working memory, appropriate behaviors of all sorts that could be deployed when necessary.

"Well, there it is." A small sound, something between the upward tone of surprise and the downward slide of disappointment, escaped from his mother as she examined the sash in question and then shrugged. "It will have to do, I suppose."

His mother was already dressed for the ceremony – had probably been so for several hours. The clothes she had chosen tended toward the gaudy. The tunic that hung over her long skirt was voluminous, a vain attempt to hide her widening girth. Silver threads glinted in the fabric, a familiar irony given his mother's name. Even her ceremonial mask, denoting her family relation to Lord Paell, had sparkles on it – an addition beyond what was actually required by tradition.

Not for the first time, Andeved wondered at the pairing that was his parents. Glitter and Sere. Names too right for humor, too opposite for comfort. The only weight his mother carried was on her skeleton. Ideas pushed against her mind and sprang out again, leaving no dent on that internal softness. The only liveliness his father managed was in the animation he gave his anger. It had a sullen existence of its own, igniting often, though seldom when expected.

"I cannot help you any more with your preparations, dear," Glitter announced as she started toward the chamber door. "You made me take too much time already worrying where you were. Your cousin has great responsibilities today. It's naughty of you to take so much of our attention on such an occasion."

That Andeved had not asked for, needed nor wanted that attention never seemed to occur to his mother. As she left, he noticed that a section of her hem had come undone and trailed behind her collecting ragged bits of thread and dust. He said nothing.

A slight, sudden sound made him start. Once again Belwether made his presence known.

"How do you do that?" Andeved growled. "Been my Observer since I was seven and you still manage to startle me at least once a day."

Belwether's expression did not change even slightly. "Yes, you still startle – though most often when you've taken the last sweet cake or broken something."

"Mother left before I could tell her about the hem."

The Fool tilted his head and blinked once, slowly. "Hem?"

Andeved felt the warmth of guilt flush up his neck. "You know very well what I mean. You saw the same thing I did and you didn't say anything either."

"Hmmm." That was the total of Belwether's reply.

Andeved's insides growled, effectively distracting him from his companion's infuriating neutrality. The prospect of a long and difficult ceremony on an empty stomach was not pleasant. If he hurried, he might be able to finagle something edible elsewhere before he was missed. Out he went, half running but hoping not to sweat in his dress clothes, toward the Outer Halls.

Down the passage, turn left, then right, then straight out a wide corridor whose rock turned from the dark gray of interior selphstone to the brown of edgestone. Light grew the farther outward he went until it burst out in fullness as he reached the terrace. The Terraces. They never failed to amaze him. Great waves of stone jutting out beyond the caverns and to each side, crowded with growing things and those who tended them.

But first he turned back to the interior hall where, of course, his Observer stood, not an arm's span away.

"You can guess what I mean to do and you know you cannot stand near me like a beacon." Andeved pointed at a darkness of shadow just inside the cavern entrance. "Stay there until I return and, if you keep hidden, I may bring you something to eat as well."

Without a word, Belwether stepped back into the darkness and Andeved plunged forward and outward toward his prospective breakfast.

"You cannot go outside today, boy." A Terracetender blocked his way. "Too much going on, what with the feast and all. Can't allow anyone in but Foodists and Terracetenders. Sorry."

Andeved wracked his memory for the woman's name.

"But I was sent by Lord Paell, especially for some sweetrounds." He peered up under the huge brim of the inevitable shielding hat and recognized the face beneath. "You know how it is, Fleeney. My cousin's all nerves and jitters. Needs something gentle to settle his stomach. I, myself, would not bother folks just now, but…"

"Nonsense, son. You need to do what you're told." Fleeney stepped aside and motioned him on. "Go on then, but be quick about it and stay out of the way. Lots of busy people—and your father's out there somewhere having an argument about visqhens that won't lay on his schedule."

His father out here? Not good at this precise moment, though usually it was one of the advantages of having Sere as a father, this access to the terraces whenever he wanted. For the edgeside farms were his father's responsibility. It was Sere who directed the guild that hauled soil recovered from the gesh excavations to the ledges, those who planted and tended, those who harvested. On the ledge farthest down was the ocean garden with its sheltered fish ponds, oyster beds and salt reclamation basins. The terraces up from that held the cool growers: mushrooms, berries and the diminutive sheep and goats of Under. Here on the topmost gardens were the warm growers: vegetables of all kinds and the threadworm and small fowl.

But Andeved was quite adept at avoiding those he did not want to meet. So he dove into the bustle of the Foodists rushing here and there, shouting for more of this and another of that. He dodged Terracetenders running up and down the narrow aisles between plants, picking what was ripe and sprinting back to the waiting baskets.

Ah, there. A long, tall row of sweetround plants. The fist-sized melons hung heavily, ripe and warm. Andeved picked four of the most likely looking ones and, stuffing them inside his tunic, turned to go back—back to the city entrance and a chance to eat.

But from the other side of the sweetround row came the sound of anger. Two people were heading down-row, just as Andeved was, hidden by the broad leaves of the trellised vines. And he knew one of the debaters. The horrible flatness of the voice, the words hitting like huge, dull rock hammers. His father. Andeved froze.

"If you have devoted your life 'til now to becoming a moron, Chasen, it is the only success you've had." His father's black temper was legendary throughout Under. "What did you do to those hens? They won't settle, they won't lay. What did you do to them?"

"Nothing, I swear Lead 'Tender." Chasen sounded frantic under Sere's verbal attack. "Something's set them off, but no one knows what. They're jumpy and cross and..."

"Nothing, I swear, master." Sere's parody of Chasen's defense was brutal, derisive. "Do you hear yourself? You admit you've done nothing. Get back to the coops, idiot, and soothe the lice-ridden fowl if you have to eat and sleep in the coop for a hundred days. Keep at it until I see eggs or I'll speak to my nephew, the Lord Paell, and he will have you and your brats exiled. You can spend the rest of your miserable life in the wideopen with no surety of stone to keep your lazy brood contained."

"But no...I can—"

"Go. Now." Sere's tone had gotten even harder. The last word could have shattered stone. As it was, it elicited the sound of footsteps hurrying away. Andeved knew the sweat and fear Chasen must be enduring. Knew it well. And because he had grown up too close to this father, a black anger grew in his own heart. His father should not hurt others this way. It was not right.

Andeved picked another melon—this one larger and heavier than the others. He drew back his arm, calculating the force needed to launch the too-ripe missile over the plant row. The sound of dirt grinding into stone meant his father was walking away. If he could just...

A huge hand caught his outstretched arm and held it hard.

"Is this one for my breakfast?" Belwether's voice was low and steady. He pried the sweetround from Andeved's grasp. "I could not see you once you entered the planting rows so I moved closer."

"You came to spy on me." The tang of anger was still bitter in Andeved's mouth.

"No. Attached Oni do not spy. They observe."

"And they are not supposed to interfere. Or do you pick and choose which traditions you will obey?"

To Andeved's astonishment, Belwether appeared to blush, if that was what the darkening of the Fool's craggy cheeks meant.

"An Attached Oni does not interfere. I was only observing my breakfast in your hand. That was all. That you held it in the manner of small boys bent on mischief, that you looked ridiculous, that you could have hurt him…or he, you…observations only."

It was perhaps the longest speech Belwether had ever made and it took Andeved by surprise. He realized his mouth was gaping. He shut it with a snap, turned on his heel and started back to the interior entrance, Belwether trailing silently behind him. There was not time to consider what this departure from the Observer's usual ways betokened. But he placed the question in a recess of his mind for later.

It was the Hour of the Second Turning. As the tiny bells hung from the mirror ropes rang the change, the light of the Chamber of Ceremony went from pewter-glinted to burnished copper.

From his place on the first balcony, Andeved watched the skin on the back of his hand go from shadowed to warmly luminescent, transfixed by the play of light on flesh. This chamber, its shape and colors, what was in it and what happened in it was a source of endless fascination. His first memories of it were filled with changing light. Of all the great halls carved out of Under's vast caverns, this one was the greatest. Not one but three levels had been carved, each of them with its own tunnel of light mirrors. The sunlight captured by the polished plates was usually diluted the farther back in the city one went. But here, in the Chamber of Ceremony, that never seemed true. Even the loftiest reaches of the vaulted ceiling were not completely enshadowed.

And when the sun shifted in the sky and the hours for turning the outer disks toward the light came, the jangling of the tiny rope bells chimed so loudly that for long moments the sound continued to careen from wall to wall.

Even now, before his eyes and ears had drunk their fill of the place, the tunnel bells died away and there was a silence made—created, he knew—for the speaking of the hour's ritual. From her position beside the Water Clock, this season's Ceremonialist, dressed in robes of deep red and decked with the black and white full-face mask of that office, spoke into the void:

"Turning and turned again.

The second solar revelation

Piercing, as a miner's candle might,

Morning's chill reflection.

Heat and light, sustenance, sight,

Turned again and turning."

The sound of the proscribed phrases sank into the ears, clothes, skin and bones of the hundreds of guests in the great cavern. Those bones and flesh knew exactly when the echo of the ritual would die. Knew exactly when to reply, "The lives of the people. Turning. Turning." And though each time Andeved swore he would be the rebel by leaving the response unsaid, he had not yet mastered the doing of that irreverence.

Then, before the reverberations of the reply had ceased, there was noise from the outer hall. All heads turned toward the cavern-high doors—but Andeved glanced back and saw Lord Paell's hands tighten into fists. How his cousin must dread this moment—to see the stranger who was to be his wife here, in the company of those who desired and those who dreaded his humiliation. And yet, in the band of light that flowed over the wide dais Lord Paell posed as calm, resplendent in a tunic of burgundy and a half-mask of green with long visqcock feathers arrayed lavishly on each side. Andeved wondered if anyone else saw that the very tips of those feathers trembled, oh so very slightly.

The doors completed their slow, stately swing open.

"Ahhh." Those who first saw what entered sighed as one. Tall as the looming doorway came branches, leaves, limbs of trees. It was if a forest moved into the chamber, bringing with it the rustle of wind playing in the open.

As the onlooking crowd moved apart to receive the procession, Andeved could see that the moving trees were, in fact, many long branches held by attendants dressed in mottled greens and browns.

"Ahhh," again from the courtiers. This time there was an undertone. Cavern dwellers could never so wantonly waste the tallest of plants. Hard enough to grow foodstuffs in a mostly sun-missed place. But this...

"Ohhh." A swelling of fragrance preceded the next of the procession. From wide baskets youngsters tossed handfuls of petals. Pink and yellow, lavender and ivory. And upon this carpet, laid on the unblemished smoothness of the chamber's stone floor, came the party of the Intended.

First came High Minister Voeller of Over. Attired in a robe the color of storms, sleeves edged with blackest fur, he held in one hand the engagement contract, its seals glinting in the bronze light. The other hand was empty—and so, too, for all purposes his face. This broker of kingdoms had not come masked to honor the customs of Under. Angry mutters stirred as he approached. Wait. Andeved looked harder. Voeller was masked—but it was painted so cunningly that it seemed the Minister's own features. As the crowd discovered the ruse, the mutters died down even as the unease grew.

Next in the procession came a woman who would not have been immediately noticed but for her place in the pageant. There was no glitter about her, no suggestion of the open sky, no haughty manner. She was short, stocky, but steady. Her gown was of deepest burgundy, made deeper as the copper-colored light of the Hour of Turning melted into it. Her mask was the half-mask of a ruling family, colored mid-dark blue-black, traced with the silver stars arranged in the pattern of... Andeved looked harder to see what it might be...ah, yes. The pattern of the Night Lord's Bow. The only star cluster seen so low in the sky that it was an icon of night protection for both demesnes. The young woman carried a small wooden chest, polished to a high sheen, no doubt containing the Overite's guesting gift.

Who was this subtle, unforward herald?

"The Lady Kendle, younger cousin to your cousin's betrothed," came a whisper from behind Andeved where Belwether had anticipated his question. "She comes as companion to the Lady Arrant. Some say there is more of the servant-to-the-master in this, but I speak as one who seeks to learn what others know." And with this, the huge Fool managed, somehow, to withdraw without actually moving at all. Andeved sighed to himself.

But his attention was again fully caught with the entrance, finally, of the Lady Arrant, the Intended.

She came, walking stiffly, in a gown of pale pastels that, in the intensity of the hour's light, had turned to muddy golds and russets. Her mask was of white and copper, made in the shape of a sunburst. Was it a dawning or a sunset? Andeved could not tell.

The attendants of the trees made a circle around the lady. And all stopped. In the silence that sprang from perceiving motionlessness when action is expected, awkwardness built. This was not the way the moment had been agreed upon in those long hours of negotiation. Paell was to have met Arrant in the center of the chamber and escorted her to the dais, each in the full focus of both the contingents. But the lady was encircled, without an access way to be seen.

It grew quiet and then more quiet, save for the susurrus of the grove whose branches were not shivered by wind but by the beat of blood. Those courtiers who had been murmuring amongst themselves or jostling for a better view fell silent.

Lord Paell stood alone on the dais in a space built of his disbelief and the terrible expectations of the crowd. Like a cautious crow, he tilted his head, listening for more than a dozen heartbeats, as if seeking direction from the empty air.

Andeved's fingers began to twitch. Three times he flinched, needing to step in, to break his cousin's paralysis. But the moment was too witnessed, too intimately observed. So the taut, unseen connection of cousin-friend between large-knuckled Andeved and fine-boned Paell stretched even tighter. To the point of pain.

Then, from beneath and within the stone of the chamber came a low, sweeping sound, a groan that shook the air and built and grew louder until it became a howl of rock. And another rumble of despair came, pushing through the very walls of the chamber. Then another, until the air could hold no more howling.

The crowd, with a single voice, moaned a word that named their fear: Bittercalls.

No sooner had that name been voiced than the rock walls creaked and crackled with bulging and pushing—here an immense forehead, there an unseeing eye as big as a cistern. Stone walls were forced by a power too large to consider into the shapes of five howling faces. The Bittercalls were present— those who existed only to be harbingers of disaster, who ate fear and drank chaos.

Courtiers scrambled into a mass in the center of the room, the pretend grove trampled underfoot. Overites and Underions alike huddled together, as if that would protect them from the doom the Bittercalls inevitably preceded.

Only Paell remained alone, his mask askew but his pose unbroken, a small dark smile on his lips. Until the last howl died he stood unmoved, one leg cocked at the knee and the other locked with the foot turned slightly outward. Then, when only the cries of the frightened broke the silence left when the nightmare visages melted once again into the stone, he raised his hands to straighten his mask. That done, he lifted his hands even higher. Carefully he uncurled his fingers from the fists they had formed, leaving the forefingers on each hand bent at the middle knuckle. In his mind he saw himself, from fingertip to pointed foot, and approved of the picture. It was time to speak. He drew in a clean, deep breath and, tightening the tendons and muscles below his lungs, pushed up the words to be heard.

"Do not fear." The echo of his voice came back to him. He listened and found it strong. "We are well and we will be well. Rise up and do not be afraid."

But immediately he saw there were no people who had fallen down and the mischoice of words irritated him. Still, those who cowered in the center of the great hall began to regroup in more normal ways. Paell scanned the balconies, too, for signs of people in distress. Slowly the crowds that had so eagerly lined the railing were returning to see what was happening on the main floor. He saw Andeved on the first level, moving among the shaken onlookers. That ludicrous boy, all knuckles and knees. No grace, no sense of duty. But loyal.

A strident voice, edged with anger, took Paell's attention from his cousin. There, in the middle of everything, the lady Arrant pointed and gestured and spoke—too loudly. He could hear every syllable much too distinctly.

"No, pick them up. All the branches. They are ruined, take them out. Kendle, come here and bring the casket." Leaving her attendants to gather the now trampled branches that had so recently been her sanctuary, Arrant strode forward. Toward him.

Before he could think to do otherwise, Paell lowered his arms. His Intended had climbed the seven steps to the dais and was almost upon him. His reaction to this unseemly haste and invasion of what was surely his place and public moment was a surprise to himself—he had begun to panic. More so the closer she got.

"The ceremony is ruined." Arrant's tone had an edge to it that suggested movement barely restrained. "We have to do something with the people. How do you want to organize clearing the hall?"

Arrant's eruption into demands and questions with so little ceremony made Paell almost ill. The whole ceremony, for that matter, was a descent into uncivilized chaos—circled tree branches, departure from the planned way, the Bittercalls, the Intended's abruptness. Was he the only one to keep to the right in all of this? With great determination he recalled the words that should have been spoken.

"Lady Arrant, as Lord of Under I welcome you to the heart of our city and to my own heart. You come today as representative of Over and as she who will share—"

Paell stopped. The lady was staring at him as if she had never seen the likes of him before. At first he could not think why she was so amazed. But he could tell from her expression that something had stunned her into silence. He could only conclude it must be himself.

"Ah, yes, Lady Arrant. You have not truly seen me before this and I do not doubt you are struck by what you see. I have been told I am a handsome man." He said the words gently so as to appear humble, but still the lady's face took on a deep ruddiness. Perhaps she was embarrassed by appearing so crude in his presence. He tried to help her.

"Those who have seen behind your mask tell me you are very beautiful. More so than the drawings sent to us could show." She did not warm to his courtesy. He tried another tack. "Perhaps you feel uncertain of what is required here. Our society is so much more…shall we say…ordered than yours. But rest assured, my people do not hold your lack of ceremony against you, for you are not familiar with our ways as yet."

"Are you mad?" The Intended waved her arm toward the rest of the great room. "Did you hear the Bittercalls? Look at all the frightened people. You must do something."

Paell looked out over the milling crowd and his heart warmed.

"They are mine and I am theirs. We can rest in that."

Arrant stared at him.

At that moment, one of the Overites, a short younger woman—the one who carried the guesting gift casket—appeared at Arrant's side.

"Cousin? Lady? Perhaps we should—"

Paell felt anticipation stir. Since he first set his eyes on that polished, wooden box he had barely been able to restrain his curiosity. What had the Overites brought him? The box alone was worth a great deal. But what was in it?

Paell inclined his head in the gracious way, though he did it a bit too quickly in his eagerness. "Yes, you want to present the guest gift. How splendid." He held out his arms.

"No...I..." The plain young woman pulled back, apparently unable to speak to her betters with any ease at all. While she spluttered awkwardly, others also began to approach the dais—several of Paell's advisors, the Chief Advisor Etcherelle, the Overite High Minister Voeller. Would they not let him be?

They closed around him, a living prison.

From his vantage point at the balcony railing, Andeved watched his cousin. And as he did so, all the fears he had tried so hard to conquer returned. Something was wrong with Paell. Something fundamental. How else to explain the man's calm hard on the heels of the Bittercalls, the strangely skewed comments and priorities of recent days?

At least he was no longer alone in his apprehension. The Chief Advisor's alarm at Paell's non-response and her charge toward the dais made that clear. Andeved's father, a late arrival to the ceremony who had stationed himself on the opposite balcony, had also registered a reaction. It was not difficult to read the black study on his father's face. Unlike Etcherelle, Sere would not step forward to help, however. As usual, he left the scene, waiting for the object of his sufferance to come to him.

Worst of all, the chamber was filled with desperately worried people who needed reassurance, counsel, someone to tell them they need not fear, to name and then prevent the disaster the Bittercalls had come to predict. Would no one step in and take charge?

Chief Advisor Etcherelle was on the dais now and, for good or ill, she signaled for the attention of the crowd.

"Quiet," she shouted over the tumult. "Quiet and listen."

Beside her the Lady Arrant frowned deeply, clutching at Paell's arm and whispering swiftly and violently into his ear. He seemed not to hear, his gaze never wavering from the shining box.

Slowly the anxious crowd moved toward the dais, though Andeved was hard pressed to know whether it was from the Chief Advisor's shouting or the peculiar tableau arrayed at the top of the seven steps. He shivered under the stress—and heard a similar movement from behind him where Belwether stood. The notion that the Oni was uneasy was unexpected and alarming.

"The Lord Paell wishes you to know that his advisors will be gathering in the next hour." Etcherelle, her sharp eyes glinting from behind her mask, arrowed her glance to one after another of the many near the dais. As if her glance was an accusation, an uneasy quiet formed in the front of the hall, spreading backward and upward.

"At the Hour of the Last Turning we will bring our conclusions and a plan back to this hall. For now, go to your home chambers." For a space no one moved. Etcherelle's native impatience asserted itself. "Go on. Go home. Now."

At last, some turned toward the doorway, worriedly muttering, reluctant to leave the comfort of numbers. The Bittercall's wordless prophecy might mean a single death or many, a small but potent disaster or one to strike down a world. Until they knew what to expect, it felt better to be with others.

And then there was the mesmerizing scene on the dais. Andeved, like many of the folk in the great hall, could not leave because he could not bear to look away from it. So it was he saw that, in her fierce whispering to Paell, Arrant gestured too broadly and jostled Kendle, causing the gift casket to fall from her hands, hit the stone floor with a loud report and fall open. A bright effervescence of light flew up from the broken box, up into the highest spaces of the vaulted dome of the chamber. Back and forth it streaked, leaving a glowing trail in the eyes of the beholders. Then down it came, over the crowd, like tiny ball lightening, zigzagging from person to person. Just over their heads, stopping for the beat of a heart at each one. Then rushing on. Then streaking toward the dais, hovering over Etcherelle, then Arrant, then Paell. And stopping above Paell. Stopping long enough that it could be identified.

Once again the crowd saw and knew and named. Flett. The word breathed up from those watching like the exhalation of a dream. Unmistakable. The sinuous body, no longer than a child's finger, a blunt, eyeless head—like a blind worm powdered with light. And the wings of shifting, oil-on-water colors, fluttering faster than the mind could grasp.

As if one body, the crowd held its breath. Nothing moved except the fey luminescence of the flett as it described an intimate circle around Lord Paell's head, closer with each revolution until, at last, it settled delicately on the top curve of the man's ear. In a movement peculiar to fletts, it nestled between Paell's ear and head, bringing both wings to one side of its body to lay them over the ear of its now-host like a gossamer coverlet of colors.

Again, as one, the crowd sighed. No matter that disaster was moving toward them all, this was a thing of wonder and awe. Only a very few times in a handful of generations had one of these mysterious beings singled out one of the grossfolk with a bonding. And they had seen it here, and it had been one of their own.

Andeved found it hard to breathe. His hands were clenched so tightly his nails dug into his palms like tiny skinning knives.

Too much had happened too quickly and his heart lurched painfully against his ribs. Was this seeming gift of grace what the Bitttercalls had some to decry? How could something so rare and beautiful be the stuff of disaster? Or was it the marriage that was to connect Under and Over that prompted the visitation? Or the off-balancing arrival of Overites to the protected realm of Under? Or his cousin's increasing strangeness?

His cousin. Andeved found that his burgeoning unease did not lessen, but grew, as he looked at Paell, now the pinpoint center of all attention. He could not help but look—and could not help but be frightened. For an expression of ecstasy had come to Paell's face and to it he had utterly surrendered. Eyes closed, mouth open, all eerily lit by the bodyglow of the worm.

Behind Andeved, Belwether was rocking back and forth in manifest distress, repeating and repeating but one phrase: "They knew. They knew, oh save us, they *knew*."

The urge to find privacy and the lust for display fought a giddy battle within him. He reached up to touch the creature but stopped just short for fear of disturbing, harming or even offending it. Paell frowned in frustration. He knew too little about fletts—though what he did know shivered him with elation. They were rare. Almost unheard of in Under. Surely the mark of a special destiny. A visible sign of what Paell had always believed. The ruin of his well-rehearsed ceremony by the undisciplined Overites and the manifestation of the Bittercalls did not seem so predictive now.

He looked around, needing to search the faces of those near him for their reaction to his wondrous addition—and found that he was almost alone, having somehow walked out of the Chamber of Ceremonies to his own rooms. Only Etcherelle remained at his side. He was disappointed. His chief advisor never showed emotion. He would get no satisfaction from her face.

Her face. Odd. Her mouth moved, as if in speech, but no sound came forth. Her brows were furrowed and the lines that splayed out from the corners of her eyes were deeper than usual. What was she doing? Did she realize she was soundless? Or was she mocking him for not paying closer attention?

"Etcherelle, I would thank you to stop—" But Paell could speak no more. His words reverberated so strangely in his head he knew immediately it was not his advisor who was voiceless but he who could not hear. Thunder crashed against his chest, hammered in his head. It was the only sound he could hear—the sound of his heart pounding out its fear.

He must regain control. In an attempt to calm, he shut his eyes. But opened them again in panic. The darkness behind his eyes was too silent, too deep without any noise to tether him to the outside. Sweat ran, hot and swift, down his spine. In front of him Etcherelle stood immobile with astonishment. In some way he must let her know his problem. He reached up and placed his fingers against his throat to at least feel the words he would try to make heard.

"There appears to be a problem, perhaps due to the physical adjustment I must make to my flett. It seems I cannot hear, at least for now." It did not feel like a whisper that went through his throat, but Paell could not tell for sure.

Etcherelle moved her lips again, then caught herself doing so and stopped. Instead she nodded so vigorously that Paell thought surely her head would snap off with the force.

"I can see you well enough. You needn't visually shout." His choice of words pleased him. He began to believe he could bring advantage from this. Then she began to speak again. It irritated him she could so disregard his state so he settled his fingers against his throat again so he might remonstrate. In so doing he brushed up against the flett as it nestled behind his ear and draped down toward the cords of his neck.

His reply died before it was born, for as his fingers touched the powdery skin of the wormlike creature he began to hear the slightest of noises. Etcherelle's voice came at him as if from a distance—not the voice he knew from his youth, first as severe foster mother and then as relentless advisor. This was gentle, soft, papery.

"…what I say? How will we—I could get pen and—"

Paell could feel the smile drift to his lips as he made to answer her. "Be calm, Chief Advisor. It seems that when I am in contact with the flett, I can hear. It must be part of this new, joined state."

The flood of relief that swept away Etcherelle's distress proved amusing to Paell. He pressed his advantage.

"So do not tarry with me. I shall, as always, be well. Go, call the Council. Bring together the guild leaders. And when all are assembled, I will come and we will calm the fears the Bittercalls created. And as soon as possible, send Andeved to the Archives. Tell him to find everything there on fletts and bring it to me."

"I shall. Indeed." Etcherelle stumbled in her reply but it was not unpleasant to hear filtered through the fey creature's perception. A great welling of benevolence filled him as he watched his second-mother leave at his bidding. All would be well. He knew it.

He brought his fingers away from his neck where they touched the flett. But his hand felt suddenly cool so he looked at it. For the second time in this strange hour, the thundering of his heart bashed against the darkness in his head. For his fingers were covered with red—blood—that could only be his.

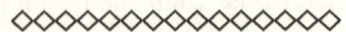

Watch for the release of *Underoveron: The Hours of Under* at www.kemacleod.com.

About the Author

K. E. MacLeod is a Pacific Northwest novelist who writes epic and high fantasy and imaginative fiction. Somewhere in her sordid past she's taught English, speech and acting. She also lays claim to having performed in and directed plays ranging from Shakespeare to modern drama, produced and provided on-air talent for educational television and radio, and narrated a symphony production of Peter and the Wolf. Then there were the years working as an administrator in a community mental health organization. Result so far: Accumulation of words, written and spoken; drama in real life and on stage; deep respect for those who walk a hard path. All of which resolves itself into a sense of humor—which is the single most potent survival tool.

You can learn more about the author and upcoming projects, including the Underoveron series, at www.kemacleod.com.